MATHER BYLES

Painting by John Singleton Copley

MATHER BYLES
WORKS

COMPILED AND WITH
AN INTRODUCTION BY
BENJAMIN FRANKLIN V

SCHOLARS' FACSIMILES & REPRINTS
DELMAR, NEW YORK, 1978

Published by
Scholars' Facsimiles & Reprints, Inc.
Delmar, New York 12054

New matter in this edition
©1978 Scholars' Facsimiles & Reprints, Inc.
All rights reserved.
Printed in the United States of America

Grateful acknowledgment is made to the following institutions
for giving permission to reproduce material
from their collections:
Boston Public Library
Congregational Library, Boston
Houghton Library, Harvard University
Library of Congress
William L. Clements Library, The University of Michigan
New York Public Library, Astor, Lenox, and Tilden Foundations
Thomas Cooper Library, University of South Carolina
John Carter Brown Library, Brown University

Library of Congress Cataloging in Publication Data

Byles, Mather, 1707-1788.
Works.

Reprint of the author's works
published in 18 v., 1727-61.
I. Franklin, Benjamin, 1939-
PS721.B5   1978   818'.1'09   78-6439
ISBN 0-8201-1309-3

To the memory of my grandparents

CONTENTS

INTRODUCTION

Mather Byles (1707-1788) was born exactly one century after the founding of Jamestown and lived for a dozen years after the signing of the Declaration of Independence. He saw America grow from a population of about 300,000 to four million, from a religious to a much more secular society, and from a British colony to an independent country: his life spanned most of the eighteenth century. But as the country grew, Byles stayed in Boston; as religion assumed a less central role than previously in the lives of many Americans, Byles continued his routine preaching in the Hollis Street Congregational Church; as his countrymen moved toward revolution and freedom, he remained content with the *status quo* and sympathized with the Crown. He was a Tory. His century and his country were expansive; he was not.

Tradition provides a sense of security while encouraging a conservative approach to life, and few men of his time possessed such deep roots in the American past as Byles. His mother, Elizabeth Mather Greenough Byles, was the granddaughter of both Richard Mather and John Cotton, the daughter of Increase Mather, and the sister of Cotton Mather. Byles's maternal great-grandfathers arrived in America within fifteen years of the Pilgrims and quickly established themselves as leaders of the Massachusetts Bay Colony; Increase Mather, one of the most important men of his generation, early opposed but later supported the Half-Way Covenant and was instrumental in eliminating the hysteria surrounding the Salem witchcraft trials; and Cotton Mather possessed the most formidable and eclectic mind of anyone in America to his time. Mather Byles was thus part of the greatest, most influential, and most powerful American family before the Adamses. Yet he was certainly not the greatest Mather. Conservative by tradition and training, this eighteenth-century gentleman was content with modest achievements.

Much more is known about Byles's maternal than his paternal ancestors. His father Josias, an English saddler, came to America with his first wife Sarah and several children in the 1690s. They had at least four more children in this country; Sarah died soon after giving birth to the last. In 1703, within a year of her death, Josias, then in his late 40s, married Elizabeth Mather, a woman in her late 30s and the widow of William Greenough; Josias died less than a year after the birth of their only child, Mather Byles. The elder Byles was a man of modest means unable to leave his widow financially secure. As a result, her family came to her aid. Cotton Mather assisted Elizabeth in rearing her son, and Increase Mather, upon his death in 1723, left Byles numerous books and money for schooling. The Mathers, then, and not the Byleses helped shape the mind, character, and values of Mather Byles. That Elizabeth's only child bore her maiden name was appropriate.

As a member of the Old North Church, Josias Byles naturally knew his ministers Increase and Cotton Mather, and Elizabeth as well. While it seems unlikely that he married her solely to guarantee his position in society, through her he became a member of the esteemed Mather family. Mather Byles was thus from birth of the social elite. Certain of his actions helped solidify his standing, especially in the eyes of British officials in Massachusetts. He first gained his credentials by following the Mather tradition of matriculating at Harvard where he took his bachelor's degree in 1725 (at age eighteen) and his master's in 1728. Five years later came the most important year of his life: he was ordained pastor of Governor Belcher's new Hollis Street Church in Boston, a position he would hold for forty-three years. In 1733 he also married Belcher's niece, Anna Noyes Gale, the widow of Azor Gale and the daughter of the Governor's sister and Dr. Oliver Noyes, a prominent Bostonian. (Thomas Prince, of the Old South Church, officiated at the ceremony held in the Province House that Nathaniel Hawthorne would immortalize a century later in four of his tales.) This assumption of leadership in Belcher's church and his marriage into the Governor's family provided Byles with a new status and established his ties with British rulers that would last,

ultimately at great cost, into his old age. In 1733 he must have
been secure within his society, profession, family, and self.
If he once felt inadequate because of his father's social
position and concomitant penurious state or because he had
to bear the Mather mantle, that feeling undoubtedly van-
ished as he turned twenty-six and as the first third of the
century receded quietly into the past. After Anna's death in
1744 (they had six children), Byles formed new ties with the
political establishment by marrying, in 1747, Rebecca Tailor,
whose father William was twice Lieutenant Governor and
once Acting Governor of Massachusetts. Before she died in
1779, she and Byles had three children. Byles thus remained
in his privileged position for several decades after 1733, but
because of his allegiance to the Crown, he necessarily fell
from prominence in the eyes of many Americans who opposed British rule during the decade from the Stamp Act to
the Revolution.

Byles became a pariah not because he changed but because the group to which he had repeatedly sworn fidelity
was overthrown. With the Revolution he lost everything,
including his pastorate. Even though Boston was the hub of
revolutionary activity, the Tory Byles chose to remain there
during the siege. He also allegedly prayed that Britain would
defeat America, consorted with British officers, and permitted the quartering of troops in the Hollis Street Church.
He should not have been surprised when his parishioners
—none of whom apparently shared his reactionary political
opinions—removed him from his ministerial position in 1776.

Complications surrounded his dismissal. Because the congregation, in its haste to rid the Church of him, denied Byles
due process by failing to have his case heard by an advisory
council of representatives from sister churches, other Congregational clergymen, who were anything but Tories, came
to his defense. They took no action against the Hollis Street
Church, but neither did they pursue the matter to the point
where they could redress Byles's procedural grievances. He
denied the charges against him, but a civil court ultimately
found him guilty of disloyalty and ordered him held secure
until he could be deported. Byles was then seventy years old

and a threat to no one, so his penalty was reduced to house arrest for a few months. Thereafter he was permitted free movement. (This confinement inspired two of his most famous puns. When asked the identity of the sentinel standing watch before his house, Byles replied, "O, that is my observe-a-Tory." Later, after his guard had been removed, returned, and finally dismissed, Byles noted that he had "been guarded, re-guarded, and disregarded.") His eventual freedom was no freedom at all because few of his old Tory friends remained in Boston (many, including his son, Mather Byles, Jr., fled to Halifax, Nova Scotia). During the war he was virtually companionless in a country in which a common energy had forged a strong bond among most of its citizenry. After 1776 Byles was a misfit: he was an old man in young America; his atrophied spirit clashed with the country's enthusiasm; his vision was directed toward the past while the new nation looked toward the millennium. He suffered a paralytic shock in 1783 and died in 1788.

Byles remains of interest today because of his ancestry, his Tory sympathies, his fabled wit (as a punster), his portraits by Peter Pelham and two by John Singleton Copley, his friendships with Benjamin Franklin and Isaac Watts, and his attempted intimacy with Alexander Pope. What recommends him most to our attention, however, is his written legacy.

Byles's sermons and poems were published in nineteen separate volumes (pamphlets, mostly) that reveal the entire scope of his literary abilities and achievement. All are reproduced in facsimile herein. The first was a poem on the death of King George (1727) when Byles was twenty and pursuing his master's degree at Harvard; the last was a funeral sermon for the former Commander in Chief and Acting Governor of Massachusetts, William Dummer, when Byles was fifty-four (1761). Elegies to the Crown and British rule thus frame his other publications and illustrate the life-long dedication to Britain that caused him to become *persona non grata* in his own country. Although he averaged one volume every other year between 1727 and 1761, only an epistle to accompany a John Seccomb sermon (1772) appeared during the last twenty-seven years of his life. He was most productive in 1744 (the year of his first wife's death) when three of his titles were published in addition to a book he compiled anonymously, *A Collection of Poems. By Several Hands.* (The title-page has 1744 as the date of the collection, but external evidence suggests it was not published until January, 1745.) All of his works except a 1758 sermon published in New London, Connecticut, were first published in Boston. Byles's fairly active writing career—at least as seen in his published volumes—was limited to the years of his greatest standing in society. At the first signs of American political unrest he ceased expressing himself. He undoubtedly saw that his loyalist sympathies went counter to the prevailing political opinion in America. Lapsing into silence, he symbolically ceased living. His publishing career thus documents his rise to and fall from prominence in a country where his roots were deep.

When compared with the sermons of his grandfather, Increase Mather, his uncle, Cotton Mather, or his great contemporary, Jonathan Edwards, Byles's appear uninspired. He was not concerned with fine theological points such as those with which the seventeenth-century Puritans had to grapple in formulating the Half-Way Covenant, with anything beginning to approach the ambitiousness of his uncle's ecclesiastical history, or with a crisis such as that Edwards had to address when confronting the Arminians in 1754. But to compare Byles too closely with the greatest early American divines disserves his work. Even though his sermons lack breadth, depth, and variety, they are superior to many of the more impassioned sermons published in America during his productive years by such a clergyman as Samuel Davies. Byles's sermons have been admired by Evert and George Duyckinck: "His published sermons . . . show him to have possessed a fine imagination, great skill in amplification, and great command of language combined with terseness of expression. Passages in these discourses would not do discredit to the best old English divines" (*Cyclopaedia of American Literature* [1855; enlarged 1875; rpt. Detroit: Gale Research, 1965], I, p. 127). Moses Coit Tyler also commends Byles's sermons: "The distinctive gift of Mather Byles was homiletical; he originated no ideas, he constructed no new argument of ideas; his function lay in the strength, warmth, and vivacity with which he grasped for himself the great familiar propositions in faith and conduct, and then, for others, held them forth in a succession of splendid and powerful pictures that inevitably drew the eyes of men, and stirred their hearts into followship of fervor" (*A History of American Literature* [1888-89; rpt. Williamstown, Mass.: Corner House, 1973], II [1676-1765], p. 196). Byles's usual approach was to cite a Biblical verse, provide exegesis, and apply his findings to life. His primary concerns were with regeneration, with being born again, and with focusing one's vision not on the imperfections of this world but on the eternal perfection of the next. His individual sermons are interesting enough, but in aggregate they reflect, at bottom, an uninquisitive theological mind.

To the reader concerned with literature as well as theology, Byles's best sermon is *The Flourish of the Annual Spring* (1741), not because it differs from the others in its call for regeneration, but because he uses Canticles (ii.10-13) as his text and comments on that book as poetry. That is, he evaluates the entire book as a creative poem and applauds it as "the finest poetical Composure now extant in the world." He also cites his reasons for so thinking. He finds bold metaphors in it, admires its dramatic nature, commends its lyricism, and approves of its pastoral qualities. Above all else he loved the Song of Solomon because the end of its poetry is to show love for Christ: it is a divine poem. Most of these qualities may also be seen in Byles's own verse, but never did he use them all effectively in any one poem. It goes without saying that nothing he wrote approaches the beauty of Canticles.

The seventeenth-century American Puritans, as well as the Pilgrims before them, inherited a specific stylistic theory from their English forebears that called for clarity above all else. They believed what they wrote in praise of God and instruction to man was true because it came mostly from the Bible, so they thought their writing needed little embellishment. While they avoided excessive and ornate imagery that might focus a reader's attention on the manner rather than the matter of a text, they were not reluctant to use figurative language their audiences would understand. The American

Puritans mastered the plain style, but while plain, it was not dull. Kenneth B. Murdock summarizes the Puritans' writing as succinctly and well as anyone: "But essential in most of it are its realism, its insistence on solid content rather than superficial form, on rhetoric as the servant of truth, and on 'Words of Wisdom' rather than the 'Wisdom of Words.' So is its habitual dramatization of spiritual truth in terms of man's struggle from darkness to light. Whatever subject is to be discussed, the Puritan writer tries to make his argument or his exhortation strike home by putting it in concrete terms that will ring true in the ears of an audience of hard-working men" (*Literature & Theology in Colonial New England* [1949; rpt. New York and Evanston: Harper & Row, 1963], p. 62). Such authors as William Bradford, John Winthrop, John Cotton, Urian Oakes, Thomas Hooker, and Increase Mather wrote majestic prose in the plain style.

With the eighteenth century came new social and literary concerns. No longer were Americans as single-minded as previously in their dedication to religion. Writers, looking to such an English model as Addison, certainly addressed more secular topics in a style less plain than did those mentioned above. Their prose, best illustrated by Franklin, was conversational and graceful. Byles was aware of stylistic theory in a casual way and wrote about it several times. In the preface to *A Discourse Upon the Present Vileness of the Body* (1732), for example, he states that he composed that piece in a plain style *"adapted to a popular Audience."* The implication of such a statement is unfortunate but telling: in so adapting his natural plain style for a popular audience he diluted it. Still, he had to compromise because his parishioners did not wish the plain prose of times past. Murdock notes that Byles's Bostonians were "fashionable and complacent" and that the town "was losing its character as the center of a Bible commonwealth and becoming a worldly, if provincial, metropolis. The old conventions were weakening, the old symbols were losing their power, and too often the preacher of Byles's time tried to compensate by the exaggerated artifices or downright sentimentality of a 'melting' style" (*Literature & Theology,* p. 178). In order to accommodate popular taste Byles wrote sermons as religious/literary exercises of no great theological significance, although they possess a certain stylistic charm. They also contain no hint of controversy. Nowhere does he betray the fervor that accompanied the Great Awakening in the fifteen years before midcentury, years during which fully half of his sermons were published. The sermons are nonetheless of value today as documents representing Byles's theological concerns and the eighteenth-century "melting" style that Murdock sees characterized by "sentimental hyperbole" (*Literature & Theology*, p. 179). The first three-quarters of the eighteenth-century was America's poetic dark age. Aside from Edward Taylor's late poems written in the first quarter of the century (but not published until the twentieth) and an occasional exception such as Ebeneezer Cook's *The Sot-Weed Factor* (1708), little meritorious American poetry was published until the productions of the Connecticut Wits and Philip Freneau around the time of the Revolution. Mather Byles was the best pre-Revolutionary eighteenth-century American poet, a distinction less significant than it might at first seem because of his lack of competition for the honor. Who today can even name one other such poet than Byles? He wears the crown by default.

Byles wrote all of his poetry before mid-century, and he was especially active publishing it in the *New England Weekly Journal* (Boston) in the late 1720s when he was in his early twenties. He discussed the composition of his poetry in the preface to *Poems on Several Occasions* (1744):

> THE Poems collected in these Pages, were for the most Part written as the Amusements of looser Hours, while the Author belonged to the College, and was unbending his Mind from severer Studies, in the Entertainments of the Classicks. Most of them have been several Times printed here, at *London*, and elsewhere, either seperately [*sic*], or in Miscellanies: And the Author has now drawn them into a Volume. Thus he gives up at once these lighter Productions, and bids adieu to the airy Muse.

In presenting a large body of his poetry to the public, he assumed the attitude of a mature man looking back on his prodigal youth. In those earlier years he was frivolous; what he produced was an escape, he is now able to see, from more serious pursuits. Yet Byles obviously saw merit in his poetry, despite its unlikely origin, and decided to offer it to the public with one hand while detaching himself from it with the other. One understands his tactic: he was willing to receive praise for his creative efforts, but he could hardly be criticized for his poems since he dismissed them himself as the productions of "looser Hours."

We know that in 1744 Byles also compiled *A Collection of Poems. By Several Hands,* a volume important for at least two reasons. First, it is technically the earliest anthology of American poetry, but in spirit it is not so much an anthology as a collection of poems by and about Mather Byles. (Elihu Hubbard Smith's *American Poems, Selected and Original,** published in 1793, is generally considered the first true anthology of American verse.) Second, Byles made a conscious effort in that volume to present to the public poems not collected in *Poems on Several Occasions,* and he also included poems in praise of his own artistry by other poets. In so doing he revealed his desire for a reputation as a poet in 1744. His two volumes of verse published in one year possibly exceed in quantity and quality (with the exception of Anne Bradstreet) the output of any American poet before him. He published no new verse after 1744. Even if he did devote himself thereafter to what he considered more serious endeavors, for which there is no evidence, he bade "adieu to the airy Muse" with a grand flourish belying the disparagement of his poems in the preface to *Poems on Several Occasions.*

Byles's poetical canon is discussed in C. Lennart Carlson's excellent introduction to *Poems on Several Occasions* (New York: Facsimile Text Society/Columbia University Press, 1940), and in the only book on Byles, Arthur W. H. Eaton's *The Famous Mather Byles The Noted Tory Preacher Poet, and Wit 1707-1788* (Boston: Butterfield, 1914). Both commentators accurately identify Byles as comfortable with the neo-classical poetical form and directly inspired by Pope. Carlson is especially effective in dating Byles's poems, and Eaton is the best source for Byles's biography. I should like,

*Reprinted by Scholars' Facsimiles & Reprints in 1966.

therefore, to focus on a representative Byles poem and its attendant problems to examine his skill as a poet. The poem is "To My Friend: Occasioned by his Poem on Eternity, Dedicated to the Author," but before understanding it fully, one must know that Byles wrote it in response to another of his poems entitled "Eternity. A Poem. Dedicated to the Instructor of My Muse." Both poems appeared first in Samuel Kneeland's *New England Weekly Journal*, "Eternity" on May 15, 1727, pp. 1-2, and "To My Friend" on June 5, 1727, pp. 1-2. Neither poem bore Byles's name, but he included both in *Poems on Several Occasions*, the earlier on pp. 106-111, and the latter, with the title "To an Ingenious Young Gentleman, on His Dedicating a Poem to the Author," on pp. 49-57. As first published in Kneeland's newspaper, however, "Eternity" was accompanied by an introductory letter by Byles that he chose not to include in his collection of poems seventeen years later. It reads as follows:

To *PROTEUS ECHO*, Esq;
SIR,

As you have given the Publick some Touches upon the Grubstreet Way of Writing Poetry, and been more large in a Criticism upon the Bombastick, I presume you will not be displeased to insert a good Poem in your Paper. The inclosed I take to be of such a Character; and, if I may be allowed to judge, there is a noble Spirit reigns thro' the whole; and, at the same time, the several Parts of it, are finish'd with much Correctness and Beauty. Several of the Thoughts are entirely New, and were never hit on before; and several are truly Grand and Sublime; such, particularly, is that,

> Time leap'd to Life, and sped its March from far,
> Seated on Motion its Triumphal Car. —

This, I think, is one of the most bold and poetical strokes that I have any where met with; and all those that are acquainted with *Aristotles* Definition of Time, *The Measure of Motion*, will be sensible of the exquisite Propriety and Magnificence of the Sentiment. But I shall not take upon me, to criticize upon the Performance, but if you publish it, I shall take it for granted that you Subscribe to my Opinion of it, when I say, No Person that has a Relish for Productions of this Kind, can read it without some Emotion.

> I am,
> SIR,
> Your most Obedient and very Humble Servant, R. S.

Byles would become well known as a wit, but as one who usually dealt in such obvious humor as puns. In this case his humor is private (or limited to a few), for he writes as another praising his own work. In so doing he is part of an American literary tradition that found greatest expression in Whitman. Here as elsewhere Byles presents a straight face to the readers while taking obvious delight in their ignorance of the true situation. (He comments further on bombastic and grubstreet styles in an untitled essay in *The American Magazine and Historical Chronicle,* January 1745, pp. 1-4.)

Byles again praised his own work when he published "To My Friend" in the *New England Weekly Journal.* He first wrote as the editor:

> MY Printer brings me, among others, the following Letter, and I think I cannot better entertain my Reader, than by presenting him with it. The Poem has already met with great Applause, and since it is finished deserves greater. The Thoughts are bold and lofty, the Similes just and surprizing, and none but a true Genius could have carried them so happily through. There is a Purity and Sublimity in the Language, and a musical Flow of Harmony in the Numbers, which have such a variety as not to tire the Ear by a constant Return of the same Cadences. The Reader will also [obser]ve beautiful Conformity of the Sound to the Sen[se whi]ch so much charms us in *Homer* and *Virgil,* and their [ad]mirable Translators *Dryden* and *Pope;* especially the latter, who'of all the Moderns seems to have attained the greatest Mastery in this happy Art. In short, there seem diffused thro' the whole of this Poem, a free, sprightly, and noble Spirit, and if any in these inclement Regions have been warmed by the Fire of the Muses, I dare pronounce it is the ingenious Author of these Lines.
>
> Thus much I think my self obliged to say, to encourage rising Merit, as well as out of Justice to the Author: And it cannot but be a Comfort to me in my old Age, to see others coming on to supply my Place to so great Advantage.
>
> X.

He then provided a letter from himself, again as R. S., to recommend "To My Friend," a poem addressed to himself as author of "Eternity":

> To *PROTEUS ECHO,* Esq;
> SIR,
>
> The *Acceptance you were pleased to give the Poem on ETERNITY, which I lately conveyed to you, together with the*

Approbation it has met with from none of the meanest Judges among your Readers, incourages me to send you the following Copy of Verses, which are addressed to the Author of the above-mentioned Poem. An imperfect Publication of them has been already made, when they stole into the World without the Consent of the Author; who imagines, that if the Lines are still bad, yet at least in that incorrect Dress, they were worse.

    I am,
        SIR,
            Your very Humble Servant,
                      R. S.

Byles as R. S. thus serves as an intermediary between the editor (Kneeland) and the poet (himself), although the editor's voice accompanying the later poem is Byles's. None of this prose is present in *Poems on Several Occasions,* a regrettable omission because especially in his words as editor Byles reveals that at age twenty he was concerned with and knowledgeable about poetics and influences. He knew the key ingredients of poetry (at least as the eighteenth-century perceived them): the thought should be "bold and lofty"; similes, "just and surprizing"; language, pure and sublime; meter ("Numbers"), flowing, harmonious, and varied. Sound and sense should be fused. He also knew good models — Homer and Virgil — although his reading of them was through the translations of Dryden and Pope, the latter of whom he considered the best of the moderns. (Byles included copies of "Eternity" and "To My Friend" with the first of his four letters to Pope in October, 1727. The texts of those letters and a commentary on them may be found in Austin Warren, "To Mr. Pope: Epistles from America," *PMLA,* 48 [1933], 67-73.)

Byles attempted to trick the readers of these two poems by presenting ecstatic commentary from people seemingly well qualified to make such judgments. But as informative as his introductory prose is, the poems, and especially "To My Friend," stand as works that, while falling short of his own purposely inflated opinion of them, have considerable merit and show him to be a poet of some ability. As with Hawthorne's best tales a century later, so too with Byles's poems: once curiosities, irrelevancies, and playfulnesses are put aside, each author is at bottom serious.

In "To My Friend" Byles establishes the author of "Eternity" as the ideal poet, addresses the poet's function, joins classical and Christian imagery to glorify both the object of his poem and Pope, and offers some of his best images. The Muses and Apollo already look favorably upon this young man who dedicated his poem to Byles. In addition to being an accomplished poet, he has the proper virtues: despite his greatness he remains modest, and even though his mind is filled with bold ideas he did not hesitate to acknowledge publicly his early mentor, although he did not mention him by name. Yet his talent is limitless, so he may acknowledge an infinite number of debts without diminishing his own luster:

> So your bright Father *Phoebus*, o'er the Skies
> Profusely scatters Light's eternal Dyes,
> Unnumber'd Worlds from him receive their Days,
> Yet still he shines with undiminish'd Rays.*

His pen will never run dry.

The young poet dedicated his poem to Byles in order to thank the older poet for nurturing him, yet Byles generously denies any responsibility for his friend's genius. Byles compares his role in the poet's development to the lowly hen caring for the young eagle:

> So the low Hen the Eagles Egg may hatch,
> And feed the callow Care, and o'er him watch,
> But when thick Feathers on his Back unite,
> He spreads his Plumes, & takes a tow'ring Flight,
> Neglects his Nurse, & claims his heav'nly Birth,
> While she, with flutt'ring Wings, hovers—and drops to Earth.

But Byles allows that even if he did help the youth grow into adulthood (into poetic maturity), Pope was the real mentor since he inspired Byles. One of Pope's great qualities, Byles thought, was his ability to make cacophony euphonious, to capture, in his couplets, the basic unity of all things, a technique Byles attempted with classical and Christian imagery in this poem. Byles here and elsewhere extols Pope as the greatest poet (the Proteus on earth). While Pope inspired him, Byles admits that he possesses none of the master's artistry: he likens his relationship with Pope to that of the moon and the sun, the former in each case merely reflecting the rays of the latter; the one is passive, the other active.

---

*All quotations are from the text in *Poems on Several Occasions.*

Byles also compares his role between Pope and the young poet to a glass between the sun and the object receiving its intense rays:

> But when to you I would the Flames convey,
> In my cold Hands the holy Fires decay.
> As when your Hand the Convex-Glass displays,
> It close collects some scattr'd solar Rays;
> Tho' cold the Glass, where'er its Focus aims,
> The Object smokes, it reddens, and it flames:
> So POPE, thro' me, shines full upon your Muse;
> So cold my Breast; and so your Bosom glows.

Proteus' sun (and son) gives life to the universe. Byles balances that classical reference with Pope's father, who is God. The bard is "Sent from high Heav'n to grace the happy Age," and when Pope's power passes through Byles, he feels "the rushing GOD." After reading Pope, therefore, Byles is in a position to urge the young poet to rise above mortal themes and "let sacred Subjects fill the Air around." In this conjoining of classical, mortal, and divine sources of inspiration, the poet cannot help but be great.

Subtly invoking the title of the young poet's poem that inspired this one (recalling once again that Byles wrote both), Byles further implores his friend to write for eternity, as all great poets must. In so doing, however, Byles finds himself writing about eternity, and to remain consistent with his earlier perception of himself as a mere poetaster, he can only interrupt his description by saying:

> But, pause my Muse; cease my unartful Song:
> The Beauties which I strive to praise I wrong.
> The Scenes so fast upon My Fancy flow,
> Convinc'd, I own ETERNITY a NOW.

Byles leaves himself and Proteus far behind and makes his final instruction to the young poet religious by urging him to follow his "pious Muse," which he may find through Pope and which will lead him to the celestial chorus. Byles concludes by portraying his friend's development as a poet:

> So some full Spring a trickling Rill bestows,
> That makes melodious Murmur as it flows;
> It widens as it wanders on its Course,
> And as it glides it gathers greater Force;
> Still on it runs, and nought its Stream controuls,
> It now a Riv'let, now a River rolls.

> Now its strong Tyde, with unresisted Sway
> Rushes impetuous down and foams away;
> It pours along, and all its Banks out-braves
> Till the vast Sea absorbs its undistinguish'd Waves.

"To My Friend" is an engaging poem even though Byles chose to misdirect his readers by the diversionary prose praising himself qua young poet. Beneath his playful deceit is serious commentary on the importance of the great poet, the necessity of superior poetic models, and the ultimate goal of poetry in society, which is to lead man to God. He was able to convey these thoughts effectively by fusing classical and Christian imagery and by using several good figures, and in so doing he showed himself capable of writing neo-classical poetry superior to most published in this country at that time and for the half-century to follow.

Pope's example governed eighteenth-century American poetry even after a call for a native literature arose following the Revolution. One cannot deny Pope's greatness, but his dominance over American poets for almost a century had a stultifying effect on our verse and was partly responsible for our poetic dark age. Such demi-Popes as John Adams, Benjamin Colman, Francis Knapp, and John Maylem were occasional poets comfortable within the limits of the neo-classical form, but they lacked Pope's energy, skill, and genius and thus produced imitative verse that, taken as a whole, is undistinguished at best. Standing well above the others is Byles. He wrote his share of bad poems, to be sure, but he occasionally created a fairly good one, as "To My Friend" surely attests.

Various librarians have helped me prepare this collection of Byles's works. I would like especially to acknowledge Howard H. Peckham, former Director of the William L. Clements Library, The University of Michigan, and Roger Mortimer, Curator of Rare Books, Thomas Cooper Library, University of South Carolina. I also wish to thank my colleague Donald J. Greiner for his assistance. This project could not have been completed without a Research and Productive Scholarship grant from the University of South Carolina.

BENJAMIN FRANKLIN V

University of South Carolina

THE
CHARACTER

OF THE

Perfe&t and *Upright* Man;

HIS

Peaceful END defcribed;

AND

Our Duty to OBSERVE it
laid down.

In a DISCOURSE

On PSALM XXXVII. 37.

By *Mather Byles*, M.A.

Phil. I. 21. *For me to live is CHRIST, and to
die is gain.*

*Quod fi putatis longius vitam trahi
Mortalis aura nominis,
Cum fera vobis rapiet hoc etiam dies,
Jam vos fecunda mors manet.*

Boet.

BOSTON : Printed for S. GERRISH in
Cornhil. MDCCXXIX.

The CHARACTER and END of the *Perfe&t Man* &c.

PSALM, XXXVII. 37.

Mark the perfe&t man, and behold the upright : for the end of that man is Peace.

THERE is nothing more becoming rational creatures, than a conſtant regard to the *end* of their ſeveral actions. It is the effect of true wiſdom, to look beyond preſent things, forward to futurity, and inquire how they will terminate ; and then to direct in the moſt proper methods, to avoid a miſchievous, and produce a happy period.

IT is the peculiar excellency of the Holy Scriptures, that they addreſs mankind in a manner thus ſuitable to themſelves, and with a rational authority and majeſty, ſtrike the human ſoul, and command aſſent and reverence.

The

THE Pſalm immediately under our view is of this character, in which the Royal Prophet undertakes to vindicate the diſpenſations of Divine Providence, from every objection of injuſtice, unfaithfulneſs, and inequality, with which the ſons of profaneſs might affront and blaſpheme them. From the conſideration of the righteouſneſs and equity in the dealings of GOD moſt high, to men upon the earth, the *Pſalmiſt* perſwades to the exerciſe of patience and holineſs, and directs us where to look for that real felicity, after which our eyes wander, and our hearts inceſſantly pant. The inſpired reaſoner concludes with an exhortation, exciting all the ſincerely pious, that they by no means be diſcouraged from the ſervice of their Lord, and enforces the exhortation by ſeveral notives and arguments. The laſt of theſe is, the *different ENDS* of the *righteous* and the *wicked.* Both the righteous and the wicked muſt *come to an end ;* For *it is appointed unto all men once to die,* and *what man is he that liveth, and ſhall not ſee death ?* But how *wide* and *diſtant* are the ends of theſe two very different parties of men ? *Mark the perfect man, and behold the upright ; for the END of that man is peace. But the tranſgreſſors ſhall be deſtroyed together, the END of the wicked ſhall be cut off.*

IN the words of my Text, there are three evident diviſions, which I ſhall diſtinguiſh into *deſcriptive, doctrinal,* and *practical.* Theſe I ſhall conſider in their order.

I. THE *deſcriptive ;* in which, we have the CHARACTER *of the good man :* PERFECT *and* UPRIGHT. *Mark the perfect man, & behold the upright.* Theſe two terms, *Perfection & Uprightneſs,* are a ſhort, but a moſt comprehenſive character of an heir to cæleſtial and unfading glories. They are a very compendious and brief epitomie of the heart and life of a ſincere chriſtian : The fair lines of his character are here drawn, but in miniature, exact, and elegant. PERFECT and UPRIGHT : Perhaps, on the one hand, ſome would confine the meaning too cloſe, and take both the words to ſignify the ſame thing.

thing. Like *Pharoah's* dreams, they will say, *the words are one, and the interpretation is one.*

OTHERS may perhaps strain them too far, and be willing to make a devout remark, which however it may entertain the Fancy, and be true in it self, perhaps may not have the weight of a demonstration with the judgment, as being otherwise than *prettily* deduced from this immediate text. PERFECT, say they, that is *internally* holy; UPRIGHT, that is *externally* religious. It is, without doubt a true character of a servant of GOD, that he is holy both in heart and life; but whether the two branches of my Text point most accurately at these two parts of sanctification, I shall not here pretend to determine.

BUT that I may consider the words in a suitable latitude and clearness, I shall show how they appear to me, in a more particular answer to the question, *WHAT is the PERFECTION which good men attain to in this life?*

IN discussing this enquiry I shall say,

I. Negatively. *BY the word PERFECT in the text we are not to understand SINLESS Perfection.* This is a degree of felicity not attainable by men, while they dwell in *this present evil world.* Of *natural* men, it is strictly true, what we read, inPsal. xiv. 3. *They are ALL gone aside, they are ALTOGETHER become filthy; There is NONE that doth good, no NOT ONE.* And even of those *renewed by the SPIRIT of our GOD,* it is as infallibly certain, I. Joh. i. 8. *If we say we have NO SIN, we deceive ourselves, & the truth is not in us.*

INDEED if we take perfection in the *rigid sense* of the word, it means something beyond what any *created Being* may assume to it self; *supremely and divinely good.* And in this respect, surely *there is none good but one, that is, GOD,* Mat. xix. 17.

BUT in a *larger sense,* moral perfection is applied to *Creatures,* and signifies *a state entirely free from all sin.* Such is the blessedness of the holy Angels, these sons of perfection, and possessors of unsullied purity: And such is the *honour of all the Saints,* in

the

the confecrated manfions above. There, in a moft exalted fenfe, they *ftand* PERFECT *and compleat in* ALL *the will of* GOD; and are moft emphatically called, *the fpirits of juft men made* PERFECT.

HOWEVER, in this world, alas, it is far otherwife: For *there is not a juft man upon earth, that doeth good, and finneth not,* Ecclef. vii. 10. This is a truth very eafy to be proved from *reafon,* from *fcripture,* from *example,* and from our own unhappy *experience.*

WAS there ever a *meer man,* upon earth, fince the fall of ADAM, that had a perfect *underftanding* of the Law of GOD. It reaches to *every action* of life ; to *every word* we fpeak or *ought* to fpeak ; to *every thought* in our minds, or that *fhould* be there. It *forbids* fin at *all times,* and there is *no reafon* but there is fome *particular duty* which it commands and exacts. In a word, *the commandment is exceeding broad :* fo broad, that the mind of no man, weakned and obfcured by the fall, can ever fo much as fully *underftand* it. It is plain then, if no man can have a compleat underftanding of the divine law, he cannot fully *practife* it : For it is firft neceffary to *know* in order to *do* our duty. Thus DAVID admires, Pfal. xix. 7. *The Law of the* LORD *is* PERFECT——and no wonder then, he exclaims, ver. 12. *Who can* UN-DERSTAND *his Errors? cleanfe thou me from fecret faults.* Thus we fee *reafon* gives it, that as the law of GOD is of too wide a compafs to be *fully compre-hended* by finful man ; fo, by confequence, it cannot be *compleatly practif'd,* any more than *ignorance* can be the *mother* of rational *devotion.* To this we may fubjoyn *another* argument, namely, that did we fully underftand the moral commands, yet *no man perfect-ly comes up to what he knows.*

WHO among the prefuming fons of men, after he has performed *one* fingle duty, dares look back on it and appeal to GOD, that he fees no *finful defect* in it, for which he defires a pardon? Not one among the deluded mortals, that boaft a perfection in this life, dares venture upon this tryal ; and truly if they did, what would it prove, but their impudence and

vain

vain conceit ? *GOD I thank thee,* faid the proud Pha-rifee, while he ftood and careffed himfelf, and run the infolent difparity, *GOD I thank thee, that I am not as other men, —— or even as this publican.*

Surely if any mortal might have afferted per-fection in this life, who would have been more likely than the admirable *PAUL,* who was the holieft a-mong the moft holy, and *came not behind the very chief of the Apoftles.* Yet this is the very man, whom the Holy Ghost felects out, to infpire his moving lan-guage with thofe pathetick and mournful fentiments, which flow through the vii. Chap. to the *Romans,* fee from the 14. ver. *For we know that the law is fpiritual, but I am carnal, fold under fin. For that which I do, I allow not ; for what I would that I do not ; but what I hate, that do I.——— For I know, that in me (that is in my flefh) dwelleth no good thing : for to will is prefent with me, but to perform that which is good I find not. For the good which I would, I do not ; but the evil which I would not, that I do.——I find then a law, that when I would do good, evil is prefent with me. —— I fee another law in my members warring againft the law of my mind, and bringing me into cap-tivity to the law of fin, which is in my members. O wretched man that I am, who fhall deliver me from the body of this death !* And is this indeed Paul ? the devout, the laborious, the moft excellent Paul ! the very fame who could tri-umph in thofe harmonious and gallant periods of in-fpiration, II. Cor. xi. from the 21 ver. —— *Whereinfoever any is bold, I am bold alfo. Are they Hebrews? fo am I : are they Ifraelites ? fo am I : are they the feed of Abraham ? fo am I: are they minifters of CHRIST ? I am more : in labours more abundant, in ftripes above meafure, in prifons more frequent, in deaths oft. Of the Jews five times received I forty ftripes fave one. Thrice was I beaten with rods, once was I ftoned, thrice I fuffered fhipwrack ; a night and a day have I been in the deep: In journeying often, in perils of waters, in perils of robbers, in perils by my own countrymen, in perils by the heathen, in perils in the city, in perils in*

B   *the*

the wilderness, in perils in the sea, in perils among false brethren ; In weariness and painfulness, in watchings, often, in hunger and thirst, in fastings often, in cold and nakedness. Besides those things which are without, that which cometh upon me daily, the care of all the churches. Who would imagine that these two, are the defcriptions of the fame perfon ! That he who *was* fo excellent, and *did* fo much, fhould cry out, *Oh ! the body of death !* Yet, this is he ; the great *Paul,* the renowned doctor of the *Gentiles.* By choofing out this diftinguifhed Hero of Chriftianity, to fill his tongue with the lamentation of fin polluting all his duties, the HOLY SPIRIT feems to have pitched upon the fitteft perfon in the world, to ftop the mouth of gainfayers. For when a character fo great and exalted as that of the Apoftle PAUL, owns the blemifhes of fin, what petty mortal prefumes to ftand up, and boaft his fuperiour attainments ? The Man, who drove on unrivalled through the race of Chriftianity, and flung even the Apoftles themfelves at an humble diftance ; to hear his confeffions of defect and fin : with what pity, and contempt, and indignation muft we hear a grovelling fet of Enthufiafts, pour out their abfurdities and nonfenfe, in felf-applaufes at their own more untarnifhed Holinefs? None of them venters to fay, *He himfelf* has attained Perfection ;. but they all it feems agree together, that it is fcattered, invifibly, fomewhere among their conceited numbers. — *No doubt they are the people, and* Perfection *fhall die with them* —

As there has been enough faid to confute this vain and arogant opinion, of a finlefs perfection attainable in this life, fo the objections and cavils againft the true Doctrine in this refpect, may be as eafily obviated and overthrown. It happens very uncomfortably for the afferters of Perfection, that all the texts they bring to eftablifh their error, lie fo near other texts which explain them in a different fenfe, that a man muft be very fenfibly *given up to ftrong delufions* before he can *believe* fo evident *a lie.*

Do

D o the *Scriptures call some men perfect* ? it happens
very well for our doctrine, that there is not one meer
man called so, but some sin of his is also recorded, to
prevent miftakes about the matter.   Was † N o a h *a
just man,& PERFECT in his generations* ?   This fame
N o a h, we are informed, * lay *drunk* and *uncovered
in his tent.*   Was A s a's *heart PERFECT with the
Lord all his days.* ‖ In the very next Chapter four
of his Crimes are tranfmitted down to pofterity. Did
H e z e k i a h *walk before GOD with a PERFECT
heart,*§ yet did the fin of H e z e k i a h *bring wrath upon
him and upon Judah,and upon Jerufalem.*   Even our Father A b r a h a m himfelf, to whom the command was
given, *walk before me and be thou PERFECT,* ‖
even H e, the faithful *Abraham,* failed in that very
grace wherein lay his chiefeft excellency. He was
twice over reproved by a heathen, for a crime into
which he was betrayed through diffidence and infide-
lity. See *Gen.* x i i. 12----. x x. —.   In a word, let the
pretenders to perfection, look over the Scriptures,and
produce from thence their meer man without fin.

P e r h a p s they will give up their argument from
example, and lie intrenched rather under fome *precept* which commands perfection. They will frame
their plea thus : Are we not plainly *commanded to be
perfect?* Now is it reafonable to imagine that we
fhould be required to perform an impracticable duty?
There needs no other anfwer to the objection, than
to cite the very text they allude to, Mat. v. 48.
*Be ye therefore perfect, even as your Father who is in
heaven is perfect.* No man can underftand this literally ;
or take it otherwife, than as a command to endeavour
after perfection, as much as ever he can.   And that
this fhould be our *endeavour* is agreed by all :   But
that ever it will be our attainment in this World,
ft.ll remains to be proved.

T h e laft argument I fhall take notice of, urged by
the afferters of perfect holinefs in this Life, is per-

---

† Gen. vi. 9. * Gen. ix. 20, 21. ‖ 2 Chron. xv. 17.
§ 2 Kin. xx. 3. ‖ Gen. xvii. 1.

verted from some texts, which seem to a careless eye, to look that way : But these too, all lie near such places, as very effectually explain their meaning. In the Epistle of *James,* Chap. iii. 2. we are told, *If any man offend not in word, the same is a perfect man.* It is well however that the very words before are, *In many things we offend all.* So that there can be no difficulty in this text. But the most noted passages which these men produce, are in the 1st. Epistle of *John,* particularly, Chap. iii. 9. *He that is born of GOD sinneth not.* Methinks this Epistle of all others, should be the most unlikely to find favour with these men. The first chapter of it, is directly armed to overthrow their tottering foundation. See 8 and 10.verses. *If we say that we have no sin, we deceive our selves, and the truth is not in us. If we say that we have not sinned, we make him a liar, and his word is not in us.* To conclude, There is no way for these men to prove their point out of this Epistle without making the inspired author contradict himself. I shall here dismiss this point,and make some *positive answer* to the Question. *What is that perfection good men attain to in this life,* spoken of in the Text?

1. *It implies INTENTIONAL Perfection.* In this particular the text explains it self,and *perfection* means *uprightness,* and sincerity. *Mark the PERFECT man, and behold the UPRIGHT.* If good men are not *positively* perfect, yet they are *intentionally* so; and though they can never in this life fully *acquire* this felicity, yet they are always *endeavouring* after it. So the Apostle *Paul* at the same time calls himself *perfect,* and yet says he *has not attained* to perfection. Phil.iii.12,13,14,15. *NOT as though I had already ATTAINED,or were already PERFECT,but I follow after it.---Brethren,I COUNT NOT my self to have apprehended.But this one thing I do,forgetting the things which are behind ; and reaching forth unto those things which are before, I press forward toward the mark for the prize of the high calling of GOD in CHRIST Jesus. Let US therefore, as many as be PERFECT,be THUS MINDED.* This was the Gospel preached by
Paul.

Paul, that though he had *not arrived* to perfection in the *strict sense* of the Word, yet, while he *pres-sed* after it, he might in the sense of the Gospel come into the number of *as many as were perfect.*

And the same conclusion rears it self, on a comparison of *Job* i. 1. with *Job.*ix.20. In the first of these *Job* is called a *PERFECT* and *UPRIGHT man,* one that feared *GOD,*and *eschewed evil.* And in the other *Job* himself pronounces, *If I justify my self, my own mouth shall condemn me; if I say I am PERFECT, it shall also prove me perverse.* Hence it plainly follows, that *Job's perfection* was only *uprightness,* and signified no more than that he *feared GOD,* and *eschewed evil;* that is, *endeavoured after perfection.*

And this is a perfection which belongs to all good men. They Desire to be perfect; their *desire* forms itself into a settled Purpose to pursue it; their *purpose* produces an Endeavour; their *endeavour* demonstrates their Sincerity, and their *sincerity* is a *Gospel* Perfection.

Indeed if we consider how sincerity operates in a good man, we shall observe some *resemblance* of a *real perfection* in it. The regards of a holy Man to the new Covenant, flame with the purest ardor, and proceed with a direct integrity. He is entirely for God, and aims at his glory, with a single eye, and an upright heart. Though he obeys the Law of GOD *but in part,* yet he obeys *every part* of it : That is; tho' he cannot *fully* come up to *any* single precept of it, yet, there is *no* single precept, which he does not *endeavour* to come up to. So that though the *obedience of faith* is not *sinless,* yet it is *universal;* and this both in regard to the *person* obeying, and the *law* o-beyed.

It is universal in respect of the *person obeying :* because he observes it with his whole spirit, soul, and body, and submits it both *externally* and *internally.* Thus runs the exhortation of the Apostle, *Jam.* iv.8. *Cleanse your hands ye sinners, and purify your hearts ye double-minded.* The *hands* and *heart* here specified, have a plain reference to the two constituant parts of man, *body* and *soul,*   It

IT is the care of the man of GOD, to prefent his *BODY* as well as *his fpirit a living facrifice to GOD*; and the feveral *members* that fupport and adorn it, he improves as the members of his LORD JESUS CHRIST. The feveral *fenfes* of his Body too, the holy man dedicates to the GOD who contrived their curious conftitution, and maintains their various powers of action and delight. His *EYES difcover* the image of the Deity clearly reflected from the glafs of nature, and the will of GOD more clearly revealed in the mirrour of his word; and are then *lifted up* to heaven, in admiration and praife. His *EARS* catch the glad tydings of the *Pulpit*,and attend devoutly at the facred place of thunder; and not only fo, but they endeavour to learn fomething forGOD in the moft trifling or vain*Company*. His Food relifhes upon his *PALATE* with a finer flavour, and a ftronger guft, when *he eats to the glory of GOD*, and therein *taftes that the LORD is gracious*. The Fields do not breathe their odors upon him, and render the air about him a perfume, without his articulating the *fcented* breath in founds of gratitude and thankfgiving. He does with his might,what his *HANDS* find to do, and his *FEET* are directed in right paths, while,like his JESUS upon Earth, he *walks about* conftantly *doing good*. He calls upon his *TONGUE*,*awake my glory* to praife the*LORD* : And to what end, *fays he*,have I my *voice*,but to praife thee *aloud with joyful LIPS*. In fine, the whole *body* of the good man, and all the *members* and *fenfes* of it, are dedicated to the fervice of GOD, and employed in the facred exercife.

AND not only does he *ferve GOD in his body*, but with *his SPIRIT alfo which belongs to GOD*. The HEART is the *principal thing*,& to this both the pious man, and his GOD have a principal regard. A conftant watch over his own heart, is *effential* in the character of the holy man. Wherever he *walks*,whatever he *does*, this is his care, and the ferious bent of his thoughts. This is a fecret and filent, but a great work, and makes the upright heart, confcious to many *joys which a ftranger intermedles not with* ; and alfo to *know its own bitterness,* and *feel its own plague,* which none elfe can be a witnefs to. Hence we read of the *hidden life of a chriftian,* Col. iii. 3. and of the *hidden man of the heart,* I. Pet. iii. 4. And indeed every *power* and *capacity* of the pious foul is confecrated to the glory of GOD. This facred employment forever furnifhes its *invention* with a pleafing labour ; renews its *memory* to a fweet recollection ; exercifes its *judgment* in a rational debate ; and kindles its *affections* with a holy rapture. Thus we fee the obedience of the chriftian to the divine Law, is univerfal in refpect of the PERSON *obeying :* that is, both parts of the man yield obedience, even every *faculty* of his Soul, and every *member* of his Body.

AND if we confider the LAW *obeyed,* the obedience is *univerfal* in regard to that too. The fincere chriftian endeavours a conformity to the *whole* moral law, without any exception, and *counts none of the commandments grievous.* Both tables of the decalogue make but one fyftem of rules for the direction of his life. His GOD, his *neighbour,* and *himfelf,* are all the objects of his becoming care and folicitude. That nicely-drawn Scheme of practical religion, *Tit.* ii. 12. is but a regular fketch of his life, *Denying all ungodlinefs, and every worldly luft, he lives foberly, righteoufly, and godlily, in this prefent world ; looking for the* glorious rewards of another. Here is contained both the *negative* and *pofitive epitome* of his *heart* and *life.* He *forbears* to do what the law *forbids, denying all ungodlinefs, and every worldly luft :* and as it *commands,* he lives *foberly* with regard to *himfelf* ; *righteoufly* with refpect to his *neighbour* ; and *godlily* with reference to his *Maker* ; while at the fame time the *internal* principle is declared *looking* to future rewards. So his bleffed LORD upon Earth, was *holy, harmlefs, undefiled, feperate from finners,* Heb. vii. 26. *Holy* before GOD, *harmlefs* towards *men* ; and undefiled in *himfelf* ; while, in a *negative* character, he was *feparate from finners.*

THIS

THIS is the picture of the *PERFECT* and *UP-RIGHT man*, spoken of in our Text ; and indeed none but he, is *universal* in his obedience to the divine law. The *hypocrite* is quite of *another character*, forever *partial* in his obedience, and still rolls some beloved lust as a sweet morsel under his tongue, which he will by no means part with. Nor can the most painted among that unhappy generation be described any further than he, Mar. vi. 20. *He did MANY things. Many* things ; not *all*. But so much for the first thing, that the good man is *intentionally* perfect.   To proceed,

2. *HE is perfect by IMPUTATION.* And in this sense, the believer is perfect in the *strictest* sense of the word, as it can be applied to *creatures: Fully*, and *completely* perfect. The imputation of CHRIST's righteousness, gives the faithful a claim to a perfection without spot or blemish. The true Christian, holy as he *is*, and perfect as he *endeavours to be*, forever renounces *his own righteousness*, and stands *perfect before GOD* in the *imputed righteousness* of the Mediator. This is most emphatically expressed in that humble devotion and ardor of our Apostle, Phil. iii. 8, 9. *What things are gain to me I count loss for CHRIST. Yea, doubtless, and I count all things but loss for the excellency of the knowledge of CHRIST JESUS my Lord --- and do count them but dung that I may win CHRIST, and be found in him, not having my OWN righteousness, which is of the law, but THAT which is THROUGH FAITH in CHRIST. the RIGHTEOUSNESS which is of GOD BY FAITH.* In like manner the ignorance and vain-conceit of those who go about to establish a *righteousness of their own*, are detected by the same Apostle, Rom. x. 4. *For CHRIST is the end of the law for RIGHTEOUSNESS to every one that believeth.* But it is not easy to express any thing more plainly than this matter is declared in the *fifth* chapter to the *Romans*. See from the 12 verse, where the Apostle treats this subject at large. I am not concerned to know what subtilties the *unlearned and unstable* may use to *wrest* this passage of *Paul's* Epistle :

But

But fure they will at leaft keep from contradicting the
Doctrine as we here lay it down ; for the fame *Trick*
which will evade the *Apoſtle's Argument*, will alfo ferve
to explain all that *we aſſert* according to their own
Scheme. I do not fee how it is poſſible to deliver
this Doctrine in plainer and fewer words than thofe,
*As by one man's DISOBEDIENCE many were made
SINNERS; fo, by the OBEDIENCE of one, ſhall many
be made RIGHTEOUS.*

In fhort, this *Juſtification* by the *imputed Righteouſneſs* of CHRIST, is fo evidently afferted and explained in the holy writings, that a man muft be
more cunning than ordinary, who can perſwade them
to a different confeſſion. No doubt the various *Racks*
of the *Critick*, or the *Commentator* (men who have a
wonderful knack to *illuſtrate away the meaning* of the
cleareft texts, and *explain them into nonſenſe)* no doubt,
but the *artificial engines* of thefe men may pervert the
plaineſt words, and extort half a dozen contradictions
from every verfe in the New Teftament : But however their ingenuity may pleafe themfelves, and gratify a few Gentlemen of their own opinions, yet they
will never be able to convince the ferious inquirer
after truth, or weaken the authority of the infpired
oracles, to a mind at the fame time devout and rational.

If then the Scriptures declare the *righteouſneſs of
CHRIST imputed to the true believer*, no wonder he
is called the *PERFECT MAN.* This is the diſtin-
guiſhing glory of the fons of GOD among men, and
this honour have all the faints. The radiant atire of
his *Saviour's righteouſneſs* fhines over the *juſtified* foul
of the *perfect man.* This untarnifhed and dazling robe,
renders it approved and beauteous in the eyes of heaven. Not the ftrict and impartial juftice of GOD can
charge it with the leaft defect, adorned fo illuftrious
and magnificent. Not an angel in the imperial city
above fparkles in the circle of fo divine a fplendour ;
nor does the whole conſtellation of morning ftars
blend their beams in an equal glory.

Stand ftill then, *Mark the PERFECT man ! and
behold the UPRIGHT !* *Take notice* and *obſerve* his

C   Character,

Character. *PERFECT*; that is, *JUSTIFIED* by the *imputation* of a *perfect righteousness*, even *CHRIST*'s. *UPRIGHT*; that is, *SANCTIFIED* by the *HOLY SPIRIT*. Thus is the good man *PERFECT as he who has called him is PERFECT*; and he walks in the *shining path of the just, which rises more and more unto the PERFECT day!*

WE come now to the SECOND main thing in the Text, which may properly enough be called the DOCTRINAL *part* of it.

II. *THE perfect and upright man has PEACE in his END.*

IT is a great miftake to imagine that there is no peace in the *way* of a true Believer; for certainly his *WAYS are ways of pleafantness, and all* his *paths are peace*; Prov. iii. 17. But it is furely a much greater error to fuppofe that the *end* of his way is not peaceful and happy. Nay, *the END of that man is PEACE*; a *PEACE paffing all underftanding*, and a *peace* without any *end* at all.

BUT for the clearer illuftration of this matter; we may here make a *conceffion*, and acknowledge that *the death of believers may fometimes be attended with uneafy and grievous circumftances.* When we affert the peaceful end of the good man, we do not always mean to banifh from his death-bed, every thing of a frightful and ghaftly afpect; and fpread fun-fhine and ferenity over the gloomy vale. No; the pious man may die in fuch a manner, as to wear quite a *different face* from that of *peace*, in the unfanctified eye. All may feem to end in a tragedy; his fun may fet in a cloud; and the grave may open a hideous mouth, and gape upon him black and difmal. The righteous and unerring Providence of GOD in this World, makes no diftinguifhing and conftant difference between the holy and impious. *For we fee that WISE MEN DIE, likewife the FOOL and the BRUTISH PERSON perifh. And HOW died the WISE MAN: as the FOOL,* Eccl. ii. 14, 15, 16. *The WISE MAN—and the FOOL—I my felf perceived that ONE EVENT happened to them all. Then faid I to*

my

my self, as it happeneth to the FOOL, so it happeneth unto ME ; and why was I then more WISE ?

THESE equal diſtributious of providence, in regard to the juſt and the unjuſt, for ever check the daring pride of the men who would judge of their neighbours uprightneſs, by the events that befall them. It is a vain arrogance to judge a man's eſtate in the *other world*, by the manner of his expiration *here :* And it is a vain preſumption to expect that all good men ſhould die with the *outward ſigns of peace*, and basking in the viſible dawn of a future bleſſedneſs. Our bleſſed Saviour has warned us againſt theſe indecent and uncharitable cenſures, Luk. xiii. 1—5. *There were preſent at that ſeaſon, ſome that told him of the Galileans, whoſe blood Pilate had mingled with the ſacrifices : And Jeſus anſwering, ſaid unto them, ſuppoſe ye that theſe Galileans were ſinners above all the Galileans, becauſe they ſuffered ſuch things ? I tell you, NAY : —— Or thoſe eighteen, upon whom the tower of Siloam fell, and ſlew them, think ye that they were ſinners above all men which dwelt in Jeruſalem ? I tell you, NAY :——* Thus the death of good men may ſometimes look with an awful and ſurprizing aſpect ; far from peace and calm. They may *die* by *caſualties;* like thoſe ſlain of *Siloam :* They may be *afflicted* with *grievous diſeaſes ;* like the upright *Job :* they may be *murdered* by the *cruelties of martyrdom ;* as the righteous *Abel :* or they may be *ſtruck* by the *immediate hand of heaven ;* as the too-zealous *Uzziah.*

NAY, what is moſt of all dreadful, a good man may die in great dejection of mind : and inſtead of peace, his whole ſoul may be in a tumult ; and the ſound of war, may alarm his laſt moments. GOD may hide his face from him ; and withdraw the ſenſe of his love. The *Devil* may be let looſe, and urge his onſets with redoubled *fury, becauſe he knoweth that he hath but a ſhort time.* In a word, the good man may die with all poſſible circumſtances of horror and anguiſh, except an *abſolute deſpair.*

C 2 BUT

BUT is this any objection to the truth of the Doctrine, *The* END *of that man is* PEACE? Surely no : even amidst all the shuddering of this agony, and though the thundering tempest beat with the utmost outrage upon the departing saint; yet is there peace and calm in it all. Faith shews the heavenly calm of paradise, far-distant, behind this momentary tumult : and let the winds rise, the waves roar, and the storm thicken and grow black in the cloudy atmosphere below : Yet above does the ether-shine ever clear and serene ; and the climate is eternally pure, and soft, and indulgent. There the sun-beams play about without the least stain or obstruction ; but the whole ample space, seems but one unbounded ocean of flame and glory. Nay, even all the present affliction ; the grief of soul, and the pangs of death ; it is all intended for the advantage of the good man ; and shall only promote his flight to the smiling regions, *where the wicked cease from troubling, and the weary are at rest.*

HAVING made this *concession,* and considered the *objection* which might arise from it, I shall now show, HOW *the* END *of the perfect and upright man is* PEACE.

1. *A good man dies in a* STATE *of* PEACE *and reconciliation to* GOD. Sin has made a terrible controversy between GOD and man; while man is become the rebel, and GOD the avenger. The deplorable condition in which the fallen race of *Adam* stand with relation to the holy GOD, is like that, Zach. xi. 8. — *My soul loathed them, and their soul abhorred me.*

BUT though the state of the unregenerate is thus unhappy and dismal, while GOD *holds them for his enemies:* Yet it is much otherwise with true believers. The difference between GOD and them is made up. GOD is at *peace* with *them,* and *they* are *reconciled* to GOD. Rom. v. 1. *Being justified by faith, we have* PEACE *with* GOD, *through our Lord Jesus* CHRIST. That blessed *Prince of peace,* has *made* peace for us; He has *bought* it with his *blood,* and *sealed* it to us by
his

his *holy Spirit*. He has drawn up the *articles* of it, in his *new and everlasting Covenant* ; and settled it upon strong foundations, forever fixed and immovea-ble. There it stands like a mighty city, of the finest symmetry and proportion: *divine wisdom* is the *archi-tect*; *divine truth* the *basis*, and it is *supported* upon the *pillars of omnipotence.* Surely the death thus defend-ed and secured, cannot but be *really* peaceable and blessed. But,

2. THERE is not only a *real* peace in the death of believers, but it is very often attended with a *SENSE of that happy and glorious PEACE.* They have frequently a *taste* of peace, as well as always a *state* of peace, when they come to die. *TO DYE!* alas, how improper the phrase for our purpose here ! Ra-ther, it is a *sleeping in JESUS* ; an entrance into rest, and into glory. A soft transition to the upper World; a short step to a full reward of our labours. *DEATH!* Tis but the opening of the gates of Pa-radise ; and though they may sometimes seem to grate upon their hinges, and affright the soul with a jarring found; yet how often do they, on the contrary, move smooth and easy, and ring their golden harmony in the ears of the dying saint. *Open, ye gates, that the righteous nation which keepeth the truth may enter in. Thou wilt keep him in PERFECT PEACE, whose mind is stayed on thee : because he trusteth in thee,*Isai.xxvi.2,3.

OH ! happy condition of the expiring good man! O peace divinely sweet, and divinely full ! Death it self is no longer an *enemy*, but a *friend* be-yond expression welcome to a triumphing soul. *O death,*he shouts aloud,*O DEATH! where is thy sting? O GRAVE where is thy victory?* His *conscience* now when he has oft need of it, appears for him, and anticipates the sentence of his Judge. It pronounces, *Well done, good and faithful servant, thou shalt pre-sently enter into the joy of thy Lord.* His SAVIOUR now speaks peace to him, *To day shalt thou be with me in paradise.* GOD his FATHER, with smiling lips, and an enlightened countenance, tells him, *SON, be of good cheer, thy sins are forgiven thee.* The HOLY
SPIRIT

Spirit becomes in him, a spirit of *adoption*, and of *consolation*; inspires him with a noble courage, and transports him with a full assurance. The attending *Angels* that hover round his curtains, to receive the dis-united soul, are busy to strengthen him in his agony. They say, *Fear not, our friend, for thou hast found favour with GOD : Hail! thou that art highly favoured, the Lord is with thee, blessed* shalt thou be for ever : And as for us, *we also are thy fellow-servants, and thy brethren.* Nay, the *believer himself* how can he choose but sing, divinely raised! *I am now ready to be offered up, and my departure is at hand ; I have fought a good fight, I have finished my course, I have kept the faith. Henceforth is laid up for me a crown of righteousness, which CHRIST the righteous judge will give me on that day.* Ah, vain *world, says he,* no more shall your gilded vanities mock my eyes: I am going to a world of substantial and unfading delights! Ah, vile *sin,* no more shall you molest and perplex me : I am just entring into the city, where *nothing entreth that defileth, or worketh abomination.* Ah, tempting *devil, yet a little while and I am with you, and then I go to* my father: *and whither I go, thither you cannot come.* These elevated flights, this triumphant language, is often heard from the quivering lips of the expiring Believer.

MARK now, *the perfect man, and behold the upright ;* and say, *ye wise observers,* say, is not the *end of that man peace? BEHOLD,* his eyes yet strive with departing light, and hang upon the ebbing day; anon, they fix, they darken, they go out : But say, *O FAITH!* what are the joys which the soul, the immortal part, sees, and converses with, while the mortal eyes are languishing in death! What visions of endless glory rise up to the smiling spirit! How is it cheer'd, how transported, by the rushing beams of a future blessedness, that break the clouds of the awful valley! *MARK,* his breast heaves, and his heart seems to labour in the final struggle : But, oh ! does the pale bosom really pant with agony ? or rather, does not the heart leap and bound with a joy unfelt till this blessed moment ;

and

and is not the breaft fwell'd and extended only by the ravifhing beginnings, of the extafy without limits, and without end.

THERE is not a more noble fight in nature, than a good man amidft all the confufions and horrors of death, relying on his bleffed Redeemer with fuch an unruffled and heavenly calm of mind. The very heathen paid this complement to virtue, as *certain alfo of their own poets* have exprefs'd it: * *The man refolute in goodnefs bears regardlefs the clamours of the defpicable rabble, and mocks the frown of the threatning tyrant. Nor ftorms, nor the thunder of God, can fhake the folid peace of his mind. Should the orbs of heaven fall crufhing about him, fearlefs would he ftand, and bear a world fhatter to ruins.* If the *Poet of the Gentiles* can fing thus, what ftrains fhall the *Apoftle of the Gentiles* raife, for the lips of the dying chriftian. Rom. viii. 35, 37, 38, 39. *Who fhall feparate us from the love of Chrift? fhall tribulation, or diftrefs, or perfecution, or famine, or nakednefs, or peril, or fword? Nay, in all thefe things we are more than conquerors through him that loved us. For I am perfwaded, that neither death, nor life, nor angels, nor principalities, nor powers, nor things prefent, nor things to come, Nor height, nor depth, nor any other creature, fhall be able to feparate us from the love of God which is in Chrift Jefus our Lord.* Thefe may well be the notes, the hallelujahs, which the Saint giving up his foul, may fend to paradife before him. Affured that nothing fhall feparate him from the love of CHRIST; and affured that his maker is his friend, HE, the GOD who manages all the wheels of Nature and Providence, what has he to fear. GOD, may he fay, is my *father*; *Heaven* is my *home*; *Death* is my *friend*; *Angels* are my *guardians*; *all things* are *inftruments of my good.*

HE may demonftrate to all about him, that there is fomething in religion able to fupport, and bear him up, under all the confufions & fhipwrecks of nature. The uproar of a *diffolving univerfe* cannot difturb the foft and fettled

---

Hor. Lib. III. Ode. 3.

tranquility of his mind, while the HOLY SPIRIT of GOD breathes and operates there.   He attends the *Thunder* as it shakes the skies over him, and he shouts to the noble sound.   O, says he, *I hear my father speak here; it is his dear voice that breaks the clouds; and bends the poles !*   And as the *Lightnings* flourish the power of his GOD, in flaming characters, thro' the gloomy sheets of midnight,*There,* he sings, *there behold the glory of my inheritance in light, stream down the skies, in every blaze, and every gleam.*   If death rushes to meet him, upon the wings of a *whirlwind,* undaunted, unappall'd ; he smiles upon the welcome angel, and hears the blasts of the hurricane, as the trumpet of the herald to proclaim his ascent to paradise.   He says * among the trumpets, *ha, ha* ; he defies the tempest afar off, the thunder of the winds, and the roaring.   He mocks at fear, and is not affrighted, neither turns he back from the blast, the shaft, that hisses along towards him, feathered with death, and commissioned for his soul. Even in an *Earthquake,* when all things about him look wild in a general shudder, compos'd and easy, he may set still, and *sing* ; and not *Paul* and *Silas* tune the air to more melodious sounds.

UPON the whole, what a glorious peace runs like a golden thread through the whole christian life, while the end of it is in a more particular manner blazon'd with the glittering fringe, like the splendid garments of *Aaron* ? †   'Behold, happy is the man whom GOD thus
' calleth away.   In six troubles and in seven shall no
' evil touch him : neither shall he be affraid of destruc-
' tion, when it cometh.   At destruction and famine he
' shall laugh ; neither shall he be afraid of the beasts
' of the earth.   For he shall be in league with the
' stones of the field ; and the beasts of the field shall
' be at PEACE with him.   And he shall know that his
' tabernacle shall be in PEACE : and he shall visit his
' habitation, and shall not sin.   He shall come to his
' grave in a full age, like as a shock of corn cometh in
' its season.

* Job. xxxix. 25. 22.   † Job v. 17, 19, 21----26.

2. *AFTER*

3. *AFTER their death believers go into EVER-LASTING and PERFECT PEACE.* If we would so *mark the perfect man, and behold the up-right,* as to have a full view of their *peaceful END,* let us look *beyond* the grave, into the *invisible world.* Isai. lvii. 1,2. *The righteous perisheth, and the merciful man is taken away —— The righteous is taken away from the evil to come. He shall enter into PEACE—.* But when will it once be that he shall *enter* into this unmolested peace ? Truly, when he is *taken away* ; and at the *END* of his life here. Rom. vi. 22. *Being now made free from sin, and becoming servants to GOD, ye have your fruit unto holiness, and the END everlasting life.* No sooner is the last gasp over, but the spirit of the believer wings away for paradise, the realms of immortal peace and triumph. A flight of Angels, watch unseen, round his dying curtains, to be the convoys of the fleeting soul : And soon as the vital thred snaps asunder, they receive it with a glad caress, and spread their pinions and soar away. If our minds could but follow the shining ascent, what a wonderful scene of glories would open upon them? How does a soul just escaped from a body of sin, and pain, and death, exult as it towers away in the midst of such bright attendants ! What Hallelujahs spread tuneful round the unmeasured Æther, as the pomp rises through it, to the regions of life, ever-fair and flourishing !

But, O the *peace,* the joy, the rapture inconceivable ! when the orient gates of the new Jerusalem shall be thrown open for the reception of the *perfect man !* O dazling splendors of the crown, that never fades or grows dim, prepared for the man faithful unto the death ! O the unknown transports, in the open immediate vision of JESUS, the very life of the good man below, and the crown of his future glory ! Here is the great *peace* we look for : The *end* of the *perfect and upright man,* is a translation to this holy and illustrious world. Here we shall have *peace* from *corruptions*; nor shall we complain any more of the *body of death,* after the *death of the body.* Here we

D   shall

shall have *peace* from *temptation* ; for there is no *serpent* in that *heavenly paradise*, no *forbidden tree* in that *beauteous garden of* GOD. Here we shall have *peace* from *afflictions of all sorts* ; for there are no *sorrows* where all *tears are wiped from the* raptured *eyes* : There is no *sickness* where the *Sun of Righteousness* shines in his meridian glory, with *healing in his wings* : There are no reviling *Shimei's* in the *New Jerusalem;* nor can any *losses* happen to those who find these *durable riches*.

THESE are faint shadows of the heavenly blessedness ! Alas, how little a portion is known of it ! No more ——— To speak of the glory of heaven fully, who is sufficient for these things ! What the perfection of it will be, *we know not now*; *we shall know hereafter.* Fitter are these themes for the Hallelujahs of a Seraph, than the faultering tongue of a mortal : better to be admired than described : to dwell for ever in a sacred meditation on our hearts ; to influence every action we perform ; and at last, to breathe a *peace* into our final hour, and inspire the instant of our death, with a joy untasted in the brightest moment of our life. *This* is the *LAST End,* of the perfect and upright man ; and *this* the *PEACE* which spreads its wings over it. ' Eye has not seen, nor ear heard, ' nor can the heart of man ascend high enough to con- ' ceive it all !

THE LAST *part* of the text, we observed was properly PRACTICAL ; and consists of a *direction* to perform a particular *duty* ; Namely,

III. *WE are to take a particular NOTICE and OBSERVATION of the peaceful end of the perfect and upright man. MARK, BEHOLD,* says the text; that is, *Take particular HEED,* and be careful to *remember,* and *fix in your minds* the joys and assurances of the *perfect man,* as he lies gasping on the bed of death : *observe* and *record* his conquest of the last enemy. I shall but just touch upon this point, and having offered a few hints to show our duty and advantage in this respect, I shall finish with a brief Reflection upon the whole. We should MARK and BEHOLD the *peaceful* END of the *perfect and upright man,* Because,   1. IF

1. *IT CONFIRMS OUR FAITH in the truth of the Goſpel.* O moſt excellent religion, we cry, that can inſpire its votaries with ſuch noble and well-timed courage ! Here ſeems to be the ſeal of GOD that it is indeed true. Bleſſed are the ways which *End* thus happily.

2. *IT ENCOURAGES OUR HOPE, that OUR END alſo may be PEACE.* We look upon the departing believer rejoycing in the hope of the glory of GOD, and raviſhed with the foretaſte of his approaching bleſſedneſs ; and we ſay within our ſelves, ‘ Who knows but GOD may thus graciouſly ſupport ‘ and inſpire *me* too, when I languiſh in the ſame con- ‘ tion. We ſee his pale lips ſmiling in a perfect calm, and his cloſing eyes lifted up in the raptures of deſire and aſſurance, while we hear the laſt notes flutter upon his dying tongue, ‘ *How long, O LORD !* ‘ *—— When ſhall I come and appear before GOD ? ——* ‘ *Come, Lord JESUS, come quickly ? —— Why is thy* ‘ *chariot ſo long a coming ? why tarry the wheels of* ‘ *thy chariot ! —— I deſire to depart, and to be with* ‘ *CHRIST ! —— Father, thy will be done ! —— Lord* ‘ *JESUS, receive my ſpirit.* We ſtand by the bed of death, and BEHOLD the ſcene of tranquility, and MARK the ſacred, and ſublime, and joyous language, and our glowing hearts argue, ‘ This ‘ good man was ſuch an one as I now am : He ſuffer- ‘ ed the ſame temptations ; laboured under the ſame ‘ infirmities ; and, it may be, ſlipt into the ſame ſins ‘ which now cauſe me to walk ſoftly and mourning. ‘ But now, GOD has forgotten all ; he is comforted, ‘ and entring upon endleſs ſatisfactions. The ſame ‘ GOD whom we both ſerve, may, as far as I can ‘ tell, deal thus with *me* too.

3. SUCH obſervations *MAKE US WILLING, and TEACH US HOW to die.* Who can behold the man of GOD amidſt the ſhades of death, thus compoſed and ſerene, thus chearful, and thus raviſhed, and not be willing to be as he is, and even wiſh to repoſe our dying heads upon the ſame happy pillow ? To look death in the face with the ſame courage, and commit

our

our fleeting fouls into the hands of JESUS with the fame confidence and ardour ?

4. WHEN we *mark* the happy *END* of the *perfect man, we are induced to* FOLLOW THEIR EXAM-PLE. While we *mark* and *behold* the happy *END* of good men-; we are excited to *mark* and *behold* their LIVES too, by a wife *imitation* of them. The felicity that glitters to the period of a pious life, powerfully urges and perfwades us, to *follow thofe who through faith and patience inherit the promifes* ; to *fhew the fame diligence, to the full affurance of hope unto the END : Their faith we follow, confidering the END of their converfation.*

BUT it is time to haften to a CONCLUSION. Let us paufe, and REFLECT.

MARK the perfect man, and BEHOLD *the upright, the END of that man is* PEACE : Go to now, MARK *and* BEHOLD *the* WAY *to* OBTAIN PEACE *in our latter END.*

To this purpofe ; Let us not be fo ftupid and foolifh as to put far from us the *thoughts* of our *end,* forget the *day of our death,* and make it an *evil day* by doing fo. Are we all *going down to the dead* ? and fhall we permit fuch *madnefs in our hearts* as to do it blindfold ; and rufh upon the flames of hell *as the horfe rufheth to the battel* ? *O that we were wife, that we underfood this, that we would confider our* LAT-TER END *!* Let us confider that we are not *far from our End,* but our lives fly fwiftly to a period. Efpecially to fuch as put off the folemn preparations for their end, to fuch is applicable that, in Ezek. vii. 5, 6. *Thus faith the Lord* GOD,—*the END is come, the END is come, it watcheth for thee, behold it is come!* And is it indeed come ; and does it thus ftand ready for the fecure finner; and fhall he ftill mock it, and fcoff it from afar? fhall he urge it on with an infolent frenzy ? will he think to dare the vengeance of heaven, and out-brave omnipotence ! Ah ! *be not* thus *wicked over-much, neither foolifh ; why fhouldft thou be deftroyed before thy time.*

MARK

*MARK the perfect man, and behold the upright,the
END of THAT man is peace : But what is the
END of those who are NOT perfect and upright ?*
Will thefe unhappy men have peace in their latter
end ? *what peace fo long as the fins* of a wicked
life remain unpardoned ! Verily,*there is NO PEACE
faith my GOD, to the wicked !* Shall I carry you to
the death-bed of a wretch who has lived without
GOD, and without CHRIST, and without hope in
the world : And who dies as he lived, without hope,
and abandoned to trembling, and agony, and defpair ? Who can utter, or what heart conceive, the
wild horror of fuch a guilty foul, juft gafping into
the hands of an almighty and inexorable judge !
Juft finking down into the place of torment, the
fathomlefs pit of perdition, and the lake which burneth with fire and brimftone, from whence the fmoke
rolls up for ever and ever ! How does the amazed
fpirit, recoil, and fhrink back into the body, at the
difmal profpect before it ! How does it fhudder upon
the edges of the vaft duration,which ftretches from its
eyes in an endlefs fucceffion of ages ! that eternity,which
waits to overwhelm and fwallow it up ! But, alas, vain
are all its tears, and out-cries ; it looks wild about for
any way to efcape in vain. The profpect of life is
wholly over; the door of mercy is for ever fhut; the
holy angels are all drawn off, and will no more defend it ; the devils ftand all hiffing around, and wait
to rufh in upon it ; hell opens its voracious jaws, and
flames of fire leap out ; the foul begins to feel the
unfufferable fcorches, and finds, that let it fhriek
and ftrive ever fo much, *IN IT MUST !* To fum
up all in a word, *GOD holds it for an enemy !* The
GREAT GOD is engaged againft it ; dooms it to
fuffer his almighty vengeance : and *who knows the
power of his anger ! even as his fear fo is his wrath.*

BUT this is only the ftate of the death-bed ; and
the picture of the fpirit fhivering on the borders ;
what are the fcenes which open behind ? *Is there
any PEACE TO COME ?* any hope of hereafter ?
alas, no. Where is the language to declare the *ftrange
plagues,*

plagues, which will continue for ever to torment the ruined finner? Not the howlings of hell it felf can exprefs its torments ; not the horrid imagination of a devil can paint his future and eternal mifery. This is the END of *all that forget GOD.* The pleafures that now flatter them, will be *bitternefs in the LATTER END* ; will *at LAST bite like a ferpent, and fting like an adder.* They fhall *mourn at the LAST* : and find *the END of thofe ways* to be *the ways of death.* He who purfues his finful pleafures, in fuch an open defiance of heaven, *fhall leave them in the midft of his days, and at his END fhall be a fool.* Numb. xxiv. 20. *His LATTER END fhall be that he PERISH FOREVER.*

SURE, it can be no indecency to fpeak with emphefis here : for who can think of thefe things unaffected ? who can let his mind loofe upon thefe awful myfteries of damnation, and not be moved at the dire idea ? who can look down into this horrible furnace, and talk of the devouring and unquenchable fire, in cool blood ? For my own part, *when* I meditate, *my* flefh *trembles* ; *my lips quiver at the* thoughts ; terrors enter into my heart ; and *I tremble in my felf, that I may find PEACE in the day of trouble* * the hour of death.

AND is this indeed the END of *all that forget GOD* ? and on the other hand, Is the *End* of the good man fo divine and glorious as we have heard ? who would not pray with him, Numb. xxiii. 10. *Let me die the death of the righteous, and let my LAST END be like his!* Would we be thus *happy* in our *end,* and *dye* the *peaceful death* of the *righteous* ? Let us be thus *fincere* in our *beginning,* and *live* the *holy life* of the *righteous.*

LET us all be at laft perfwaded to fue for *peace with GOD,* that we may have *peace in our latter end.*

WAS there ever more affecting words uttered among men, than thofe, II. Cor. v. 20. *We are ambaffadours for CHRIST, as tho' GOD did befeech you by*

_____
* Hab. 3. 16,

215

us : we pray you in CHRIST's *stead, be ye* RECON-
CILED TO GOD ?

WITH what pathetick language did our blessed
Saviour mourn over *Jerusalem,* who had outstood its
day of grace ; and had an eternal bar fixed to its peace
with GOD! Luk. xix. 41, 42. *And when he was come
near, he beheld the city, and wept over it, saying, if thou
hadst known, even thou, at least in this thy day, the
things which belong unto thy* PEACE ! *but now they
are hidden from thy eyes !* O let us not *delay* our
endeavours after a peace with GOD, least *This condition,* also *become ours.*

BUT in our transactions about this great affair, let
us by no means forget ourLord JesusCHRIST ; but do
all *through* him, *depending upon* him, and *ascribing
all to him.* Of him it is declared, Mich. v. 5. THIS
MAN IS THE PEACE. Having secured a part in
his friendship and mediation, we are happy for ever :
nothing can hurt us ; all things will work together
for our good.

LET the *end of our lives* come now as soon as they
will, the *day of our death,* will prove better than the
day of our birth. Then shall unmolested, — smiling,
immortal *peace* spread her heavenly wings over us.
We may throw our selves upon the bed of death, and
sing, in the notes of the psalmist, Psal. iv. 8. *I will
lay me down in* PEACE *and sleep, for thou* LORD
makest me dwell in safety.

F I N I S.

Mr. *Byles*'s

Two S E R M O N S

A T

Dorcheſter.

A

DISCOURSE

On the Prefent

Vilenefs of the Body,

A N D

Its Future Glorious Change by

C H R I S T.

To which is added

A SERMON

O N T H E

Nature and Importance

O F

CONVERSION.

Both occafionally deliver'd at *Dorchefter April* 23. 1732.

By MATHER BYLES, A. M.

Hic neque concepto fetu, nec femine furgit :
fœunda morte reformat
Et petit alternam totidem per funera vitam.
Claud. Phœnix.

B O S T O N:

Printed by S. KNEELAND & T. GREEN, for N. PROCTOR.

M D C C X X X I I,

PREFACE.

IF any enquire into the Reasons of this Publication; the Importunity of some Friends, and the Judgment of others, together with some Desire to do good, are the general Arguments of a modern Preface: And the Author hopes he has some Right to this common and useful Train of Thoughts.

The Sermons are Plain, & adapted to a popular Audience. They were composed without any Tho'ts of the Press, and when they were perswaded out of the Author's Hands, he could not find Leasure from his other Studies to transcribe them: for which Cause the Reader will not expect to find any thing laboured or uncommon. The Author imagines that lively Descriptions, a clear Method, and pathetick Language best become the Desk: And this possibly may be one Reason why he insisted no more upon
Philosophical

Philosophical Arguments in his Discourse upon the vile Body changed. Tho' he believes the Doctrine of the Stamen will as easily account for a Resurrection, as for Generation, yet he suppses such Talk in the Pulpit serves more to amuse the Auditory, and complement the Preacher himself, than to honour CHRIST, or do good to Souls.

If by looking over the ensuing Pages, any Christian shall have one more holy or proper Tho't, the Writer will think his Pains well rewarded.

T H E

THE

Glorious Change of the vile Body.

PHILIP. iii. 21.

Who shall change our vile body, that it may be fashioned like unto his glorious body.

He Apostle *Paul* in the Chapter open before us, after some Precepts laid down, concludes with Two Motives to perswade Men to the Practice of them : And these are, the *Coming of* C H R I S T, in the Verse preceeding my Text ; and the *Resurrection of the Saints* now read unto you. Both of them are very solemn and sublime Thoughts : But it is only the latter which comes immediately within the Compass of our present Meditation.

The *Resurrection of the Dead*, and, which is much the same thing, the *Transformation of those found alive* at the coming of CHRIST, are very clearly revealed in the New Testament, especially by the Apostle *Paul*. But the Glory of a Believer's Raised Body is not, nor indeed can it be any where more fully express'd, than in the Words under our immediate View. *Who shall change our vile body, that it may be fashioned like unto his glorious body.*

The Apostle tells us, Our Bodies are now *vile* ; our vile Bodies shall be *changed* ; it is our Lord JESUS CHRIST *who* shall change them ; and they shall be *fashion'd like unto his glorious body.* How much is crowded into a few Words ! how emphatical are they ! how copious ! how sublime ! How amply do they fill the Mind, and exhaust the Imagination, inspire our Faith, and awaken our Joy ?

In

In handling thefe Words, I fhall only have Time to fpeak to Three of the Four Articles (or if you pleafe, *Doctrines*) which you fee are plainly contained in them.

I. *Thefe Bodies of ours, in their Prefent State, are* VILE BODIES. *Who fhall change our vile bodies?* Shall we here let our Thoughts loofe upon a few Particulars, which will render it plain, and humble us with the fad Conviction. Thefe Bodies, of whofe Beauty and Vigour we are fo apt to boaft, alas, they are vile Bodies.

1. Their *Original* is mean and defpicable. In the Senfe of the *Greek* Text, our Body was vile, even in the Purity of its firft Creation. The Word which we tranflate *vile*, is ταπεινώσεως: The Body of our *Humility*. 'Tis a *humble* Body. It carries *Humiliation* even in its Origin and Conftitution. It comes from *Humus*; the *moift Ground*; The *Clay*, the *low Earth*. The Firft Principle of *Humane*, is *Humus*. Humiliation and Vilenefs is thus entail'd upon our Body, even from the primative Materials out of which it was framed. Even *Adam* in Paradife and Innocence, might in this facred fenfe, have own'd a Vile Body.

And now, Let the Proud Creature look down to the Earth, & view the Duft from which he fprung, & then confefs his Body Vile. *And the Lord God formed man out of the duft of the ground* †. Out of the Clay was this living Frame fafhioned; here it had its humble Original; and from this abject Earth, did it arife and fhoot up, thus curious in its Form and Conftitution. This beauteous Arrangement of finer Duft, was taken from the common Glebe, into which it muft quickly fall, and refolve again. The Limbs which now fhew the exacteft Symmetry and Proportion, the Pulfes which beat with the ftrongeft Energy and Life, and the Afpect that is flufh'd with Health and Beauty, owe all their Exiftance to the fame Clods of Earth which harbour our Brethren, the Worms: The Worms, which wait to Feaft upon our moulding Carcafe; and riot in our wafting Flefh. The Body *is of the Earth, earthy*: *Duft it is, and to Duft it fhall return.* Let us reflect thus, & then confefs, This VILE BODY.

2. It is a *finful* Body, and therefore a vile Body. It has in it a Body of Death; and no wonder it looks ghaftly, and loathfome, and vile. All its Appetites are vitiated, and diforder'd, and it leads the Soul about like a Malefactor in Chains. The Spirit which God *infufes*, is depraved and polluted by it: and Original Sin is *communicated* thro' the Veins of the guilty Parent. The feveral *Senfes* of the Body, prove fo many Traitors to the nobler Faculties of the Mind, and continually captivate and debafe it. How many Sins enter at the *Eyes*? and how many idle Ideas pafs in at the *Ears*, for ever open

---

† *Gen.* ii. 7.

to the Vanity of empty and corrupted Air. The Luxuries of the *Palate* debauch the enslaved Mortal, and drag him on to Excess and Intemperance. He wanders among sensible Appearances, and forgets spiritual and divine Realities. He is hardly brought to consider, that the *things which are SEEN are temporal, but the things which are not seen are eternal.* Is not the Body, that thus abuses the Soul, the Rational principle within, a vile Body? The Body, the beautiful Workmanship of an Alwise Artificer, how is it sunk beneath the Level of the brutal World, by its Sin against God? *O wretched that we are! who shall deliver us from the Body of this Death?*

3. Our Body is a weak, *infirm* Body, and therefore a vile Body. It is a feeble House of Clay that totters to every Blast. Disease and Mortality lurk in every Member, and Vein, and Muscle. It is liable to Contagions and Distempers of all Sorts. They March silent and unseen, in the fine Air about us. They lie brooding in their Venom, thro' all the Fluids within: Latent Destruction! Death in Ambuscade! A Thousand different Fevers stand ready to seize this Body; to torment it, and to burn away its Life: To lick up the finer Spirits, and snap the Vital Cord. It may be at once *blinded* by a Defluxion of Rheum, fetter'd with the Tortures of the *Gout*, and broken in the Agonies of the *Stone*: Like *Sampson* in the Philistian Prison-house, at the same Time *blinded*, and *shackled*, and *grinding*. Every Nerve about us, is capable of Pains too great for us to bear, too strong for us to resist, and too subtil for us to escape. The Strength of the most athletick Body, is still on the Wing; may fly away suddenly; will do it speedily; and must at last wholly leave it. The Beauty of the most amiable Body, is every Day hasting to fade, and go out in obscure Darkness. Our daily eating and drinking, proclaim a feeble Body, that would faint and die if these were omitted. Every Time we set down to a Table, or take a Cup in our Hand, we confess we are Creatures that need constant Support and Nourishment. When we lie down to the necessary Sleep of the Night, we own the Sleep of the Night must relieve us a little from the long Slumber of the Grave. Every Breath we draw insinuates, in a silent Whisper, our Frailty, our Dependance on God, and our short Continuance: It warns us that our *Life is Wind.* —— So Weak is our Body, that it takes away much of our Thought from our Souls, to contrive for its Life, and Health, and Sustenance. —— Let us look now upon the brittle Frame, and exclaim, O the vile Body!

4. It is a *dying* Body, & therefore a vile Body. Here our Bodies now stand, perhaps flourishing in all the Pride and Bloom of Youth: Strong our Sinews; moist our Bones; active and supple our Joints; our Pulses beating with Vigour, and our Hearts leaping with a Profusion of Life and Energy. But oh! Vain Appearance and gaudy Dream! Surely every Man at his best Estate, is altogether Vanity. He walks in a vain Show; he glitters with delusive Colours; he spends his Years as an Idle Tale. What avails it, that he is now

B   hardly hardy and robuſt, who muſt quickly pant upon a Death-bed. What avails it, that his Limbs are ſprightly in their eaſy Motions, which muſt quickly ſtretch in the dying Agony. The Lips now fluſh'd with a Roſey Colour, will anon quiver and turn pale. The Eyes that roll with a ſparkling Vivacity, will fix in a ghaſtly Horror. The moſt muſical Voice will be ſtop'd ; and the tuneful Breath fly away. The Face where Beauty now triumphs, will appear cold, and wan, and diſmal, rifled by the Hand of Death. A Cold Sweat will chill the Body ; a hoarſe Rattling will fill the Throat ; the Heart will heave with Pain and Labour, and the Lungs catch for Breath, but gaſp in vain. Our Friends ſtand in Tears about our Bed : They weep ; but they cannot help us. The very Water with which they would cool and moiſten our pearched Mouths, we receive with a hollow Groan. Anon we give a Gaſp, and they ſhriek out in Diſtreſs, ' Oh ! *He's gone,——He's dead !* ' The Body in that Inſtant ſtretches on the Sheets, an awful Corpſe. This is the End of our Body for this World : Pronounce now ; Is it not a Vile Body ? But this brings me to the laſt Article.

5. Our Body will quickly be a *dead* Body, and this proclaims it a vile Body. The Silks and ſoft Linnen which now fold and adorn theſe Bodies, muſt be changed for a winding Sheet. The Applauſe and Complement which now flatter us, are not heard in the Retirements of the Grave, to diſturb its aweful Silence : Nor ſhall Reproaches and Revilings break in upon our Reſt there. Our pleaſant Habitations will be left for others, while we have no Apartment left us, but a Coffin, or a Tomb at moſt. We ſhall forſake our Diſhes and our Tables ; and our ſelves become Food for the crawling Vermin of the Duſt. How quickly ſhall we haſten to Clay and Aſhes, in the ſolitary, and dark, and cold Grave ?

In a few Years, the moſt beautious, or learned, or pious Head will grin a hideous Skull. Our broken Coffins will ſhow nothing but black Bones, and black Mould, and Worms & Filth. The Places that know us ſhall know us no more. The Perſons who were moſt intimate in our Acquaintance ; who ſooth'd us with their Viſits, or careſs'd us in their Boſoms, will now forget us. When they ſhall perhaps enter our Tombs and take up our Bones in their Hand, they'll not ſuſpect the frightful Carcaſe to be Ours, ſave by the Letters on the broken Coffin, or the Inſcription on the mouldring Monument.

And now, *Man giveth up the Ghoſt, and where is he ?* What becomes of the Dream of Worldly Happineſs ? Where are the Houſes, and the Coffers ? The Great Name, the loud Applauſe, and the Brutal Pleaſure ? His Riches are left to others : And to whom he knows not ; whether a Wiſe Man or a Fool. He forſakes his numerous Houſes, and is confined to a narrow Coffin, in a lonely Vault.

Out

Out of all his Lands he retains but a few Foot of Earth to cover him from the Sight. His boafted Name is forgot among
the living, and fcarce once in an Age cafually read upon his
Grave-ftone. *His Breath goeth forth, he returneth to his Earth, in
that very Day his Thoughts perifh.*||

The Spirit is given up ; and fee the Body drops down, pale,
and ftiff, and cold. The Eyes are fixt; the Teeth are fet; the
Breath is fled. Is this the Face we once gaz'd upon with fo much
Pleafure ? Are thefe the Cheeks that glow'd fo frefh, and bloom'd
fo lovely ? Are thefe the Lips that fmil'd fo graceful, and pour'd
out fuch a gliding Stream of Eloquence and Mufick ? Where's
the tuneful Voice that once held the liftening Ear, and rais'd the
attentive Eye ? Where are the proportioned Limbs, the fupple
Joints, the vigorous Pulfes, the beating Heart, the working Brain,
and the breathing Breaft ? Lo, the Body is laid in the Duft, and
the Worms cover it. Polluted Vermine crawl over every Part
of the elegant Form, and the beautious Face. It is folded in a
winding Sheet, it is nailed in a black Coffin, and it is depofited
in a filent Vault, amidft Shades and Solitude. The Skin breaks
and moulders away ; the Flefh drops in Duft from the Bones ;
the Bones are covered with black Mould, and Worms twift a-
bout them. The Coffins break, and the Graves fink in, and the
difjointed Skelliton ftrows the lonely Vault. This fhapely Fabrick
muft leave its Ruins among the Graves ; lie neglected and forgot ; moulder away without a Name, and fcatter among the E-
lements. ' And were thefe Bones once living like ours ? and
muft ours be as they ' ? This hideous Skull, the frightful Jaw
fallen, and the black Teeth naked to the Eye, was it once a
thinking Frame, covered with a beauteous Skin ? Strange Alteration made by Death ! And are not our Burying-Grounds
full of fuch Spectacles ? What do they but illuftrate and con-
firm the Doctrine ? Methinks every Grave, with open Mouth,
preaches upon my Text, *This Vile Body.* O Vile Body ! under
what infamous Difhonours of Loathfomenefs and Corruption art
thou ? Thou muft be laid away in the dufty Galleries of the
Grave, the gloomy Chambers of Death, unregarded and unknown ;
loft in deep Retirement, and awful Silence. O Vile Body !

Thus we have feen with what Propriety Vilenefs belongs to
thefe Bodies. How fuitable and emphatical the degrading Epi-
thet ? Let us here paufe, and improve, and fet Limits to the
Defcription.

Is this Body fo Vile and Wretched ? *How vain and foolifh is
it to be Proud of our Body.* τό σω̂μα τη̂ς ταπεινω̂σεως ἡμω̂ν :

The Body of our Humiliation. Vain Men ! Proud of the very Body of Humiliation ; Vile, debasing, sinful Clay. Why should we let our Eyes upon that which is not ; or in a little Time will not be ? Why should we prefer our Bodies, and forget our Souls ? Cloath and adorn those, while we are regardless of the Salvation of these ? Why, ye *Fair*, should ye be proud of a Beauty destin'd to the embrace of Worms ? Or why, ye *Strong*, should ye boast the hardy Nature, which must quickly faint, and drop down breathless. O far be the Tho'ts from us, to be vain of such vile Bodies ! Away, the haughty Mein, and the disdainful Glance ; the conscious Smile, and the assuming Brow. Away the artful Movements and manag'd Airs of Wantonness and Pride. No more let airy Fashions and looser Modes of Dress expose the Body. Nor let it be lost in the studied Disproportions of an ambitious Garb. Why need we affect an Apparel, fantastically Demure, on the one hand ; or choose on the other, Pomp, and Glitter, and empty Show ? We may appear decent in the Polite World, without running thro' all the quick Succession of Fopperies : The *round Attyre like the Moon*, in a perpetual Circle of Changes. Let the vile Body, be CLOATHED *with* HUMILITY : ✝ Modesty and Sobriety are the best Ornaments.

But let us set Limits to the Exclamation, and not carry it too far. No ; our Bodies, vile as they are, are, to be honoured and respected by us. They are the wonderful Production of Omnipotence, the curious Workmanship of an alwise Artificer. Let the Body of the Sinner be as vile as it will, your Bodies ye happy Believers, are raised above the common Clay in nobler Honour. *What, knew ye not,* (says the Apostle) *that your Bodies are the Members of* JESUS CHRIST ? —— *Know ye not, that your Bodies are the Temples of the Holy Ghost, that dwelleth in you.* ✝ Our Bodies, it is true, are in many respects vile ; But yet, under all their Humble Circumstances, they are the Members of our Lord JESUS. Let us always then, when we call our Bodies vile, remember that they are noble too, and intituled to the sublimest Honours. Let us take Care of them, cherish them, view them in the Light in which CHRIST looked upon his own Body. For he *spake concerning the Temple of his Body,* Joh. ii. 21. Let us respect and reverence our Bodies, as the Temples of the HOLY SPIRIT ; the Members of JESUS CHRIST, and the Candidates of a glorious Resurrection. When we wash, or feed, or cloath, or adorn our Bodies, let such Meditations as these, produce, and sanctify the Act.

But we come to the second Doctrine.

✝ 1 Pet. v. 5.   ✝ 1 Cor. vi. 15, 19.

II *Thess.*

II. *These vile Bodies of ours shall be* CHANGED. The greatest
Part of Believers on CHRIST shall be changed at a Resurrection from the Dead : But not all. Some shall never die,
but be found alive at the Appearance of CHRIST : These shall
be caught up to meet the descending Judge, and shall be
changed in the shining Ascent. See in the 1st Epist. Cor. xv,
Chap. where the Apostle treats this Subject at large, ver. 51, 52.
*Behold I shew you a mystery; we shall not all sleep, but we shall all
be chang'd, in a moment, in the twinkling of an Eye, at the last
Trumpet, (for the Trumpet shall sound) and the dead shall be raised
incorruptable, and we shall be changed.* So that in the End, there
will be very little Difference between the dead Believers, and
those whom our Lord finds alive at his coming. Both shall be
changed at our Lord's descent ; caught up to meet him in the
Regions of Air, as his fiery Chariot rolls down amidst Thunder,
and Clouds, and Whirlwinds. The Living Saints shall be snatched
from the Earth, and changed from the feeble State they are
now in : Those who are Dead, and sleep among the Tombs,
shall shake off the Dishonours of the Graves, and be changed
from the Vileness of Dust and Worms. Of these in their Order.

1. This vile Body shall be changed from the STATE *of*
DEATH. What though our Bodies die ; they shall revive from
the Condition of Curse and Corruption. *If a man die, shall he
live again ?* Yes ; at the Resurrection of the Dead shall he be
raised. GOD shall raise the Dead, by the Man whom he hath
ordained, whereof he has given Assurance unto all Men in that
he raised him from the Dead. So long ago as the Time of
Job, the holy Man could look to a Redeemer, who should call
him from the corruptions of the Grave, and renew his consumed
Limbs to Strength, and his Eyes to Light. [Job xix. 25, 26, 27.]
*For I know that my Redeemer liveth, and that he shall stand at the
latter Day upon the Earth. And tho' after my Skin, Worms destroy
this Body, yet in my Flesh shall I see GOD ; whom I shall see for
my self, and my Eyes behold, and not another, tho' my Reins be consumed within me.* We must die, but what then, we are as sure
of a Resurrection as we are of Death. But Oh ! what a blessed
Change will the Resurrection make upon our dead Bodies. Perhaps the Worms have feasted themselves upon our Last Dust ; but
they shall refund it, and give back every Attom : All that really
belongs to our numerical Body. The Fishes perhaps have eaten
the Carcase, buried in the Waves, and lost in the Depths of the
Ocean : But *the Sea* also shall return it back, † *and give up the
Dead that is in it.* These Bodies may dissolve, and scatter a-
mong the Elements. Our Fluids may forsake their Vessels ; the

† Rev. xx. 13.

Solid

Solid contract, and fold up in its primitive Miniature. And even after that the little invifible Bones may moulder to finer Duft, the Duft may refine to Water, wander in a Cloud, float in a River, or be loft in the wide Sea, and undiftinguifhed Drop among the Waves. They may be again fucked up by the Sun, and fall in a Shower upon the Earth ; They may refrefh the Fields with Dew, flourifh in a Spire of Grafs ; look green in a Leaf, or gaudy in a Flower or a Bloffom. For we know Matter is continually changing, and one Element perpetually loofing it felf in another. But let our Duft wander where it will, thro'out the whole material Creation, yet at the firft Blaft of the laft Trumpet, it fhall all at once rufh together, and ftart up a compleat Man. The vile Body fhall be changed, where-ever it lay hid : The Duft fhall be called together ; the Bones fhall harden, and the Joynts connect ; a new, unknown, incorruptible Fluid fuddenly fill the Veffels; the Sinews fhall brace with an immortal Strength, no more to be parted ; and the Skin cover all with everlafting Beauty, never to fade any more. This fhall be the Change from the *State of Death*, which our vile Bodies fhall pafs through. —— The prophetick Vifion of *Ezekl*, fhall be literally fulfilled at that day. *Ezek.* xxx. 1,--14.

2. This vile Body fhall be changed from its PRESENT STATE. Tho' it fhall be raifed from the Dead, it fhall *not* revive to its *prefent* mean and difhonourable Condition, but fhall be changed. Now it is a Body full of Uncleannefs and Corruption, Difeafe and Death. But it fhall be changed. *Tho' it is fown in corruption, it fhall be raifed in Incorruption.* * Now our Body is mean and vile, and upon many Accounts difhonourable ; But it fhall be changed *Tho' it is fown in Difhonour, it is raifed in Glory* Now they are weak, and faint, and foon exhaufted, and fpent with long and clofe Labour. But they fhall be changed from their feeble ftate. *It is fown in Weaknefs, it is raifed in Power.* Now how grofs and heavy are our Bodies? How fluggifh and unactive the unweildy Flefh? But it fhall be changed. *This I fay Brethren, Flefh and Blood cannot inherit the Kingdom of God ; neither doth Corruption inherit Incorruption,* ver. *It is fown a natural Body, it is raifed a Spiritual Body,* ver. What can we fay more to illuftrate the bleffed Change? Our Body is now in a thoufand refpects an infirm and dying Body : But, O glorious Transformation ! *This corruptible muft put on Incorruption ; and this mortal muft put on Immortality,* ver. This is the Change from the *prefent State*, of which thefe very vile Bodies are the Candidates. But we will not prevent our felves from faying

---

* 1 Cor. xv. 42. 5c, 44, 53.

III. *This vile Body of ours shall be* FASHIONED LIKE UNTO CHRIST's GLORIOUS BODY. They shall be changed from the corrupt and unclean State of Death. More than this : they shall be changed from all the Dishonours and Meanness of the Present Life : But O sublimest Glory of all ! O divine Expectation, and sacred Hope ! They shall be *fashioned like unto his glorious Body.* Like the illustrious and immortal Body of our blessed LORD JESUS CHRIST. Observe ; CHRIST still has a Body. His Body has a Form and Shape belonging to it. It is not our Bodies shall be *made* like unto CHRIST's glorious Body ; but shall be *fashioned* ; συμμορφον, shall receive a like *Figure* and *Shape,* and *be changed into the same Image.* So says the Apostle, 1 Cor. xv. 47, 49. *The first man is of the Earth earthy ; the second Man is the Lord from Heaven. And as we have born the Image of the Earthy, we shall also bear the Image of the Heavenly.*

But what is this Image ? and what is implied in that most expressive Idea, our vile shall be changed ; and fashioned like unto CHRIST's glorious Body ? I shall just hint at a few Particulars very briefly.

1. To have the vile Body fashioned like unto CHRIST's glorious Body, implies in it, that it be made *splendid and illustrious.* The Body of CHRIST is a shining Body, and *scatters Light and Glory round about it. Saul* was struck blind, dazled with the unsufferable Blaze, that rush'd in a Tempest upon his Eyes, from the Body of the Son of GOD. *John* beheld him, with his Face shining like the Sun in its meridian Flame, and his Body beaming in an answerable Glory. The Angels and the glorified Saints beheld him, as the great Ornament and the Light of Heaven : *For the Lamb is the Light of it, and they need no Sun, or Moon, or Candle.* †

If CHRIST's Body be thus splendid, our's shall be so too ; for they shall be fashioned like unto his glorious Body. They shall put on a shining Form ; shoot like a Flame from the Grave, and glitter like a Ray of Light up the Ether. Dan. xii. 3. *They that be wise, shall shine as the brightness of the Firmament, and they which turn many to Righteousness, as the Stars for ever and ever.*

2. It implies that our Bodies shall be *immortal.* CHRIST's Body is immortal ; *Being raised from the Dead, he dieth no more,* Rev. vi. 9. He pronounces with a Voice of Triumph, Rev. i. 18. *I am he that liveth, and was dead, and behold, I am alive for evermore ; Amen.*

---

† Rev. xxi. 23.

Is the Body of CHRIST immortal ? our Bodies shall be fashioned like unto his own immortal Body. *This Mortal must put on Immortality.* We must all die ; we shall die but once: Being raised from the Dead, Death shall be swallowed up in Victory ; and *there shall be no more Death.* *

3. It implies that our Bodies shall be glorified with very *mysterious and astonishing Powers.* The Body of Christ could ascend and descend with equal ease. It could stand aloft in the Air, without any visible Support ; So he looked down thro' the opened Heavens, upon the expiring *Stephen* ; *Act.* vi. 56. So he dazled the Eyes of *Saul* in the Road to *Damascus* ; Act. ix. 3. It could rise up gradually from the Ground, and tower away thro' the upper Skies, to the World above. So he ascended in the View of the Men of *Galilee*, till a Cloud fail'd under his Feet, and ravished him from their gazing Eyes; *Act.* i. 9. The Body of CHRIST could shift its form as their was Occasion, and vary its Shape and Dress, according to the Disposition of his Soul. To *Mary Magdalene* he assumed the Form and Habit of a Gardener ; *Joh.* xx. 15. While the same Day, the Two Disciples going to *Emmaus*, mistook him for a Traveller, from his Air and Dress.† *For after that he appeared in another Form unto two of them as they walked, and went into the Country.* In a Word, the Body of CHRIST could appear or vanish just as he pleased, and it should seem without Resistance from grosser Matter. Thus to his Disciples met together, with the Door shut, on a sudden, he stood confess'd in the midst of them, to their Wonder and Amazement. ‡ I can see nothing tending to Heresy in this conjecture : Nor do I think we have any reason to read the Passage, *after the Time of shutting the Door.* But it is indifferent to our present Head, whether the Body of our Lord penetrated thro' the Pores of the Wood, as Light, which is a Body, does thro' the much finer Pores of Glass ; or whether it had a power so marvellous, as to open and shut the Door; at once so swift, and so soft, as to be entirely unperceived both by their Sight and Hearing. Either the one or the other, shows the wondrous Powers of the raised Body.

And are these the Glories of CHRIST's Body ? our's shall be fashioned like it. When we are raised from the Dead, our Bodies will be active as the Flames, and vigorous as the Sunbeams. They will be able to command their Shape, or to shift their Place as they please: To glide over Oceans, rise thro the Clouds, dart like a Stream of Lightning from East to West, and range suddenly over the whole Creation.

---

* Rev. xxi. 4. † Luk. xxiv. 13. Mark xvi. 12. ‡ Joh. xx. 19, 26. Luk. xxiv. 36, 37.

4. It implies, That our Bodies shall be renewed, *holy* Bodies. CHRIST's Body is holy, and always was so. *He knew no Sin*; and tho' he was made in the likeness of sinful Flesh, yet without Sin. He was *holy, harmless, undefiled, seperate from Sinners.* His Body was sacred, and consecrate, and perfectly holy from its Birth. So the Angel blessed the Womb of the pregnant Virgin, *The Holy thing which shall be born of thee, shall be called the Son of GOD.* *

Is the Body of CHRIST holy? our's shall be so too; shall be fashioned like unto his own holy Body. These Senses shall be refined, these Passions rectified, and these Appetites adjusted to a perfect Order and Oeconomy. O divine Felicity, when this sinful Flesh, shall be changed into a perfectly holy Temple! Our Sanctification displays it self upon Spirit, Soul, and Body. But in this Life, we are sanctified but in Part, in each of these. But our Souls are wholly sanctified, upon the last happy Gasp of Death: Our Bodies will be so too, at the final Note of the great Trumpet, that shall call them from the dusty Bosom of the Grave. Then shall they be raised holy Bodies, fashioned like unto CHRIST's most glorious Body.

But why should we proceed any further? Shall our Bodies be fashioned like to CHRIST's glorious Body? It is enough! We can go no higher; can wish no more! We make a vain essay to describe the Glory, which the Fancy cannot paint, nor the Heart conceive. Our raised Bodies will shine with a Splendour, which, at present, we can have no equal Idea of. *Beloved, now are we the Sons of GOD; and it doth not appear what we shall be: But we know, that when he shall appear, we shall see him as he is.* ‡ *It does not yet appear what we shall be:* We can't imagine or conceive the Brightness of our future Glory. No matter; It is enough for us, that we shall with these Eyes behold the beauteous and majestick Face of JESUS, and *see Him as he is.* If we may but *with open Face behold the Glory of the Lord,* we shall irresistibly catch the Beams, and be *changed into the same Image from Glory to Glory.* The Vision will be a transforming Vision. *We shall be like Him, for we shall see Him as he is.* Be like Him; How? who can say how? It is above our mortal Language to declare how. *It does not appear what we shall be, but we know that when he shall appear we shall be like Him, for we shall see Him as he is.* O happy Vision! O blissful Change! O mysterious Glory.

The Fourth Proposition of the Text, is; It is our LORD JESUS CHRIST *who* shall change our vile Body, and fashion

---

It like His glorious Body. This is the Work of the great GOD our SAVIOUR. He *can* do it, and he *will* do it, Here is the *Power* ; here is the *Goodness* of a GOD. He is *able* and he *will* keep, and raise, and glorify, even the Dust committed to Him. From the Hints of the Context I might fetch Arguments enough to enlarge here. ——— But I see the Time expires, and I desist.

I come now to make a short Improvement of the noble Doctrines.

I. *How unhappy are Wicked Men !* He *shall change* OUR *vile Body that it may be fashioned like* his. Ours ; none but *ours.* The Unbeliever and Impenitent has no Interest at all in this *blessed hope* ; none but the sincere Christian can apply it to himself. It is true, the wicked must be raised from the Dead, as well as the holy. But Oh! how wide the Difference between the one and the other, at the great decisive Day ! The wicked shall be *raised to shame and everlasting Contempt.* No Glory shall shine about them, no Image of CHRIST shall appear upon them. They shall be changed, 'tis true, but O the dreadful Change ! Their *feeble* Bodies must be changed into Bodies *strong* to bear the Wrath of an Almighty GOD. Their *dying* and *dead* Bodies shall be changed into Bodies of an *immortal* Constitution ; Bodies that must live forever in unsufferable Anguish ! That must measure Eternal Ages with Groans and Out-cries, and Execrations and Despair. Their *corrupt* and *filthy* Bodies shall be changed into ten thousand Times more *hideous* and *loathsome* Figures : Fit to be Inhabitants of Hell, and Companions for Devils. Their *healthy* and *pleasurable* Bodies shall be changed, be seized and rack'd with an unknown Variety of Pains and Torments ; shall feed the Flames of the horrible Furnace ; kindled with the Wrath of GOD, that burneth as an Oven, and endureth for ever. And Oh! *who can dwell with devouring Fire ? who can inhabit everlasting Burnings ?* The *darkness of a Grave* shall be changed for the *outer Darkness, where shall be weeping and gnashing of Teeth.* Instead of being fashioned like unto CHRIST's glorious Body ; they shall be blacken'd with the finish'd Image of the Devil, and be consigned over to *everlasting Fire, prepared for the Devil and his Angels.* O the fearful Change, which the Resurrection will make upon the Bodies of the wicked !

II. *Let us learn to set a due Value upon our Bodies.* Tho' we may not idolize them, as the Crime generally is, we ought to honour them, and cherish them with a proper Care. What Honours are they coming to in a future State ? They shall be raised, and changed, and fashioned like to CHRIST's glorious Body.

III. *Learn*

III. *Learn the Honours of our Lord* JESUS CHRIST. 'Tis
HE who shall raise these vile Bodies, and fashion them like his
glorious Body. Herein is the dear Saviour *mighty* as a GOD ; Herein he is *good* as a GOD too. Not only *can* he, but he *will* do this
for us. O what Love should beat in the Hearts of these Bodies, to him who shall change them, and be the Strength of
these very Hearts, and their Portion for ever. What Thanks
shall we pay this adored JESUS ! What grateful Returns shall
we make him ! Let every Breath arise tuneful in his Honours,
who shall quickly inspire these Nostrils with Breath that will
never scatter or gasp away. Let every Pulse in our Blood, beat
Time to Musick of his Praise, who will anon give the Pulses to
leap thro' this living Frame, unfainting and immortal. Let every
Member of these vile Bodies, grow honourable, by Employment
in his Service, who shall change our vile Bodies, and fashion
them like his own. Our *Eyes*, be ye exhausted in viewing the
Works of GOD, in Reading his Word, and be lifted up to Heaven in his Praise ! These Eyes which shall see GOD ! Our
Ears, employ all your curious Organs in hearing his dear Voice :
These Ears which shall quickly be changed ; which shall hear
the Voice of the Son of GOD, in the Graves where they lie,
and be transported with endless *Hallelujahs*. Shall not these
Tongues of ours be redeemed from the silent Grave, and utter the
Anthems of Heaven ? Awake up then, our Tongue, our Glory ;
and bless and praise the LORD. These *Lips* shall forget the Pale
of Death, and be changed, and bloom afresh : what can we do
less than praise thee aloud with joyful Lips, who shall renew
their faded Beauty. O Let *all* the Body which shall be changed by CHRIST, be employed in the Service of CHRIST. How
was CHRIST's Body employed upon Earth ? Let our Bodies
be *employed* like *his now*, which shall be *fashioned* like *his hereafter.*

IV. And to conclude. *Rejoice*, O Believer, *Thy dead
men shall live, together with my dead Body shall they arise :
Awake, and sing ye that dwell in the Dust : for thy dew is as the
dew of Herbs, and the Earth shall cast out her dead.* * Shall our
Body be raised from the Grave, let us not be afraid to put off
this Body ; Let us meet Death with Triumph ! Death ! which
shall only change this vile Body for a glorious one. What glories are to come even upon this vile Body of ours. Our Souls,
the noblest Parts, they are safe. Nay, but our Body too, the vile
Body, shall be all glorious . Now, perhaps, these Bodies are in
Pain ; but quickly they shall know no more Pain. Now they
are weary with Labour ; quickly, they shall rest from their
Labour, and rise to constant Exercise without Weariness. Now

* Isai. xxvi. 19.

they

they weep and figh in many Sorrows: Quickly, all Tears fhall be wiped from our Eyes, and Sorrow and Sighing fhall flee away. Now they fhall die, and go down to the Graves which wait for us: But tho' we die, yet fhall we live; we fhall be redeemed from the Power of the Grave, and arife to die no more. *Therefore my heart is glad, and my glory rejoyceth; my flefh alfo fhall reft in hope. For thou wilt not leave my Soul in the* Grave; *nor fuffer thy holy one always to fee corruption. Thou wilt fhew me the path of Life,* in a Refurrection from the Dead; *In thy Prefence is Fulnefs of Joy, and at thy Right hand are Pleafures for evermore.*

AMEN.

THE

THE
Nature ana Necessity
OF
CONVERSION.

MATTH. xviii. 3.

Verily I say unto you, Except ye be converted, and become as little Children, ye shall not enter into the Kingdom of Heaven.

HE main Subject which our Lord JESUS CHRIST insisted on in the constant Course of his Ministry, was, the Necessity of Conversion and the New Birth. When *Nicodemus* came to converse with him, he took the First Opportunity to surprize the Honourable *Rabbi* with this most important Doctrine: *Except a man be born again he cannot see the Kingdom of* GOD, Joh. iii. 3. And here in my Text, when the ambitious Disciples came to him to determine a Dispute which they had been no doubt warmly engaged in ; *Which of them should be the greatest in the Kingdom of Heaven ?* Nay, says our Lord, Not too fast: *Except ye be converted, and become as little Children,* ye shan't so much as *enter in* there at all. Pride, and Strife, and Emulations, are no Preparatives for that World. Nor the Kingdom of Grace below, nor the Kingdom of Glory above, is to be enter'd with this unmortified, aspiring Temper. Conversion, Humility, and a new Life, must make us meet for that Inheritance in Light. CHRIST himself has determined this Matter, and it therefore comes to us with all Authority and Conviction. Let us then attend earnestly to the Illustration and Application of the Words.

The

The Doctrine of CHRIST now before us is this,

DOCT. *Conversion is of absolute Necessity in order to our Entrance into the Kingdom of Heaven.*

In the clear and profitable Handling of this Doctrine, I shall endeavour these three things. I. To explain to you the Nature of Conversion here spoken of. II. To shew what we are to understand by the Kingdom of Heaven. And III. To prove that this Conversion is absolutely Necessary in order to our Entrance into this Kingdom. And to make some practical Inferences.

I. I am to *explain the Nature of True Conversion. Except ye be converted,* says the Text. Conversion, and to be converted, are Phrases often found in the Holy Scriptures ; and our Salvation turns upon our right understanding what they mean. The Literal Sense of the word *Conversion* then is no more than this, *turning about.* And this is the meaning of the Word in this Place : and so it is explained in many other Texts. Sinners are called upon to *turn* : and this Short Word comprizes in it all Salvation. Let us meditate a little here, and endeavour to understand it well.

Man was at first created holy and happy in the Enjoyment of GOD. The Soul of *Adam* was filled with Thoughts of GOD, and love to him. The Glory of GOD was his End in all that he did. The Sense of GOD, Love to GOD, and Satisfaction in the Will of GOD, made up the Happiness of *Adam* in Paradise. The Soul was satisfied and crowded with the Enjoyment of the Infinite Being ; and a Sense of his Glories, and his Love.

Well : But no sooner did *Adam* sin, and renounce this Happiness, than GOD forsook him, and he was left destitute and empty. That Soul that was once filled full of GOD, has now in it a vast Casm We feel indeed our want of Happiness : But our dark Minds know not where to find it. The Desire remains ; but the Satisfaction is lost and gone. Our Souls feel something wanting. There's a vast Hollow there without any thing to fill it up. It is constantly craving, *Give, Give.* That's the Reason that Men are never perfectly easy and at Rest. They are forever pursuing that Happiness which they constantly miss of. GOD is gone, and Happiness with Him : and they try to fill up the empty Space, with every thing they can lay their Hands on. Riches, and Honours, and Sensual Pleasures, these they fancy will make them happy. They try ; and try again ; and repeat their Tryal : But they still meet a Disappointment. They think ; If ever I obtain such a thing I shall be satisfied. If ever I get into such Circumstances, I shall set down contented. They obtain what they desire

fire, and are juſt where they were before. Then they put off the Point of Happineſs a little further, and ſtill think on ſome Temporal Good which they have not yet enjoyed. If they obtain this too, they are ſtill diſappointed. Thus they go on from one Deceit to another, till Death overtakes them, before they have tryed their laſt Projeƈt. This has been the Caſe of all Mankind from *Adam* until now: Nor will Men take Warning after all. All paſt Examples, and all their own Experience to this Moment, will make no laſting Impreſſion on them. They have loſt Happineſs in GOD: they wander from Creature to Creature in Purſuit of it. Madneſs is in their Hearts while they live; and after that they go down unto the Dead. I am not at all wandering from my Text, in theſe Obſervations, but making clear the Way to it.

Converſion then lies here. The Man as he is purſuing Happineſs in Creatures, is ſtop'd ſhort, and convinced that theſe will not do. GOD gives him a New Sight of things. He ſees an End of all Perfeƈtion below GOD. He ſees he is undone every where elſe. Now his Will is renewed. He *turns about* : (THAT's CONVERSION) he TURNS ABOUT to GOD, and from this Time ſeeks all Happineſs in Him alone. He ſays, *Who ſhall ſhew me any Good?* and he replies, *Lord, lift thou up the Light of thy Countenance upon me. Whom have I in Heaven but Thee? and there is none upon Earth that I deſire beſides Thee.* For ever after this Turn of Soul, the Man is ſet upon pleaſing GOD : upon yielding to the Will of GOD : upon approving himſelf in the Sight of GOD. He never ſeeks his Happineſs in the Creature any more. He may indeed, under the Power of Temptation, caſt a wiſhing Look at them. But he recalls it in a Moment. He never can reſt eaſy one Moment ſhort of the Favour of GOD. Like the Needle touch'd by the Magnet, ſtill pointing Northward. When it is ſhaken indeed, and toſt about, it trembles, it wavers, it vibrates, it varies a Point this way and that, but it never fixes but right North again. So a Soul thus touched by the SPIRIT of GOD, may be toſt by Temptations, and the Hurries of the World, and look this Way and that among the Creatures, till the Violence of the Shock is over, but he never fixes; never reſts, till he points full and ſteady to GOD again. This ſhort Paragraph is, I think, a full and clear Account of Converſion.

We all are ſeeking Happineſs. Every Natural Man ſeeks for it ſomewhere below GOD. Converſion is, The Man ſeeing he is infinitely wrong, *turns about* to GOD again to ſeek his whole Satisfaƈtion there. I hope I have now ſaid enough in a few Words to explain the Matter, and ſhew what Converſion is. Before we proceed to the next Head, we may make one or two ſolemn and affeƈting Inferences.

1. From

I. From what we have heard, we perceive that *Conversion is out of our Power*. It is impossible for us to convert our selves ; or for all the Angels in Heaven to do it for us. To convince you of this, Let the Natural Man make the Experiment. Try this Moment. Try and see whither you can bring your Hearts to this, to renounce all Happiness in every thing but the Favour of GOD; to let GOD order for you; to have no Will of your own ; to be swallow'd up, and ravish'd with his Will, whatever it is. Can you forego every Creature-Comfort ? Can you leave this World, and all the Delights of it, to go to a World where you will have none of them, but the Love of GOD will swallow you up ? These things are so distant from an unrenewed Heart, that they look like wild Paradoxes to it. The Man finds he can't bring his Heart to this ; and he thinks no Body ever could. And yet, there is not a Good Man upon Earth, but knows a little what this means. He knows a little what it is to love GOD ; to have his Happiness in GOD ; to exult that the Will of GOD is done. Not a Good Man upon Earth, but would gladly leave all the Delights of Life, only to be made perfectly holy. Nay, all he fears in Death is, lest it should not convey him to a World of perfect Holiness. Could he be sure consummate Holiness would be to him the immediate Consequent of Death, he'd die chearfully , without a Struggle or a Groan. Seeing then that Conversion is not in our own Power, let us seek to GOD for it. Sensible, and amazed at our own Incapacity, let us go to GOD, and take to our selves Words and say with repenting *Ephraim*, Jer. xxxi. 18. *Turn thou me, and I shall be turned ; for thou art the Lord my* GOD. Be sensible of the sinful Nature which still carries us away from him. Be sensible of that first Sin, by which we departed from him, and pray, Psal. lxxx. 19. *Turn us again, O Lord* GOD *of Hosts, and cause thy Face to shine and we shall be saved.* To see our own Impotency is the first Step towards Conversion.

2. From what we have heard we learn *our Necessity of* JESUS CHRIST. We can't turn again to GOD without Him. No man can come to the Father but by Him. The Enmity between GOD and us is irreconcilable but by CHRIST. Out of him GOD is a consuming Fire. We may indeed feel the Want of Happiness, but we should never dare to go to GOD for it. He would be our Enemy, and we should hate him for it. *False Notions* of the Divine Justice and Mercy could never bring us truly to him : And *true ones* would only drive us farther from Him. So that set CHRIST aside, and there can be no Conversion.

3. We Infer *the Honours of the* HOLY GHOST. He is the Agent who performs this Work. One Reason that Men fall Short of this saving Change, is the not acknowledging him as they ought. Did men regard the Operation of the Holy SPIRIT more, there would be more frequent Converts. Men are apt to trust to
their

their own Strength when they set about the Work of Conversion. They rob the Spirit of GOD of his Glory, and so it all comes to nothing. He it is who makes this great Change in men. He must be the Almighty GOD then : and we should honour him as so.

4. You see *how many mistake in their Notions of Conversion* Some think that to be converted is only to profess the Christian Religion. They fancy that to turn from Heathenism to Christianity is all that is implied in it. To talk of a Baptised Person's being afterward converted they think is Cant and Superstition. This is the modern (I wish I could not add, the obtaining and fashionable) Scheme. If we speak of our being *Converted,* they ask, why what were you before ? *Jews,* or *Turks,* or *Heathen* ? Alas, the fatal Mistake ! We are all undone in our Natural State, unless we know what Conversion means. We are all naturally departing from GOD, and seeking Happiness in something below him. If ever we are happy then, it must be by our stopping here, and turning about to him. Conversion does not consist, in embracing a new Sect, or Party : in Baptism, or Approach to the Lord's Table ; or any external Privilege, or Advantage, or Alteration. No ; it consists in turning from the Creature to GOD.

5. From what we have heard, we learn the Propriety of the Expression in the Text, Except ye *become as Little Children.* Conversion implies such a Change as will bring us to begin our Life anew. We must become as Little Children : modest, unambitious, teachable as they. Like them, we must begin to live again : begin another kind of Life : pursue a quite different End, by quite different Measures. Like a weaned Child, must be weaned from Creatures, and the things we were formerly fond of. But I would not enlarge here. I proceed to the Second thing proposed.

II. To shew *what we are to understand by the Kingdom of Heaven,* spoken of in the Text. *Except ye be converted, and become as little Children, ye shall not enter into the KINGDOM OF HEAVEN.* I shall not be long in explaining this Phrase. The *Kingdom of Heaven,* and the *Kingdom of GOD,* are principally used in the Evangelists for the State of the Gospel in This World ; or the Rewards of it in the Future. Sometimes it means the Kingdom of Grace ; and sometimes the Kingdom of Glory. And I suppose that tho' the Text may ultimately refer to the Latter, yet it takes in the former also. And therefore we shall consider them both in our Handling the Third Proposition : Which is this,

III. *Except we be converted and become as little Children, we shall not enter into the Kingdom of Heaven.*
1. Without this we cannot enter into the *Kingdom of Grace.* God cannot receive us as his Favourites even in This World, till

D

we

we have had this Change paffed upon us. He will take no Delight in us, while we openly neglect him, and fet up Self and Creatures in his Throne. We may indeed belong to his Kingdom of *Mercy*, and he may have Defigns for our Salvation before our Converfion: But we are by no means Subjects in this Kingdom of *Grace* before this. By no means intitled to his Special Favours, and the Objects of his peculiar Delight.

We may indeed belong to the Vifible Kingdom of CHRIST in the World, and not be favingly Converted. We may be Members of his Church here, and eat and drink in his Prefence, and yet he know nothing of us. But here too, in order to our being worthy Guefts at this facred Feaft, Converfion is neceffary.   But

2. Without this Converfion before we cannot enter into the *Kingdom of Glory.* Rev. xxi. 27. *There fhall In no wife enter into it, any thing that defileth, either whatfoever worketh abomination.* And not only has GOD *declared* this, all over his New Teftament, but it is impoffible even in the *Nature of the Thing.* The principal Happinefs in the Kingdom of Glory is, in being perfectly conformed to the Will of GOD: And this, we know, is only attainable by Converfion. We entertain jufter Ideas of Heaven, when we apprehend it as a *State* than a *Place.* There is indeed fuch a glorious Place ; but we know not where, or what it is. But as to the Temper and Happinefs of this Holy World, this every Good Man feels a little of in his own Breaft. What do they do in Heaven ? What do they Enjoy there ? Truly they praife GOD ; they love GOD ; they feek their whole Happinefs in GOD ; and are perfectly conformed to his Will. And now, how can an Unconverted Man enter that glorious World. His whole Soul is bent upon Self and Creatures ; here he terminates, and he knows nothing further. Should fuch a Soul but once get into the Manfions of Glory, he would be like a Swine in a Golden Palace : He'd be quite out of his Element ; and long for the Puddle and the Mire again. Like *Uzziah* with his Leprofy in the holy place, 2 Chron. xxvi. 20. *And Azariah the chief P.ieft, and all the Priefts looked upon him, and beheld he was leprous in his Forehead, and they thruft him out from thence, yea, himfelf hafted alfo to go out.* So would he the Cafe of the Polluted Soul in the Holy Heavens. Not only would the *Angels,* and *Juft Spirits* drive him out from among them, but he *himfelf* would *hafte* alfo to go out. What fhould he do there ? His Soul has no turn to this Sort of Happinefs. Unmortified Lufts, and raging Appetites ; Pride, and Senfuality, and Self-Will would be a Hell in his own Bofom, amidft all the Glories of Heaven. His whole Nature muft be changed ; he muft be converted, and begin a New Life, or he could never enter into that bleffed State.

Verily

Verily I say unto you, Except ye be converted, and become as little Children, ye shall not enter into the Kingdom of Heaven.

Thus I have endeavoured as clearly as I could, to explain and demonstrate the Doctrine, and I come now to the Solemn Application.

I. Shall not the Unconverted enter into the Kingdom of Heaven, *Where then shall they go* ? They must go somewhere. They are in Being, and they must exist for ever. *Here* they cannot always live : In a few Days more they must leave this Earth ; not suffered to tarry by Reason of Death. To *Heaven* they cannot go. They have no Part there ; nothing to do there ; The Voice of CHRIST, like a Flaming Sword, guards the Passage against them. *Verily I say unto you, they shall not enter* there. Well then, what will become of them ? O fearful, destitute, ruined State ! The infallible Word of GOD informs us where the miserable Creatures must take up their Eternal Lodging, Matt. xxv. 46. *These shall go away into everlasting Punishment.* Mark ix. 43. 48. into *the Fire that never shall be quenched : where the Worm dieth not, and the Fire is not quenched.* Rev. xiv. 10,11. *The same shall drink of the wine of the wrath of GOD, which is poured out without mixture, into the cup of his Indignation, and he shall be tormented with Fire and Brimstone, in the presence of the holy Angels, and in the presence of the Lamb ; and the Smoke of their Torment ascendeth up for ever and ever ; and they have no rest day nor night.* He that overcometh, indeed, shall inherit all things : He that is converted and has his Nature changed, shall enter into the World of Glory : *But the fearful, and unbelieving, and the abominable, and murderers, and whoremongers, and sorcerers, and idolaters, and all liars, shall have their Part in the lake which burneth with Fire and Brimstone which is the second Death,* Rev. xxi. 7, 8. See now the Place to which the unconverted must go ! See the gloomy Landskip of that infernal World ! And O, are we not amazed ? are we not in Agony, about our escape from this Ruin ? Who can dwell with devouring Fire ? who can dwell with everlasting Burnings ? Is not the Case awful and dreadful ? And do not our Hearts quiver, and our Souls sink and die within us. Behold, Life and Death set before us : Eternal Life, and Eternal Fire ; and are they insignificant Things ! O stupid ! O mad ! if they make no Impression upon us. On the one Hand we are informed, *Repent and be converted, and your Sins shall be blotted out ; and Except ye be converted ye shall in no wise enter into the Kingdom of Heaven.* Nay, on the Contrary, we must take up our eternal Abode in the World of Darkness, and Fire, and Chains. Ah ! miserable Case of Unconverted Men ! Who would not fear, who would not fly their Doom ? And therefore,

2. From

2. From what we have heard, O *let us labour inſtantly after ſaving Converſion.*

Turn ye, Turn ye, why will ye die. Conſider the matter, and debate it with your own Hearts. Converſion begins in ſerious Conſideration. *I thought on my ways, and turned my Feet unto thy Teſtimonies,* was the good old way, Pſal. cxix. 59. Let us then go alone, and put the Caſe to our ſelves, " Am I con-
' verted or not ? What Happineſs am I purſuing ; a Happineſs
' in the Creature, or a Happineſs in the Enjoyment of GOD ?
' Can I think that the Poſſeſſion of any Temporal Good can
' make me Happy ? Have I not often made the Experiment al-
' ready ; and have I not as often been diſappointed ? And why
' ſhould I try any more ? Is it not high Time for me to *turn*
' *about,* and ſee if I cannot find that Happineſs in GOD, which
' till now I have in vain ſought for in Objects below him ?"
Propoſe theſe Queſtions to your own Souls, and ſee what anſwer your Conſcience will frame upon them.

Now be convinced that you cannot give this Turn to your ſelves. Learn to feel and be ſenſible how atached to Self and Creatures you are. Mourn it and confeſs it before GOD : and tell him how undone you are without his Almighty Grace. Plead with Him in Tears and Agony to change your vile Na-ture : to turn you ſavingly to Himſelf. Be importunate, be reſt-leſs till you find this done for you : Till you find a Soul in-tirely forſaking the Creature and purſuing its whole Satisfaction in GOD alone. Till CHRIST appears tranſcendently dear and lovely to you ; and you can joyfully leave this World to go to His Arms and his Boſom. This divine and ſaving Turn of Soul, may be given to you, as you are in the Uſe of theſe appointed Means labouring to obtain it.

3. *O let thoſe of us who have been converted, live becoming the Change we are under.* Be thankful, be joyful : thankful to the GOD who has turn'd us, and joyful that we are paſſing to Hea-ven. Let us labour more and more after the Heavenly Temper ; Love GOD more ; think on him, work for him, long and wiſh to be with him. If ever we find a prevailing Fondneſs for Crea-tures after this ; if ever we find our Wills going to rebel, or our Deſires tend to this World ; let us immediately check the inordi-nate Affection, and ſay, ' No, I have renounced theſe long ago.
' I have choſen GOD for my Portion, and his Will for my Law
' long ago. GOD forbid, that after having eſcaped the Snare, I
' ſhould be again taken and entangled therein. No, No, farewell
' Creatures; no more ſhall you tempt me from my true Happi-
' neſs. Farewell the Riches I once coveted ; the Applauſe I once
' graſp'd after ; the Pleaſures that looked ſo charming. Farewell
' Felicity on Earth : and welcome the Will of my GOD : welcome
' Everlaſting Life. Welcome the Good Things of Earth, which my
　　　　　　　　　　　　　　　　　　　　　　　　' GOD

' GOD pleafes to give me: But adieu all Thoughts of Happinefs in
' the Poffeffion of thefe. Welcome Afflictions too; the Gifts of
' my GOD, and the Purchafe of my SAVIOUR ? Shall I receive
' Good at his Hands, and not receive Evil ? 'Tis the Cup which my
' Father gives me, why fhould I not drink it ! Other Lords
' have had Dominion over me : But what have I any more
' to do with Idols ?

And while are thus awakening the Piety of our own Souls, how
fhould we pity a miferable World about us ? Poor Creatures! they
know not what this Love to GOD means. They never felt what it
was to be refigned to the Will of GOD, and fwallowed up in his
Love and his Praifes. They are, as we once were, glewed to Senfe
and Creatures ; and have no Idea of Converfion and the New Birth.
You may talk them eternally of thefe things ; but they difcern
them not : you had as good go to explain the Myftery of Colours
to a Man born blind. Ah, Poor Men ! how fhould we pitty and
pray for them : How fhould we contrive to fhew them their Danger and Mifery ; and labour with them to make their efcape ? Remember, *He that converteth a Sinner from the Error of his Way,*
fhall fave a Soul from Death. Sure we never need envy them the
little Good they poffefs: But O how fhould we admire the Free
Grace which has diftinguifhed us from them ! There's no Room
for boafting in the Cafe. 'Tis all fovereign, and all free : To
GOD belongs the Glory ; and to us Wonder, and Gratitude, and
Humility.

We draw on towards a Conclufion. And how can we leave off
better than with a View of that Heavenly World, fpoken of in
the Text. This then fhall be the laft Inference from the whole.

4. *What a Holy and Happy Place is the Kingdom of Heaven ?*
There is not one *finful Perfon*, not one *finful Frame* in that World.
The Spirits of *Juft men* are *made perfect* before they are admitted
there. Tho' the Good Man *here* loves GOD above all, and choofes
his Portion in him, yet this gracious Temper is often fhock'd and
broken by Temptations and Indwelling Sin. But *There* is no Sin,
no Corruption, no Tempter. All the Employment, all the Converfation, and every Thought is about GOD and his Glories. *Alle-*
luia, for the Lord GOD omnipotent reigneth ; This is the Language,
the Temper, the Work, the Felicity of Heaven. There, they
are *fill'd with all the Fulnefs of GOD.* There, GOD *is all in all.*
In that happy World, every Inhabitant, and every Object, glori-
fies GOD, and is filled with his Glory. His Perfections, and his
Love takes them intirely up ; and nothing elfe is feen, or heard,
or thought of. O happy, happy State ! The Converted Soul
knows a *little* what this means; but what it *fully* is, we *know not*
now, we *fhall know hereafter. Eye has not feen, nor Ear heard, nor can*
the Heart of man conceive it all.

These,

These, ye Converted Souls, are the Joys set before you! These are the Glories, and this the Felicity reserved in Heaven for you. Here you perceive a *little Taste* of it, in your Conformity to the Will of GOD; There you shall set down to the *full Feast*, and be *perfectly* conformed to his Will. Here the Joy of the LORD *enters into you*; There *you shall enter into the Joy of your Lord.*

F I N I S.

An HYMN to CHRIST for our Regeneration and Resurrection.

I.

TO Thee, my LORD, I lift the Song,
　Awake, my tuneful Pow'rs :
In conftant Praife my grateful Tongue
　Shall fill my foll'wing Hours.

II.

Guilty, condemn'd, undone I ftood ;
　I bid my GOD depart :
He took my Sins, and paid his Blood,
　And *turn'd* this wand'ring Heart,

III.

Death, the grim Tyrant, feiz'd my Frame,
　Vile, loathfome and accurft :
His Breath renews the vital Flame,
　And Glories *change* the Duft;

IV.

Now, SAVIOUR, fhall thy Praife commence;
　My Soul by Thee brought Home,
And ev'ry Member, ev'ry Senfe,
　Recover'd from the Tomb.

V.

To Thee my Reafon I fubmit,
　My Love, my Mem'ry, LORD,
My Eyes to read, my Hands to write,
　My Lips to preach thy Word.

Mr. *Byles's*
Artillery Election
SERMON
June 2. 1740

The Glories of the LORD *of* HOSTS,

A N D

The Fortitude of the Religious Hero.

A

SERMON

Preached to the ancient and honourable

Artillery Company

June 2. 1740.

Being the Anniverſary of their Election of Officers.

By MATHER BYLES, *A M.*

Paſtor of a Church in *Boſton.*

II King, ix. 4, 5, 6. *So the Young Man, even the young Man the Prophet, went.——And when he came, behold the Captains of the Hoſt were ſitting; and he ſaid, I have an Errend to thee.—— Thus ſaith the* LORD GOD *of Iſrael.*

BOSTON Printed, and may be had at the Shops of *Thomas Fleet* and *Joſeph Edwards,* in Cornhill. 1740.

(5)

The Glories of the Lord of Hosts,

AND

The Fortitude of the Religious Hero.

I Sam. xvii. 45.

——*THOU comest to ME with a SWORD, and with a SPEAR——But I come to THEE in the NAME of the LORD of HOSTS, the GOD of the ARMIES of Israel.*

IT is a hardy Enterprize, my Fellow Souldiers, to which you appoint us, in your annual Elections of us, to preach upon these Occasions. More than an Hundred Years, have called for as many Military Discourses from the Desk, to sanctify your Arms, and add the peculiar Glory of Religion to your Elections, and your Exercises. In order to gratify your Desires, and answer your Expectations, your Ministers have at these returning Seasons, chosen their various Subjects, suited to the Sons of Battle, and have in a Manner exhausted all that can be said, proper for you to hear, and for the

Pulpit

Pulpit to fpeak. Some have led you up to the Origin of War in general, expoftulating with the Apoftle, *From whence come Wars and Fightings, come they not from hence, even of your Lufts*; at the fame Time proving the Neceffity to learn the Art of War, fo long as thefe Lufts remain in Men to occafion it. Some have urged our own Danger as an expofed People in our defencelefs, carelefs Pofture, *and far from Zidon*. Others have treated on the Nature and Neceffity of Weapons, and led you into a glittering Magazine of Armory. Some have reprefented the *Lord* as a *Man of War*, to reflect a Glory upon your burnifhed Arms, and infpire you with religious Fortitude. Some have lifted up JESUS as the *Enfign to the Nations*, and preft you to Battle under this Triumphant Banner. Some have tranfported you with the Examples of former *Heroes*, who *by Faith fubdued Kingdoms*, and bore victorious through all the Conflict of human Life, that you might be animated by fo great a *Cloud of Martyrs*. Some have inftructed you in the Glories of the *Captain of your Salvation*; *Gird thy Sword upon thy Thigh, and ride forth O moft mighty*. Others have drawn out his holy Armies upon the March; *The Armies of Heaven followed him*. Some have exhorted you to be *good Soldiers of JESUS CHRIST*, others have called on you to *put on the whole Armour of God*, others have told the *Soldiers what they fhould do*, and defcribed the Man *expert in War*, and others explained and argued the Doctrine of Valour, *only be thou ftrong and very couragious*; while others have taught you to encounter the laft Enemy, for *there is no Difcharge in that War*.*   AFTER

---

* Since the preaching of the above, I have been more critical in fearching for the feveral Texts which have been improved upon this Occafion. And as far as the Records of the Military Company could affift me, they ftand thus: Mr. *Willard*, Prov. 4. 23. Mr. *Moodey*, Prov. 16. 32. Mr. *Bel-*

AFTER all the pertinent, and pious, and sublime Things, which so many of my Fathers and Brethren have advanced upon this Occasion, there seems to be nothing new for me to add ; nor do I readily think of any one proper Topick which has not been touched upon by others before me. However, it has been sometimes observed that the Art of Writing, among us in these latter Days, consists not so much in starting new Matter, (for that were almost impossible after all the Authors and Volumes which have gone before us) as in setting old Thoughts in a newer, or stronger, or more agreeable, or at least in *different* Lights ; and as every Author has something of his own, a *Specifick Quality* which distinguishes him from others, this must be my Excuse for yielding to your unanimous Desire, and irresistible Importunities, and appearing at your Head this Day,

AND

Belcher, 1 Cor. 9. 26, 27. Mr. Willard of Boston, 1 King. 9. 22. Mr. Wadsworth of Boston, Isa. 3. 2. Mr. Pemberton of Boston, Luk. 3. 14. Dr. Colman of Boston, Heb. 11. 33. Mr. Rawson, Eph. 6. 11. Mr. Gibbs of Watertown, Psal. 44. 6. Mr. Bridge of Boston, Dan. 11. 32. Mr. Cotton, Mat. 11. 12. Mr. Daniforth of Taunton, Heb. 12. 4. Dr. Increase Mather, Josh. 1. 7. Mr. Walter of Roxbury, Act. 5. 39. Mr. Thatcher of Weymouth, 1 Sam. 18. 14. Mr. Stoddard of Chelmsford, 1 Sam. 2. 30. Dr. Sewall of Boston, Rev. 19. 14. Mr. Stephens of Charlestown, Isa. 2. 4. Mr. Baxter of Medfield, Rom. 8. 37. Mr. Blowers of Beverly, 1 Sam. 16. 18. Mr. Barnard of Marblehead, Rev. 3. 21. Mr. Webb of Boston, Eccl. 8. 8. Mr. Symmes of Bradford, 1 Chron. 12. 33. Mr. Prince of Boston, Psal. 122. 6. Mr. Cooper, Psal 45. 3, 4, 5. Mr. Foxcroft, 1 Chron. 5. 18, 19, 20. Mr. Thayer of Roxbury, 1 Tim. 6. 1. Mr. Checkley of Boston. 2 Sam. 22. 35. Mr. Swift of Framingham, Act. 10. 7. Mr. Waldron of Boston, 2 Sam. 10. 12. Mr. Gay of Hingham, Zech. 2. 8. Mr. Welsted of Boston, Isa. 55. 4. Mr. Hancock of Lexington, Prov: 21. 31. Mr. Peabody of Natick, 1 Sam. 2. 18. Mr. Appleton of Cambridge, Jam. 4. 1. Mr. Chauncy of Boston, Judg. 18. 27, 28. Mr. Abbot of Charlestown, Exod. 15. 3. Mr. Clark 1 Cor. 16. 13. Mr. Williams of Weston, Eccl. 9 18. Mr. Mather, 1 Sam. 17. 39.

AND if this be a juft Apology for the *Author*, it is much more fo for the *Preacher* : For it is a plain Direction to us, *as wife Stewards to bring out of our Treafury Things new and old.* You will therefore hear with Candor; and though I fhould *deliver the fame. Things,* to you *they will not be grievous.*

ATTEND then to the Voice of my Text. The Words are a gallant Speech of young *David,* rufhing to encounter the tall Giant of *Gath.* Long had the huge Monfter daily ftrode towards the Camp of *Ifrael,* and roared his Challenge over the Campaign, to the Ears of the frighted Army. An univerfal Panick run through the Ranks, chilled their Blood, and fhook. their Fabrick. Not a Man, not a Captain bold enough to iffue from their Ports, and engage the bravery Champion. They all fhrunk behind their Entrenchments, and retreated from the thundering Defiance. Then it was that *David,* by Accident in the Hoft, heard the Menaces of the godlefs Giant, and a generous Indignation fired his Breaft. Away goes the blooming Hero to the intimidated Monarch, and demands the Combat with Goliah. The King is furprized at the daring Genius that glowed in a Heart fo young, and undifciplined to the Dangers and Art of War, and hardly confents to the unequal Fight. " *Thou art but a Youth,* my Son, and he, *a Man of War from his Youth.*" " Why, replied the Rofey War-" riour, why may I not venture? Thefe unpromifing " Arms of mine, tender as they feem to you, are not " unufed to rugged Encounters. I am the Stripling, " that have wrefted a Kid of my Flock from the Paw " of a Bear, and from the rubid Jaws of a Lyon; " and my God fhall alike deliver this Philiftine into " my Hand." Aftonifhed, *Saul* gives a faint Confent; and *David* with a Sling, and a few Pebbles, runs out to the glorious Expedition. *Goliah* faw; and in a
Tranfport

Tranfport of Difdain, curft the little Adventurer by his Gods; " Come hither, Youth, and by Dagon, will I fcatter thy Limbs a Prey to the Beafts of the Field, and to the Fowls of the Air." To this boafting Period, the Words of my Text are the ardent Reply; *Thou comeft to me with a Sword, and with a Spear, and with a Shield; but I come to thee in the Name of the LORD of Hofts, the God of the Armies of Ifrael, whom thou haft defied.*

THERE's a noble Bravery in the Expreffion. The ardent young Champion takes no Notice of the Bulk and Terror of his Rival's Perfon, but feems rather to upbraid him with Cowardife. Tall and broad, and athletick as you are, fays he, it feems you dare not truft your felf againft your little Enemy, without abundant Arms and Armour. *Thou comeft to me with a Sword, and with a Spear, and with a Shield; but I come to thee in the Name of the LORD of Hofts, the God of the Armies of Ifrael.*

MORE than this had been unbecoming the manly Genius of a Warriour. Actions and not Words muft decide the Difpute. The mighty *Philiftine* hafted onward, and *David* rufhed to meet him with undaunted Eyes, while the Sling in his Hand whirled round, and away fung the Victor-Stone towards the broad Front of the Enemy. It ftrook, it crufhed, it funk, and down fell the proud Boafter thundring to the Plain.

THIS was the Courage, and this the Succefs of *David*; and Devotion and Religion was the Spring and the Bafis of all. A Zeal for the GOD of *Ifrael* infpired his glowing Breaft, and a firm Truft in Him animated him, undaunted in the Undertaking, compounded of Religion and Enterprize.

B   Two

Two glorious Characters *David* here gives of his GOD; *the Lord of Hosts*, and the *God of the Armies of Israel*; and all on Fire while he marches on in this great and fearful Name, he faces every Danger interested and victorious. *In the Name of GOD I will destroy them; in the Name of GOD I will destroy them.*

And as in the glowing Sentence are comprized the Glories of GOD, and the Fortitude of a pious Man: So the Words lead us to discourse, First of the *Lord of Hosts*; Secondly, of the *God of the Armies of Israel*; and Thirdly, of the *Nature* of *true, rational and religious Fortitude*, as taking hence its Origin, a Regard to this glorious GOD.

I. I am to discourse a little of the *Lord of Hosts*, and consider the most high GOD under this Character.

This is one of the magnificent and favourite Titles which he wears; and it is about Sixty Times applied to him in the inspired Writings. *The Lord of Hosts, he is the King of Glory: The Lord of Hosts is his Name.* Take a View of his extended and potent Armies, and see him in his Glory at the Head of all.

The Heavenly Hosts are his. So are the Angels in all their shining Forms and un-numbered Regiments: An immeasurable Front, and an endless Rear! No Army of so exact Discipline, such invincible Courage and fatal Execution. Our painted Troops are a meer Mock Show to these resistless Legions. Our Chariots and Horses make no Figure at all before these Chariots of Fire and Horses of Fire. *The Chariots of God are Twenty Thousand, even Thousands of Angels,*
Psal.

Pfal. lxviii. 17. and he maketh his Angels Spirits, his Minifters a Flame of Fire. A whole Hoft of our menal Warriours fhall wither in a Night before one of them; and ftrew the pale Camp with an *hundred and fourfcore and five thoufand Corpfes.* II King xix. 35.

Below thefe, the Stars keep their Military Watch, the Out-Guards of the Cæleftial Army. And what a glittering Hoft of them range themfelves over the Blue Plains of Æther? *Lift up now thine Eyes to Heaven, and tell the Stars if thou art able to number them.* Thefe, in all their immenfe Dominions, are under his abfolute Command. *He bringeth out their Hoft by Number, he calleth them all by their Names,* Pfa. cxlvii. 4. *Ifa.* xl. 26. *The Stars in their Courfes fight againft* his Enemies. How myfterious and unknown are the Laws of thofe unnumber'd Squadrons; and how irrefiftible their Movements? *Canft thou bind the fweet Influences of Pleiades, or loofe the Bands of Orion? Canft thou bring forth Mazzaroth in his Seafon, or canft thou guide Arcturus with his Sons?* But he, the great Monarch of all, commands with infinite Eafe, and every rolling World fubmits with exact Obedience. *Behold, even to the Moon and it fhineth not; and the Stars are not pure in his Sight. — Sun, ftand thou ftill upon Gibeon! and thou Moon in the Valley of Ajalon!* (Jofh. x. 12.) *Sun, go thou back!*—and wondering Nations fhall gaze, and enquire the meaning of the aftonifhing Retreat. II King. xx. 8. ——

Below thefe, and failing along our Atmofphere, the Clouds make their majeftick Appearance: A flying Camp; or a moving Magazine of Divine Artillery. *Haft thou entered into the Treafures of Snow or haft thou feen the Treafures of Hail; which I have*

B 2   *referved reserved against the Time of Trouble, against the Day of Battle and War.* Job xxxviii. 22, 23. There the Northern Tempests plant their impetuous Batteries, there the fierce Engines of the Sky play in various Forms of Destruction.

> *There like a Trumpet, loud and strong,*
> *Thy Thunder shakes the Coast;*
> *There the red Light'nings wave along.*
> *The Banners of thine Host!* *

He is alike Lord of the Terrestial Hosts, while every Species of Creatures, and every Individual is under his exact Command. But who can call over the List of these extended Colours? *Is there any Number of his Armies?* The Earth is full of his Legions; so also is the great and wide Sea, with all the Tribes and Colonies there, from the fearless *Leviathan* in all his Terrors, to the minute, invisible Swarms and Shoals in every Drop, unnumber'd and unnam'd So on the Surface of this our Earth the Lion leads up the Van among the Four-footed, and the fiercer Animals form the foremost Line: Among which the Horse "paws the Valley, and rejoices in his Strength, tosses the Thunder of his Neck, and shakes the Lightning of his Main. The Glory of his Nostrils is terrible; he goeth on to meet the armed Men. He mocketh at Fear, and is not affrighted, neither turneth he back from the Sword. The Quiver rattleth against him, the glittering Spear and the Shield. He swalloweth the Ground with Fierceness and Rage; Neither believeth he that it is the Sound of the Trumpet. He saith among the Trumpets, Ha! ha! He smelleth the Battle afar off, the Thunder of the Captains, and the Shouting."   But

---

* Dr. *Watts.*

But need we fpeak of the greater Animals to raife our Terror at the Hofts of GOD. Nay, the moft fordid Remile, the moft contemptible Infects can form a moft triumphant Army, and proclaim themfelves *God's huge Hoft.* Never was an Allegory better work'd up, more forcibly and elegantly carried on, and finifhed, than the Defcription of the Plague of Locufts in the Second Chapter of *Joel.* One would imagine it a March of Nations, or a Mufter of Angels fent upon the Execution of Divine Vengeance. Turn to it, and read it: For it would affront the Divine Eloquence of the Original to defcribe it in any other Words.— So grand appears the Lord of Hofts, before the moft defpicable of his Armies.

And where's the Creature that he cannot commiffion, or that dares to mutiny againft his Sovereign Edicts. He fhall *hifs for the Fly,* Ifa. vii. 18. and they fhall crowd rufhing round his lifted Standard. The very Lice fhall overpower his proudeft Enemy, and bend even the haughty Soul of a *Pharaoh.* His Air fhall fcatter Venom Plagues and Death over devoted Nations. His Water fhall rife from its filent Fountains beneath, and overwhelm a guilty World. His Fire fhall rage through a frighted City with inexorable Violence, or drive down from Heaven in a Tempeft of fhowering Flame. His Earthquakes fhall hurl fplintered Rocks from their Bafis; and Mountains fhall be caft into the midft of the Sea: The Earth itfelf fhall be broken down and diffolved before it, " and wander like a blazing Star about the Ether", a Standard difplayed to other Worlds denouncing almighty Vengeance.

On the contrary, the moft voracious Animal, and lawlefs Element fhall grow tame and placid at his Order, renounce its ravenous Nature, and protect inftead of deftroying. Hungry Ravens fhall fly with

Rapture,

Rapture, and drop the Prey from their Beak to feed the favourite Prophet. Foaming Waves shall roll fluid no longer, but open to the Right and Left, and rise in Heaps, to guard the Wings of his chosen Armies marching under his Conduct. Devouring Flames shall refuse to burn when he gives the Order, and shine round his distinguished Worthies a lambent Glory. Rapacious Sea-Monsters shall be a safe Convoy to the Man whom he appoints to go upon his Embassy: And inhospitable Lions restrain their Appetites, gaze with Pleasure upon the welcome Stranger, couch at his Knees, and lick his Feet. Behold, what a Lord of Hosts is here, even the Wind and the Seas obey him. He rules

———amidst the War of Elements
The Wrecks of Matter, and the Crush of Worlds.

Even the Devils are subject to him. He commands the unclean Spirits, and they obey him, through their warlike Regiments. Their Name is Legion, for they are many. But their very Wrath shall praise him, and the Remainder of it shall he restrain. *Behold, I saw the Lord sitting upon his Throne, and all the Host of Heaven standing on his Right Hand and on his Left.* II Chron. xviii. 8. And lo, a certain lying Spirit comes and asks Permission but to bring about his high Designs.

'Tis no Addition to him then to add, he is the Lord of our Hosts, and not an Army gathers on this Earth without his Councils and Providence. *The Lord of Hosts mustereth the Host to Battle.* He unfurls his Ensigns, and calls for the March of Nations in universal Tumult, and ranges half the Globe on a Side, confederated to a decisive Battle. What amazing Numbers have pour'd together when he has unsheathed
his

———————————————————————
* Addison.

his Sword, and flung away the Scabbard? Armies uncounted!

Whose Reer lay hid in Night, whilst rising Dawn
*Rous'd the broad Front, and call'd the Battle on.**

AND the *Battle is the Lord's*; and the *Greatness, and the Power, and the Glory, and the Victory, and the Majesty.* Isa. v. 26,—— *And he will lift up an Enfign to the Nations from far, and will hiss unto them from the End of the Earth : and behold they shall come with Speed quickly. None shall be weary nor stumble amongst them : none shall slumber nor sleep : neither shall the Girdle of their Loyns be loosed, nor the Latchet of their Shoes be broken. Whose Arrows are sharp, and all their Bows bent, their Horses Hoofs shall be counted like Flint, and their Wheels like a Whirlwind. Their roring shall be like a Lion, they shall rore like young Lions : yea, they shall rore and lay hold of the Prey, and shall carry it away safe, and none shall deliver it. And in that Day they shall rore against them, like the roring of the Sea : And if one look unto the Land, behold Darkness and Sorrow, and the Light is darkned in the Heavens thereof.* He can strike an unaccountable Panick through the boldeft Cohorts, defeat the moft numerous and potent, by the glare of a few Lamps, the crafh of a few Pitchers; and hurl down the proudeft Bulwarks thundring to the Ground, with the Blaft of a few Tempefts.

I have hardly Time to apply this. Suffer me a Word or two.

1. FROM

---

* Dr. *Young.*

1. FROM what we have heard, how desperate their Hazard who are in a State of War with the Lord of Hosts! So are all who are in a State of Nature; for we are born Children of Wrath. All Nature is armed against you to revenge the Quarrel of its Maker. Not an Element, not a Creature, but stands ready to destroy you; and with Vehemence urges, *My Father, shall I smite them? shall I smite them?*

How necessary is it for us to fling down our Weapons, and sue for Reconciliation in the Merits of JESUS; for *this Man is THE Peace.* Agree with thine Adversary quickly, while thou art in the Way with him, left he anon tear thee in pieces, and there be none to deliver thee.

2. LET us pay an humble Submission and Obedience to the Lord of Hosts, in every Rank, and in every Post where he has placed us. To one he has committed the Sword of the Magistrate, and you, my Fathers, must by no Means *bear his Sword in vain.* Another he has posted at the Head of a Family, and we must acknowledge it to him, *With my Feast I passed over this Jordan, and now am I become two Bands.* Us has he constituted as Leaders to his Church, and it becomes us to *endure Hardship as good Soldiers of JESUS CHRIST.* And *you,* my Brethren, are called to the Glories of the Field; *Be of good Courage, and play the Man for your People and for the Cities of your GOD.* Others are Brethren of low Degree, and but private Centinels in his Hosts: Murmur not; be contented upon Duty; and *let every Man wherein he is called therein abide with GOD.* You to the Sword and Spear; and we to the Service of the Temple.

THE

THE Second Thing to be fpoken to is,

II. THE Lord of Hofts, is in an eminent Senfe, the *God of the Armies of Ifrael.*

HE ftands in a peculiar Relation to his Favourite People. So he defcended with his drawn Sword in his Hand, and made his Claim to *Jofhua,* when the intrepid General faw him, and bravely demanded, *Art thou for us, or for our Adverfaries? Nay,* replied the illuftrious Vifion, *but as Captain of the Hoft of the LORD am I come.** —— And the adoring Hero fell proftrate and kift the Ground. This feems to be litterally the Glory of our Lord JESUS CHRIST, the Meffiah who was to come, and by a clofe attention to the holy Scriptures will, I believe, be found appropriated to him. Compare *Exod.* xxiii. 20, 21. with *Exod.* xxxiii. 2, 3.

WHILE *Ifrael* was litterally a People, he was immediately their LORD. He chofe them from among the Nations, led them through the Wildernefs, and pitched his *Shekinah* among them, his Pavilion of Clouds and Fire. And what People was there fo great, who had GOD fo nigh to them? The Ark was a Symbol of his Prefence; and by it he led them in their March, and by it they halted. *Numb.* x. 35, 36. *And it came to pafs when the Ark fet forward, that Mofes faid, Rife up. LORD, and let thine Enemies be fcattered, and let them that hate thee, flee before thee. And when it refted, he faid, Return, O LORD, unto the many Thoufands of Ifrael.*

C   AND

AND this favourite Nation was only a Type of the Church to the End of the World. GOD, in the Incarnate Son, is the Captain of their Salvation. He has chosen them out of the World, they are lifted under his Banners, he marches before them conquering and to conquer, and they follow, whitherfoever he goeth, more than Conquerors through him who loveth them. *The Armies of Heaven follow him.* And who is she that looketh forth as the Morning, fair as the Moon, clear as the Sun, and terrible as an Army with Banners. And who is he at their Head, that cometh from *Edom*, in dy'd Garments from *Bozrah*, glorious in his Apparel, travelling in the greatnefs of his Strength; and why are his Garments red, but in the Blood of his Enemies. He propofes Rewards to the Souldier, and leads the Way through the Labour to the Triumph: *To him that overcometh will I grant to fit down with me upon my Throne, even as I alfo overcame, and am fit down with my Father upon his Throne.*

IN every Light he is their GOD. They are all *chofen Men.* He preft them into Service; and they are alfo Voluntiers in his Caufe; bound by Military Oaths and Sacraments. *He is thy Lord, and worfhip thou him.*

A Theme this for noble Difcourfe and Entertainment; but I muft with Regret leave it, with one or two Reflections.

1. WE learn hence the Immunities of the Church of JESUS CHRIST. No Monarch has any Authority to make new Laws for his Church, or to bind a Burthen on that Confcience over which he claims an undivided Empire. The Armies of Ifrael, in this Senfe, own no other Lord. Stand faft therefore in the Liberty wherewith CHRIST hath made you free.

2. HOW

2. How victorious fhall the Hoft of GOD be under fuch a Leader? *David* in the Triumphs of my Context, was but a little Emblem of it. Though a Troop may overcome them, they fhall overcome at laft. He that hath clean Hands fhall wax ftronger and ftronger; as did the Houfe of *David.* They fhall overcome in the Blood of the Lamb, and reign till all Things are put in Subjection under him. *The laft Enemy to be conquered is Death. But Thanks be to God who hath given us the Victory through our Lord JESUS CHRIST.* The whole Church Militant fhall fo triumph. *He that falleth on it fhall be broken; but he upon whom it fhall fall it fhall grind him to Powder.*

——*All the Fowls that fly in the midft of Heaven, come, and gather your felves together unto the Supper of the great God; that ye may eat the Flefh of Kings, and the Flefh of Captains, and the Flefh of mighty Men, and the Flefh of Horfes, and of them that fit on them, and the Flefh of all Men, both free and bond, both fmall and great.**

THE laft Thing now remains, *viz.*

III. To fpeak of the Doctrine of true Fortitude, as taking hence its Origin, a Regard to the glorious GOD, in every hardy Enterprize.

COURAGE is a Moral Virtue, and a Thing very different from a flufh of Animal Spirits, or a firmnefs of Fibres in the Heart and Brain. It muft have its Foundation in Reafon, (and, fhall I add, in Religion; which is the beft Reafon) or it fubfides into Stupidity, or foams up in Frenzy. There are fome Things indeed obfervable in the Brutal World, which by way of Analogy we call by Names taken from Moral Vir.

---

* Rev. xix. 17, 18.

Virtues. But by no Means are they to be strictly under-
stood. So we speak of the *Courage* of the *Lyon* and
the *War-Horse*, and even the *Charity* and *Piety* of the
Stork feeding its aged Parents. But if we understand
litterally these Virtues, the pure Effects of Nature in
Creatures incapable of Moral Government; methinks
one had as good finish the Scheme at once, applaud
the *Patience* of a *Log*, and compliment a *Block* for
Passive Obedience and Non Resistance,

No ; Courage is that Firmness of Mind which will
enable a Man, from Principle, to abide by the
Dictates of his Rational Nature against all Opposition.
Some Men, indeed, have a natural Constitution that
is a Mechanical Aid to this Virtue : Others, from the
unhappier Fabrick of the Body, and the feebler Con-
sistence of the Fluids are more liable to Temptations
from the contrary Vices of Diffidence and Cowardise.
But still the Virtues and Vices are distinct from these
material Operations : Their Foundation is Principle ;
and their Subject is the Mind of a Moral Agent.

How many Actions have been applauded among
Men as highly Heroick, which examined to the Bottom will be found really mean ; I will venture to add,
the pure Effects of a dastardly Spirit. Such I pronounce *the SPIRIT OF A DUEL.* I believe upon
impartial Enquiry it will be found that a Duel has
been seldom undertaken but from the ignominious
Power of Fear. Reason, and Religion, and the Man's
own Inclinations have all conspired to forbid the Fact,
but the poor Paltroon has not had Presence of Mind,
and Bravery of Resolution, to stand by the Dictates of
his Understanding and Conscience, only for *Fear* of
being laugh'd at.   Call you this *Courage,* whose Original and Spring is all paltry Fear ? So many a
Coward has kept the Field, purely by being afraid to
run,

run, or afhamed of the Hifs of his Companions. Valour indeed, that can't ftand the Shock of a little Banter !

THE Fortitude of the true Hero difdains to afk any Queftions, but,—*What is the prefent Duty?* But 'tis the true Character of a Coward to confult,—*What Evil can I beft bear?* And if from a diftracted Judgment, Death and Divine Vengeance at a diftance, do not fo much fright him as the prefent Contempt of Mankind, the Daftard chufes *Damnation* rather than *Ridicule.*

> *VALOUR's a noble Turn of Thought,*
> *Whofe pardon'd Guilt forbids her Fears :*
> *Calmly fhe meets the deadly Shot,*
> *Secure of Life above the Stars.*

> *But FRENZY dares Eternal Fate,*
> *And fpur'd by Honeur's airy Dreams,*
> *Flies to attack th' Infernal Gate,*
> *And force a Paffage to the Flames.**

How foon fhall all this Flefh defert the Man ? The Day haftens, when the great Men, and the chief Captains, and the mighty Men fhall fly to hid in the Dens and Rocks of the Mountains. Then rejoice ye Righteous, lift up your Heads with Joy, for your Redemption draweth nigh.

IF Reafon muft be the Bafis of true Courage, who can lay fo fair a Claim to it as the Hero of Religion ? No Reafon like his who marches on in Obedience to his GOD, and vanquifhes all the Reluctances within, nor will allow them fo much as to parley. No tall
Cham-

---

* DR. *Watts.*

Champion of the Field so terrible as to drive him from his Post, or cause him to desert his Colours. This is the little Stripling that shall issue out with a Sling against an armed, gigantick Warriour, without a Thought of Retreat. This the Man that shall bear up to the Battery of Cannon, and be the first to leap over the Trench, and rush into the Breach, sustaining with a steady Mind all the Tumult, and Havock, and Horrors of the Storm. Not so *the Horse rusheth to the Battle.* Not so the *Lyon* faces the *Lybian* Hunters. Not so the *Leviathan raiseth up himself* the *Terror of the mighty*; *laughs at the shaking of the Spear*, and the *stubble of the Darts*, and *scatters the Weapons upon the Mire.* But (in the Words of the correct, the delicate, the sublime *Addison*)

> *So when an Angel, by Divine Command,*
> *With rising Tempests, shakes a guilty Land;*
> *(Such as from Heaven o'er pale* Britannia *past)*
> *Calm and serene he drives the furious Blast,*
> *And pleas'd, th' Almighty's Orders to perform,*
> *Rides in the Whirlwind and directs the Storm.*

After so grand a Set of Images, and such a Pomp of Eloquence, nothing can sound well but In-spiration itself. And *David* himself, the Hero of the Day, full of the Holy Ghost, has given us a most animated Description of religious Fortitude, in a Song for the Edge of Battle. Psal. lxvi. 1. *God is our Refuge and Strength, a very present Help in Trouble. Therefore will we not fear, though the Earth be re-moved, and though the Mountains be thrown into the midst of the Sea; though the Waters thereof roar and be troubled, though the Mountains shake with the swelling thereof.* — *The Heathen raged, the Kingdoms were moved, he uttered his Voice, the Earth melted. The LORD of Host*

Hosts is with us, the God of Jacob is our Refuge.
Happy stands this Man, while Heaven it self draws
his Character. *He shall deliver thee in six Troubles :
yea, in seven there shall no Evil touch thee. In Famine
he shall redeem thee from Death ; and in War from the
Power of the Sword. Thou shalt be hid from the Scourge
of the Tongue : neither shalt thou be afraid of Destruction
when it cometh. At Destruction and Famine thou shalt
laugh : neither shalt thou be afraid of the Beasts of the
Earth. For thou shalt be in League with the Stones of
the Field : and the Beasts of the Field shall be at Peace
with thee.**

THUS fearless may stand the Man secure of his
Maker's Friendship. The greatest Mortal General
needs to be supported by Numbers, animated by
Trumpets and Shouts of Applause, inspir'd Examples
of Bravery all round the Field, and hurried out of
himself from a cool Survey of Death and Eternity.
How many a Coward hath stood his Ground, supported by such little Arts. But the Christian can go
alone, calmly, insulted, to a burning Stake, that most
indisputable Tryal of thorough Courage. Persons the
most unlikely have been so inspired. The tenderest
Age, and the softest Sex have in this way encountered
and mocked the King of Terrors; and *at her Feet he
bowed, he fell, he lay down ; at her Feet he bowed, he
fell ; where he bowed there he fell down* vanquished
Guilt and painful Fear came into the World together.
Assoon as our Fore-Father fell, he cried out, *I heard
thy Voice in the Garden, and I was afraid.* If there's
a Conscience of Guilt removed, then the *Love will cast
out the Fear.* So that Courage in this Light appears
to be *a Grace of the Spirit of GOD.*

THUS,

---

* Job v. 19,—23.

THUS, my Brethren of the Field, I have led you up to the Head-Spring of true, manly, and Christian Fortitude. In this, I have not deserted my Station, but acted as became a Minister of CHRIST, and agreeable to the Text I have chosen. Had I treated of Skill in Arms; of Facings, Advances and Retreats, of Evolutions, Counter-marches and Military Figures, I had descended from my Rank, and you could easily drive me back to my Line, keep the Field, and out-preach me. But *every Man to his Post. Thou comest to me with a Sword, and with a Spear; but I come to thee in the Name of the Lord of Hosts, the God of the Armies of Israel.* While *You* are called to the glorious below, *We* appear in the Mount and lift up our Hands, and the Rod of GOD there. Or if need be, we will come down and share your Hazards, and animate you to the Battle in the Name of GOD. Deut. xx. 1, 2, 3, 4. *When thou goest out to Battle against thine Enemies, and seest Horses and Chariots, and a People more than thou, be not afraid of them : for the Lord thy God is with thee—. And it shall be when ye are come nigh unto the Battle, that the Priest shall approach and speak unto the People, and shall say unto them, Hear, O Israel, you approach this Day unto Battle against your Enemies : let not your Hearts faint, fear not, and do not tremble, neither be ye terrified because of them. For the Lord your God is he that goeth before you, to fight for you against your Enemies, to save you.*

BUT I must hasten to a Close. And in the First Place you will allow me to preach to my self, and improve at least something by my own Discourse.

AND from what we have heard, *How becoming is Courage to a Minister of CHRIST?* None go forth more immediately in the Name of the Lord of Hosts than we. None are called to bolder Services, *knowing we are set for the Defence of the Gospel.* The Priests bearing the Ark of GOD muſt be the firſt to ford the Swell of *Jordan,* and upon the deepeſt Sands below muſt they take their gallant Stand till the meaneſt *Iſraelite* be paſſed over. What a poor Figure makes a cowardly Miniſter! Shall he be afraid of the Faces of Men, who comes upon Embaſſeys from the great GOD! Ezek. iii. 8, 9. *Behold, I have made thy Face ſtrong againſt their Faces; and thy Forehead ſtrong againſt their Foreheads. As an Adamant, harder than a Flint, have I made thy Forehead: Fear them not, neither be diſmayed at their Looks.* This was the brave Character of the intrepid Prieſts that withſtood the Monarch in his impious Invaſion upon their ſacred Office. II Chron. xxvi. 16,—20. *But when he was ſtrong, his Heart was lifted up to his Deſtruction: for he tranſgreſſed againſt the LORD his God, and went into the Temple of the LORD, to burn Incenſe upon the Altar of Incenſe. And Azariah the Prieſt went in after him, and with him Fourſcore Prieſts of the LORD, that were valiant Men: And they withſtood Uzziah the King, and ſaid unto him, It pertaineth not unto thee, Uzziah, to burn Incenſe unto the LORD, but to the Prieſts the Sons of Aaron, that are conſecrated to burn Incenſe: go out of the Sanctuary, for thou haſt treſpaſſed, neither ſhall it be for thine Honour from the LORD God. Then Uzziah was wroth, and had a Cenſer in his Hand, to burn Incenſe: and while he was wroth with the Prieſts, the Leproſie even roſe up in his Forehead before the Prieſts in the Houſe of the LORD, from beſide the Incenſe-Altar. And Azariah the chief Prieſt, and all the Prieſts looked upon him, and behold, he was leprous in his Forehead, and they thruſt him out from thence, yea, himſelf haſted alſo to go out, becauſe the LORD had ſmitten him.* And this was the Magnanimity and Reſolution of our Apoſtle, Act. xx. 22, 23, 24. *I go bound in the Spirit unto Jeruſalem, not knowing the Things that ſhall befal me there: Save that the holy*

Ghoſt

Ghost witnesseth in every City, saying, that Bonds and Afflictions abide me. But none of these Things move me, neither count I my Life dear unto my self, so that I might finish my Course with Joy, and the Ministry which I have received of the Lord Jesus, to testify the Gospel of the Grace of God. So sings he in inimitable Periods, and with more than mortal Eloquence, *We are troubled on every side, yet not distressed; we are perplexed, but not in despair; persecuted, but not forsaken; cast down, but not destroyed; always bearing about in the Body the Dying of the Lord Jesus;— alway delivered unto Death for Jesus sake.** So JESUS himself led the Way ; and on the Paschal Night when the Vengeance of Heaven was marching through the Land, and GOD had given Warning, *None of you shall go out of the Door of his House until the Morning* ; then it was that our Lord went forth as from between the sprinkled Door-Posts, to encounter Divine Justice upon the March. This was his Work, and he has left us his own Example of Courage upon Duty. My Brethren, let the same Mind be in us. *Fight the good Fight of Faith, lay hold on eternal Life.* As *we wrestle not against Flesh and Blood, but against Principalities and Powers, against the Rulers of the Darkness of this World, against wicked Spirits in high Places* ; so let the *Weapons of our Warfare, which is not carnal but spiritual, be mighty through God to the pulling down of strong Holds.* Anon, you shall put off the Harness, and glory, *I have fought a good Fight, I have finished my Course, I have kept the Faith, I go to the Reward.* The Kingdom of Heaven suffereth Violence, and the violent take it by Storm : And these shall, as Victors through a Breach, have an abundant Entrance into the Joy of their Lord. Here shall we receive immortal Lawrels. Not a withering Chaplet, or a fading Garland, the transient Crown, or an Olympick

---

* II Cor. iv. 8, 9, 10, 11.

pick Victor; but the Crown of Life that fadeth not away.

IN the mean Time let our Examples and our Diſcourſes inſpire Courage into the Breaſts of the Militant Hoſts of GOD below: And while *Iſrael* encounters her Enemies let the Prieſts blow the Trumpets.

II. LET us all, from what we have heard, liſt our ſelves Volunteers in the Hoſts of GOD. Let us make ſure of our Maker's Friendſhip through JESUS CHRIST; and this be the Foundation of our Courage, *I know whom I have believed.* There's nothing irrational or enthuſiaſtick in this. A Man may upon the moſt ſolid Principles be aſſured of the Truth of the Chriſtian Religion: And he may be as rationally ſatisfied of his own being a true Chriſtian. And theſe being aſcertained,—*The Lord is my Light and my Salvation, whom ſhall I fear? The Lord is the Strength of my Life, of whom ſhall I be afraid.* Nor Life nor Death can hurt us; all Things ſhall conſpire our Good. *Watch ye, ſtand faſt in the Faith, quit you like Men, be ſtrong.* Look with a diſdainful Smile upon all your armed Enemies, you have more numerous and powerful Auxiliaries. There is more with us than with them. The Angel of the Lord encampeth round about them that fear him; and lo! the Mountain crowded with Chariots and Horſes of Fire.

III. From what you have heard you infer, a Man may lawfully engage in War. He may go in the Name of the Lord of Hoſts. This is a Subject that has been often handled upon theſe Occaſions, and to cut ſhort the Matter, the Proof may take this direct Courſe. Is there any Man upon Earth, who does not own that a Criminal ought to be puniſhed? But ſuppoſe this Criminal ſtands upon his own De-

fence,

fence, and is refolved to attack every one that fhall attempt to punifh him: Suppofe he engages a Number of others to ftand by him, and to fight for him rather than deliver himfelf up; what fhall be done in this Cafe? Shall the Officers of Juftice let him alone, if they cannot perfwade him to Chaftifement by Dint of Eloquence? This were to let the moft egregious Criminal go free, and correct only the more modeft: The harden'd Villain would efcape, and, in a Senfe which *Solomon* never meant, *The Rod would be only for the Fool's Back*. It muft then be lawful by Force, to make a Thief, for Inftance, refund his unjuft Gains, and by Punifhment deter him from future Ravages. This is the Cafe of a Nation engaged in a lawful War. It has been pillaged by a Combination of Thieves: Thefe unreafonable Banditti ought to make Reftitution and for many Reafons, fubmit to Difcipline, but the refractory Men ftand upon their Defence. There's no other Way left then but to march out in the Name of GOD, and overpower them by Force. And as the Laws of particular Kingdoms have appointed fuch and fuch particular Men, as the Minifters of GOD to ex cite Vengeance; the Law of Nations in general gives to every People Authority to protect themfelves, and to punifh thofe who injure them as far as they are able, as their own Executors. So that Fighting may be as neceffary as Laws themfelves; for what fignify Laws without Sanctions.

But I have ftood longer than I intended, and muft now difmifs you.

Gentlemen,

You profefs Skill in Arms, and would be afhamed of any thing like Cowardife. You are a Band of chofen Men, the Head and the Flower of all our Militia.

To

To honour Arms, and add a Glory to your Order, I have fet before you the great GOD as the Lord of Hofts. And at the fame Time I have recommended to you the fureft way to arrive at true Fortitude, that greateft Glory of a Souldier : A religious Regard to the great GOD the Bafis of rational Courage ; without which all Pretences to it are no better than the Stupidiy of a Stock, or the Rage of a Brute. Be ambitious of this Title, THE CHRISTIAN HERO.

YOU may now bear on fearlefs of every Danger, fhould the GOD of Armies call you to immediate Service. How foon this may be GOD knows ; for your Mufters are now fomething more than pretty Amufements, while the Sword of an injur'd Nation is unfheathed, and Vengeance is thundred from the Mouth of her Cannon Hark ! to the Sound of the Trumpet and Alarm of War! Hear the rufhing of Nations, that make a Noife like the Sea, a rufhing, like the rufhing of mighty Waters ! Methinks I can therefore addrefs you with a better Grace, than when thefe things only appeared at a diftance, and your Exercifes looked lefs in earneft. Sure you will not make a Flourifh in a Game, and when the Field gleams with hoftile Terrors bear to be infulted with the keen Sarcafm Judg. ix. 38. *Where is now thy Mouth, wherewith thou faidft, who is Abimelech —? Is not this the People that thou haft defpifed? Go out now and fight with them.*

WE are certainly a moft expofed People and in our unfortified Pofture feem to lye an eafy Prey to the firft Invader. 'Tis not for me to charge the Fault of this any where : Only to pray GOD that fome happy Method may open for the Redrefs of this Grievance. *Do good in thy good Pleafure unto Zion ; build thou the Walls of thy Jerufalem. David* himfelf, with

all

all his Courage and Divine Commiffion, would not
encounter his Enemy without fome Arms; a Sing
and a Stone at leaft, the Weapons which he knew beft
how to manage. To have gone in the Name of the
Lord of Hofts without, had been an unwarrantable
Prefumption. While we have been fitting at Eafe
amidft the Ruins of our falling Batteries, without fo
much as a Sling-Stone to defend us: Or rather have
feen our disjointed Fortifications dropping into feperate
Stones of no ufe but for the Sling: Inftead of Bulwarks a few loofe Pebbles. My Brethren, thefe Things
ought not fo to be. However, *the Name of the LORD
is* ftill *our ftrong Tower, the Righteous fly to it and are
faved.* So *our Place of Defence fhall be the Munitions
of Rocks.*

But You, Gentlemen, will do what in you lies to
diffufe Skill and Valour through your feveral Regiments and Companies; that at leaft we may keep our
Country, fhould we be obliged to give up our Fron-
tiers on the Sea. A fmall Number of difciplined
Troops will over-match a Rout of Thoufands. So a
few Men uniting their Strength, fhall be able with
eafe, to lift a Weight, which Ten times the Number
trying feperately fhall not be able to move. This is the
Reafon that all the military Movements and Fires fhould
be exactly together, that the whole Battallion may act
as one, with irrififtible Forces. The Drum and the
Trumpet fhould be articulate to every Souldier, and
he fhould know at the firft Notes, the Charge, the
Retreat, and the Parley. Every Man fhould be acquainted with his Duty, and be exact to the Word of
Command. The whole Succefs of an Engagement,
and the Fate of a Country, under GOD, depends upon
this one Military Maxim.

And

AND with how much Calm of Mind may you attend to it, in the midſt of the moſt hazardous Enterprize, if you can but aſſure your ſelves you are venturing in the Name of the Lord of Hoſts; and he is engaged for you. Then, to advance will not be terrible; to retreat will not be ſhameful; for all will be under the ſerene Conduct of Reaſon and Duty. You will not be meanly elated by the compleateſt Victory; nor afraid to fall in the hotteſt Battle; but with an equal Mind hear the Shouts of Triumph and the Groans of Death. *Thou ſhalt not be afraid for the Terror by Night, nor for the Arrow that flyeth by Day. A thouſand ſhall fall at thy Side, and ten thouſand at thy right Hand,* and thou ſhalt not be moved. *Thou ſhalt tread upon the Lyon and Adder; the young Lyon and the Dragon thou ſhalt trample under Feet.* —*Go up and proſper: The LORD is with thee, thou mighty Man of Valour.*

F I N I S.

THE Author having neither Leaſure nor Inclination to tranſcribe his Notes for the Preſs, when the Gentlemen of the Artillery asked his Copy, it has occaſioned many Errata. Some of the groſſer the Reader is deſired to correct as follows:

Page 8. Line 15. for *their* read *the.*
  l. 5. from Bottom, for *rubid* read *rabid.*
P. 11. l. 3. for *menal* read *mortal.*
P. 12. l. 13. for *Colours* read *Cohorts.*
P. 13. l. 3. for *Remile* read *Reptile.*
P. 16. l. 12. from Bottom, for *Feaſt* read *Staff.*
P. 21. l. 6. for *What* read *Which.*
  l. 11. from Bottom, for *Fleſh* read *Fluſh.*
P. 24 l. 9. for *Line* read *Lines.*
  l. 13. after *glorious* add *Labours.*

AFFECTION on Things ABOVE.

A

DISCOURSE

Delivered at the

Thursday-Lecture

In *BOSTON*,

December 11th 1740.

By MATHER BYLES, V. D. M.
And Paſtor to a CHURCH in *Boſton.*

REV. xi. 12. *They heard a great Voice
from Heaven, ſaying unto them,*
COME UP HITHER. ——

BOSTON, Printed by G. ROGERS and
D. FOWLE, for J. EDWARDS and H.
FOSTER in Cornhil. 1740.

Affection on Things above.

COLOSSIANS iii. 2.

*Set your Affection on Things above,
not on Things on the Earth.*

THE great Error that all Mankind are prone
to, and which indeed ruins the larger Part of
the World, is their placing their Happiness
in this Earth. The great Realities of another World, strike their Minds but weakly,
and appear at a wide Distance, and a strange Uncertainty
to their unbelieving Hearts. But the Things present,
and that are seen, the Objects that we converse with every Day, make a deep Impression upon us. We fancy
they are solid, and would fain believe they are lasting;
nor do we care to detect their Falshood and Treachery;
their Vanity and Emptiness. We have never been in
the other World; and therefore we don't know how to
reallize the Existence of it: It appears to us a Novelty
and a Dream. But the Earth we converse with every
Day;

Day ; we live upon it, and it is the conftant Object of all our Senfes. We have been a long Time ufed to it ; and the very firft Impreffions of our Infancy, have prejudiced us in its Favour. But the news of another World, comes to us by hear-fay ; and after we have been firft attached to this Earth, by our Sight and Familiarity. But above all, our Fall from GOD has brought a Cloud upon our Minds as to fpiritual Matters, and rendered our Appetites after carnal Things raging and impetuous. We all need then the Addrefs of the Text, *Set your Affection on Things above, not on Things on the Earth.* They are the Words of an *Apoftle* ; they are then weighty and folemn : But they are the Words of the HOLY GHOST in the *infpired* Apoftle ; they come then armed with divine Authority and Command, with the Power and Name of GOD. They are very plain and eafy to be underftood ; and no Subtlety or Artifice can obfcure or elude the Evidence of the facred Law. They are agreeable to the Maxims of eternal Reafon ; and they are expreffed in a very forcible and emphatical Manner. To render it beyond all Doubt or Hefitation, the Phrafe runs both Negative and Pofitive. *Set your Affection on Things above, not on Things on the Earth.* All the Circumftances tend to demand our moft awakened Attention, and ready Obedience.

The DOCTRINE of the Words is this,

DOCT. *It is the great Duty of Chriftians, to withdraw their Affections from the Things of the Earth, and fix them on the Things of Heaven.*

In handling this Doctrine, need I go about to prove to you,

I. That *the human Soul has in it many Affections ?*

This you feel in your felves ; and your own Hearts, and your own Experience are beforehand with me.
You

You are all confcious to the Paffions and Appetites of your own Minds. You know that you love and hate ; defire and abhor ; rejoice and grieve, hope and fear. That you have fuch Things as the Language of Scripture and Philofophy and common Life, call Affections, is a felf-evident Propofition, and can need no Proof. To pretend a Demonftration of it, would only be to obfcure it. I fhall drop this then, and purfue another, alas ! that it is fo plain a Propofition.

II. *Our Affections are naturally fet on the Things of Earth.*

We need fuch a Call as this of my Text, *Set your Affection on Things above, not on Things on the Earth.* The Matter of Fact is plain in our felves, and has been fo through all the Generations of Men, that this Earth ftrangely allures and engroffes our Affections. We feel in our Hearts a prevailing Fondnefs to the Things we poffefs, and a prevailing Defire to thofe we expect. And we fee the Cafe is the fame with all about us, who are earneft to get and to keep the vain Treafures of the Earth : And it has been fo from the firft Ages even until now. All the Children of Men are born the Slaves of this World ; and its Empire is univerfal and continuing, like that of Death. It has reigned over all Men from *Adam* even until now. If the Matter of Fact is fo plain then, what are the Reafons ? How comes it to pafs that our Affections are fo linked to earthly and mortal Things ? Alas, it is eafily and fadly accounted for. Our Fall from GOD has corrupted our Tafte, and blinded our Underftandings, and brought us into this deluded and bewildered Condition. *Adam,* our firft Father, fat his Affections on the Things below ; and now the juft Judgment of GOD has left us his Offfpring to do fo too. He was led away by his Senfes to forget the Things which were above, and difbelieve and difo-

bey

bey his GOD. The forbidden Tree allured his
Sight, and appeared *fair to look upon* : It tempted
his *Palate* ; and appeared *good for Food* : It excited
his *Desire*, and raised his *Ambition* : *A Tree to be
desired to make one wise* : So he *took the Fruit of
it, and did eat.* Gen. iii. 6. Thus were our first
Parents led away, and ever since then, the guilty
Progeny have been cheated by their Senses to place
their Affection on earthly Things. The holy GOD
immediately withdrew the Restraints of his SPIRIT,
and gave up the Race to follow the Senses which
they chose to follow. And now, the Fetters are
made strong upon many Accounts.

For Instance,
Earthly Things are the *first* we converse with ; and
as they are beforehand with our Reason, they insi-
nuate themselves into our Affections, before we are
aware of their Treachery and Falshood. The Child
learns to gratify his Senses before he comes to exercise his Reason ; and the first Impression is the deep-
est, and lasts the longest. His first Acquaintance is
with earthly Things ; and therefore his Affections
are placed upon them, before Reason can set a Guard
upon his Mind.

And as we converse *first* with earthly Things, so
we do it *constantly* ; and this is another Reason why
our Affections are fixed upon them. Earthly Things
are sensible Things, and familiar to our Eyes every
Day : And constant Familiarity begets Love. 'Tis
a sufficient Reason how we come to prefer the
Things of Earth, before Things above : Because
Things temporal are seen, but Things eternal are
invisible. Things unseen, are the Objects of our
Faith ; but the Things of this World, are the Objects of Sight and Sense. Faith is the Evidence of
Things not seen ; the Substance of Things hoped for.
But the Things below strike us more immediately ;
they bribe our Senses, and captivate our Souls. Hence
'tis

'tis that we feek the Things which are below, and
not the Things which are above. And need the
Warning and Exhortation of the Text ; *Set your Affections on Things above, not on Things on the Earth.*

The very Expreffion of the Text infinuates the Tendency of our Minds to earthly Things, and the Difficulty to tranffer them to heavenly. 'Tis becaufe
one is *below*, the other *above*. 'Tis like panting up
Hill, or fliding gently down. The Things of Heaven are *above*, and we rife to them with Pains and
Labour ; but the Things on Earth are about us, and
beneath us, and we may fit ftill, or fink down and
enjoy them. So that in every Light the Propofition appears evident, that our Affections are naturally
fet on Things below, and not on Things above.

III. *'Tis our Duty to fet our Affection on Things
above, and not on Things on the Earth.*

'Tis our Duty for fo has the Command of GOD
made it. The Will of GOD is the Rule of our
Duty. Whatever he enjoins immediately becomes
our Duty. 'Tis enough to enforce our Obedience
and Compliance, that GOD has given his Orders,
and declared this to be his Will. A Thing may
on other Accounts be our Wifdom, and our Inte-
reft, our Honour and Safety, but 'tis the Command
of GOD alone that can make it our Duty.

And befure this is the Cafe here : For GOD has
commanded it at our Hands, that we fet our Affections
on the Things above, and not on the Things below.
This is the great Defign of the Law of GOD, to
take our Affections off from Earth, and draw them
up to Heaven. In the New-Teftament this Matter
is more fully explained, and more frequently and
more ftrongly inculcated. Here we are inftructed,
I. John ii. 15, 16, 17. *Love not the World, neither
the Things that are in the World ; if any Man love
the World, the Love of the Father is not in him. For*

B *all*

all that is in the World, the Lust of the Flesh, the Lust of the Eye, and the Pride of Life, is not of the Father, but is of the World. And the World passeth away, and the Lust thereof ; but he that doeth the Will of GOD abideth for ever. 'Tis the Will of GOD then, that we set not our Affections on the Things of the World ; and 'tis then our Duty not to do it. Rom. xii. 2. *Be not conformed to this World ; but be ye transformed by the renewing of your Mind, that ye may prove what is that good, and acceptable, and perfect Will of GOD.* It is impossible to obey GOD ; to comply with the Will of GOD, without proclaiming War with the World ; without weaning our Affections and withdrawing our Friendship from it. James iv. 4. *Know ye not that the Friendship of the World is enmity with GOD ? Whosoever therefore will be a Friend of the World is an Enemy of GOD.* Thus the New-Testament, which has more fully brought Life and Immortality to Light, is, you see, full of the Matter.

But the Old-Testament is not without sufficient Indications of this too ; and tends to lead our Affections from the Things of Earth to those of Heaven. Indeed the Promises of the Old-Testament, do for the most part refer literally to the Land of *Canaan* : But they were ultimately regarded by the wise and good Men of those Days, to signify the Blessings of the heavenly World. Hence the believing ancient Patriarchs, all along professed that they were but *Strangers and Pilgrims here*, that they *sought a better Country, that is, an heavenly.* They looked upon the earthly *Canaan*, but as a Type of the heavenly ; and applied the Promises in the Letter temporal, to Things spiritual and eternal. And this is the Spirit that breathes in the pious Patriarchs till the coming of their blessed SAVIOUR, whom they all regarded and lived upon in the Prospects of Faith. They all believed a future World ; a State of Recompence, and eternal Rewards : And they withdrew their Affections from the Things below, and placed them

them on thofe greater above. Is not this the Language of *Mofes,* when he *chofe rather to fuffer Affliction with the People of* GOD, *than to enjoy the Pleafures of Sin for a Seafon?* Is not this the Confolation of *Job,* when *I know* (fays he) *that my Redeemer liveth, and though after my Skin, Worms deftroy this Body, yet in my Flesh fhall I fee* GOD ? Is not this the Infinuation of the Pfalmift, when he fpeaks of the *Men of this World, who have their Portion* only *in this Life* : And what elfe could comfort him when he *walk'd through the Valley of the Shadow of Death,* but that he knew for him *to die would be Gain.* Even *Balaam* himfelf, when he came to have his Eyes open, could wifh to *die the Death of the Righteous,* convinced that the *Day of his Death was better than the Day of his Birth.* So that upon the whole, all the facred Pages reprefent this bleffed Truth to us, that GOD therefore calls us to fet our Affections on thofe Things, and not on Things on the Earth : And that accordingly this has been the Practice of good Men in all Ages, who have fo underftood the Duty, and fo perform'd it.

Set your Affection on Things above, not on Things on the Earth. This does not forbid us *having* an Affection for the Things below ; but indulging an inordinate Affection. We may have an Affection for earthly Things, but we muft not *fet* them, muft not *fix* them upon thefe Things ; muft not fet our *Affection* ; not *all* of them as ONE ; not *wholly* upon earthly Things. We may *defire* worldly Good ; but not too vehemently ; but it muft be with profound Submiffion. We may love and be glad of our outward Bleffings ; but it muft be a fubordinate Affection ; we muft fet loofe by them, and be willing to part with them. We muft fet a much *bigher* Value upon the Things *above* ; and look upon *them* to be by far better. This is the State of the Cafe : You may *have* an Affection for the good Things in

the

the World ; but you muſt not *ſet* your Affection on theſe lower Things, but on Things above.

It were high Ingratitude in us, to have no Re-gard at all for the good Things which a bounte-ous GOD, on this Earth gives us. 'Tis he that beſtows on us, our Riches, and our Relatives ; our Health, and our Life ; and it were Diſreſpect to the Giver to diſreliſh the Gifts. So an abſent Friend ſends us Tokens of his Friendſhip, by which we ſhould remember him : As it would be ſtrange that thoſe Marks of Affection ſhould be lov'd in-ſtead of our Friend to the Prejudice of our Fond-neſs for him, ſo it would be baſe and ungrateful not to eſteem the Tokens and remember our Friend by them. Let us reliſh the Creature for GOD's Sake then, and there will be no Danger of an inordinate Affection.

Some have made ſtrange Work with a Paſſage in the New-Teſtament, where our SAVIOUR tells the young Man in the Goſpel, *Sell all thou haſt and give it unto the Poor*, as though this were a Command that reached unto every Chriſtian, and a Rule to hold univerſally as a Criterion to try our Love to the World by. 'Tis a Wonder ſuch Genius's for Expoſition have not commented on that Paſſage in the Old-Teſtament, where *Abraham* is commanded to ſacrifice *Iſaac* ; and demonſtrated that a Man could not be a true Believer who did not deſtroy his Chil-dren for Burnt-Offerings ; for the Ground for both is pretty near the ſame. In one Caſe and the other, GOD gave a particular Command to try the Truth of Grace in the Heart of a particular Perſon, and all the Difference was, one ſtood the Trial, as every good Man would, and the other ſunk under it, as would be the Caſe of every Hypocrite. And had the young Man in the Goſpel with the ſincere unrelucting Heart of *Abraham*, given up his Poſſeſſions, no one can ſay how far they might have been given back again to him, as *Iſaac* was to *Abraham*, or

as

as *Job's* Estate was doubled. However that may be, all we can infer from both the Stories is this, That if GOD does really call for all our outward good Things, a good Man so loves his GOD, that he would make a ready Surrender of them : And not that he is now oblig'd either to slay his Son, or give away all his Estate. It is plain this cannot be the Meaning in the latter Case, because it is a Duty impossible to be perform'd : For how could every Man sell all his Estate and give it to the Poor ? Where would be the Poor to receive it ! 'Twould indeed serve to level all Mankind, destroy all Order, and break up the Community : As though we should contrive that the Body natural should be all Hand, or all Eye : And then where were the Hearing and the Taste ?

And yet, after all, nothing is more certain than this Truth, that the Man who has ever felt what a Work of Grace upon the Soul means, loves his GOD and his SAVIOUR beyond any Creature. And if he does not sell all he has and give it to the Poor, 'tis purely because he knows it would not please GOD ; and if he sacrifices not his only Son, 'tis purely because GOD requires it not, but forbids it.

But would you know whither this be the real Principle of your Actions, and not the governing Love of the Idol-Creature, the best Way of discovering the Matter, will be, not to try your selves in Instances, where, as GOD has not commanded, so has no where promis'd to assist you : But to examine, do you without Reluctance comply where his Commands are plain. 'Twas that young Man's Duty to sell all. He cou'd not do it : 'Tis plain he was not a sanctified Man. 'Twas *Abraham's* Duty to sacrifice *Isaac* : He set about it immediately : 'Tis plain he was truly faithful. Neither of these are Commands to you. So that if you are not assisted to do Things which are not your Duty, you have no need of Discouragement at the Reluctance. The Rule is, Do you do
what

what is your Duty ?   Do you chearfully give GOD
his Dues out of your Eſtates ? Do you give up
this Part of your Gains with a peculiar Pleaſure,
and far from any Regret ? If you have the Teſtimony
of your Conſciences here, you may be ſure that as
your future Days ſo your Strength ſhall be.   And
your whole Eſtate, or your only Son you ſhall be
enabled to part with, if ever GOD really demands
them.   GOD will either keep you from the Temptation, or make Way for your Eſcape. ---All our
Projections about future Tryals proceed from our vain
Confidence as though our Strength was our own. ---
Take no Thought for the morrow, but do the Duty of the Day, and that is all GOD requires.

Thus I have briefly explain'd and evinc'd the Duty
to you ; and I come now to improve and apply it.

*Be exhorted, my beloved Brethren, to ſet your Affection
on Things above, not on Things on the Earth.*

Conſider,
1. *CHRIST is above.* Is not this a ſufficient Reaſon why you ſhould place your Affection there. Who
is worthy of all your Love but he ?   The Creatures
you are ſo fond of, were made by him, and derive all
that is lovely in them from him.   And if from
his Fulneſs they have all received all their Graces,
how ſuperiour muſt his Fulneſs be ? Beſure then, if
we are apt to ſet our Affections on Things below,
we have infinitely higher Reaſon to ſet them on Things
above ; for CHRIST is there in his more abundant
Glory.   And ſo ſays the Apoſtle, in the preceeding
Context, *Seek thoſe Things which are above, where
CHRIST ſitteth on the right Hand of GOD.* CHRIST
is above ; and the right Hand of GOD is above ;
is not this then a Place worthy your Deſire and
Choice ? *At his right Hand are Pleaſures for evermore.*

2. Set

2. Set your Affection on Things above, not on Things on the Earth : *For ye are dead,* fays the Context : Ye are dead ? What a Shock does it give to our Security in earthly Enjoyments ? We fet our Affections on Things below : Alas! we muft prefently be fummon'd by Death to leave them all. So certain is it that we muft die away from them, that it may be pronounced, we are already dead. Death *has* paffed upon all Men, in that all have finned. In the *Day* thou eateft thou fhalt furely die. It proved true, becaufe in that *fame Day* the Sentence took Place, and we became liable to Death : Dead in Law. Ye are dead then. 'Tis as certain you muft be fo, as if you were already dead. Set not then your Affection on the Things below. *When GOD requires your Soul, whofe fhall all thefe Things be?*

But befure this is not the principal Intention of the Text, when it fays, *Ye are dead,* therefore fet your Affection on the Things above, not on Things on the Earth. Ye are dead : that is, the corrupt Principle in you is dead. The reigning Power of your Lufts is dead ; your inordinate Paffions and Appetites are mortified and dead. You are dead to this World. By the Crofs of CHRIST the World is crucified unto me, and I unto the World. And now why fhould you revive the Dead Affections, and fet them on Things below ? Having efcaped the Pollution of the World through Luft, why fhould you be again taken and entangled therein ? Remember how the World treated your bleffed SAVIOUR, and let the Crofs of CHRIST crucify the World to you. Let the Remembrance of his Sufferings wean you from the execrable Place.

3. But fays the Text, *Your Life is hid with CHRIST in GOD.* Is CHRIST your Life ; the vital Principle of Thought and Action in you ? Befure we fhould have our Hearts and Affections where our Life is. Where fhould Life be, but in the Heart ? the Seat of the Affections ? Now,

CHRIST

CHRIST our Life is above, on the Throne, and in
the Bofom of G O D.   Our Affections fhould be
there too then :   Our Life is hid with CHRIST in
GOD.   Your Life is hid indeed ; but this Way
you may difcover it to others, by your Indifference
to the Things of this World, and your Ardor to
thofe of another.   Your Life is *hid* ; laid up out of
Sight.   But O realize it ;   Look for a future Life.
Remember *this is not your Reft*, why then fhould
fhould you terminate your Affection here ?

4. Another Motive in the Context, is, *If ye then
be rifen with CHRIST, fet your Affection on Things
above, not on Things on the Earth.*   If we were always to live among fuch Objects and Enjoyments,
it were more excufable fhould they feize our Affections ; but when we expect fo different, a Refurrecti-
on-State, what Madnefs is it,   to circumfcribe our
Acquaintance in fuch narrow Limits ?   We are made
for the R:furrection-World,   widely different from
the prefent Scene of Things ;   why then fhould we
learn to love thofe fhort-liv'd Objects, and neglect
the future and eternal ones ?   CHRIST is rifen :
No Truth is more capable of Proof than this.   And
we are rifen with CHRIST, we fhall as furely rife,
as if we were already rifen.   *For if the Dead rife not,
then is not CHRIST raifed.* ---- we are rifen in Type,
in Earneft and Pledge.   'Tis Folly then, 'tis the greateft Folly, to fet our Affections on the World of
Death, when we are made for the quite different
Refurrection-World.   Nay, but further, *Ye are rifen
with CHRIST* :   It fignifies a fpiritual Refurrection.
A Refurrection from a Death in Sin, and a Refto-
ration to the Life of Holinefs.   Here now is the Argument, *If ye then be rifen with CHRIST, fet your
Affection on Things above, not on Things on the Earth.*
If you have experienced this blefled Refurrection with
CHRIST ; if you have been renewed, and brought
into the Life of GOD, Oh feed the divine Life,
and cherifh it ; by no Means ftifle it by an inordinate

dinate Affection to the groffer Things below. This Principle of Life in you, like a Flame, tends *upwards* : You fmother it when you fet your Affection on the Things below. 'Tis worfe in you to do fo than for others : For the natural Man cannot difcern to do at all otherwife. It is better not to have known and felt the Power of the Truth, than after that to difobey it, and love the Things contrary to it.

5. Another Motive in the Context is, *when* CHRIST *who is our Life fhall appear, then fhall ye alfo appear with him in Glory* ; *mortify therefore your Members, which are upon the Earth. Set your Affection on Things above, not on Things on the Earth.* The fecond Appearance of CHRIST, and the Rewards which he will then beftow on his Faithful, are a fufficient Reafon why we fhould fet our Affections and Expectations on Things future and above. CHRIST will appear the fecond Time : Behold he comes, and his Reward is with him. He will give the Crown of Righteoufnefs in that Day. Wherefore, *forgetting the Things which are behind,* and calling our Affections back from them, *let us reach forth to thofe Things which are before, and prefs towards the Mark for* this Prize. The *Account* we are to give *to* CHRIST our Judge, this methinks is a moft awakening Motive to fet loofe by the Things of this World, and fet our Affection on the Things above. The *Glory* that we fhall receive *from* CHRIST our Judge, this methinks fhould raife our Expectations, and attract our Defires and fix our Affections ; for when CHRIST who is our Life, fhall appear, then fhall ye alfo appear with him in Glory. My Brethren, are we not ambitious of this Honour ? Do we not long for this Glory ? Is it not enough to call up and fire all our Affections ? Are the Things below worthy to be Rivals here ? Are they, think you, worthy to be compared with the Glory which fhall be revealed ? Think on the Appearance of CHRIST ; on the Glory of CHRIST ; and that you fhall appear with him in Glory ; and fee if this has not a pre-

vailing

vailing Charm to draw your Affection from the Things
below, and set them on Things above. If this will
not do, consider,

6. *The Wrath of GOD cometh on the Children of
Disobedience.* So says the Context very emphatically :
Ver. 6. If your Affections are let loose upon the
Things below, they will lead you on to all excess
of Uncleanness, for which Things sake the Wrath of
GOD cometh on the Children of Disobedience. And is
not here fair Warning against inordinate Affection? The
Wrath of GOD, is it, do you suppose, a light Matter?
Can you easily bear it? Dare you confront it with an
intreped Air? Can you resist, or can you escape? Nay, be
not deceived, GOD is not mocked : It is indeed a fearful Thing to fall into the Hands of the living GOD.
Can thy Heart endure, or can thy Hands be strong
in the Day when he shall rise up in his Vengeance
and Flame! And this will be the amazing Danger,
and this the swift Destruction that shall pour upon
the Head of those, who seek earthly Things and
neglect heavenly. The Things on the Earth are dying
Creatures; and those who set their Affection on them,
go down to the Dead : What wonder then, that
they should be gathered with the Congregation of the
dead? GOD commands you to set your Affection
on Things above, and not on Things on the Earth;
You disobey GOD, and you set up Creatures in the
Throne of GOD, when you let your Love loose below Him. And will not this justly provoke GOD?
For this Cause the Wrath of GOD cometh on the
Children of Disobedience.----Thus far I have confin'd
my self only to the Motives of the Apostle in the
Context.

7. And to conclude, Set your Affection on Things
above, not on Things on the Earth : *For the Things
on Earth are temporal, but the Things above are eternal.*
This is the great and finishing Stroke of all : And
though this Motive is not expressed in the Context,
yet

yet it is implied in it, and urged in innumerable other
Places. The Things in this World are fading, tran-
sitory and perishing. Why should we set our
Eyes then, upon that which is not; or presently will
not be. Look upon the Things you are so fond of,
in this Light, and see how worthless they are of your
warm Affection. You have an Affection to *Wealth*
and *Plenty*; you look with Joy upon your large Pof-
fessions, and let your Wishes loose for more. Alas,
*Riches take themselves Wings, and flee away as the Eagles
towards Heaven.* You have an Affection to the *Pleasures of Sense and of Sin,* and are very loath to withdraw your Desire and Choice. Alas, *the Pleasures of
Sin are but for a Season.* You are fond of *worldly
Fame and Honour,* and pant after Dignities and a great
Name. Alas, *Man being in Honour abideth not.* You
feel a glowing Affection to your *Relatives,* and your
Heart beats with the Ardors of *Love* and *Friendship.*
Alas, *Lover and Friend must forsake you, and your Acquaintance retire into Darkness.* You desire *long Life,*
and love many Days that you may see Good. Alas,
*If by reason of Strength you should reach fourscore Years,
yet,* ---*'tis soon cut off, and we flee away.* Thus you see
how very temporary, how vanishing and transient are
all Things here below! But now set your Affection
on the Things above, and they will last boundless as
your Wishes, and immortal as your Souls. The *Riches*
there, are *durable Riches.* The *Pleasures* are *Pleasures
forevermore.* The *Honours* are, *Salvation by* CHRIST
with eternal Glory. The *Inheritance* is *incorruptible, undefiled, and fadeth not away.* The *Companions die no
more : Death is swallowed up in Victory, there shall be
no more Death :* And so shall we all be *forever with
the Lord.* The *Rewards* are an *everlasting Crown,* and
Life eternal.

And now, who would not try to set their Affections on Things above, and not on Things on the Earth?
Who would not take Pains for the new Nature, that
he might do this? Though you go through Diffi-
C 2   culty

culty and Labour in this great Work, and meet with many Oppositions, Temptations and Afflictions in it, yet remember and take Encouragement from that Word of GOD, which I leave with you, and conclude, II. Cor. iv. 17, 18. *For our light Affliction which is but for a Moment, worketh for us a far more exceeding and eternal Weight of Glory ; while we look not at the Things which are seen, but at the Things which are not seen ; for the Things which are seen, are temporal, but the Things which are not seen, are eternal.*

FINIS.

THE

The *Comparison*, the *Choice*, and the *Enjoyment*.

I.

WHO on the Earth, or in the Skies,
  Thy Beauties can declare?
Jesus, dear Object of my Eyes,
  My Everlasting Fair.

II.

Mortals, for you this is too great,
  Too bright, and too sublime:
This Angels labour to repeat,
  And sink beneath the Theme.

III.

Behold, ye Beauties here below,
  And clasp him in your Arms:
Can ye such heav'nly Graces show,
  Or rival him in Charms?

Though

IV.

Though now, delighted, we can trace
 Your Colours as they ly,
When he appears, from off your Face
 The fading Colours fly.

V.

When all your Charms in vain we feek,
 And all your Joys are fled,
Beauty blooms rofey on his Cheek,
 And dances round his Head.

VI.

In vain your fofteft Smiles appear,
 Or lovely Blufhes rife :
Eternal Tranfports center here,
 Heav'n brightens in thefe Eyes.

VII.

Unveil, almighty Love, thy Face,
 Thy Features let me fee ;
At once I'll rufh to thy Embrace,
 I'll fpring at once to Thee.

Thus

VIII.

Thus fix'd for ever,—O the Joys !
  Th' unutterable Blifs !
Now where's your Pleafure? earthlyToys?
  Can ye compare with this ?

IX.

No more from thy Embrace I'll roam,
  My LORD, my LIFE, my LOVE,
I fee the Scenes of Joys to come
  In long Proceffion move.

X.

Now, vaft Eternity, roll on,
  O fathomlefs profound !
Ye endlefs Ages, fwiftly run
  Your never-ceafing Round.

Mr. *Byles*'s

SERMON

ON THE

Spring of the *Year.*

THE
FLOURISH
OF THE
Annual Spring,
Improved in a
SERMON
Preached at the ancient THURSDAY
LECTURE in *Boston*, May 3. 1739.

By MATHER BYLES, A.L.M.
Paſtor of a Church in *Boston*.

Numb. xvii. 8. --- *Behold, the Rod of*
AARON--*budded, and brought forth*
Buds, and bloomed Bloſſoms, and
yielded Almonds.

BOSTON, Printed and Sold by ROGERS
and FOWLE at the Printing-Office
over-againſt the South-Eaſt Corner
of the TownHouſe. 1741.

THE
FLOURISH
OF THE
Annual Spring.

CANTICLES II. 10---13.

--- Rise up--and come away. For lo,
the Winter is past, the Rain is over
and gone. The Flowers appear on
the Earth, the Time of the singing of
Birds is come--arise--and come away.

O F all the meer Men who have
lived since the Fall of *Adam,*
the Author of this beautiful
Passage is pronounced the wis-
est, by the GOD of Heaven. And of
all the Books which he wrote, this is,

without Difpute, the moft elegant,
fublime and devout. The three Books
which *Solomon* wrote, are refembled to
the three Divifions of the Temple which
he built ; of which the *Holy of Holies*
is compar'd to this admirable Song. His
Proverbs contain an excellent Scheme
of Morality ; and to this anfwers the
outward Enclofure, called the *Court of
the Gentiles*. His *Ecclefiaftes* contains
the Difquifitions of a philofophical and
religious Genius after true Happinefs ;
and the folemn Reflexions and pious
Arguments render it a *holy Place*.
But this *Divine Song* is all confecrated
Rapture ; 'tis the *Holy of Holies :* It
muft be approach'd with Reverence and
Trembling, and it admits of no unhal-
lowed Feet to tread its awful Recefles.

The Title of the Book is, *The Song
of Songs* ; and it well deferves the
Name, for it is the fineft poetical Compofure now extant in the World. It
is not every where over-nice and exact
in its Metaphers and Allufions ; but
they are bold and grand, elevated and
lofty, all Fire, all confecrated Rapture and Infpiration !

The

The Criticks in the Art of Poetry will prefently fee that it is a *Drama-tic* Compofition of that kind to which perhaps the Moderns would give the Name of a *Paftoral Opera.* That it is a *Dramatic* Performance is eafily difcerned, inafmuch as it confifts wholly of Action, Dialogue, and Character: It is a perfonal Reprefentation of Paffion and Hiftory, all which are the exact Defcription and Character of the *Drama.* It is an *Opera*; it feems to confift of three Acts; The Numbers are of the Lyrick Kind; and it has in it the evident Intimations of Mufick, and a Chorus. And it is a *Paftoral*; for the Scenes are moftly laid in the Country; and the Characters and Images are principally rural.

But more than this, 'tis a Divine Poem *. It contains a fine Picture of

---

* *I purpofely avoid the vain Difputes of late raifed, about the Canonical-nefs of this Book. The Teftimony of the Jewifh Church, and the Forty-fifth Pfalm are a fufficient Vindica-tion of it, if we had not other abun-dant Evidence.*

the

the Loves of CHRIST and his Church;
He is the heavenly Bridegroom, and
she the beautiful Shepherdess, that are
the principal Speakers in the Song.
With how much Admiration does
the sacred Spouse look up to the lovely
JESUS, and how full of Passion and
Transport are her Expressions about
him! And on the other Hand, with
what Tenderness and Delight does the
blessed SAVIOUR overlook the Defects
of his Church, and applaud the Graces
which he had before lighted up in her
smiling Form? *Who is she that looketh
forth as the Morning? Fair as the
Moon, clear as the Sun, and awful as
an Army with Banners?*

Among the many fond and endear-
ing Sentences, my Text is none of the
least remarkable. There are a thousand Beauties glowing in the Sentiments and Expressions. 'Tis a Speech
that well suits with the graceful Lips
of him, who spake so as never Man
spake; that well sutes with the heavenly Form of her, who is the chosen
Bride of JESUS CHRIST --- O thou
fairest among the most elegant of the
Works of GOD!

The

The Words are a Defcription of the Spring of the Year, in the Land of *Canaan.* Great Part of it may be literally applied to our Spring : But in fome Refpects it varies. The Winter there, as in our Mother-Country, ufed to be cloudy and rainy, and a fteady fair Weather ufed to fmile on the Face of the Spring. Indeed it is otherwife in our inconftant Climate, where we fee the Clouds fo frequently returning after the Rain.

Without going into the myftical or prophetical Way of explaining thefe Words, I fhall only obferve, That they are the Invitation of Christ to his beloved Church. Every true Believer in Jesus, and Follower of the Lamb, may apply the Addrefs to himfelf. He may take up his Bible, and fay, I hear the dear Words of my Lord Jesus, *Arife up, and come away.* --- Before when the Flowers appear on the Earth; when the Rain and Cold of the Winter is paft, and the Spring begins to blof-fom and flourifh, and renew the Face of the Ground, this Call is in a peculiar Manner to be heard, from our bleffed Redeemer, *Arife and come away.*

The

The Doctrine then that I shall offer from the Words, is this.

DOCTRINE.

When we see the Spring open upon the Earth, we may hear the Call of CHRIST *to us, to rise up from the Earth, and repair to him.*

In the Illustration of this Point of Doctrine, I shall do two Things. I. *Show what is implied in the Call of* CHRIST, *Rise up, and come away.* II. *Why this Call is in a peculiar Manner seasonable when the Winter is past, and the Spring opens.*

I. *What is implied in the Invitation of* CHRIST, *Rise up, and come away?*

I shall be but brief here, that I may hasten to a more seasonable and uncommon Set of Meditations. And in short then, when we hear the Call of CHRIST, *Rise up, and come away,* we presently discover the Condition of those who are addressed! They are indolent and supine and sleepy Creatures: They want to be roused and quickned; and are by Nature bowed down, fo-
cure

ture and dead. The Voice is, *Rise up.*
Shake off the mortal Lethargy that
hangs upon your Eye-lids. Arise from
the dead, and CHRIST shall give thee
Life. Awake thou that sleepest, and
call upon thy GOD. And indeed, all
Mankind need such a Call as this, for
they are dead in Trespasses and Sins.
They are cold and lifeless Corpses, unable to help themselves, and can do
nothing spiritually Good. They are
not able as of themselves, to think so
much as a good Thought : And they
have only a Power of chusing which
Sin to commit. They may if they
please talk of a *Free-Will,* and amuse
themselves with the idle Notion. But
alas, they are *free amongst the dead* :
Free 'tis true, in their Choice of Wickedness, but it must be the infinite Power of GOD that can incline them to
any Thing spiritually good. Our
preaching to them is indeed only pro-
phesying over dry Bones : Though
this sometimes does Wonders. In one
Word, they act entirely from selfish
Principles, negligent and forgetful of
the Glory of GOD. They are
bowed down to Earth and Creatures,

and

and their own abject Will ; and have need to be awaked, *Rife up*.

And what is implied in this Phrafe, when it is fpoken by our Lord CHRIST to his People ? In a few Words, It comprifes in it, our Duty to our LORD JESUS. We are called to *believe* in CHRIST. To rife up from a vain Earth, and raife our Eyes to invifible and eternal Realities. To walk by Faith, and not by Sight.

Rife up ; 'tis a Call to *Repentance* that we are by Nature fo bowed down. It comes with a Voice of Conviction and Awakening ; to roufe our drowfy Faculties, and fhake us from our Security and Indifference. *Rife up*, or we fhall lie down among the dead ; flide down to the Congregation of the damned.

'Tis a Call to *Holinefs* and Obedience. *Rife up* and walk : It demands a holy Walk of us ; and tells us that our Converfation fhould be in Heaven ; that we fhould feek the Things which are above, and carry our Treafure over into the other World. The Path of the Juft-- fhines brighter as it rifes higher.

Rife

Rife up, it befpeaks our *Meditation* and *Prayer.* Lift up your Eyes and Hands, your Hearts and your Souls. Is it not aShame that this Earth fhould feize our Thoughts and Affections, and GOD and CHRIST have fo little of them. There is not an Object we fee, but may ferve to raife ourThoughts to GOD. His glorious Name is divinely impreffed upon all his Works; and with one Voice, they all call out to us, GOD! GOD! " I was made " by GOD! I am fupported byGOD! " I am a Servant of GOD! and anIn- " ftrument in his Hand! *Rife up!* " Arife and adore GOD. Contem- " plate him, pray to him, adore and " blefs him.

But to finifh this Point, It will be the Call of CHRIST to us quickly *to leave this World; Rife up and come a- way.* Death fhall arrive with this welcome Meffage, *The Mafter calleth for thee.* This will finifh ourLife upon this Earth, the Voice of CHRIST inviting us to his Kingdom and Glory. *Rife up and come away, the Winter is paft, the Rain is over and gone.* Every Evil will be concluded forever, and we fha'l

B

enter

enter into Reft : The *Winter* of Affliction, Temptation and Sin, will no more
moleft us : The Evils of this World,
which fell on us like a continual dropping in a very rainy Day, will defcend
no more about us. *The Rain is over
and gone.* No more Storms will roar
in our Air ; nor Clouds intercept our
Sunfhine. The laft Tempeft of Death
will beat after us but a little Way ; and
rapid we fhall leave it behind. And
now, welcome everlafting Delights !
Welcome the opening Dawn of Paradife ! *The Time of the finging of Birds
is come.* Angels tune their Harps, and
join their Voices about us. *The Flowers appear upon the Earth* ; and the e-
verlafting Hills lift up their flowry Tops
before us. Joys unfelt till this bleffed
Moment, will now feize our beating
Hearts, and our Souls will leap out,
obedient to the dear Voice that calls
us, *Rife up, and come away.*

These, I think, are natural Heads
for Meditation from the Words : But
that which I principally intend to allude to, in theProcefs of this Difcourfe,
is, that when we fee the annualSpring
open upon the Earth, we have a Call

to

to *Rife up to* CHRIST *in holy Meditations* : To come away from lower
Objects to him the higheft and moft
worthy of all. The Beauties which
fmile around us, at this lovely Seafon
of the Year, unite to lead our Thoughts
to CHRIST. And this is the fecond
Point to be fpoken to.

II. *How is the Invitation of our bleffed
Saviour to rife up aud come away, peculiarly adapted to the Spring of the Year?*

1. *The Spring looks like the natural
Beginning of the Year* : And before
we are to begin our Year with GOD.
The Demand and Expectation of the
bleffed GOD is, for the *firft-ripe
Fruits.* And it is reafonable that our
firft Care fhould be to pleafe him, our
firft Hours confecrated to him. He
demands of us the firft Day in every
Week, and why fhould he not for the
moft part have the firft Hour in every
Day ; and the firft Seafon in every
Year. *Seek firft the Kingdom of* GOD,
is the Direction of CHRIST. A Year
begun with GOD, is a Year well begun, and it will yield a comfortable

B 2   Re-

Reflection all the Year, for us to call to Mind how we have been enabled to spend the first Months of it.

2. *The Temptations of the Spring afford another Argument for us to obey the Call of CHRIST, Rise up, and come away.* That the Spring is attended with many Circumstances to tempt away our Minds from GOD and Duty, will very easily be rendred plain and evident. Then 'tis that the Face of Nature puts on the most gay and alluring Smiles ; and the beautiful Prospects about us are apt to catch away our Thoughts, and possess and fill up our Minds. Then 'tis too, that our animal Spirits are most sprightly and vigorous ; and our fermented Blood pours along its rapid Current more warm and impetuous. The Chains of the Winter are melted off : and the *Bands of Orion are loosed* : And from this Flush of Blood and Spirits, there arises a Variety of Temptations. Our Appetites are most raging and violent; and our inferiour Faculties most apt to usurp the Throne of Reason and Conscience. We are now most easily deceived

ceived with the tempting Profpects of
Futurity ; and we prefume upon a vain
Earth, and Happinefs here below, from
a Warmth of Temper, and the Difpofition of our Blood and animal Spirits.
Thus we fee the Temptations of the
Spring both external and internal. External, from the alluring Face of Nature ; Internal, from our own Frame
and Conftitution. How proper then
the Call ? *Rife up and come away.*
Does the *low* Face of the Ground
tempt us ? *Rife up.* Get above the
Earth. Leave the Molehill for the
Emmits to inhabit ; but let us take to
our felves Wings, as Angels, and fly
away. Have we our Temptations in
our felves ? Come away then ; let us
get out of our felves into CHRIST ; feparate our felves from our felves, and
mortify and root out the corrupted felf-
ifh Principle in us.

And indeed nothing will have a
greater Tendency to demonftrate our
Sincerity in Religion, than our Refolution to defeat the ftrongeft Temptations which affault us in this World.
When Sin fpreads all its Snares, and
lays all its alluring Bates in our Way,

if

if we have then Power to overcome all, and pass unhurt amidst all, it will be a good Evidence that we are infpired with a Power superiour to our own : That the Holy Spirit is in us ; and that we are in good Earnest in Religion. The same Arguments to persuade Youth to serious Piety, are in the same Sense proper to perswade us to Religion in the Spring. Because we may all the Year look back on it with this concomitant Satisfaction, When Temptations were most universal, and most impetuous, I stood the Shock, and was carried graciously thro' them.

And what an Honour will it be for us to overcome Temptations when they are at the strongest ; and regulate our Appetites when they are most raging and lawless ? So *Joseph*, fortified with the Grace of GOD, withstood Satan and himself together, joined in the most dangerous League ; he broke loose from the Toils of Death, and by a wise Retreat, rushed away, pursued by Victory and Triumph. This is more to the Honour of young *Joseph*, than a Monument of Brass, and the Trophies of conquered Nations ! When
the

the *Cæfars* and the *Alexanders*, and the Conquerors of the Eaft, blufh and hide, *Jofeph* fhall ftand applauded by the Judge of the World, and faluted by fhouting Armies of Men and Angels. And it will be an Honour of the fame Nature, for us to be moft firm and refolute, when Temptations are moft frequent and violent. So that if it has been proved, that the Spring of the Year, is a Seafon lying moft open to Temptations, it plainly follows, that Religion in this precarious Seafon, is attended with additional Honours.

Befides, the Rewards of our future Glory, will be proportioned to our Labours and Difficulties. We know that *he who foweth fparingly fhall reap fparingly*; and they who take the greateft Pains, fhall reap the fulleft Harveft. Now he who ftands his Ground againft moft Oppofition, who beats through the thickeft Temptations beft, fhall receive the brighteft Crown, and hear the loudeft Applaufe. So that if we would attain the higheft Degrees of Glory, one Way is to fpend that Time beft, which is fulleft of Temptations. When it was afferted, that the Spring

is

is the Seafon fulleft of Temptations, a vain Mind would perhaps have drawn another Confequence : Let me then wait for a more convenient Seafon for the Duties of Religion and Holinefs. But it is you fee eafily retorted. Is the Spring of the Year fulleft of Temptations, fure then we have moft need of gracious Hearts. This will be attended with the higheft Pleafure in the Reflection here ; This will be followed with the ampleft Rewards of Heaven hereafter. This will prove our Sincerity to us with the fulleft Evidence. For, as one fpeaks, if there is no Enemy, there can be no Fight ; if no Fight, no Victory ; if no Victory no Crown. And on the contrary, if there be powerful Enemies, there will enfue a fharper Fight, a greater Victory, and a brighter Crown. But to take the Objectors in their own Way ---

3. *The Advantages of the Spring afford another Argument why we fhould obey the Call of* CHRIST, *Rife up and come away. Rife up and come away, for the Winter is paft, the Rain is over and gone* ; many Difadvantages are over and gone ; *The Time of the finging of Birds*

Birds is come, and the Flowers appear upon the Earth ; many Advantages come pouring round us, and call, and awaken, excite and quicken us.

If it can be proved that there are peculiar Advantages in the Spring for the Duties and the Delights of Piety, it will follow of Courfe that we ought to make Ufe of thefe Advantages, and improve them while they laft : For they are all but fo many Talents committed to us by the GOD of Nature, which he will call us to a ftrict Account for, and miferable we, if we can give no good Account of them.

And that the Spring of the Year is indeed attended with fuch Advantages for the Labours and Delights of Piety, will be evident upon a very little Reflection. Now it is that the Days lengthen apace, and the Light increafes over us. The Morning awakes us early ; and the Day-fpring from on high, the rifing Sun, calls us betimes from our Slumbers, *Rife up, and come away.* Now it is alfo, that the Weather grows moderate, and we blefs the Indulgence of the mild Skies, and the temperate **Air.** We are not chained up with Cold,

Cold, or confined by the bleak Winds.
We may live more in one Day now,
than in many that are numbed with
Froft, and chilled by the Rigour of the
Winter. Now it is alfo that our Spirits awaken, and our Blood has a cheer-
ful and lively Flow, fo that our Souls
are moft fprightly, vigorous and active.
Our Bofoms kindle with new Delights,
and we enjoy the fmiling Hours that
glide fmoothly by us. It is a moft happy Seafon to revive the Joys of Piety,
and raife our Satisfactions in the bleffed GOD to a renewed Ardor and Vehemence. Add to this, now it is that
our Health is at its beft Eftate, unmo-
lefted by the cold Rheums of the Winter, or the faint Heats of the Summer-
Noons. Befides, the opening of the
Earth by the Plough, and the Odours
of the various Bloffoms fcattered from
every glowing Tree around, confpire to
call back the declining Health, or eftablifh the found Conftitution. So that
we fee new Advantages arife in every
Light, and are convinced how many
Opportunities we have for the Service
of GOD, and the Raptures of Devotion,
let us look where we will. Whether
we

we confider the lengthened Days, and the many Hours of Light and Bufinefs: The moderate Weather, and fine Temperature of the Air and Skies : The Chearfulnefs of our Spirits, and our confirmed Health ; ---- they all with one Voice agree in the Call, *Rife up, and come away.* Rife up to GOD; ferve him in thefe golden Seafons, thefe fmiling Moments, which though they dance along fo fmoothly, wing away fo fwiftly. Lovely as they are, they will be quickly gone and over. Let them not pafs without this additional Delight in the Reflection, that we ferved GOD in them, and tafted the fublimeft Tranfports of Devotion, while we filled them up in Communion with GOD.

Befides, in the Spring of the Year, we have many *Advantages for Medition,* and are furrounded with *Objects* for this holy and bleffed Employment. Now the Works of GOD fhine in our Eyes, with the moft finifhed Beauty, and raife our Thoughts to the infinite Artificer, who has poured out fuch a Profufion of Charms and Graces on the wide Creation. *The Flowers appear upon the Earth, and the Time of*
the

the finging of Birds is come, rife up, and come away. To be particular here, I fhall offer a Set of Meditations peculiarly adapted to the Spring of the Year, and raifed out of the Objeﬁs which then fmile around us.

First of all, See the *Perfeﬁions of the glorious GOD.* Who gave the Face of Nature thefe flowery Charms ? How beauteous then, and how divine the Being whofe fcattered Rays fo adorn the blooming Earth ? The glowing Raptures of divine Love and facred Meditation may well be lighted up by thefe wondrous Works which we behold about us. See the Glories of *creating* Power difplayed in the Flourifh of the Spring! * *And GOD faid, Let the Earth bring forth Grafs, the Herb yielding Seed, and the Fruit Tree yielding Fruit after his Kind, whofe Seed is in it felf, upon the Earth. And the Earth brought forth Grafs,-- and Herbs,-- and Trees, -- and GOD faw that it was good.* And it is his unwearied Providence that ftill demands our Afcriptions, † *Thou reneweſt the Face of the Earth.*

---

* Gen. i. 11, 12. † Pfalm civ. 30.

Look

Look abroad in the Spring, and fee the Beauty and Beneficence of *Divine Providence,* and learn to adore and truft GOD. † *Therefore I fay unto you, take no Thought for your Life, what ye fhall eat, nor for your Body, what ye fhall put on---Behold the Fowls of the Air---Your Father provides for them---Confider the Lillies of the Field, how they grow ; they toil not, nor do they fpin, and yet I fay unto you, that* Solomon *in all his Glory was not arrayed like one of thefe. Wherefore if GOD fo cloath the Grafs of the Field, which to Day is, and To-morrow is caft into the Oven, fhall he not much more clouth you, O ye of little Faith ?* How proper fuch a Truft in GOD, and fuch a confecrated Meditation, when the Time of finging of Birds is come and the Flowers appear upon the Earth ? ‘ My GOD feeds the Birds, and ‘ adorns the Flowers, fhall he not much ‘ rather feed and cloath me ? Does he ‘ not love me better than thefe?

Look abroad in the Spring and rife our Thoughts to the *Refurrection of the Dead* at the laft Day. Thefe

† Matth. vi. 25.---

C   Fields

Fields were once covered with Snow like the Pale of Death. These Trees were difrobed of their flowry Honours, and appeared bare and naked. The Rofes droped away, and the Lillies hung down their Heads and died, but fee how the Year revives again, and blossoms, and brightens, and lives. † *And when ye fee this, your Heart fhall rejoice, and your Bones fhall flourish like an Herb.* Juft as thefe Groves revive, and as this Grafs renews its Green, fo fhall our fcattered Bones flourish from their prolifick Graves. When CHRIST the Judge fhall defcend from Heaven, our dead Bodies fhall hear his Call, *Rife up, and come away, for lo, the Winter is paft, the Rain is over and gone, the Flowers appear on the Earth, the Time of the finging of Birds is come.* ‖ *He fhall come down like Rain upon the mown Grafs : as Showers that water the Earth. In his Days fhall the Righteous flourish--They that dwell in the Wildernefs --- the* burying Place--- the wild and folitary Retreats

† Ifaiah lxvi. 14. ‖ Pfalm lxxii. 6.---
of

of Death and the Grave, --- *ſhall bow
before him.*† In what a living Repre-
ſentation do we ſee the Reſurrection
of the Dead, exemplified in the Reſurrection of the Year. † *They of the
City, ſhall flouriſh like the Graſs of the
Earth.* Who can count it a Thing
incredible that GOD ſhould raiſe the
Dead, who ſees him ſo renew the
flowery Fields, and the blooming
Trees! Cannot he as eaſily make our
Graves, as our Gardens to bloſſom?
*The Wilderneſs and the ſolitary Place
ſhall be glad for them, and the Deſert
ſhall rejoice, and bloſſom as a Roſe. It
ſhall bloſſom abundantly, and rejoice even
with ſinging; the Glory of Lebanon ſhall
be given to it, the Excellency of Carmel
and Sharon : They ſhall ſee the Glory of
the LORD, and the Excellency of our
GOD.* ‖

Again, See the fair Scenes about
you, and lead your Meditations to the
final Judgment of the World. ‡ *Let
the Heavens rejoice, and let the Earth
be glad : let the Sea roar, and the Ful-*

† Pſalm lxxii. 16.   ‖ Iſaiah xxxv.
1, 2.   ‡ Pſalm xcvi. 11, ---

nefs thereof. Let the Field be joyful, and all that is therein: then shall all the Trees of the Wood rejoyce. Before the LORD ; for he cometh, for he cometh to judge the Earth : he shall judge the World with Righteousness, and the People with his Truth. And indeed, well may the Earth, and Fields, and Woods rejoice, which are to be renewed, and bloom in a perpetual Spring. All the Creatures Groan, for this Restitution of all Things. * *Nevertheless, we according to his Promise, look for new Heavens and a new Earth, wherein dwelleth Righteousness.*

See the Flowers appear upon the Earth in the Spring, and rise up to Meditations on the *swift Progress of the Gospel* through the World. The Sun of Righteousness so arose with healing in his Wings ; and the Church of GOD sprouted and sprung up, and flourished at the reviving Heat. So was the Prophefy of the mystical Israel, ‖ *Israel shall blossom and bud, and fill the Face of the World with Fruit.* So the typi-

* II. Pet. iii. 13. ‖ Ifaiah xxvii. 6.
‖ Numb. xvii. 8.

cal

cal Rod of *Aaron, budded, and brought forth Buds, and bloomed Blossoms,* and yielded *Almonds* †. So *the Sower goes out* in the Spring, *to sow* ; and O what a large Harvest covers the Fields a-round him. This World lay in the Cold and Darkness of a long Winter-Night, till the Gospel, like the Day-spring from on high, visited the Nations, and a sudden Spring covered the Face of the Ground. * *Thus saith the LORD GOD, I will also take of the highest Branch of the high Cedar, and will set it, I will crop off from the top of his young Twigs a tender one, and will plant it upon an high Mountain and eminent. In the Mountain of the height of Israel will I plant it : and it shall bring forth Boughs, and bear Fruit, and be a goodly Cedar : and under it shall dwell all Fowl of every Wing : in the Shadow of the Branches thereof shall they dwell. And all the Trees of the Field shall know that I the LORD have brought down the high Tree, have exalted the low Tree, have dried up the green Tree, and have made the dry Tree to*

* **Ezek. xvii.** 22, --- 24.

C 3

flourish : I the LORD *have spoken and have done it.* The GOD of Heaven called to the Nations that lay in Ignorance and Wickedness, *Rise up, and come away,* and at once the Shades scattered, and the Darkness fled away ; and the Nations of them who are saved walked in open Light.

See the gay Appearance of the Spring, and learn the *Destruction of the wicked.* The beautiful annual Flourish which now so charmingly guilds the Fields, shall quickly fade away, and die. So the last Spring was scorched by the Summer-Sun, and frozen by the Winter-Cold. And do we not here behold the lively Emblem of a wicked Man, and the sudden, and the dreadful Change which must pass upon him. * *When the Wicked spring as the Grass, and when all the Workers of Iniquity do flourish, it is that they shall be destroyed for ever.* So Nebuchadnezzar stood † flourishing in his Palace and at once fell down deprived of humane Reason, and howled like a wild Beast, through the blasted Desart. How often does it happen that the im-

* Psalm xcii. 7.   † Dan. iv. 4.
‖ Job xv. 32.

pious

pious Youth is cut off at once, like a
fudden Froft, withering the whole
Spring in its Infant-Bud ? ‖ *It ſhall be
accompliſhed before its Time, and his
Branch ſhall not be green. He ſhall
ſhake off his unripe Grape as the Vine ;
and ſhall caſt off his Flower as the Olive.*
What though the wicked Man glitters
in all his gaudy Pride, and has every
Beauty fmiling round him ; what
though his filken Apparel be gay like
the Spring ; and like the flowery
Crown on every waving Tree, yet is
Deſtruction from GOD nigh to the
unhappy Criminal. * *Wo to the Crown
of Pride, --- whoſe glorious Beauty is
a fading Flower, on the Head of the
fat Vallies.* This is the great Woe of
an almighty GOD, denounced againſt
the moſt pompous Sons of Earth ; and
as it is denounced it ſhall come on. ‖
*Behold the Day, behold it is come, the
Morning is gone forth, the Rod hath
bloſſomed, Pride hath budded ; Violence
hath riſen up into a Rod of Wickedneſs :
None of them ſhall remain, --- the Time
is come, the Day draweth near, let not
the Buyer rejoice, nor the Seller mourn ;*

* Iſai. xxviii. 1. ‖ Ezek. vii. 10.

for

for Wrath is upon all the Multitude thereof. Let the Wicked then look frefh as the green Herb, and chearful as the opening Spring, yet, rife up, and come away our Thoughts from his prefent Glory to his future Ruins. The Epitaph on the moft flourifhing wicked Men, will be that, ‡ *They were as the Grafs of the Field, and as the green Herb, as the Grafs on the Houfe Tops, and as Corn blafted before it be grown up.*

Look abroad upon the opening Spring, and behold a beautiful *Emblem of humane Life. For all Flefh is Grafs, and the Glory of Man as the Flower of Grafs, the Grafs withereth, and the Flower fadeth away.* * See the glowing Bloffoms, how foon they drop to the Ground ; and what are we our felves better than they ? ‖ *He cometh forth as a Flower, and is cut down.* In the Spring we fee the verdent Grafs, and the blufhing Flowers ; but to fade and die is common to both, and equally to us with them. † *As for Man*

‡ II. Kings xix. 26. * I. Pet. i. 24. ‖ Job xiv. 2. † Pfalm ciii. 15.

his

his Days are as *Grafs*, *as a Flower of the Field fo he flourifheth* ; *for the Wind paffeth over it and it is gone, and the Place thereof fhall know it no more.* Nay, fhould we efcape Death in our Youth, and out live the Spring of our Time, yet Old-Age will come on, when our hoary Heads fhall be covered like the Groves with white Bloffoms. So is the beautiful and accurate Defcription of Old-Age by *Solomon*, ‡ *The Almond Tree fhall flourifh.* And in a little Time muft the Silver Crown be thrown at the Feet of Death, and the *Bloffom go up as Duft.* † Here then is the Life of Man exactly; no more than a fading Spring. ‖ *In the Morning they are like Grafs that groweth up. In the Morning it flourifheth and groweth up, in the Evening it is cut down and withereth.* When the Winter is paft then, and the Flowers appear, and the Birds fing, do we not hear the Voice of Christ to us ? A Voice that calls us to rife up ? * *The Voice faid, Cry,*

‡ Eccl. xii. 5.   † Ifaiah v. 24.
‖ Pfalm xc. 5.   * Ifaiah xl. 6.

and

and he said, What shall I cry? All Flesh is Grass, and all the Goodliness thereof as the Flower of the Field. The Grass withereth, and the Flower fadeth. Surely the People is Grass.

The Winter is past, the Flowers appear, the Time of the singing of Birds is come. Rise up, and come away. Consider the *blessed and happy Condition of the holy;* they are under the mild Influence of a perpetual Spring ; and Paradise it self breathes in their transported Breasts. ‡ *The Righteous shall flourish like the Palm Tree, he shall grow like the Cedar in Lebanon. Those that be planted in the House of the LORD, shall flourish in the Courts of our GOD. They shall still bring forth Fruit in Old-Age : They shall be fat and flourishing.* The good Man *himself* shall be chearful and prosperous as the youthful Spring. ‖ *The Righteous shall flourish as a Branch.* And even the *House* of the good Man shall be blessed, even his Children shall shoot up as *Olive-Plants about his Table.*

‡ Psalm xcii. 12. ‖ Prov. xi. 28.

The

† *The Tabernacle of the Upright shall flourish.* O happy Man, thrice, yea, four Times happy ; ---- Blessed art thou, and blessed are thy Children, and thy Servants. * *Thy Tabernacle shall be in Peace.* --- *Thy Seed shall be great, and thy Off-spring as the Grafs of the Earth. Thou shalt come to thy Grave as a Shock of Corn in its Season.* This is the Man beloved by his GOD, the Darling of Heaven, and fair and beauteous as an immortal Spring. *He shall grow as the Lilly, and cast forth his Roots as Lebanon ; his Branches shall spread, and his Beauty shall be as the Olive-Tree, and his Smell as Lebanon.* And the descending *Dews of Heaven,* shall still refresh and cherish him. ‡ *He shall revive as the Corn, and blossom as the Vine.* This is your Portion, ye holy People, and shall we not rise up from the lower Spring, and rejoice in our GOD, who gives us to vie with it, and assert our superiour Beauty. ▌ *Although the Fig-Tree shall not blossom,*

† Prov. xiv. 11.   * Job v. 24
‡ Hosea xiv. 5.   ▌ Hab. iii. 17.

neither

neither shall Fruit be on the Vines, the Labour of the Olive shall fail, and the Field shall yield no Meat, yet will I rejoice in the LORD, *I will joy in the* GOD *of my Salvation.* This GOD, may the good Man say, will shower his Blessings round me with a lavish Hand, and though the Year die in the Spring, I shall be satisfied with good Things. † *He maketh me lie down in green Pastures, he leadeth me beside the still Waters.* ‡ *See ! the Smell of my Son is as the Smell of a Field which the* LORD *hath blessed.* GOD *shall give thee the Dew of Heaven, and the Fatness of the Earth, and plenty of Corn and Wine.*

Again, See the Spring ; and what a proper Meditation rises out of it, on the Sufferings of our LORD JESUS ? *The Flowers appear on the Earth* ; *Rise up and come away :* Contemplate the Bitterness and Sorrows of the bleeding JESUS, in the Garden of his Agony. *We* behold the charming Aspect of Nature all about us ; and are ra-

† Pfalm xxiii. 2. ‡ Gen. xxvii. 26, 27.
viſhed

vished with the Beauty of Prospect
from the green Grafs, and the Rofey
and the Silver Bloffoms : *He* had
fomething elfe to do, when he lay
weeping on the Ground, and cried,
*My Days are like a Shadow that de-
clineth : and I am withered like Grafs* ‖.
So the Lilly of the Valley lay, hung
down his Head, drooped and languifh-
ed. *He bowed his Head, and gave
up the Ghoft.* Bleffed SAVIOUR !
Is not this the Call we hear from
thee, in the Spring, To rife up and
confider, *If thefe Thirgs be done to the
green Tree, what fhall be done to the
dry ? Adam* finned in a Garden, and
for this our LORD fuffered in a Garden.

Look on the amiable Landfkip, and
remember the *Eden* we have loft.
*The Time of the finging of Birds is paft ;
and of flowry Fields.* The very
Ground is under the Curfe. *Thorns
alfo and Thiftles fhall it bring forth unto thee.*

To conclude, *The Winter is paft,
the Rain is over and gone ; the Time of*

‖ Pfalm cii. 11.

D   *the*

the singing of Birds is come, and the Flowers smile over the Ground : Rise up, and come away : Lift up your Eyes to the *Joys prepared for good Men after Death.* The Glories and Delights of Paradise, how sublime and magnificent are they, when even this lower World can look so beauteous from the Flowers of the Spring! This Earth, polluted by Sin, and devoured by the Curse of GOD, does yet retain so much of its Ornament and gay Aspect. But, O the ravishing Glories of the Place where no Curse lays waste, no Sin defiles ! The Paradise of holy Souls ; the Mansion of blessed Angels ; the imperial Seat and Residence of GOD! In our low Spring of Earth, all our Senses are agreeably entertained with a Variety of Delights and Satisfactions. *The Winter is past,* and as the Cold decays, a moderate Warmth diffuses thro the Air, we *feel* it, and are refreshed by it. *The Time of the singing of Birds is come,* and our *Ears* are regaled by all the Harmony of the Groves and Forests. The idle Musicians of the Spring fill the Fields and the Skies with their artless Melody. A thousand Odours are
thrown

thrown from every Bough ; and ſcatter through the Air, to gratify our *Smell.* *The Flowers appear on the Earth*; and the opening Buds, and the riſing Graſs dreſs the rich Landſcape, and paint the Scene to delight and charm our *Eyes.* Theſe are the Pleaſures of an earthly Spring : But, O the Joys of the upper Paradiſe ! There the *Eyes* are delighted with Sunſhine ever bright, and Fields ever fair, and never fading. The Angels, and not the Birds, ſing ; and nothing addreſſes the Ear but *Hallelujahs* and Anthems to GOD : The Fruits of the Tree of Life ſatisfy the Taſte ; and Rivers of Pleaſures and the Breath of GOD, baniſh Thirſt, and cool the deathleſs Region. From the Things that we ſee then all below us, *Riſe up, and come away,* to the future State of eternal Rewards, reſerved in Heaven for us. --- *Ariſe, let us go hence.*

And now what remains but the Exhortation and the Motives in my Text. *Riſe up, and come away, for the Winter is paſt, the Rain is over, and gone, the Flowers appear on the Earth, the Time of the ſinging of Birds is come.* Lo,

D 2 the

the Seafon of the Year, and every fragrant Breeze of Air, confpire to awaken us to Thoughts on GOD, and to quicken our Love to him, and truft in him. Univerfal Nature about us with one Voice, fings *Hallelujah* aloud. Glory to GOD in the Higheft, is refounded by every tuneful Bird, every warbling Brook, and bubling Fountain. Incenfe to the GOD of Heaven is offered by every opening Lilly, and glowing Bloffom, which perfume the Air with their ambient Sweets. The wide Earth we tread on feems but one great Altar, covered with Incenfe and Offerings to GOD its Maker. And fhall not we alfo offer our felves upon it ? *Rife up, and come away.* It belongs to us, as the Priefts of GOD below, to exprefs the Praifes of the fubordinate Creatures in articulate Sounds, and utter their filent Voice in intelligible Language. *For all thy Works praife thee, O LORD, and thy Saints blefs thee.*

But the Application may more particularly be directed to young People, who exult under the Indulgence of a *double Spring.* To you, my Brethren,

I

I turn my Addrefs; and fuffer, I pray
you, the Word of Exhortation. Will
you as wafte thefe golden Moments,
that glitter in the Spring of Life, which
once fled away, can never return more?
Rife up, and come away ; leave the lower Objects that allure and tempt you.
Give your felves up to GOD. *Seek
firft the Kingdom of GOD and his Righ-
teonfnefs, and all other Things fhall be
added unto you.* Rife up, for lo, the
Winter [---*is paft* fhall I fay ? Nay] it
is *coming on,* and the evil Days of Rain
and Tempeft are haftening over you.
*Remember now thy Creator in the Days
of thy Youth, before the evil Days come,
or the Years draw nigh, when thou
fhalt fay I have no Pleafure in them.*
Rife up, out of the Way of thefe defcending Evils, by a Flight to the dear
SAVIOUR, who invites you with his
gracious Voice, and opens his tender
Arms to receive you. My Brethren,
Your Life will decay, like the fading
Spring, O let it not before your eternal Well-being is fecured, and a fure
Foundation for happy Reflection laid
in thefe pleafant Hours.

Thus have I taken you with me *to meditate in the Fields.* We have been furveying the beautiful Scenes of the Spring : And fhall we have no good Effect of the foft Profpects ? Shall not a rival Glory open and dawn in our ravifhed Hearts, while all the Fields flourifh about us ? O for aSpring now ! and that even while I am fpeaking, every confenting Breaft may feel new Delights in GOD kindle with a fudden Flame, and glow with immortal Ardor ! That is the Defign as of all the Meffages from the Pulpit, fo particularly of thisDifcourfe on the fpringing Year. I would call your Sou's in to flourifh like the Earth about you. * *My Doctrine fhall drop as the Rain, my Speech fhall diftill as the Dew ; as the fmall Rain upon the tender Herb ; and as the Showers upon the Grafs. Away ! thou North-wind, and come thou South, blow upon my Garden, that the Spices thereof may flow out.*

* Deut. xxxii. 2.

Thofe

Thofe of us who have recovered
from theSick-Bed, methinks, may hear
the loud Call, *Rife up,* --- *Arife, and
walk !* Tafte the renewed Bounties
of Heaven with redoubled Pleafure,
while we redouble our Labours
for GOD, and his Kingdom. But,
ah ! Let us not think the *Danger is all
paft, and the Rain is over and gone* ; for
the Clouds return after the Rain ;
Death fhall quickly fhut the pleafing
Scene, and the *Days of Darknefs
fhall be many. Do therefore with thy
Might, what thy Hand findeth to do.*
If all the Care of Heaven to manure
and cultivate you be loft, the Voice
quickly will be that, *No Fruit be found
on thee for ever ! Cut it down !*---Ah !
*rejected and nigh unto Curfing, thy End
is to be burned.*

And indeed, The Addrefs of Heaven is proper for us all : For we are
all in the Spring of our Being, while
we are in this Life. Eternity is like an
endlefs Year, of which this Life is like
the buddingSpring. And, as the Spring
is, the Year will be more or lefs fruitful and bleffed. If in this Life we difobey GOD ; the Spring of this Life
will

will end in the Heat of a withered Summer, the Flames of eternal Fire. If, on the contrary, we serve GOD from a Principle of Faith in CHRIST, our Spring will end in a blessed Harvest : And we shall enter upon the Feast of the Fruits that adorn Paradise. Death it self will but convey us to the Regions of immortal Life : And our LORD JESUS CHRIST the good Shepherd, will lead us through the dark Valley, to the green Pastures, and the still Waters. There the Groves ever blossom, the Flowers ever flourish, and the Fields are ever green. There JESUS himself blooms in unveiled Charms, and invites us to him, with his dear Voice. We may lie upon the Bed of Death, and see the endless Glories shine behind the Glooms, and guild and break away the awful Shadows. We may see our dear SAVIOUR at a Distance, encouraging our desired Flight. We may hear his Voice sound charming through the dark Length of the Vale of Death ; *Rise up, and come away!* And the last Words we utter, when we leave the Flourish of the lower Spring

may

may be like that,* *It is the Voice of my Beloved : He flourisheth through the Windows, shewing himself through the Lattess.* Then shall be compleatly fulfilled to you, that blessed Promise, † *For as the Rain cometh down, and the Snow from Heaven, and returneth not thither, but watereth the Earth, and maketh it bring forth and bud, that it may give Seed to the Sower, and Bread to the Eater : So shall my Word be that goeth forth out of my Mouth : it shall not return unto me void, but it shall accomplish that which I please, and it shall prosper in the Thing whereto I sent it. For ye shall go out with Joy, and be led forth with Peace : the Mountains and the Hills shall break forth before you into singing, and all the Trees of the Field shall clap their Hands. Instead of the Thorn shall come up the Fir-tree, and instead of the Brier shall come up the Myrtle-Tree : and it shall be to the LORD for a Name, for an everlasting Sign, that shall not be cut off.* ‖ --- In

* Cant. ii. 8, 9. † Isai. lv. 10--13.
‖ Isai. xxxv. 6. ---

the

the Wilderneſs ſhall Waters break out, and Streams in the Deſert. And the parched Ground ſhall become a Pool, and the thirſty Land Springs of Water: In the habitation of Dragons, where each lay, ſhall be Graſs with Reeds and Ruſhes. ------- No Lion ſhall be there, nor any ravenous Beaſt ſhall go up thereon, it ſhall not be found there: but the redeemed ſhall walk there. And the ranſomed of the LORD ſhall return and come to Zion with Songs, and everlaſting Joy upon their Heads: they ſhall obtain Joy and Gladneſs, and Sorrow and Sighing ſhall flee away.

FINIS.

An Evening-Lecture.

Mr. *Byles*'s

SERMON

From Joh. III. 2. *The same came to JESUS by Night.*

THE
Visit to JESUS by Night.

AN
Evening-Lecture.

〰〰〰〰〰〰〰〰〰〰〰〰〰〰〰

By Mr. BYLES.

〰〰〰〰〰〰〰〰〰〰〰〰〰〰

〰〰〰〰〰〰〰〰〰〰〰〰〰〰〰

Joh. xx. 19. *The same Day at Evening ---
where the Disciples were assembled---came
Jesus and stood in the midst, and saith
unto them, Peace be unto you.*

BOSTON, Printed and Sold by ROGERS
and FOWLE, at the Head of Queen-
street, near the Town-House. 1741.

AN

Evening-Lecture.

JOHN III. 2.

The same came to JESUS *by Night---*

THESE Words are spoken of *Nicodemus,* a Man of Honour and Authority among the Jews, and secretly a Disciple of our Lord JESUS. *The same came to* JESUS *by Night,* to hear about his Soul, and the Mysteries of the Kingdom. 'Twas *Nicodemus's* Fault that he feared to profess CHRIST openly; that he chose the Darkness to approach him undiscovered : But it was his Happiness that he came at all ; and it was infinite Compassion in our Lord that he accepted the cowardly Visit, and instructed the weak, but sincere Disciple. I should

be

he glad if the Arguments brought by some
to vindicate *Nicodemus* from the Imputation of Cowardize in this Visit, were of
more Significance. The Words are big
with Entertainment and Instruction :
And from the various Hints which they
afford us, I propose to give you an useful
and brief Discourse.

The same came to Jesus. The Doctrine is, That *for us to come to* Jesus
Christ *is our Interest and our Duty.*

It is our *Duty.* So *Nicodemus* was convinced, when he made his serious Approach. He was convinced that he was
the great Teacher come from GOD.
And therefore he knew that he ought to
wait upon him for Instruction and Wisdom.
And as this was the Duty of *Nicodemus*
in his Day, so it is no less ours at this
Distance. We are under the same Obligations, and our Lord Jesus is still the
same Prophet and Teacher that he was
then. Indeed we cannot go to Christ
as *Nicodemus* did, and have the Pleasure
and the sacred Curosity to hear from his
Lips the divine Language. He is now
gone to his Father, and is no more
visible

visible on Earth. But yet have we his Spirit to lead us into all Truth: and they are His Instructions, which the Spirit gives us. And we are equally obliged to repair to him now for this spiritual Instruction as *Nicodemus* of old. Joh. xvi. 7,---14. *It is expedient for you that I go away: For if I go not away the Comforter will not come unto you; but if I depart I will send him unto you.--He shall receive of mine, and shall shew it unto you.* CHRIST then speaks as much to us by his Spirit, as if we saw his Face, and heard his Voice, as they did when he was upon Earth. And we are as much obliged to attend the gentle Whispers and obey them. In every divine Institution we are to seek that we may find him.

And as this is our Duty, so it is our *Interest* too. *Nicodemus* found it so when he came desirous to learn, and went home instructed, wise unto Salvation. Our Duty and our Interest are inseperably linked together, by the Law of Nature, and the GOD of Heaven. Heaven and eternal Happiness will be the future Reward of our Obedience to the divine Commands: Nor is this all, nor shall we wait so long for a Recompence; for they carry their
own

own Wages in them, and *IN keeping of them there is great Reward.* The believing, humble Soul, that comes to Jesus Christ, shall find a blessed Peace and Satisfaction attending, and succeeding the sacred Labour. A divine Ease, and Relief of Mind, will be the sweet Consequence of a Visit to Jesus. Matth. xi. 28, 29. *Come unto me all ye that Labour, and are heavy laden, and I will give you Rest --- and ye shall find Rest unto your Souls.* This then is the *First Doctrine* observable in the Words: and happy if we obey it.

The *Exhortation* here is, *Let us come to* Jesus Christ, as *Nicodemus* in the Text; *and be incouraged by the Reception he found.* Let us pray for the Holy Spirit to instruct us in the Mysteries of Godliness; and be afraid to grieve and sin away his Influences. Whenever we find the blessed Spirit at work upon us, let us cherish the holy Thoughts, and labour to keep them alive in us. We must find a Time every Day for Retirement to *pray* for this, and the better to *attend* to it. *If we seek him he will be found of us, but if we forsake him, he will cast us off forever.* He has said, *My Spirit shall not always strive with Man.* And *woe to us if he depart from us.* Nay, he he has *limited it to a certain Day ; where-fore, To Day if ye will hear his Voice, har-den not your Heart, lest he swear in his Wrath ye shall not enter into his Rest.* Be-hold now is the accepted Time, behold now is the Day of Salvation. Escape for thy Life this Night, for to morrow thou shalt be slain.* And now does the Saviour incourage our Labour, *I love them that love me, and they that seek me early shall find me.* Nicode-mus went to CHRIST in Body ; but we cannot. He is gone away above our af-pectable Skies : And *where he is gone, thi-ther we cannot come,* till Death shall give us Wings to *fly as the Eagles towards Heaven.* But though we cannot approach In Person to his bodily Presence, yet we can come to him as truly and as effectu-ally as *Nicodemus.* Let us then do so, by *Repentance, Faith, Prayer,* and *Meditation.*

But to proceed to another main Branch of the Text : *The same came to* JESUS *by Night.* The DOCTRINE is, *No Season is improper or unsuitable for our solemn Ap-proach to* JESUS CHRIST. Our Lord accepted and rewarded the Visit of *Nico-demus,* though he chose the Night to be-friend his Cowardise, and came in the un-seasonable Hours of Darkness. Tired and

spent

spent as our LORD was won't to be with
the Affairs of the Day, he sent not the
feeble Disciple from him, but redeemed
Time from his natural Rest, to discourse
with, enlighten and instruct him. That
we may reap the Benefit of this Passage in
sacred Record, I have formed this *Doctrine*
for you, *That at every Season we are welcome to our* LORD JESUS.

1. There is no Season improper for us
in which to *believe* on JESUS CHRIST :
that is, to come to him by Faith. Faith
in JESUS CHRIST is the great Doctrine
of the Gospel. And as it is to be preached to all Nations ; to all Men, in every
Place, so at every Season too : *In Season,
and out of Season* And the Practice is
like the preaching : it should be universal in Time, Place and Person. The
youngest is not too young for this, nor the
eldest too old. The first Essay at Understanding and Will should be employed in
believing on CHRIST, and the Acts should
be continued and repeated to the latest
Gasp of Breath. Those who have never
yet savingly complied with the Offers of
the Gospel, are obliged to do it now : So
long as you have an Inclination to do it,
you may safely conclude the Season for it

B

is not over. In every various Circum-
stance of Life : In the Sunshine of Prof-
perity, or in the Gloom of Affliction, like
Nicodemus in the Night, Faith in JESUS
CHRIST is your Duty, and should be
your Practice.

2. There is no Season improper for us
in which to come to CHRIST by *Repentance.* The Discourse between *Nicodemus* and our blessed Saviour in the Night,
turned upon Repentance and Conversion.
They were the mysterious Doctrines of
Regeneration which were the Subject
of Debate between our LORD and the
young Disciple. It naturally, methinks,
leads our Thoughts to this, that the most
improper Season is still proper for our Concern about Repentance and the New-
Birth. This before was the Sentiment of
the Psalmist, when he thought that the
Night was better improved in devoting
himself to GOD, than in the soft Refresh-
ment of Slumber and Sleep. Psal. cxxxii.
4. *I will not give Sleep to my Eyes, nor
Slumber to my Eye-lids, till I find out a
Place for the* LORD, *an Habitation for the
mighty* GOD *of Jacob.* 'Tis dangerous
delaying one Night.

3. There

3. There is no Season improper in which to come to CHRIST by *Prayer.* Prayer is a coming to GOD, and to CHRIST who is GOD. 'Tis called a *drawing near* to him ; and a *seeking* him ; and *coming before* him. *They that be far from thee shall perish* : *But it is good for me to* DRAW NEAR *to* GOD. *O that I knew where I might* FIND HIM, *that I could* COME NEAR *even to his Seat, I would order my Cause before him, and fill my Mouth with Arguments. Let my Prayer* COME BEFORE *thee as Incense, and the lifting up of my Hands as the Evening Sacrifice* And as Prayer is a coming to CHRIST, and to GOD the Father by him, so this Way of sacred Access is never impertinent or unseasonable. We are commanded to *pray without ceasing* : To *pray always with all Prayer.* We are incouraged that *the Ears of the LORD are always open to our Prayer* ; and that *the Prayer of the upright is his Delight.* Even in the darkest Times we are allowed to pray. Nay the darker the Season, the more necessary the Prayer. *Is any afflicted ? Let him pray. Nicodemus* in the Darkness of the Night ; and *Jonah* in the Darkness of his Affliction, and in the Belly of Hell, may both alike approach to GOD. --- *WATCH and pray.* 4

4. There is no Seafon improper for us in which to come to CHRIST by *Meditation.* In our Thoughts we may travel from Earth to Heaven in a Moment. Our Souls may approach to CHRIST, in the Twinkling of an Eye. We have no need, like *Nicodemus,* to wait for the Night for this : But a thoufand Times every Day we may lift our Thoughts to Heaven. So was the Law of GOD fweet, to the devout Pfalmift ; and his *Meditation all the Day.* Night as well as Day, this was his dear and happy Employment. *In it does he meditate Day and Night.* So *Ifaac went out to meditate in the Field at Even Tide.* Thro' the dark and folitary Hours of the Night, holy Contemplation may find us fweet Employment. Pfal. lxiii. 5,6. *My Soul fhall be fatisfied--- when I remember thee on my Bed, and meditate on thee in the Night Watches.* Not *Nicodemus* himfelf fitting at the Feet of JESUS, might conceive diviner Satisfaction ! The Believer converfing with his LORD in holy Contemplations, amidft the Shades and Darknefs, has Light arifing in his Darknefs. He may triumph in the Glooms and the Solitude, and raife his *Songs in the Night.*

And to affift our Meditations in the Night, fee how full of *Subjects* the holy Scriptures appear, to cultivate and adorn

B   the

the Work. How many wonderful Transactions have happened in this Season, to distinguish the Shades and render the Night glorious. Should we, like *Ahasuerus,* linger through the Night without the Comfort of a Slumber, we have nobler Records than of *Media* and *Persia* to entertain and delight our Thoughts. Let us reflect back upon the sacred Pages on such Scenes as these, as the Night slowly slides away, and the Morning forgets to dawn. So let us like *Nicodemus,* pay a Visit to our LORD by Night. This is the best Way not to *possess* Nights *of Vanity,* when it may be *wearisome Nights are appointed unto us.* Why need we say, *Would GOD it were Morning! In Evening Time it shall be Light. The Night shall be Light round about me, and the Darkness shall shine as the Day.*

What a glorious Night was it when our Father *Israel* seized the strugling Angel and wrested the Blessing from his Grasp.

How solemn and memorable was the Night, in the Mixture of Salvation and Ruin, which instituted the ancient Passover? GOD marched through the Darkness; and the Pestilence stalked before him. Round about all the First-born gave a Gasp, and stretched out Breathless: While the Destroyer saw the Blood upon the spring

:ed Door-Posts, & smiled and passed over: *A Night much to be remembred throughout all Generations.*

How illustrious was the fatal Night, which poured the Red-Sea upon the Armies of *Egypt,* and landed *Israel* on the opposite Shore. With what a terrible Magnificence might you then have seen the *Shekinah* blaze through the Ranks of *Israel,* and confound *Pharaoh* with its tremendious Gloom ? Before, the Waves broke, divided, and fled away in haste, to open a Path for the favourite People : Behind, they tost, and foam'd, and roar'd; they watched the Signal from the Rod of *Moses,* and rush'd thundring down.

'Twas in the Night that the Angel was commissioned against the Host of *Assyria.* He flash'd out swift as a Ray of Light, silent as a lambent Flame, but resistless and distructive as the feather'd Lightning. An hundred and fourscore and five Thousand Souls were lick'd up in a Moment; and the Field look'd pale with Corpses. What dismal Night did the whole World lie, till the Gospel spread its Light, and the *Day-Star arose. They sat in Darkness and saw no Light.* O the wondrous Night that gave the Saviour to the perishing Earth ! the Glories of that illustrious Hour !

'Twas

'Twas to you, ye admiring Shepherds, that the heavenly Messenger brought the joyful Tydings! They were watching their Flocks in the Night, when, all on a sudden, a Light broke from Heaven round the Mountains, and the Voice of *Gabriel* proclaimed the Saviour born. Then was heard the Musick of Paradise tuneful round the Sky; and *Glory to GOD in the Highest.* trembled on a Million of Strings.

'Twas on the fatal Night (-- *that same Night in which he was betrayed*--) that he sat retired in the upper Chamber with the Twelve, and instituted for us the sacred Supper, the dear Memorials of his dying Love.

A few dark Hours after you might have seen him lie in his bitter Agony, bleeding on the Ground, praying and weeping, with the *Cup of trembling* in his Hand: The dear JESUS, who had spent so many Nights in Prayer to GOD!

'Twas the same execrable Night (but blessed Hours for us) that they came to seize him with Lanthorns and Torches; and poured upon him Indignities and Torments.

The *next Day* there was a *miraculous Night* while there was Darkness over the whole Land, and the mourning Skies were hung in black at the Anguish of his Crucifixion.

Th

The Night after, he lay, a pale, bloody Corps, among the awful Mansions of the dead. And what a proper Meditation does this naturally lead us to, on our own Death and Grave?

In theNight, how eafy may be theTranfition of Thoughts, to that long Darknefs between us and the Refurrection: That refrefhingSleep in theDuft, whichChrist has confecrated for us, and will raife us from. *A Land of Darknefs, as Darknefs it felf, whofe Light is as Darknefs.* But O bleffed Dawn after the long Darknefs! The Meditation may tranfport us; and like *Paul* and *Silas*, we may raife our Voice of Harmony and Praife in all the Terrors of the hideous Night. *Are there not twelve Hours in a Day, let us work while the Day lafts, for the Night cometh wherein no Man can work.*

But to draw toward aClofe. Let us often redeem ourHours in theNight, to meditate upon that difmal, glorious Hour, when our Lord fhall come again. *Behold he cometh as a Thief in the Night. At Midnight will the Cry be heard*; and a general Horror ran through every human Breaft. Now fhall the Shades fcatter away, and the Heavens glitter with an unknown Glory. O tremendious Night! O awful Shades and

B 3   Darknefs,

Darkness, difpell'd by devouring Fire, and purfued by dazling Deftruction! And who can fay when this folemn Scene of Things muft come on ? Perhaps this Night ; perhaps all on a fudden the Judge may break in upon the fecure World. *Watch therefore, for ye know not the Day, nor the Hour ; whether at Even, or at Midnight, or at the Cock-crowing, or in the Morning.*

But, to add no more : In the Night, how naturally may we transfer our Thot's to the Place of Darknefs : The Hell prepared for wicked Men and Devils. Here is a Night without any Hope of a Morning to end it ; or a fingle Ray of Light to refrefh it. A Night confifting of Darknefs and Fire : But as the Fire affords them no Light, the Darknefs allows them no Reft. And as the Volume of Revelation affords us Matter for Contemplation in the Night, fo alfo does the Volume of *Nature.*

See the dark Earth and the dufky Skies brightened by Star-light, or filver'd over by Moonfhine : And when ye fee the blue Ether; the Stars twinkle at a Diftance and the Moon, the fair Emprefs of th filent Shades, ferenely gleeming, reflect inward and fay, LORD, *when I behold th Heavens, the Work of thy Fingers, the Moo and the Stars which thou haft ordained*
wh

*what is Man, that thou art mindful of him?
and the Son of Man that thou visitst him?*

Think too on the kind *Providence* that
preferves you everyNight. The*Peſtilence*
may *walk in Darkneſs* innocently by me,
and I am *not afraid of the Terror by Night.*
I lie down in Peace & ſleep : I awake,for
theLORD ſuſtained me. His holyMiniſters
attend my Curtains and guard my Slumbers. *There ſtood by me this Night,the Angel of GOD whoſe I am, and whom I ſerve.*

It were eaſy, you ſee, to enlarge ;
and to add many other pertinent Topicks for Meditation in the dark Hours,
by which, like *Nicodemus,* we might come
to JESUS by Night: But here I ſhall ſtop.

I might add a third Doctrine. That
*Fear in a good Cauſe is a diſhonourable
Thing.* 'Twas *Nicodemus's* Weakneſs that
he came to our LORD by Night. He
was afraid of the *Jews,* and aſhamed of
Reproach and Perſecution : and it is recorded to all Generations, as a Blemiſh
upon the good Man's Character. We
learn by it not to be like him in this :
Never to be aſhamed in a good Cauſe, or
afraid to profeſs it openly. Though we
are not to be oſtentatious in Religion, yet
we are never to be aſhamed of it. We
muſt*let our Light ſhine before others,*There is

a happy Medium betwixt Impudence and Bashfulness : and as they are *both* ill-breeding in civil Life, so they are *both* detestible in Religion. But I shall not enlarge here. I could not have done Justice to my Text without hinting at this; I have done it the rather, because this is a Crime too common, especially among young People, to be ashamed in Matters of Religion. Things that are most worthy and honourable they perform with a most awkward Air, and are willing to put the amiable Name of Modesty upon this ungraceful Blush. Modesty, it is true, is very charming : but a Shame in Matters of Religion, is dastardly and clownish, and far from this fine and delicate Temper. There is as much Difference between Modesty and Bashfulness as between Courage and Frenzy. Fortitude the Virtue of an Angel ; Rashness the Rage of a Brute. How mean is it for a Person, educated in a Christian Land, to be asham'd to pray in a Family, or ask a Blessing at a Table ; ashamed of what my Brother !--- to acknowledge thy Maker ! So that while a hypocrital Showyness is to be avoided, yet on the other Hand we are to remember, that our LORD has said, *He that is ashamed of me & of my Words before Men, of him will I be ashamed before my Father who is in Heaven.* Nicodemus was
ch nge l

changed from this coward Temper, upon his
underflanding what the New-Birth meant:
And went afterward and boldly honoured
the dead Body of JESUS. *Joh.* xix. 39.

Thus I have finifhed the *Doctrinal* handling of the Words. I fhall now conclude
with a brief Improvement of the *Second
Doctrine.*

Is it as we have heard? Did *Nicodemus*
come to JESUS by Night? And does it
preach to us our Duty to approach to our
LORD at every Seafon? Let us then *receive
the Word of Exhortation,* & practice the Duty.
Let us wait upon the bleffed Saviour Day
and Night, and his Praife be continually in
our Mouth. In our darkeft Hours let this
refrefh us, and brighten all the Shades: In
every Affliction, and every Temptation, and
every Darknefs; in every Day, and the
Gloom of every Night. Let us ufe ourfelves
to the noble Comfort; and fo learn Expert-
nefs in it. Let us furnifh our Minds with
innumerable Subjects pertinent for Contemplation in every Kind of Darknefs. And let
us repair to CHRIST as *the Sun of Righteoufnefs: A Light unto the Gentiles,* and *the
Glory of his People Ifrael.*

This, I hope, has been your intent at this
Seafon. CHRIST has met you in this Difcourfe: and like *Nicodemus,* you have come

to him by Night : O may you go away enlightned & renewed as he did. Happy will
this Night then be, memorable & blessed ;
and with Joy will you look back upon it
through the Ages of eternal Day.

But, my Brethren, if you refuse and rebel'
at your own Peril be it. Better had you not
come hither this Night, than going away,
continue Strangers to CHRIST. The golden Opportunities will become a Curse :
and the higher your present Privileges are
the deeper will be your future Fall : Even
from this Sermon you'll sink but the lower
into Ruin. So while *Paul continued his
Speech till Midnight*, the sleepy *Eutychus* fell
headlong *from the third Loft, and was taken
up dead*, Act. xx. 8,9. From succeeding
Days and Nights here upon Earth, you must
quickly be banished to perpetual Night ; to
Blackness of Darkness for ever : The *outer
Darkness*, where is *weeping and wailing and
gnashiug of Teeth.* And *in Chains under
Darkness, you'll be reserved to the Judgment
of the great* Day. This must be your Condition quickly : How quickly you cannot
say. *The Day goeth away, the Shadows of
the Evening are stretched out. Then Fool,
this Night may thy Soul be required of thee.*

On the other Hand : If you will indeed
be perswaded truly to come to CHRIST,
you

you will find the moſt bleſſedSucceſs & Joy.
At preſent you'll come to him in theNight:
The Darkneſs of this World : But in a little
Time the darkMinutes will all be over and
endleſsLight will dawn.*Weeping may endure
for a Night,but Joy cometh in the Morning.*
You'll leave the Darkneſs of Earth for the
Inheritance of theSaints inLight. For truly,
*Light is ſown for the Righteous,and Joy for
the upright in Heart. The Night is far
ſpent, the Day is at Hand.* There you'll
ſet in eternal Sunſhine, without a Night,
and without aCloud. 'Tis true, you muſt
walk thro' theValley of the Shadow of Death
to arrive at this : But all on a ſudden the
Day will break and the Shadows flee away,
the *Shadow of Death* will be *turned into the
Light of the Morning.* Angels ſhall convey
your Souls to Paradiſe, the fair Regions of
everlaſting Day.

And anon yourBody ſhall aſcend glittering from the Grave : and *tho' it is ſown in
Diſhonour,it ſhall be raiſed inGlory.* You'll
ſing over your ſleeping,but quickningDuſt,
*Ariſe and ſhine, for thyLight is come,and the
Glory of the* LORD *is riſen upon thee.* Then
ſhall you *ſhine as the Brightneſs of the Firmament,and as the Stars for ever and ever.*

O how different this magnificentGlory,
from the Gloom of the preſent World !

Here

Here we need the Moon and Stars to brighten the Shades ; and the Sun itself shines at a *Distance*, and with *Intermissions*, and through *Clouds*. And to supply his absent Beams we have Recourse to the little Arts of Lamps and Candles. But of that World we read, Rev. xxii. 5. xxi. 23, 24, 25. *There shall be no Night there, and they need no Candle, neither the Moon to shine in it ; neither the Light of the Sun: For the* LORD GOD *giveth them Light, and the Glory of* GOD *did lighten it, and the* LAMB *is the Light thereof. And the Nations of them which are saved, shall walk in the Light of it.*

F I N I S.

G O D Glorious

In The

Scenes of the Winter.

A

S E R M O N

Preach'd at *B O S T O N.*

December 23. 1 7 4 4.

By Mr. Byles.

John x. 22, 23.——*It was Winter. And* Jesus *walked in the Temple.*——

B O S T O N:

Printed by B. Green and Company for D. Gookin, over against the old South Meeting-House. 1 7 4 4.

G O D Glorious

IN THE

Scenes of the Winter.

P S A L M cxlvii. 16, 17.

He giveth Snow like Wool; he scattereth the hoar Frost like Ashes.
He casteth forth his Ice like Morsels; Who can stand before his Cold?

 H E Glories of God the Creator, are every where seen in his Works, and preached in his Word. Look where we will in his World, we see them; and attend where we will to his Word, and we hear them. The holy Scriptures begin with the Declaration, That *In the Beginning God created the Heavens and the Earth;* and the Account is carried on, and interspersed thro' all the sacred Pages. The Honours of God are here celebrated, in his

Power

Power andSovereignty,and creatingAttributes. Pſal. lxxiv. 16, 17. *The Day is thine, the Night alſo is thine : Thou haſt prepared the Light and the Sun : Thou haſt ſet all the Borders of the Earth : Thou haſt made the Summer and the Winter.* The great Frame of Nature is the Work of God : He orders all the *Motions* of Nature, and is himſelf the firſt Mover. He is the Owner and Proprietor of Nature then ; and the Day and Night, the Light and Sun, the Summer and Winter are his.

But it is the Winter Scene that now opens: And the Skies and the Earth around, and the ſacred Volume before us unite to claim our Honours to the God of Glory, as he appears grand at the Head of this Part of Nature and Providence, *He ſendeth forth his Commandment upon Earth ; his Word runneth very ſwiftly. He giveth Snow like Wool ; he ſcattereth the Hoar-froſt like Aſhes. He caſteth forth his Ice like Morſels ; who can ſtand before his Cold?*

The Theme before us is, *GOD is adorable in the Scenes of the Winter.* How does it appear ? And what Evidence can we bring for it ? It is proved every Way : And Conviction pours in upon us from all Quarters. He has created it ; He has eſtabliſhed it ; He ſtill continues to bring it upon the Eartn ; He gives us the Senſation of it ; a Capacity to feel it, in the Diſpoſition of our Bodily Organs : And he acts, and operates in all the ſecond Cauſes, that conſpire to form it.

1. *He has created it.* The Cold it ſelf is a Creature of God. Some have argued Cold to be only the Privation of Heat, as Darkneſs is only the Privation of Light. But even in thisSenſe, God who forms the Heat and the Light, is the Author of the Cold and the Darkneſs. He lays his Claim, in the Letter as well as the Metaphor, *I form the Light: I create Darkneſs.* But there is ſomething further in the Nature and Philoſophy of Cold, than a bare Privation.

on. A Non-entity and Cold one would think were different. A *cold Nothing* were an abfurd fort of Curiofity.
Cold has really fomething material in its Nature; and it
is not barely the Privation of Heat. The God of Nature
has filled the Air with the Nitre, which fo penetrates the
Pores, and even cuts the Skin, in the bleak Winds of the
Winter. By this he fwells and fixes the frozen Water,
and binds the Sea and Rivers in Fetters of Ice, bringing
the Globules of the Fluid into that Attraction which we
call Cohefion. He created the Caufes of the Cold.

2. *He has eftablifhed the Winter.* He formed all the
Caufes, and contrived all the Laws of it : And he has proclaimed the Laws, and keeps them in Force and Authority.
Gen. viii. 21, 22. *The Lord faid, While the Earth re-
maineth, Seed-time and Harveft, and Cold and Heat, and
Summer and Winter, and Day and Night fhall not ceafe.*
We know not how far the Flood it felf contributed to
this Inequality of Seafons, and brought the Sun and Earth
to flant to one another, as we find they now do : But this
we know, that at the Flood the Law of Summer and Winter, was confirmed and eftablifhed.

3. 'Tis he who *ftill continues to bring it upon the Earth.*
He keeps up the Performance of his own Laws, and leads
on the Summer and Winter in their perpetual Circle.
The Wheels of Nature would ftand ftill, were it not for
his powerful and unerring Hand : But having firft communicated Motion to them, he maintains it, and keeps
them rolling to this Day. The *fteady* Return of the annual Cold, is a Proof that there is fome intelligent Agent at
work, to bring it fo orderly and ufefully onward. The
whole Voice of modern Philofophy, is aloud for this, that
the Motion of the heavenly Globes is owing to the perpetual Energy of God. It is demonftrable from Principles of Nature, that fhould the great God fufpend his

Power one Moment, all the Planets would leave the Sun, and fcatter thro' Immenfity. Summer and Winter would ceafe in a Moment, and the Inhabitants of the Earth would wonder to fee the Sun leffen fo faft to them, as our Globe fhot off in a right Line, into eternal Cold and Darknefs. What fhall I fay? Should the great God withdraw his Operations, we fhould no more have the Sun go off and return as the Caufe of Winter and Summer: But on the contrary, the Earth and Sun would feparate forever, and retire to further and further Diftances in the immenfe Space, to all Eternity. God, then, who ftill keeps the Sun, (to fpeak in the Language of the Vulgar) in its Circle, and makes it approach and retire; makes it fhine aflant, or direct, is the Author of the Summer and the Winter. He made the Winter: For he is ftill forever at Work to bring it on us. Not only did he create it at firft; and eftablifh it by a ftated Law; but he ftills puts this Law in Executien. He *makes* the Winter: He made *This* Winter. He does not leave the Year to run Riot; but ftill orders and produces and changes all the Seafons.

4. *He has made the Power in us to perceive the Scenes of Winter.* He has given us the Faculties of Senfation, to hear the Tempefts roar, to fee the Snows defcend, and to feel the chill and cutting Blafts. To what Purpofe would the material Scenes of the Winter be, if our Organs were not difpofed and adapted to perceive them? Nay, if our Souls were not furnifhed with a Power of forming Ideas from them, different from what are in the Objects themfelves? There is, in our Perceptions of Cold and Heat, no Connexion between the material Object, and the conceived Idea, but the unaccountable Will of God. He it is, who has made the Snow, and the Winds, and the Cold; and he it is that gives us the Power to perceive them. *He* has filled the Winter Sky with the pointed Froft, and
impregnate*d*

impregnated it with the Particles of Nitre : And he has given us the Power to apprehend Cold, from thefe different Caufes. We depend upon him to keep thefe Senfes in Exercife ; for it is the continual Exertion of his Power by which they act. Our Senfes are the Springs of thefe Perceptions ; and in this Senfe, *All our Springs are in him.* He keeps them acting, as he at firft awakened them in us. He ranged and modified our Nerves ; he filled them with the animalSpirits ; he formed theImagination & Fancy in us, by a Combination of all which, we feel the Cold, and fhudder at the keen Winter. He firft contrived the fmall pointed Matter, and then he contrived our Pores to receive thefe little Particles ; then he formed our animal Spirits to convey the Senfation to our Brain ; and after all he lighted up the Imagination, to perceive the Idea, and pronounce upon it, *Cold.* Thus is the great God adorable in the Winter. 'Tis all his ftrange Work, within us, and without us. 'Tis intricate, and myfterious ! We know but Part of his Ways ; nor can we find them out unto Perfection. We amufe our felves, and wonder, and adore. Our Philofophy reaches a little Way : And where that ceafes, our Devotion goes on, and our Afcription to God muft ftill be, 'Tis *His* Ice, 'tis *His* Cold.

5. He has *made all thofe Things which unite to form the Winter.* The Cold, the Snow, the Winds, the Froft and Ice, the Nitre in the Air, the Obliquity of the Sun, and all the fhivering Attendants of the Winter, are the Productions of his Hand. *For he faith to the Snow, be thou on the Earth.*-----Job xxxvii. 6,---10. 'Tis all afcrib'd to God, to the Voice of God, to the Breath of God. The Snow falls, and the Ice thickens at his great Command : And by his Cold he feals up the Hand of every Man, and puts a Stop to his Work. As foon as ever his Word is

B　　　　　　　　　　　　given,

given, all the Terrors of the bleak Winter, collect and muster together. *He sendeth forth his Commandment upon Earth, his Word runneth very swiftly :* Swift as his Command, his Creation obeys him, and performs his sovereign Order. He bids his Wind blow, and the stormy Wind fulfills his Word. It rushes out, and roars aloud ; it blusters and sweeps the Earth, and battles in the Air ; it raises the Ocean, tosses up the Billows in white Foam, and dashes Wave upon Wave, and Cloud upon Cloud. If he enlarges his Commission, it roots up Forests, and a whole Grove shall fly before it's Rage ; and Cities shall be overturn'd and laid waste in an Instant. In all this, the lawless Tumult of the Winds is strictly govern'd by God : They do but blow his Praises, as with the Sound of a Trumpet. When he Commands, they retire, and are hush ; a profund Calm ensues ; not a Whisper, not a Breath of Air moves a Sprig of the Trees, or bends the Smoaks of the Chimneys : The Sea smooths its shining Surface, and the Sky gleams serene in Silence. 'Tis this same God, who orders his Cold to chill the Air, and strip the Forests : To arrest the Rivers in their rapid Motion, and bind them in Fetters of Ice : To seize the living Creation, slacken the Motion of the Blood, and make the Limbs shake, and the Teeth chatter. 'Tis this same God, who makes his snows gently descend, sport in the light Air, and whiten the soft Ground. At his Order, the beautiful Fleeces cover the Fields with a dazling and a warm Robe. He it is, that forms the slippery and glistering Paths, and finishes the Looks and the Form of the rugged Lanskip. Every little Rising about us, the Banks of Snow, or the shining Ice, are the common Works of him, the God who made the Winter. He has made all the various Parts of it, and furnished and compleated the whole Scene.

Thus

Thus I have illuftrated and confirmed the Doctrine; I come now to apply it to the holy Ends of Piety and Devotion.

1. Learn the *adorable Perfections of this GOD.* See his Grandeur and Majefty, in the terrible Work! How contemptuous is his Challenge to mortal Man, in thofe Operations of his Hands? Job xxxviii. 22, 23. *Haft thou entred into the Treafures of the Snow? Or haft thou feen the Treafures of the Hail? Which I have referved againft the Time of Trouble, againft the Day of Battle and War?* How grand and majeftick is the God who has fuch Magazines of Artillery; fuch Armies of various Deftruction all at his uncontroulable Command. See the Winter, and own the almighty Power and of the God who produced it. What a refiftlefs Arm muft he have, who rolls on the Seafons in their Order, and forms all the ftrong Cold, and Wind, and Froft of the Winter? *Who can ftand before his Cold?* Who then can ftand before him when once he is angry? Who knows the Power of his Anger? Even as his Fear, fo is his Wrath.

See the Winter, and own the Mercy of God, to bring Good out of Evil, and make it beneficial to the Fruitfulnefs of the Year, and the Health of Mankind. See his Mercy in providing us Shelter from the keen Air, and Cloaths as the Covering from the Cold. He has built our Houfes for us; elfe had the Artificers laboured in vain. He has given us Fire to oppofe the Cold, and defend us from its unfufferable and mortal Rigour. He gave our firft Father Coats of Skin, and he gives us all our ufeful and beautiful Raiment, to hide us from the fatal Cold. The Winter all over fhews the Mercy of the God who made it.

See the Winter, and behold his Juftice alfo. 'Twas for Sin that Cold became painful, and executes part of the Curfe upon the barren Earth. 'Tis not improbable, that

the

the Pofition of the Earth to the Sun, has been altered fince
the Sin of *Adam* : And how far the Flood which came upon the World of the Ungodly, has contributed to this, is
difputed among the Learned.   'Tis no unfair Conjecture,
that the Difruption of the Abyfs, and the general Con-
cuffions of the Globe at that Time, might unhinge the
Poles, and alter the Courfe of the Year.   Perhaps this is
hinted at, when God faid to *Noah* immediately after the
Flood, that now there fhould be no Ceffation of Winter
and Summer, and Cold and Heat.   However that may
be, we know the Curfe on the Earth for Sin, became
more compleated by the Flood, which has very much
alter'd the Form of the Earth, and the Healthinefs of the
Air ; and fhortned the Life of Man.   And we know
the Painfulnefs and Unfruitfulnefs of the Winter Cold, is
Part of that Curfe brought upon us by Sin.   But I would
not enlarge ; let us fee the Perfections of God in his
Work.

2. Let us *ferve God in the Winter.*   It is his Time :
We ought then to render it to him, and fill it up in his
Service.   'Twas for his own Glory that he made it : For
this is his End in all his Works.   *For his Pleafure they are
and were created.*   'Tis juft then that we fhould make the
Winter conduce to his Glory, and glorify him in it, and
for it.   We are apt indeed to be rendred fluggifh and
floathful by the Winter-Cold.   Prov. xx. 4. *The Sluggard
will not Plough by reafon of the Cold.*   But far be this Character from us !   Amidft the Cold let us be diligent :
not flothful in Bufinefs, but fervent in Spirit, ferving the
Lord.   Let not our Love wax cold with the Seafon.
Away with the invidious Proverb, *Cold as Charity.*   Let
us now, as far as God gives us Capacity and Opportunity,
relieve the Neceffities of our poor Neighbours.   If a
Brother of Sifter be naked and deftitute of daily Food,
and

nd one of you fay, Be ye warmed, be ye cloathed, notwithftanding ye give them not thofe Things which are
neceffary for the Body, what doth it profit? Your Faith
is dead, unlefs it infpires thefe Works. And the great
Demand of Chrift at laft will be concerning thefe Works
and Labours of Love. And as we, in thefe Inftances,
real by his Members, he will look upon himfelf honoured
or abufed.---*I was naked, and ye cloathed me not*---Or, *I
was naked, and ye cloathed me. Inafmuch as ye have done it
unto one of the leaft of thefe my Brethren, ye did it unto me.*
Then fhall not a Cup of cold Water lofe its Reward,
much lefs fhall a warm Garment, or a comfortable Fire,
or a refrefhing Meal.---And as there are Duties peculiarly
adapted to Winter, I fhall conclude with a few profitable
Meditations pertinent to the Seafon. We may ferve
God, in his Winter, by making the Winter itfelf con-
tribute to our facred Contemplations.

For Inftance, When we feel the *Cold* of the Winter,
let us fear the God who made the Cold. How eafily can
he kill us by this one Creature? There have been Inftances of Perfons paffing over the northern Mountains,
feized and ftiffened at once, and left like *Lot's* Wife, a
Pillar to be wonder'd at in after Years. In a dreadful
Senfe, they *ftand* before his Cold; ftand *by* it, and are
kept ftanding, the Monuments of his awful Power. *
Who would not fear this God!

When we fee the *Snow* around us, let us meditate on
unfpotted Holinefs of the God who made it. The

So Dr. WATTS has defcribed them.
Fly to the polar World, my Song,
.n the Pilgrims there, (a wretched Throng)
Seiz'd and bound in rigid Chains,
f Statues on the Ruffian *Plains.*

Snow

Snow is not pure in his Sight. Let us reflect on our own Guilt & Blackness, & take up the Prayer, Pfal. li. 7. *Wash me, and I shall be whiter than the Snow.* Let us plead the Promise of God, *Though your Sins be as Scarlet, they shall be white as Snow.* Let us repair to Chrift for his unfullied Righteousnefs, as the fine Linnen white and clean, which is the Righteoufnefs of the Saints. Let us feek Sanctification of the Holy Spirit, that we may be *Nazarites purer than Snow.*

When we fee the Ice fhine in the flippery Paths, let us be caution'd to walk with Care; and remember the Admonition of God, *Let him that flandeth, take Heed leaf he fall.* Let the fhort Days of the Winter admonifh us, to work in hafte, and what we do, do quickly. Let the flippery Paths and the fhort Days unite to perfwade us, to walk circumfpectly, redeeming the Time. This I fay, Brethren, the Time is fhort; Oh! fhall we not fill up the fhort Time as full as ever we can. Let the cold Day put us in Mind of the Cold of Death; and the fhort Day of our fhort Life.——But I confider the Cold, and I would *not fland too long before it.* Let us improve the Winter well in this World, and quickly we fhall be taken to that blefled State, where the *Winter* fhall ceafe from troubling, and the Weary are at reft. Death will arrive to us with that Meffage from Jefus our Lord. Cant. ii. 10, 11. *Rife up and come away, for lo, the winter is paft, the Rain is over and gone, the Flowers appear on the Earth, and the Time of the finging of Birds is come. Rife up, and come away.*

F I N I S .

THE

Glorious Reſt

OF

HEAVEN.

A

SERMON

At the *Thurſday-Lecture* in
Boston, *Jan.* 3. 1744,5.

By Mr. Byles.

Publiſh'd at the Requeſt of many of the Hearers.

Matth. xvii. 4. They *ſaid* —— *It is good for
us to be here.*——

BOSTON:

Printed by B. Green and Comp. for D. Gookin, over
againſt the Old South Meeting-Houſe. 1745.

THE

Glorious Reſt

OF

HEAVEN.

ISAIAH XI. x.

——*His Reſt ſhall be glorious.*

T H E Prophecy of *Iſaiah*, is one of the moſt ſublime and noble Pieces of the Old Teſtament, whether we conſider the Force of Thought, the Magnificence of the Deſcriptions, or the Majeſty and Importance of the Subjects with which they abound. Among the latter of theſe, *viz.* the Subjects, there are none that ſhow with a diviner Brightneſs, or caſt a more radiant Luſtre thro' tne Book, than thoſe which concern the Advent of the *Meſſiah*, and the illuſtrious Tranſactions that ſhould attend it.

This

This is a Theme that the Prophet delights to dwell upon, and introduces throughout the whole of his lofty Predictions.

The Chapter before us is of this Kind, in which the inſpired Man gives us the Character of the *Meſſiah*, and deſcribes his powerful and happy Kingdom. This is done with an Eloquence and Beauty peculiar to himſelf. At the 10*th* Verſe, our Saviour is deſcribed as lifted up as an Enſign, and the Gentiles ſeeking to him, while he thus purchaſes a Reſt for them. *And in that Day there ſhall be a Root of* Jeſſe, *which ſhall ſtand for an Enſign of the People ; to it ſhall the Gentiles ſeek, and his Reſt ſhall be glorious.* That is, the *Meſſiah*, who is the Root of *Jeſſe*, ſhall by his being lifted up on his Croſs, obtain a bleſſed Reſt for his choſen People ; among whom ſhall be the *Gentiles*, who ſhall ſeek to him for it. The Diſpenſation he brings is a Reſt compared with the Yoke of *Jewiſh* Ceremonies. It brings with it a Reſt of Mind, an *Heart fixed truſting in the Lord.* There is alſo a glorious Reſt for the Church upon Earth in the latter Day : *The new Earth, wherein ſhall dwell Righteouſneſs.* And there is beyond and above all, the Reſt that remains for the People of God, in the heavenly World.

The Text that is under our Conſideration, includes in it, all the Reſts that the bleſſed Jeſus beſtows on true Believers, whether in this World, or the World to come ; for Time, or for Eternity ; to the Soul, or to the Body. However, we will, if you pleaſe, confine it to the Reſt after this Life, in the heavenly World. That *Reſt will be glorious* without diſpute ; and the Words contain a very juſt Deſcription of it. It is call'd a *Reſt*, which is a negative Deſcription ; and excludes all manner of Uneaſineſs or Diſturbance. It is called a *glorious Reſt* ; which is a poſitive Deſcription, and implies all poſſible and real Bleſſedneſs fedneſs. And it is called *His Reſt*, that is, Chriſt's Reſt, inaſmuch as he is the Owner of it : For *the Son of Man is Lord alſo of the Sabbath*. The Doctrine that the Words preſent us with, is this,

DOCTRINE.

The Reſt of our Lord Jeſus Chriſt, which he has laid up in the heavenly World for his People, will be a glorious Reſt.

There are three Propoſitions contained in the Doctrine.
I. *There is a Reſt laid up for the People of God, in the heavenly World.*
II. *This Reſt will be a glorious Reſt.*
III. *That it is the Reſt of our Lord Jeſus Chriſt ; he is the Owner of it.*

I. *There is a Reſt laid up for the People of God, in the heavenly World.*
In ſpeaking to this Head, I ſhall ſhow, what the Reſt is not, what it is, and endeavour at a Scripture Proof of it, as I go along.
It may here be premiſed then, That by this Reſt, *We are not to underſtand an idle Ceſſation from all Employment*. The holy Souls in the heavenly World, do not ſpend their E-ternity in a drowſy Indolence. They are not waſting thoſe golden Ages in a ſupine Negligence and Idleneſs. No, in this Senſe, they are never unactive, but we read of them, Rev. iv. 8. *They reſt not Day nor Night, ſaying, Holy, holy, holy, Lord God Almighty, who was, and is, and is to come.* That is, they are never idle, but always diligent in glorifying and admiring the Perfections of God. Not one Hour of their happy Duration rolls unuſeful away ;

away ; not one Moment is loft to them in that endlefs
Succeffion of Ages.

But as a pofitive Anfwer, we fhall fay, that the Inhabitants of the Paradife above, reft from all *painful Labours*,
Tho' they do not ceafe from acting, yet their Induftry is
not labourious and difficult to them. It is true, they are
conftantly taken up with the Bufinefs of Heaven, but it is
no longer arduous and uneafy. They perform the moft
exalted Services, with the clofeft Application, and without
Intermiffion ; and at the fame Time enjoy the fereneft
Tranquility, and Compofure of Mind. The Works of
former Years, when they lived upon our Earth, are now
no longer able to perplex and moleft them. No longer
will they *ftrive to enter in at the ftraitGate*, when they are
already poffeffed of the Happinefs of the Kingdom. No
more will they *give Diligence to make their Calling and
Election fure* ; when their Fa h is turned into Vifion,
and their Hope concluded in Enjoyment. Never will
they again weary and tire themfelves in the Exercifes of
Religion, or the Duties of their fecular Employments ;
but will inhabit a Quietnefs and Peace, without the leaft
Moleftation or Difturbance. Heb. iv. 10. *He that is
entred into his Reft, hath ceafed from his own Works, as God
did from his.* Nay, they are gone to the Reward of their
paft Actions, and have their Labours crowned with an
ample Retribution and Recompence. Rev. xiv. 13. *I
heard a Voice from Heaven, faying unto me, Write, Bleffed
are the Dead which die in the Lord, from henceforth : Yea,
faith the Spirit, that they may reft from their Labours, and
their Works do follow them.*

Again, the bleffed Spirits of the Juft in Heaven, reft
from all *Sorrow* and *Affliction.* In this World, all Men
meet with Griefs and Woes, and every Child of *Adam* is
born to Trouble as the Sparks fly upward.

And

And as all Men in general are fubjeƈ to the unhappy Incidents of humane Life ; fo the pious Man in particular is peculiarly obnoxious to many fupernumerary Tryals, which a *Stranger* to true Piety *intermeddles not with.* Perfecutions and Abufes from a degenerate World, are no fmall Part of the Pains that encompafs him. He has an Awe of that Eternity upon his Mind, which the fecure Sinner never fuffers to give him an uneafy Refleƈtion. He is grieved at the Withdraw of God from him, and when his Saviour *hides his Face he is troubled* ; while the unregenerate Wretch goes quietly on, and glides fmoothly to the End of his Journey, unruffled with fuch Cares, and entirely ignorant of every Fear and Concern of fuch a Nature. In a Word, the good Man *thro' much Tribulation enters into the Kingdom of God,* befides the Sorrows common to all Men in *this prefent evil World.*

This is the Condition of the Children of God here, but in the heavenly World, they are removed at an infinite Diftance from every uneafy Thought ; and they leave all the Anguifh of their temporal Life behind them, when they enter that Place of Reft. And not only do good Men when they die, go to a World where there is *no more* Affliƈtion, but they receive a Reward for the former Anxieties that they have met with, and have born with a decent Refignation and Patience. That Beatitude is fully accomplifhed unto them, Pfal. xciv. 12, 13. *Bleffed is the Man whom thou chafteneft, O Lord, and teacheft him out of thy Law : That thou mayeft give him Reft from the Days of Adverfity.* And agreeable to this is that magnificent Defcription of the Paradife of God, in *Rev.* vii. from the 9*th* Verfe, where the Apoftle *John* gives us an Account of a glorious Vifion he had of it. And he tells us exprefly, that the happy Inhabitants of it came out of great Tribulation, Verfe 14. And he concludes the

B   fublime

fublime Narration, Rev. vii. 16, 17. *They ſhall Hunger no more, neither Thirſt any more, neither ſhall the Sun light on them, nor any Heat.---And God ſhall wipe away all Tears from their Eyes.* And in the ſame beautiful Manner, is the new *Jeruſalem* repreſented, Rev. xxi. 4. *And God ſhall wipe away all Tears from their Eyes ; and there ſhall be no more Death, neither Sorrow, nor Crying, neither ſhall there be any more Pain ; for the former Things are paſſed away.* Thus do the bleſſed Spirits in Heaven, reſt from all Sorrow, and every afflictive Evil.

Again, The *Spirits of juſt Men made perfect*, reſt from *Sin*, and are entirely freed from the Guilt and Power of that Worſt of all Evils.

In this World, the beſt of Men are full of Imperfection and Sin ; and have Cauſe to go Mourning all the Day, becauſe of the Oppreſſion of that great Enemy. The holy *Paul* himſelf, under a ſad Conviction of it, cries out, Rom. vii. 24. *O wretched Man that I am, who ſhall deliver me from the Body of this Death.* Thus that bleſſed Apoſtle complains of the Tyranny of original Sin. And even, in the moſt ſincere and devout Frames of his Mind, when he was engaging in the ſolemneſt Exerciſes of Religion, he laments it, that he was ſtill infeſted by his innate Corruptions, verſe 11. *When I would do Good, Evil is preſent with me.* And thus it is with every good Man, while he lives in this World of Sin and Miſery.

But in the heavenly World, there is no more Sin. Rev. xxi. 17. *There ſhall in no wiſe enter into it any Thing that defileth, or worketh Abomination.* There is no Guilt in thoſe pure and deathleſs Regions, to blaſt the Beauty of the Place, or caſt a Gloom over the immortal Day that crowns it. Not one *Action* performed in that Mountain of Holineſs, has the leaſt Mixture of Sin to ſtain or fully it : Not one *idle Word* intrudes it ſelf into

the

the raviſhing *Hallelujahs* that inceſſantly echo there: Nay, not ſo much as one *vain Thought* pollutes or diſcompoſes the Minds of the Saints in thoſe ſpotleſs Realms of Felicity.

We might add here, That the Spirits in Paradiſe, are not only entirely free from Sin, but they are alſo at Reſt from every *Temptation* to Sin. They have no Luſts within to ſollicit them; no enſnaring Trifles from without to allure and ſeduce them. The Devil, their grand Adverſary, cannot come at them, to uſe his Fraud and Subtilty, when once they are removed to that ſinleſs Kingdom: Nor can his fiery Darts reach to thoſe glorious Heights that they are advanced to, in thoſe lofty Abodes. Tho' the pious Soul, while it is linked to the Body, is hurried and buffeted with a numberleſs Variety of Suggeſtions from *Satan*; yet, no ſooner has it enter'd into thoſe everlaſting Doors, but it has an eternal Deliverance from them; it ſhall never be diſtracted with one of them more. The dying Believer may ſay to Sin, and Satan, and all his Temptations, as our Saviour ſaid to the *Jews*, John vii. 33, 34. *Yet a little while and I am with you, and then I go to him that ſent me,---and whither I go, ye cannot come.* In this Manner may the pious Man ſing in the laſt Moments of his Life: His failing Pulſe, and decreaſing Breath, may inſpire a new Delight into his Soul; and he may kindle with a heavenly Tranſport, at the Approaches of his own Mortality.

Thus we have ſeen what that Reſt is, that the Children of God have prepared for them, beyond the Confines of the Grave. We have ſhewn that they have a Diſmiſſion from all painful Labour, from all afflictive Evil, from all Sin, and from every Temptation. We come now to the ſecond Thing in the Doctrine.

II. *The*

II. *The Reſt that is laid up for gracious Souls in another World, will be a glorious Reſt.* This will appear if we conſider the following Particulars.

   1. *The Place of Heaven is a glorious Place.* Where this glorious and divine Place is, perhaps may not abſolutely be determined ; nor will it be ſafe and decent for us to aſſign any determinate Space in the Fields of Immenſity, as the Spot where the Souls of good Men are made happy, when they leave this World. Whether we ſuppoſe that theſe dazling Courts of Immortality lie within the Limits of the blew Sky, that eludes the Penetration of our Sight; and to be diſpoſed ſomewhere in that Firmament of Luminaries ; or whether we imagine that happy City to ſpread it ſelf beyond the Circumference of our Creation ; yet be it where it will, it is a Place of inconceivable Splendor and Majeſty.

   The very Heathen had a Notion of the Glory and Beauty of thoſe Regions to which good Men were carried after their Death ; and they uſed to be very gay and ornamental in their Deſcriptions of it. They ſpeak of it in their Writings as having all the Charms of Art and Nature to furniſh and ſet it off. They tell us the Fields are in perpetual Verdure ; the Hills are forever crown'd with Flowers ; and the Trees at one Time bloſſom and bear Fruit : While the Meads are refreſhed with an innumerable Variety of cool and flowing Springs. Thus the heathen World uſed to dreſs their Paradiſe, and paint it with all the Luxuriance of a lively Imagination. But how vaſtly ſhort are theſe Repreſentations to thoſe which we find made uſe of in the holy Writings, that give us a Proſpect of the heavenly World ?

   If we conſider what the ſacred Scriptures relate concerning the Receptacle of the departed Spirits of the Saints, we ſhall find ſufficient to convince us of the Truth of this.

It

It is called a *Houfe of many Manfions,* John xiv. 2. *A Building of God, an Houfe not made with Hands, eternal in the Heavens,* 2 Cor. v. i. *A City which hath Foundations, whofe Builder and whofe Maker is God,* Heb. xi. 10. But the moft fublime and finifh'd Defcription of it, we have in the xxi ft. Chapter of the Revelations, in which the holy City blazes in its greateft Strength and Perfection. It is there built up after a moft exquifite Manner, and fparkles with Gold and Jewels. The Apoftle fpeaks of it, as fhining without the Aid of the Sun ; as adorned with every Glory and Splendor : And indeed the Pomp and Riches of that City, is carried as far as our Imaginations can reach, in the Word of God ; and the *Reft* is glorious, becaufe the *Place* of it is glorious.

2. *The Company of Heaven is glorious Company.* Heb. xii. 22, 23, 24. *But ye are come to Mount Sion, and unto the City of the living God, the heavenly Jerufalem, and to an innumerable Company of Angels, to the general Affembly and Church of the Firft-born, which are written in Heaven, and to God the Judge of all, and to the Spirits of juft Men made perfect, and to Jefus the Mediator of the new Covenant.* There is fomething very beautiful and natural in this divine Rapture of the Apoftle, that expreffes more of the noble Tranfport he was in, than one would at firft imagine. He is fo taken up with the Theme, that he quite forgets the little Niceties of Method and Order, and produces the Images as they come to his Mind, without a ftrict Regularity of Arangement. He is ravifh'd with the Thoughts of his Subject, and is born away with the Current of Joy and Delight, that pours down upon him in his Contemplations. He begins his Defcription with the *innumerable Company of Angels* : Then he takes the whole Hoft of Heaven together, and calls them, *the general Affembly and Church of the Firft-born* : Next he rifes to the great God himfelf, and

adores

adores him as *Judge of all* : Then defcends and tells of the *Spirits of juft Men made perfect* : Laftly, he again foars away, and fings of *Jefus the Mediator*. Thus the bleffed Apoftle is fo full of the Matter, that he is hurried along with a holy Violence; and gives a more ftrong and fublime Account of that gloriousCompany, by an artlefs and rapid Run of Thoughts, than if he had obferved the moft fcrupulous and exact Order of Difpofition.

And furely the *Reft* that is fill'd with fuch divine Company, muft be a glorious *Reft* ; and it is certainly no little Satisfaction that they afford one to another. What big Delight will it be, to go to thatWorld, where we fhall fee all the truly great and good Men that ever have lived upon Earth ! When *Peter*, and *James*, and *John*, faw *Mofes* and *Elias*, at the Transfiguration of our Lord, how were they overpowered with the Extacy of the Vifion ? Mark ix. 5. *And* Peter *faid, Mafter, it is good for us to be here: And let us make three Tabernacles, one for thee, and one for* Mofes, *and one for* Elias. If the Sight of one or two glorified Saints upon Earth, could caufe the Hearts of the Apoftles to beat with fuch a folemn Delight, what will be the Satisfaction to go to the numerousAffembly of Heaven, and fee that dazling Company all glitter together.

But then, if the Sight of the holy Souls, will adminifter fuch Joy, furely the beholding fuch a radiant innumerable Company ofAngels,muft fill us with a proportionableGladnefs and Felicity. In the heavenly World, we fhall have a View of thofe very Angels that we read of in theScriptures, as defcending on the Earth, with Meffages from God, and for the Service of his Children. There we fhall behold the Angel, that fwift as Lightning, flew *Senacharib*'s Army in one Night. There we fhall fee thofe Convoys that roll'd the Prophet *Elijah* up the Skies in a fiery Chariot. *Gabriel*, who clap'd his Wings, and fhot away like a

Ray

Ray of Light with the News of our Saviours Birth, will there attend upon the Throne of the bleſſed Jeſus : While *Michael,* who drove down the rebel Angels thunder-ſtruck from the Battlements of Heaven, into the deep Abyſs of Damnation, will there move along thro the Ranks of Seraphim, with the Port and Aſpect of the Warriour Arch-angel. The Sight of ſuch glorious Company as this, will be a bleſſed and raviſhing Sight indeed.

But O where ſhall we find Words to expreſs the Beatifick Viſion of Chriſt ? How raviſhing, and glorious, and unutterable will that bleſſed Lord appear, who is the *Brightneſs of his Father's Glory, and the expreſs Image of his Perſon ; and in whom dwelleth the Fullneſs of the God-head bodily !* When the Apoſtle *Paul* look'd upon Death in this Light, as only the Meſſenger that would call him to his dear Lord Jeſus, how does he even pant, with an holy Impatience, for the pale Monarch to come on. No more is he afraid of that King of Terrors ; no more does he ſhrink back at his Approaches. He looks upon the Face of his Chriſt, and forgets the Horrors of Death : His Sting is blunted, his Darts broken ; and that grim Tyrant of the Grave wears the Aſpect of an Angel. 2 Cor. v. 6, 8. *Wherefore we are always confident, knowing that while we are at Home in the Body, we are abſent from the Lord. ---- We are confident, I ſay, and willing rather to be abſent from the Body, and to be preſent with the Lord.* Phil. i. 23. ----*Having a Deſire to depart and to be with Chriſt, which is by far better.* Now if the Faith of going to Jeſus, can inſpire ſuch a Courage and Joy into the Mind of the good Man, and baniſh the Shades from the Vale of Death ; ſurely the immediate Sight of that Glory will be tranſporting beyond Conception.

And indeed 'tis no little Part of the Happineſs of Heaven, that there we ſhall behold the Lord Jeſus Chriſt,

unveil'd

unveil'd, in the full Bloom of heavenly Glory. This adds a Force and a Rapture to *John's* Defcription of it, in the xxift and xxiid Chapters of the Revelations, *And I faw no Temple therein : For the Lord God Almighty, and the Lamb, are the Temple of it. And the City had no need of the Sun, neither of the Moon to fhine in it : For the Glory of God did lighten it, and the Lamb is the Light thereof.* ----- *And there fhall be no more Curfe, but the Throne of God and of the Lamb fhall be in it, and his Servants fhall ferve him. And they fhall fee his Face, and his Name fhall be in their Foreheads. And there fhall be no Night there, and they need no Candle, neither Light of the Sun, for the Lord God giveth them Light, and they fhall reign for ever and ever.* Thus divinely glorious is the Company of Heaven : Holy Souls departed ; Holy Angels, and God reveal'd in the Face of the holy Jefus, all confpire to adorn the Kingdom, and fpread a Felicity over the whole Place.

3. *The Employment of Heaven is glorious Employment.* As the Company is fo excellent and illuftrious, fo no lefs is the Converfation with which they gratify and entertain one another, in thofe delightful Habitations. Doubtlefs thofe happy Spirits will difcourfe together, on the Actions of their paft Lives ; the Bleffings they were favour'd with, the Miferies they are efcaped from : and Glory that they now poffefs. Thofe that knew one another upon Earth, will be much better acquainted there ; and where any have been inftrumental in forwarding and helping on one another in their Way to Heaven, they will be mutual Joys to one another when they meet there. How bleffed and pleafing an Intercourfe muft it be, for Friends to congratulate the Arrival of Friends, to that holy World ; to talk over the Prayers they have perhaps formerly made together ; the pious Converfation they have carried on upon Earth ; and the ferious Religion they promoted in each o-
ther

ther's Minds, by their Word, and their Examples. It
will certainly be no little Satisfaction, for them there to
renew to one another, the Thoughts and Discourses they
once entertained concerning the Glory and Happiness of
the Kingdom where they will then reign. They will say
one to another, How dark and obscure were our Conceptions of this Felicity! How low and mean the Talk we
formerly had about it! How inadequate and trifling the
most exalted Strokes of our mortal Discourses to these
sublime Enjoyments!

And as the Conversation we shall have with those
which we were familiar with on Earth, will be so plea-
sant and happy, so no less will that delight us, which we
shall have with those who have gone to Heaven before us.
To mix in the divine and sinless Companies there, to hear
the improving Expressions of their Tongues, and attend
to the soft Perswasion that sits upon their Lips, this will be
a very noble Entertainment. How glad shall we be, to
hear *Paul* give us an Account of his Conversion with his
own Mouth ; or *Noah* himself be the Relator of the Flood
which bore him up in his Ark, over the Tops of the
Mountains! To hear *Moses*, in an improved Sublimity of
Style, tell of the Wonders of the Creation, and relate the
Pomp and Terror of Mount *Sinai*, when its Summit
blaz'd with Fire unto the midst of Heaven ; and the black
Smoke arose like the Smoke of a Furnace, and roll'd a-
way thro' the Air; while the Voice of the Trumpet
echo'd louder and louder, and the whole Mountain shook
to its Foundations. And will not JESUS himself tell us
of his own Love, and Sufferings for us, in *Words which it
is not lawful or possible for a Man to utter.* These noble
Themes will without Doubt, employ much of the Conversation of Heaven ; and gratify and enlarge the Minds of
the glorified Saints.

They

They will there also confider the feveral Works of God, and admire the furprizing Difplays of the Godhead in them. The *Creation* throughout its vaft Extent, will be a Field on which they will expatiate, and afcribe due Praifes to the infinite Contriver and Author of fo aftonifhing a Piece of Workmanfhip. Rev. iv. 10, 11. *The four and twenty Elders fall down before him that fat on the Throne, and worfhip him that liveth for ever and ever, and caft their Crowns before the Throne, faying, Thou art worthy, O Lord, to receive Glory, Honour, and Power, for thou haft created all Things, and for thy Pleafure they are, and were created.* To trace the Mazes of *Providence,* with exalted Strains of Rapture and Devotion, will be another Exercife of the heavenly World. The fupream Lord who manages the Wheels full of Eyes, will be adored as his wondrous Works to the Children of Men, come to have the Clouds taken off, and appear in all their Harmony and Beauty.

In fome Defcriptions that the holy Writings give us of Heaven, we find the glorified Spirits celebrating the Praifes of God, for his Judgments on Earth. Thus the Deftruction of Antichrift tunes their Harps, Rev. xix. 1,— 6. *And after thefe Things I heard a great Voice of much People in Heaven, faying, Alleluia, Salvation, and Glory, and Honour, and Power unto the Lord our God; for true and righteous are his Judgments, for he hath judged the great Whore, which did corrupt the Air with her Fornication, and hath avenged the Blood of his Servants at her Hand. And again they faid Alleluia, and her Smoke rofe up for ever and ever. And the four and twenty Elders, and the four Beafts fell down and worfhipped God that fat on the Throne, faying, Amen, Alleluia. And a Voice came out of the Throne : faying, Praife our God all ye his Servants, and ye that fear him, both fmall and great. And I heard as it were the Voice of a* great

great Multitude, and as the Voice of many Waters, and as the Voice of mighty Thundrings ; *saying, Alleluia* ; *for the Lord God omnipotent reigneth.* To be fure in the heavenly World, the Wonders of our *Redemption*, will be the Subject of the higheft Delight and Praife. We fhall there be fwallow'd up with the Contemplation of that myfterious and un-fearchable Production. Rev. v. 8, 9. *The four living Creatures, and four and twenty Elders fell down before the Lamb, having every one of them Harps, and golden Vials full of Odours, which are the Prayers of Saints. And they fung a new fong, faying, Thou art worthy to take the Book, and to open the Seals thereof : For thou waſt ſlain, and haſt redeemed us to God by thy Blood, out of every Kindred, and Tongue, and People, and Nation.*

The laft Thing we fhall take Notice of under this Head, fhall be, That one principal Part of the heavenly Bleffednefs will confift in the beholding of GOD. This will be no fmall Article of the Employment and Felicity of the Saints in Glory ; but will improve and brighten every other Delight. Not that we are to fuppofe it poffible to have a Sight of the divine Effence it felf ; but fuch a Confcioufnefs of his Prefence, and fuch Communications from him, as may in fome Senfe be efteemed Sight ; and this is what is called *the beatifick Vifion.* It is in this Senfe that thofe Texts of the holy Scriptures are to be underftood, that fpeak of *beholding the Face of God*, and *feeing him as he is.* The Eye of the Underftanding, has a View of the glorious God, and grafps in as much of the glorious Prof-pect, as it can poffibly wifh. Thu divine and happy are the Exercifes of the heavenly World.

5. *The Progreffion and Increafe of that celeſtial Bleffed-neſs, will add perpetually to its tranſcendant Glory* The Saints do not immediately upon their Entrance into Para-dife, fhoot up to the higheſt Point of Felicity and Blef-

fednefs,

fedneſs, but go on continually making new Aquiſitions in Knowledge, and enlarging their Capacities for Happineſs. This may be proved by plain and evident Arguments ; and particularly from the Make and Conſtitution of the humane Soul. The Mind of Man is like a Fire, which ſpreads and encreaſes as it finds Materials to feed and ſupply it. So that tho' the Spirit of a Believer, as ſoon as it arrives to thoſe Realms of Tranquilityy receives as much Joy and Bleſſedneſs as it is then capable of, yet it is not happy in ſo great a Degree, as it will be afterwards, becauſe it will then be able to ſupport, and bear up under, a larger Proportion of Glory. When the Soul of a good Man has enjoy'd the Felicity of Heaven for ſome long Period of Duration, every Faculty will be widen'd, and many additional Advantages will neceſſarily ariſe, as the Soul ſpreads it ſelf into more ample Capacities. Tho' the Spirit of the Believer is made perfect in Hollneſs and Glory, as ſoon as it leaves the Body, yet it does not arrive to thoſe *greater Degrees* of Perfection, that it will ſtill go on to acquire, as it ſinks further into the Depths of Eternity. The Memory will then be an inexhauſtible Magazine of Delight, as they paſs onward thro' the vaſt Variety of Satisfactions that they meet with in the heavenly World : And they will be able to look back, and reflect with renewed Joy upon that wonderful Train of Pleaſures, which has extended it ſelf in ſuch a beautiful Order, and to ſo immenſe a Diſtance. And to think over ſuch a mighty Round of Years, and renew in our Minds all the pleaſing Scenes of Felicity, which paſs'd in a gay Succeſſion before us, in ſo great a Space of Duration, muſt needs be an Happineſs which will be unſpeakably great ; and impoſſible to be enjoy'd at our firſt Entrance into Glory.

But to difmifs a Speculation fo abftracted, we may here take Notice of two Steps of Progreffion, which every one will allow at firft Sight, that the Souls of good Men take in their glorious Happinefs.

Firft, At their Death. They no fooner leave their dying Bodies, but they are borne upon the Wings of holy Angels to the Paradife of God. A Flight of thofe fhining Spirits attend the Death-Bed of the Saints, and immediately upon the laft Gafp, receive the departing Soul, and convoy it to the World of Glory. If our Minds could but follow them as they fly along, what a wonderful Scene of Delight would open to us? How does a Soul juft freed from a Body of Sin and Death, exult as it tow'rs away, in the Midft of fuch bright Attendants? How do the refplendent Angel-Guards fing round it, as they bear it thro' the Regions of the Air, and theEther, to the Habitations of unfading Blifs and Triumph! And when it enters the orient Gates of that City, what are the Acclamations and Hallelujahs that congratulate its fafe Arrival! Here it joins its Brethren of the Skies, in their immortal Anthems of Rapture and Praife, in a joyful Hope and Expectation of the Refurrection of the Dead at the laft Day.

And this is a fecond Step of the Believer's Progreffion in Glory, which is acknowledged by all, without Hefitation or Paufe. When our Lord Jefus Chrift makes his fecond Appearing, *the Dead in Chrift fhall arife,* and thofe Souls who have been many Ages happy in the Paradife of God, fhall now attain to a more compleat and extenfive Felicity at the Refurrection of their refpective Bodies; which will be glorified and adorn'd for the Habitation of fo finlefs Spirits. It will without Difpute, be a moft glorious Advancement in Bleffednefs, for the raifed Bodies of the Saints, to be again united to the Soul, and become

more

more intimate and infeparable Companions than ever they
were before. How will the ravifh'd Soul of the good
Man triumph, when he hears the Voice of the Son of
God, *Arife ye Dead !* How will his quickning Body rejoice, at the new Entry of the Spirit into it ! The whole
Man will be fwallowed up in an unknown Delight : His
Heart will leap with Tranfport in his Bofom, and beat
Time to the founding Echo's of the laft Trumpet. Thus
when our Lord Jefus Chrift fhall *come, to be glorified in his
Saints, and admired of all them that believe,* the Language
of the holy Soul, as it flies down to the Grave that contains its Duft, will be, *Arife, O my Bcdy, arife and fhine,
for thy Light is come, and the Glory of the Lord is rifen upon
thee.*

I might add to thefe two Steps in the Throne of Glory,
a Third, *viz.* that after the final Judgment, the deathlefs
Bodies and Souls of the Children of God, will in an in-
diffoluble Union, afcend to the heavenly World, with
new Additions of Splendor, and Pomp, and Happinefs.
But, alas ! What Words can bear up under this *Weight
of Glory.* What Conceptions are equal to this dazling
Solemnity, and Magnificence. When the Judge of the
World, rifes from his laft Sentence on the Righteous and
the Wicked, and returns to his Throne in the Heavens,
who can tell the Joys of the glorified Saints, and the Songs
of Thankfgiving that hang on their Lips ? They will
fhout round his Chariot Wheels, as they roll along, and
all Heaven will refound with their Acclamations. Thus
will they enter the Place of their holy and glorious A-
bodes, and receive a higher Degree of Bleffednefs, than
ever they were before capable of imagining.

Thus we fee there is a Progreffion of Bleffednefs enjoy'd by the Saints in Glory. At Death they are made
perfect in Happinefs ; At the Refurrection they arrive a-

ai

an additional Felicity, by a Re-union to their glorified
Bodies ; At their Afcenfion to the Manfions of Delights,
after the Conclufion of the great Day, they arrive at ftill
higher and nobler Degrees of Perfection ; and they then
go on adding Joy to Joy, and one Degree of Glory to
another to interminable Ages.

5. *The Duration of the Reſt remaining for the People of
God in the heavenly World, will be an inconceivable Addition to
the Glory of it.* And what is this Duration but even Eternity it felf ? Had it been but a few Years, that the glorified Saints were to enjoy the Bleffednefs of Heaven, yet
even then it would beyond Expreffion have furpafs'd all
the Pleafures of this Earth. But what an infinite Addition of Happinefs is given to the tranfported Souls there,
by the Conftancy and Laftingnefs of the Glory ! What
ftrange Delight does that Reflection ftrike into the Mind
of thefe Bleffed ? Eternity ! How does it employ their
Thoughts, how does it even overwhelm and fwallow up
all their Contemplations, in Delight and Wonder ! It not
only continues the Felicity without Ceffation, but it encreafes it every Moment. For when the Soul affures it
felf, that the Happinefs it enjoys fhall endure forever, that
very Thought doubles every Delight which rolls in upon it ;
and gives a new and an unknown Bleffednefs to every
Pleafure of Heaven. Were the happy Spirits in Paradife
to know that their Joys were in fome Period of Duration
to be finifhed ; and that then they muft leave their Glory,
how would it damp their Felicity, and caft a Veil and a
Cloud upon all their Raptures ? How diftant foever the
End might be, it would methinks ftill be prefent to their
Minds ; and, like a Man poffefs'd of an invaluable Treafure, the very Fear of loofing it, would in a great Meafure obftruct the prefent Comfort it might otherwife af-
In a Word, Did the bleffed Saints know that the

Time

Time would arrive, in which he muſt part with all his Happineſs, the very Thought would blunt the fine Edge of his Delight ; and would ſpread a Gloom, never before confeſs'd in thoſe Realms of immortal Day. Our Lord Jeſu himſelf cried out at his Father's Withdraw from him, And in like Manner, on the other Hand, the Meditation of the Eternity of the Enjoyments of the heavenly World, infuſes new Satisfaction in every Moment that rolls thro' thoſe golden Ages. It doubles every Pleaſure they taſte ; and gives an additional Splendor to every Gem in the Crown of Glory. Dan. xii. 3. *They that be wiſe, ſhall ſhine as the Brightneſs of the Firmament, and they that turn many to Righteouſneſs, as the Stars forever and ever.*

Thus we have conſider'd the heavenly Reſt, and ſhown, in ſome Meaſure, how it was glorious. That every Thing we could ſay of it, was to its Advantage and its Honour. That the *Place*, the *Company*, the *Employment*, the *Progreſſion*, and the *Duration*, all unite their Beauties together, and conſpire to ſet it off with the utmoſt Pomp and Magnificence. But alas, how little a Portion known of it. To ſpeak of the Glories of Heaven fully, who is ſufficient for theſe Things ! What the Perfection of it will be, we know not now, we ſhall know hereafter. Fitter are theſe Themes for the *Hallelujahs* of a Seraph, than the faultring Tongue of a Mortal ; better to be admired than deſcribed ; to dwell forever in an holy Meditation upon our Hearts, to influence every Action we perform, and at laſt, to make our very *Deaths* the moſt delightful and raviſhing Moment of our *Lives*. *Eye hath not ſeen, nor Ear heard ; neither hath the Heart of Man aſcended to conceive the Glory which God hath prepared for them who love him.*

III. The third Thing was to have evinced, That *the Reft of Heaven is Chrift's Reft : He is the Lord of that Sabbath.* This we might have proved in feveral Particulars, as, That he *made* it ; That he is the *Heir* of it, and it is the *Gift* of his Father to him : That he has *bought* it, and paid his own Blood the Price for it : That he has *afcended* and taken *Poffeffion* of it : That he has *promifed* it ; and muft furely therefore be its Owner. And finally, that he has *actually beftowed* it upon many of his Saints already. But thefe Things I muft at prefent omit. I haften to the Application.

And Firft, Is there a *Reft to come*, let us *Labour Now*. Our Text fpeaks of fomething future, *His Reft* SHALL BE *glorious* : And what more forcible Motive can there be for prefent Labour, than a fucceeding Reft. Do we not fee People about us fpending their Time, their Strength, and their Lives in the Labours and Fatigues of this World, and all in Hopes to have their old Age eafy, and in their declining Years to fet down and reft? And fhall thefe earthly and procraftinating Souls, be thus affiduous in fcraping their Dirt together, in the vain and empty Expectation of an idle Old Age : And fhall the Chriftian do no more to prepare himfelf for the Happinefs of Heaven, the Reft that remains for the People of God ? What a Shame is it, that fo trifling and tranfient a Reft in this World, fhould have ftronger Allurements than the eternal Tranquility of Paradife ? Can the Chriftian bear the Thoughts of This : To be thus out-done in Labour, upon fo flender a Foundation, fo trifling a Reward ?

Let every Soul of us then receive the Exhortation of the Apoftle, Heb. iv. 11. *Let us Labour therefore to enter into that Reft.* And let every *pious Soul* in particular,

labour

labour more earneftly, and affiduoufly, and give Diligence
to make our Calling and Election fure, and do with our
Might what our Hands find to do, as knowing that our
Labour fhall not be in vain in the Lord.

Inf. II. Is *this Reft* a *glorious Reft*, let us *rejoice in the
Hope of the Glory of God.* What is there that can rationally obftruct or diminifh the Believer's Joy, when he knows
that this glorious Reft is laid up for him! Why do we
not long to be poffefs'd of that everlafting Glory? Why
are we not impatient for our Tranflation to that better
that diviner World of Blifs? Whence is it, that the good
Man can even content himfelf till Death invites him to
his Inheritance! But Oh! whence, that inftead of Content he is fo fupinely Indolent, and has fuch fmall and
glimmering Notions of the Glory of that State! Inftead
of the holy Flames of Defire, there is the heavy Smoke
of Unbelief; and while he fhould be afpiring on eager
Wings up to that World, he is link'd to Earth; and
grovels in the low and contemptible Enjoyments of Time
and Senfe! The Exhortation to you is that in *Micah* ii.
10. *Arife ye, and depart; for this is not your Reft.* Happy
would it be, could we all look up to the heavenly Glory,
and fee the glittering Preparations made for us there;
and *happy,* could we hear the Bleffed there pronounce to
us, 2 *Thef.* i. 6, 7. *God fhall render Tribulation to them
which trouble you. And to you who are troubled reft with
us.* If we could look on this World, as full of Labour
and Sorrow; and turn our Eyes upon the World where
God is, and where our bleffed Jefus invites *us* to be, and
wifh, and break out, *O that I had Wings like a Dove!
then would I fly away, and be at Reft.*

Inf. III. Does this *Reft* remain for the *People of God,*
what will become of thofe who are *not his People?* If the

Righteous

Righteous scarcely be saved, where will the Ungodly and the Sinner appear? *The Wicked are like the troubled Sea, when it cannot Rest ; whose Waters cast up Mire and Dirt. There is no Peace, no Rest, saith my God, to the Wicked,* Isai. lvii. 20, 21. This is their State both in this World and the World to come. In this World, they are still pursuing imaginary Fantoms of Happiness, with constant Pains and Application ; till at last Death seizes them in the Midst of their eager Pursuits, and consigns them over to the World of Fire and Torment.

'Tis in this miserable Place, that Sleep flies their aching Eye-lids ; and Rest and Ease are utter Strangers. Alas ! What Hope of a peaceful Lodging in a Bed of Flames ? What Expectation of a quiet Abode in those dismal Regions of Sorrow ! If they cast their Eyes towards Heaven, they do but Curse God and look upwards. *They see* the beauteous Realms of *Halleiujah,* and the Doors of the holy City closed against them with everlasting Bars. *They feel* the kindling Torment inflame their impious Tongues ; and plead in vain for a Drop of Water. *They bear* the Sentence thundred from the Mouth of the great God himself, *He that is unjust, let him be unjust still. He that is filthy, let him be filthy still.* Their unsufferable Condition has a very awful Description, Rev. xiv. 10, 11. *They shall drink of the Wine of the Wrath of God, which is poured out without Mixture, into the Cup of his Indignation, and they shall be tormented with Fire and Brimstone, in the Presence of the holy Angels, and in the Presence of the Lamb : And the Smoke of their Torment ascendeth up forever and ever : And they have* NO REST *Day nor Night.* Darkness is indeed a Season for Rest ; But tho' they are banished into utter Darkness ; into Blackness of Darkness forever ; yet are they ignorant of any Rest ; they know no Cessa-

tion

tion to their Deſpair and Anguiſh. As their Flames
give them no Light, their eternal Night affords them no
Sleep. They ſpend the gloomy Ages that roll over them
in Lamentation and Woe: They rore, loud as the Fires
that wave about them ; and are unquiet and reſtleſs as
they.

There is a dreadful Diſparity between the Puniſhments
of Damnation, and the Glories of Heaven, and this will
ſerve to ſhow the Wretchedneſs of the Wicked there.
Is the *Place* of Heaven ſo bleſſed and divine, Hell is compared to a Priſon, to a bottomleſs Pit, to a Place of Torment, to a horrible Furnace, and to a burning Oven.
Iſai. xxx. 33. *The Lord hath prepared Tophet of old,—He
hath made it deep and large: The Pile thereof is Fire and
much Wood, the Breath of the Lord, like a Stream of Brimſtone, doth kindle it.*

In like Manner, the Company of Hell alſo, what a hideous
and infernal *Company!* Nothing to converſe with, but
Devils and the Damned. Their Fellow-Sinners upon the
Earth, will be their Fellow-Sufferers in Hell ; and thoſe
who formerly were Partners in Guilt, will now become
Sharers in Torment. Satan who once tempted them,
and their Companions who harden'd them in Sin, will add
to their future Miſery, and blow up the Flames to a greater Vigour upon them. The Sentence that will break
upon them from the Mouth of our Lord Jeſus Chriſt, and
that will ſweep them down to Perdition, will be that,
Matth. xxv. 41. *Depart from me ye Curſed, into everlaſting
Fire, prepared for the Devil and his Angels.* Miſerable
Souls ! to be *conſumed from the Preſence of the Lord, and the
Glory of his Power.* To be baniſhed from the bleſſed
Company of Heaven, and of Jeſus the Glory of Heaven ;
while a Portion is aſſigned unto them with *Hypocrites and
Unbelievers,*

Unbelievers, where is *Weeping*, and *Wailing*, and *gnashing of Teeth*, without Remedy, without Measure, and without End. The unhappy Company is defcribed, Rev. xxi. 8. *But the Fearful, and Unbelieving, and the Abominable, and Murderers, and Whoremongers, and Sorcerers, and Idolaters, and all Liars, fhall have their Part in the Lake which burneth with Fire and Brimftone, which is the fecond Death.*

Again, The *Employment* of Hell, what is it, but the keen Reflections of their paft Lives, and a future Eternity? What but bitter Out-cries and Execrations, while they curfe one another, and blafpheme God? Inftead of the Anthems of Heaven, they pour out Groans, and Shrieks, and Ejulations. They gnaw their Tongues for Pain ; and howling fupplies the Place of Hallelujah.

Again, The Pains of Hell have a horrible *Progreffion* . and as a Fire kindles by Degrees, and at laft Blazes with the largeft Expanfion, and the intenfeft Heat ; fo it will be with the Flames of Hell. We fee great Pains, the longer they laft, become the more intollerable. Where then will be the Sinner's Patience, after Millions of Ages fpent in thofe tremendous Agonies! How will his *Memory, Faithful Tormentor!* look back into the paft Periods of Defpair, and renew all the dreadful Lafhes of that vaft Duration. How will he effay to meafure the never-ending Succeffion to come, as the Line of preceeding Miferies lengthens out furtber and further. His *Underftanding* will be a wider Affliction, as he comes by the dire Experiment better to *know the Power of almighty Anger.* His *Affections,* particularly that of *Fear,* will be a more ftinging Anxiety, after he has felt in fome Sort, what he will hereafter expect to be more violent and infupportable. His *Will* will grow more defperate and hardened, as he ftill ufes himfelf to unpardonable Blafphemies. Finally, His *Imagination* will

will grow more unhappily capacious & artfull, to reprefent hisCondition of paft, prefent, & to come,in the moft lively and amazingColours.But to draw on to a Conclufion,in the laftPlace,the*Duration* of theTorments of Hell, is, *AllEternity*. What a boundlefs and overpowering Conception is here! The Miferies of the Damned will laft for ever. Never will thofe undone Souls be able to break Prifon ; never will their Agoniesceafe, or the Wrath of God give over raging againft them. The Day of the Fiercenefs of almighty Anger being come, it will remain, and the Indignation of God will rufh down refiftlefs and inceffant upon the guilty Rebels, and beat upon them in an eternal Tempeft. Eternity ! it adds Weight to every Chain, Heat to every Coal, and Gloom to every Cloud in that doleful Vault. It not only continues their Anguifh without End, but encreafes it every Moment. When they look forward into its unfearchable Mazes, and loofe themfelves in the ftrange Extenfion, O the Lamentation ! O the Defpair ! it is impoffible for us to form any equalConception of it.

Inf. IV. And I have done, Is *this Reft Chrift's Reft*, as I have hinted, O let us all go to him for it. If we refufe to do this, we fhall be miferable forever. *For there is no other Name given under Heaven, whereby we can be faved.* He is the mightySaviour. But *how fhall we efcape if we neglect fo great Salvation.* All Things elfe will fail us. We may wander among the Creatures, like *Noah's* Dove along the Surface of the Flood, but like her fhall find no REST *to the Sole of our Foot*, till we return to this Ark. *Gen.* viii. 9.. But if we repair to him by an humble Faith, we fhall there have Reft in the Day of Trouble. The greateft Sinner of us all is Welcome here ; and nothing but our Unbelief can hinder our Acceptance with
him.

him. Our eternal *Rest* or *Torment* depends then upon this one Thing, whether we are willing to give our selves to Christ or no. If we believe on his Name, we shall have such Dispositions infused into our own Souls, as will be a Heaven begun ; and an Earnest of the Rest to follow. If not, we shall not be qualified for it ; nor can we enjoy it. For without Holiness no Man shall see the Lord, nor enter into the Rest of his People. How foolish are those miserable Souls, who after so many Invitations to accept of the Rest of Heaven, go away unresolved whether to strive for it or no ; refuse it, and despise it ? Who can say but if you now think to put it off, and delay your Endeavours after it, an angry God may for ever banish you from it. Are you sure you shall ever have another Opportunity to sue for Mercy ? Nay, Death may strip you of all before To-morrow. What is the Language of the holy God upon such Procrastination ? Heb. iii. 7, 8, 10, 11. *Wherefore saith the holy Ghost, To-day, if ye will hear his Voice harden not your Hearts.——They do always err in the Hearts, and they have not known my Ways. So I sware in my Wrath, they shall not enter into my Rest.* But to those who with penitent Eyes, and awakened Souls enquire, *What shall I do to be saved ; to be delivered from this Wrath to come,* and obtain this glorious Rest ? To those I answer (yet not I, but the Lord JESUS CHRIST himself) in that most divine and affecting Language, Matth. xi. 28, 29. *Come unto me, all ye that labour, and are heavy laden, and I will give you Rest. Take my Yoke upon you, and learn of me, for I am meek and lowly in Heart, and ye shall find Rest unto your Souls.* And will you not echo to the dear Voice, *Return unto thy Rest, O my Soul.*

F I N I S.

Mr. *Byles*'s

S E R M O N

Before the Execution of a

Murderer.

THE

Prayer and Plea of *DAVID*,

To be delivered from 𝕭𝖑𝖔𝖔𝖉-𝕲𝖚𝖎𝖑𝖙𝖎𝖓𝖊𝖘𝖘,

Improved in a

S E R M O N

At the ancient *Thursday-Lecture* in *Boston*,
May 16ᵗʰ 1751.

Before the Execution of a Young 𝕹𝖊𝖌𝖗𝖔
Servant, for Poisoning an Infant.

By Mr. *BYLES.*

Psal. XL. 9, 10. *I have preached thy Righteousness in* the GREAT CONGREGATION.—*I have declared thy Salvation : I have not concealed thy Loving-Kindness, and thy Truth, from the GREAT CONGREGATION.*

B O S T O N :

Printed and Sold by SAMUEL KNEELAND, opposite the Prison in Queen-Street, 1751.

David's Prayer and Plea for Pardon from Blood-Guiltinefs.

PSALM LI. 14.

Deliver me from Blood-guiltinefs, O GOD, thou GOD of my Salvation: and my Tongue fhall fing aloud of thy Righteoufnefs.

THEY are the penitent Words of *David*, reflecting upon his barbarous Murder of *Uriah*: A moft earneft Prayer to GOD to forgive his Crime, and reftore the Peace of his Soul. You have the dreadful Story in II *Sam.* xi, & xii, Chapters. After his great and complicated Wickednefs, *Nathan* the Prophet is fent to him with a Meffage from GOD; a Meffage full of Conviction, Refentment, and Mercy. The Prophet, in the Name of GOD, charges home his Sin upon his Confcience; *Thou art the Man!* He denounces the Judgments of Heaven againft him, and againft his Houfe. He aggravates his Wickednefs to him, in all its Circumftances of Darknefs & Horror, and informs him of the mighty Anger of GOD burning and raging againft him. And now the poor King has his Heart melted within him. He has nothing to fay in his own Excufe. He had carried on his Impiety, with Hypocrify, Deceit & Lies: But the Spirit of GOD feizes him; He is overcome; He has no Heart to proceed any further. *And David faid unto Nathan, I have*
finned

finned againſt the Lord. And Nathan ſaid unto David, the Lord alſo hath put away thy Sin; thou ſhalt not die. Here's Penitence! Here's Mercy! The weeping David at once condemns himſelf; owns his Guilt; falls down before GOD, in Shame and Self-loathing. But Oh! How ſurprized was he to hear the Pardon pronounced, ſoon as his Repentance was declared?

When *Nathan* left him, he retired to faſt & pray for the Life of his Child: And now, a ſudden *Afflatus* from GOD came upon him, and inſpired he writes the Pſalm before us. The Spirit of GOD comes back again to his Soul: and tho' perhaps he intended to make a Prayer for the Recovery of his Infant, the Words are altered in his Mouth, and in his Pen; And he gives us the moſt noble Proceſs of Repentance that is any where to be met with. That Part of the Pſalm that I am upon, ſuited to the awful Occaſion of this Day, is the Addreſs of the humble Penitent to GOD, to pardon his dreadful Murder: *Deliver me from Blood-guiltineſs, O GOD, thou GOD of my Salvation: and my Tongue ſhall ſing aloud of thy Righteouſneſs.* — In diſcourſing on theſe Words, I ſhall in the Name of GOD, endeavour the following Things.

I. I ſhall deſcribe the *Crime* of *David: Blood-Guiltineſs.*

II. I ſhall conſider his *Prayer: Deliver me from Blood-Guiltineſs.*

III. I ſhall ſtate the *Argument of his Hopes: O GOD, thou GOD of my Salvation.*

And laſtly, His *grateful Reſolution* in Caſe God forgave him; *My Tongue ſhall ſing aloud of thy Righteouſneſs.*

I ſhall endeavour to be as brief as I can upon theſe Points, that I may haſten to that particular and ſolemn Application, which I am call'd to by the affecting Object before us.

I. I am to deſcribe to you the Crime of *David;* expreſs'd in that Word *Blood-Guiltineſs.* The original Word litterally tranſlated is *Bloods—From Bloods.* 'Twas an involved Crime, a perplex'd Piece of Villany. It had in
it

it a Plurality of darkCircumftances & Murders. *Bloods :* There was more than one it feems in it. Perhaps when *Uriah* was fet in the Front of theBattle, it was fo order'd that others fhould fall with him to difguife the Bufinefs. II Sam. xi. 25. *Then David faid to the Meffenger — The Sword devoureth one as well as another : Make the Battle ftronger* next Time. However, *Joab* was guilty as well ˑ David ; and it all refted in the End upon the Head of *David,* who caufed *Joab* to fin. So that the Guilt of two fell upon him fingly, and in this Refpeft, he might well fpeak of *Bloods.* Befides this, the poor innocent Infant muft die for his Father's Sin ; fo that in fome Sort he was the Author of his Child's Death too. But it may be *David* ufed the plural Number here, reflefting upon his murderous Defigns once or twice before : For he had the Guilt in his Heart, tho' GOD with-held him from compleating the Aft. — What a Madman was he in the Cafe of *Nabal !* 'Tis true, the Son of *Belial* ufed him unjuftly and fcuriloufly : But was that any Reafon that he fhould murder him, and his whole Family with him ? Becaufe *Nabal* was a Churl, muft *David* turn a revengeful, bloody Ruffian ? And yet what a Speech did he make upon this Occafion, when he heard *Nabal* had affronted him ? He was all on Fire. 'Twas but a Word and a Blow with him. In an Inftant he flies out in a Frenzy, curfes all his Enemies, profanes the Name of his GOD, and vows to kill *Nabal* and all his Family before Morning. 1 Sam. xxv.12. *SoDavid's young Men turned their Way, and went again, and came and told him all thofe Sayings. And David faid unto his Men, Gird you on every Man his Sword ! and they girded on every Man his Sword, and went up after David four hundred Men. And David faid, Surely in vain have I kept all that this Fellow hath in the Wildernefs — And he hath requited me Evil for Good, So and more alfo do GOD unto the Ene-mies of David, if I leave of all that pertain to him by the Morning Light, even fo much as a Dog.* And did you ever hear fuch Language as this from the Mouth of any
but

but a bloody-minded Madman ? And tho' a good GOD prevented the Execution of this rash Vow, who can excuse *David* from having Murder in his Heart ? Well then might *David* in his Penitence, reflect upon more Murders than one, and pray to be delivered from *Bloods*.

But to confine our Selves to this particular Crime, and if you please, to keep to the English Translation, *Bloodguiltiness*: O what a Scene of Impiety opens to our View! 'Tis one of the most dismal Histories in all the Scriptures. The strangest Instance of a Fall from GOD that was ever before known. *David*, a poor unregardable little Shepherd, chosen by the peculiar Grace of GOD, distinguished from, and advanced above all his goodly elder Brethren, preserved by a constant Series of Miracles, raised to the Throne of the peculiar People of GOD, surrounded by all the Blessings of Earth and Heaven ; inspired by the vast Possession of the Holy Spirit ; and in one Word, declared to be, *The Man after GOD's own Heart*. This *David* now ; (would you think it !) This very *David*, falls into Adultery and Murder. The least Sin, had in him been great, who was under so many Obligations to GOD : But Adultery & Murder ! What could a Heathen, or an Atheist do worse ?

And yet this is the very Case before us. *David*, under all his indissoluble Obligations, and matchless Advantages, thus fouly falls, an eternal Reproach to human Nature, and an Instance what frail Creatures we are, even the best Men upon Earth.

David then goes up to the Battlements of his Palace, and there walks idly from Side to Side ; and having no Business to employ him, falls a Prey to the Temptations of Covetousness and Lust. Happy had it been for thee, *David*, hadst thou now been employed in the Affairs of the Kingdom, or in thy Retirements address'd a Psalm to Heaven. But he was idle ! And O what an Inlet is this cursed Vice to all Mischief & Wickedness ? Being idle he stood as it were a Man in the Devil's Market Place, waiting to be set to Work. Here *Satan* found him out of God's Way ; and this which appears to many

fo little a Sin, lead the Way to all the Excefs and Li-
centioufnefs following. He was tempted and he fell.
The generous *Uriab* was now in the bloody Field, fighting the Battels of the Lord, & maintaining the Honour of
this *David*; while he bafely betrayed his Wife. Afraid
the Matter fhould be difcovered, he ufes the meaneft
Artifices, and the vileft Hypocrify to cover his Wickednefs : But when he found none of his bafe Schemes took
Effect, then (wonder O Heavens, and be aftonifhed O
Earth, be ye horribly afraid, and be ye very defolate !)
then he confpires the Death of *Uriab*, one of his braveft
and moft gallant Friends. He who merited to be ranked with the thirty Worthies, muft be ranked in the Fore-
front of the Battel, that he may be numbred to the Sword
of the Enemy. Was ever any Thing more treacherous
and perfideous ! The vile Confpiracy took Effect, and
the brave *Uriab* falls a Victim to the Cruelty and Luft
of *David*. The *Adultery* was deteftible ; But nothing
could be more barbarous and curfed than the *Murder*.
Confider the Criminal, the Manner, and the Subject,
and *there was no fuch Deed done nor feen from the Day
that the Children of Ifrael came out of the Land of Egypt,
unto this Day : Confider of it, confer together, and fpeak
your Minds.* How often muft *David's* Confcience check
him, while he was confpiring this Wickednefs ? How
many Reluctings muft he needs have within ? And yet,
deliberately, and bearing down all, he compleats the
Guilt, and the gallant Hero bleeds a Sacrifice to his
lewd Defires.

Now *David* began to make himfelf eafy. The Murder was committed, and he thought that it would be
concealed : There could never be any Proof of the Matter, and he fancied himfelf fecure. But Oh, poor Man,
thy GOD, and thy Confcience know the Affair, and in
vain wouldft thou difguife it from the World, while the
Guilt and the Anguifh corrodes within. Alas ! there are
no more quiet Hours for *David*. His Heart fmites
him, his GOD withdraws, the Ghoft of the murdered

B   *Uriab*

Uriah haunts his Dreams, and perplexes his waking Hours. He turns pale and ftarts at every Noife, and hears the Blood cry from the Ground, for Vengeance to the GOD of Heaven. He who a few Nights ago could fall afleep in the Raptures of his Mafter's Love, now has no Reft in his Bones becaufe of his Sin. He who was wont to remember his GOD with Joy upon his Bed, now waters his Couch with his Tears. The Anguifh of his Mind was infupportable long before *Nathan* was fent from GOD to him. He quickly begun to repent after the Fact was over.

I know 'tis the general Opinion, that *David* lived in his Sin, for feveral Months, and was never brought to Repentance 'till this Vifit from *Nathan.* But, with all Submiffion, I think the Cafe was much otherwife. It appears as tho' feveral Paffages of the penitential Pfalms were written after the Murder of *Uriah,* and before *Nathan* had faid, *The Lord alfo hath put away thy Sin.* † Would *David,* do you imagine, have written in fuch difponding Terms, after God himfelf had affur'd him that he was pardoned ? No : tho' this Pfalm wherein is my Text, was written after *Nathan*'s Meffage, yet it fhould feem from the different Air, that other of the penitential Pfalms were compofed in the Depth of Penitence, before *David* could perfwade himfelf that GOD had forgiven him.

See the poor King in his dark Retirements! Adultery and Murder lay upon his Soul. He complains of Difquietude, Wounds, and broken Bones. He weeps and rores with inward Diftrefs. His Tears are his Meat Night and Day, and he finds no Relief as yet from GOD or Man. However, his Penitence is fincere, tho' he fees it not. He would not commit the Wickednefs again for a thoufand Worlds. As yet, the Crime was concealed from the World, and as GOD had conceal'd it, he had no need to blaze it abroad. But however, he is brought into this fubmiffive Temper, as every true Penitent

† Pfal. 6. 32. 38. 51. 102. 130, 143.

tent is, if ever Providence fhould bring it out, his Repentance fhould be as publick as his Sin. This is the true Difpofition of a fincere Convert. And now the fulnefs of Time was come for a merciful GOD to regard his Diftrefs, and fend theWords of Pardon to him. The Prophet comes at the divine Order,and charges his Guilt home upon him, *Thou art the Man!* At onceDavid confeffes withoutHefitation orReluctance. He burfts into Tears, and cries out, *I have finned againft the Lord.* Now you fee *David* again. He appears like his former Self. Full of Faith, and Love, and Prayer, and Gratitude, he returns to his GOD, and rifes in all his Glory. *Nathan* goes away, and *David* retires to Fafting and Prayer, to afk theLife of his unlawfulChild. But GOD meets him in the miraculous Infpiration, and he forgets his own particular Requeft, and writes this penitential Pfalm, for the Benefit of the Church in all futureAges.

We have thus confidered theCrime of *David,*and how vaft was it! How dreadful in *itfelf,*and how aggravated in *him!* And yet,hoping in GOD,he makes this Prayer, *Deliver me from Blood-guiltinefs, O GOD,thou GOD of my Salvation: and my Tongue fhall fing aloud of thy Righteoufnefs.* And this is the fecond Thing to be confidered.

II. I am to obferve upon the *Prayer of David,* with Regard to his dreadful Sin. He *prays*; and 'twas the beftThing he could do. The wifeftCourfe we can take after we have fallen into Sin, is at once to pray for Repentance. If ever *Satan* can keep us from praying, he has us faft enough. If *David* had reftrain'd Prayer, after his Sin, what had become of him then indeed! then he had been ruined without Hope. But he prayed to his GOD: and what faid he; *Deliver me from Blood-guiltinefs, O GOD, thou GOD of my Salvation &c.* Deliver me from it. Happy had it been for *David,* had he made this Prayer, when he was firft tempted to it. But now 'tis paft, he is convinced, that if GOD will pleafe to forgive him, he may yet be delivered. The Man who is pardoned, is in the Sight of GOD, as pure as he who never finned. B 2 III.

III. You obferve the *Argument* which *David* makes ufe of in his Plea for a Pardon. *O GOD, thou GOD of my Salvation.*— Paft Experiences are Arguments for future Favours.—The Name of GOD is his ftrong Tower, to which he flies for Protection. His Name is the GOD of Salvation : Wherefore, for his Name's Sake, *David* urges for a Pardon. *Thou GOD of my Salvation ;* 'Tis as if he had faid, *Thou GOD my SAVIOUR.* This was the Name for the MESSIAH. And under that dark Difpenfation, 'twas as tho' he had faid, *For CHRIST's Sake.* And thus are we to feck Pardon from GOD. Not for the Sake of our own Prayers and Tears, and good Works : But only on the Account of our Saviour's Merits : *O GOD, thou GOD of my Salvation.* Of his own Mercy he faved us. Eph. ii 8. *For by Grace are ye faved, thro' Faith, & that not of your felves ; it is the Gift of GOD.* 'Tis a fatal Miftake, to pray for a Pardon, and think we fhall obtain it for the Sake of the Prayer. Or if we endeavour to repent of Sin, & reform our Lives, it overfets the whole Work, if we depend upon this Repentance and Reformation, and not on GOD our Saviour. Rom. x. 3, 4. *For they being ignorant of GOD's Righteoufnefs, and going about to eftablifh their own Righteoufnefs, have not fubmitted themfelves unto the Righteoufnefs of GOD. For CHRIST is the End of the Law for Righteoufnefs to every one that believeth.* Our whole Argument for a Pardon then, muft be, *O GOD, Thou GOD of my Salvation.* We muft depend upon the Mercies of GOD, and the Merits of our Saviour, for Pardon, and Acceptance, and Reconciliation. After all the vile Crime of *David,* he could make this his Confidence, and take Sanctuary here. There's no Sinner fo great, but here's enough for him, upon his fincere return.

The laft Thing I obferv'd in the Text, was

IV. *David's grateful Refolution* in Cafe GOD forgave him ; and the bleffed *Effect* of pardoning Mercy *My Tongue fhall fing aloud of thy Righteoufnefs.*

Says the Penitent *David,* I am under the Guilt of Bloods—But O my GOD forgive me, and my Tongue fhall shall sing aloud of thy Righteousness. Praise & Thanksgiving are the immediate Practice of every pardoned Sinner. O when a poor Creature has been shaken over the Mouth of Hell, and then sees himself delivered, he is swallowed up in the Love of GOD, and burns with the most lively Gratitude to him. O, says he, what has my GOD done for me! and what shall I render to him! Thou GOD of my Salvation, how can I praise thee enough! Never can I requite thee ; but how shall I testify the Sincerity and Ardors of my Love!

But in the original Text, the Particle *And* is omitted: It runs, *Deliver me from Bloods, O GOD, Thou GOD of my Salvation;—My Tongue shall sing aloud of thy Righteousness.* This expresses the Assurance the Psalmist had, that GOD *had* heard him, and the Joy of Pardon was breaking in. It teaches us, that where-ever true Repentance is, there is certainly Forgiveness. The *English Translation* expresses the *grateful Resentment* of a *Pardon :* the *original Hebrew* declares, the *certain Effect* of *Repentance.* As *David* prays to be delivered, he stops short and says inward, *I am so :* My Tongue *shall* sing aloud of thy Righteousness.

You observe ; If we are pardon'd 'tis because of the Righteousness of GOD our Saviour. This must be imputed to us, if ever we are forgiven by GOD. If after all our Sins, we are again received into Favour, we must not attribute it to our own Merits, but sing aloud of his Righteousness.

You observe, That it is an Act of Justice in GOD to forgive the believing Penitent. CHRIST, in a Word, has paid the full Price of a Pardon for all that repent and believe. 'Tis then a Debt upon GOD's giving us Faith and Repentance : GOD is Righteous when he receives us upon our Repentance and Faith. He may be just, and yet justify him that believeth. 'Tis a great Word, and if GOD had not said it himself, we should not have dar'd to ; I Joh. i. 9. *If we confess our Sins, he is Faithful and Just to forgive us our Sins, and to cleanse us from all Unrighteousness.* Convinced of this, *David* assur'd

of

of the divine Pardon, prepares to fing aloud of the Righteoufnefs of GOD, which firft purchafed, and then beftowed it.

I have now gone thro' the feveral Points of Doctrine
which I intended, and am arriv'd to my Application.

I. From what has been faid, you fee into what dreadful Sins human Nature may fall ; even the beft of Men,
a *David* himfelf, off his Guard, and loofing his Hold of
God, falls into Adultery, Perfidy, Ingratitude, Hypocrify and Murder ! O what Caufe have we to walk
cautioufly and humbly with our God.

II. Let none venture to Sin from the Example of
David. Would any feek to juftify or excufe their own
Wickednefs from this difmal Hiftory ? Do they fay,
David did as bad as we can ? Vain Men, is *David* to be
imitated or no ? If he is, why do you not follow him
in his Repentance, his Devotion, his fteady and long
continued Courfe of Holinefs, as well as in one Act which
he himfelf pronounced deteftable. So that, thou Hypocrite, out of thy own Mouth fhalt thou be condemned. But
if you fay he is not to be imitated, then pray never mention
his Name to paliate or foften thy own Crimes.—'Twas one
of the greateft Agravations of his Sin, that it *gave Occafion to the Enemies of the Lord to Blafpheme.*

III. Let none applaud his own Innocence, when he
compares himfelf with the Falls of *David*. Say not,
how pure am I, who never committed fuch enormous
Crimes ? The Law fays, *Thou fhalt not kill, thou fhalt
not commit Adultery.* Say not, *Thefe have I kept from my
Youth.* 'Twas the proud *Pharifee* who utter'd the profane Boaft, *God I thank thee that I am not as other Men
are, Extortioners, Unjuft, Adulterers, or even as this Publican.* Nay, let him that thinketh he ftandeth, take Heed
leaft he fall. Whilft I have been Preaching of Adultery & Murder, let not the bigger Part of the Audience
think that they have little to do with it. Alas, in this
vile Heart of mine, are the Seeds of all thefe blackeft
Sins. So faid the bleffed Martyr *Bradford,* ftriking
on

on his Breaſt; when he heard of the great Sins of
others. If God ſhould leave us to ourſelves, there's no
Sin ſo vile but the very beſt of us would preſently commit. Nay, who can pronounce himſelf clear, when the
Lord Jesus Christ himſelf, that beſt Expoſiter of the
divine Law, has poſitively declared, *Whoſoever is angry
at his Brother without a Cauſe* is a *Murderer : Whoſoever
looks with irregular Deſire is an Adulterer.* Matth. v. 21,
27. Nay, in the Name of God, I indiĉt every impenitent
Sinner in this great Aſſembly, of Murder, moſt execrable
Murder! You have your Share in the Guilt that has
murdered all Mankind. For *as by one Man Sin enter'd
into the World, and Death by Sin, ſo has Death paſſed upon
all Men, in that all have ſinned.* More than this, every
Time you have committed a Sin, you have given a deadly
Stab to your ruin'd Spirits. He that doth it, deſtroyeth
his own Soul. When you have been about to commit
Sin, how have you once and again felt your Heart miſ-
give, your Conſcience ſmite you. You were that Moment going to kill your Souls : And had you attended,
you had heard them cry out, Murder! And yet, you
have ſtop'd your Ears to their bitter Shreeks, and have
gone on, 'till now perhaps they are wholly dead, quite
inſenſible, and the Spirit of GOD may never work upon
them any more. But what ſay you to that Indiĉtment
of the Apoſtle, Heb. vi. 6. *If they ſhall fall away, it is
impoſſible to renew them again unto Repentance : ſeeing they
crucify to themſelves the Son of GOD afreſh, and put him
to open Shame.* Or what ſhall the profane Approacher to
the Lord's Table ſay to that Indiĉtment, *He is guilty of
the Body and Blood of the Lord.* To every impenitent
Sinner, who ſhall aſk, What has a Sermon to a Murderer
to do with me ? I tell him, as the Prophet from GOD
to *David, Thou art the Man.* The Blood of your murdered Souls cries to Heaven againſt you. Againſt thy
own Life haſt thou done this Thing ! All of us then have
need enough to make the Prayer of my Text, *Deliver me
from Blood-guiltineſs, O GOD, Thou GOD of my Salvation.*
&c.

But

But, I come now to the more particular Application of the Day ; and addrefs the Word of GOD to the poor Malefactor before us in the Terrors of the Shadow of Death.

Ah! poor Daughter of Death, Hear what Meffages I bring you from Heaven, and GOD give you Faith in the Hearing.

Poor Criminal, here you ftand condemned before GOD ; within a few Moments of Death and Eternity. Need I fay any Thing to excite *your* Attention to the Admonitions of Heaven. *You* are too nearly concerned to be a fleepy Hearer. I fhall fpeak to you, as to One juft launching into the invifible World, with the utmoft Fidelity to GOD, my own Soul, and yours.

This is not a Time to give flattering Words, but as far as I can, firft to convince, to affect, to awaken you ; and then to fhew you the right Way to a Pardon, and encourage you to *lay hold* on it.

Ah, unhappy Malefactor! The Voice of the innocent Blood cries aloud from the Ground to Heaven. In many Regards my Text is fuited to you, and your Circumftanc.s are like *David's*. GOD has blefs'd you with a religiousEducation. Like *David* you have been diftinguifhed among your Nation by peculiarFavours ofGOD.

And now, what Improvement did you make of your Advantages ? What Returns did you make to the good GOD that diftinguifhed you ? You are ready in fome Sort to own how difobedient & falfe & mifchievous you have been. GOD gave you a Space to repent,and tried you from Day to Day : But you repented not ; you were hard and incorrigible. GOD provok'd, left you : and you fee what is come of it : Young as you are, ripe for the Vengeance of a capital Execution ! However, He was good to you ftill : and in your long Confinement, in Darknefs & Solitude, he has given youOpportunities to feek his Favour ; and GOD knows how miferably you have improved them.

But, O poor Malefactor, I would not drive you to Defpair. I bring you good Tydings of great Joy, unto
you

you is offer'd a Saviour; Pardon and Life & Salvation.
You know what the Law of GOD says exprefly, Exod.
xx. 13. *Thou ſhalt not kill.* You have read what awful
Words GOD ſpake to *Noah*, Gen. ix. 5, 6. *Surely your
Blood of your Lives will I require : at the Hand of every
Man's Brother will I require the Life of Man. Whoſo ſhed-
deth Man's Blood, by Man ſhall his Blood be ſhed.* You
have been told of that unalterable Sentence of Heaven, Numb. xxxv. 16. *If he ſmite him (ſo that he
die) he is a Murderer : the Murderer ſhall ſurely be
put to Death.* Here, in the Word of GOD, you read your
Crime and your Puniſhment. It would be a Sin in any
ſo much as to wiſh for your Life Prov. xxviii. 17. *A
Man that doth Violence to the Blood of any Perſon, ſhall
flee to the Pit, let no Man ſtay him.* Numb. xxxv. 31.
*Moreover, ye ſhall take no Satisfaction for the Life of a
Murderer, which is guilty of Death : but he ſhall be ſurely
put to Death.*

But tho' you have loſt your Life for this World, there
is yet ſome Hope remaining that you may obtain a bet-
ter. Indeed they are dreadful Words, I Joh. iii. 15. *No
Murderer hath eternal Life.* 'Tis a dreadful Deſcription,
Rev. xxii. 15. Shut out of the holy City, *are Dogs, and
Whoremongers, and Murderers, and whoſoever loveth and
maketh a Lie.* 'Tis a dreadful Declaration, Gal. v. 19, 21.
*The Works of the Fleſh are theſe, Adultery, Fornication,
Uncleanneſs, Murders, Drunkenneſs —— They that do ſuch
Things ſhall not inherit the Kingdom of GOD.* 'Tis a
dreadful Account, Rev. xxi. 8. *The Unbelieving, and the
Abominable, and Murderers, and Whoremongers, and all
Liars, ſhall have their Part in the Lake which burneth
with Fire and Brimſtone ; which is the ſecond Death.*
This, miſerable Creature, muſt be your certain Doom,
if after all, you die impenient. You have fallen into the
Hands of Men, and they have condemned you as not fit
to live : But O you'l find it a fearful Thing to fall into the Hands of the living GOD.

C

But

But yet, after all thefe dreadful Words, I am here, in the Name of CHRIST, to make you another Offer of a Pardon. Like *Nathan*, I would firft convict you: And then, like him, I am to inform you of the Mercies of GOD, and the Hopes of Forgivenefs. You muft be in Agony, but you may not Defpair. Tho' Murder is fuch a flagrant Crime, and the Word of GOD fpeaks fo terribly of it, yet, 'tis no more than what you fee *David* has been pardon'd for before. So was *Manaffeh*, who is now in Glory, after all his Wickednefs & Murders. He fhed innocent Blood very much, which the Lord would not pardon, fo as not to punifh it in this World: No more did he *David's* Murder, but for ever after this was he purfu'd by one Affliction after another, 'till he died: But yet *David* and *Manaffeh* are both now in Paradife, bleffing and admiring the Grace of GOD together: You, poor Criminal, may in a few Hours be with them. 'Twas long before *Manaffeh* repented. Not 'till he was bound with Fetters, and held in Cords of Affliction: II Chron. xxxiii. 11. *And when he was in Affliction he befought the Lord his God, and humbled himfelf greatly before the God of his Fathers, and prayed unto him, and he was entreated of him, and heard his Supplication: Then* Manaffeh *knew that the Lord he is God.* Nay, what Incouragement would you defire, difconfolate Prifoner! The very Men who murdered the Son of God, were pardoned and are now in Heaven. See *Act.* ii. 23. 36 —41.

'Tis true, the innocent Blood cries from the Ground for Vengeance: But yet, the Blood of Sprinkling fpeaketh better Things than the Blood of *Abel*, and this lifts up a prevailing Cry for Pardon & Forgivenefs for you. When the frightned Jailour was going to Murder *him felf*, and cried out, trembling, *What fhall I do to be faved?* The Apoftle anfwered him, *Act.* xvi. 31. *Believe on the LORD JESUS CHRIST, and thou fhalt be faved.* So I fay to you, Prifoner of Death. I fhall explain your Duty in this Thing, and fo conclude my Difcourfe.

Spend

Spend fome of your few Moments in calling to Mind your Sins, in their feveral Argravations, and confefs them as particularly as you can to GOD. He that covereth his Tranfgreffion fhall not profper : But he that confeffeth and forfaketh *fhall find Mercy.*

As you fee yourfelf thus ruin'd on all Hands, now betake yourfelf to GOD in CHRIST. Here, poor Criminal, here's Mercy and plentious Redemption for you. Here's Pardon and Righteoufnefs, Sanctification & eternal Life. Say, O GOD, thou GOD of my Salvation, for thy Names Sake, and for thy Son's Sake, forgive me, and renew me. Submit to GOD your Saviour, and chufe and truft in the bleffed JESUS, as your Prophet, Prieft and King. Renounce your own Righteoufnefs, and depend upon his. Say, *Tho' he flay me, yet will I truft in him.* If God enables you to be fincere and thorough in this, there fhall after all be Joy in Heaven over you. The Prodigal returning fhall be met and embraced by the tender Father.

And now let your Tongue fing aloud of his Righteoufnefs. Plead the Righteoufnefs of your Saviour for your Juftification ; praife and admire this : Adore the Righteoufnefs of GOD, who gives you up for this World ; but offers you a Pardon for the next. Juftify God, and condemn yourfelf. Submit and refign, and fall down before this fovereign and juft GOD. Thus fpend the few Moments of your Life here, and if GOD fhould indeed give you fuch a Heart, in that Hour when you leave this World, the LORD JESUS CHRIST who himfelf fuffered without the Gates, fhall fay to you, as once to the Malefactor at his Execution. *To Day fhalt thou be with me in Paradife.*

But I now turn me to this very great Congregation : And Oh ! Let the chief of Sinners here before GOD, hence learn their Duty, and take Warning. Flee inftantly from the Wrath to come, the Evil which purfue Sinners.

Defpair

Defpair not, my Brethren, but remember *David*, after all his moft horrible Guilt, coming back and receiving Pardon. Sinner as thou art, look into the World of the Bleffed, and there fee the perfected Spirit of this once enormous Offender, amidft Millions of others, once firft in the Ranks of Mifery and Wickednefs, but now the divineft Triumphs of the Redeemer's Blood, and the moft illuftrious Workmanfhip of the Sovereign Spirit. Look into the World of the Bleffed, I fay, and the Holy Ghoft has taught you to repeat, I Cor. vi. 9, 10, 11. *Neither Fornicators, nor Idolaters, nor Adulterers, nor Self-Polluters, nor Abufers of themfelves with Mankind, nor Thieves, nor Covetous, nor Drunkards, nor Revilers, fhall inherit the Kingdom of GOD; and fuch were fome of you: but ye are wafhed, but ye are fanctified, but ye are juftified, in the Name of the Lord Jefus, and by the Spirit of our God.* O Glories of my Context! *Thy Mercy, O GOD! thy Loving-Kindnefs! The Multitude of thy tender Mercies!*

Like *David* then forfake your Sins with the utmoft Abhorrence; retire to plead unbounded Mercy, and lay hold on it for a Pardon. Be convinced of your Tranfgreffions as he was, confefs them with Freedom and Fulnefs, and deep Conviction: But fee the Provifion which a merciful GOD has made for you, in a Sacrifice infinitely preferable to all Burnt-Offerings, in the Death of his Son for you. O unbounded Grace, that gave you this Saviour! And if he fpared not his own Son, but delivered him up freely for us all; how fhall he not in Him freely give us all Things? Pardon, Grace and Glory, and every good Thing?

O the Joys among the Bleffed, at the Converfion of fuch a Sinner as *David*, and as You! More than over ninety nine juft Perfons who need no Repentance. With how much Affection will your heavenly Father run out to meet you; and in Embraces and Kiffes, proclaim, *This my Son was dead and is alive, was loft and is found.*

F I N I S.

GOD the Strength and Portion of His People, **under all**
the Exigences of Life and Death :

A

𝕱uneral Sermon

On the HONOURABLE

Mrs. *Katherine Dummer,*

The LADY of His HONOUR

WILLIAM DUMMER, Efq;
Late Lieutenant-Governour and Commander in Chief
over this Province.

Preach'd at BOSTON, *January* 9. 1752.

The LORD's-DAY after her Death and Burial.

By Mr. 𝕭ylc𝕤.

Pfal. lxxxviii. 18. *My Friend haft thou put far from me ; and my Ac-*
quaintance into Darknefs.
2 Cor. i. 3, 4. *Bleffed be GOD, even the Father of our Lord JESUS*
CHRIST, the Father of Mercies, and the GOD of all Comfort ; who
comforteth us in all our Tribulation, that we may be able to comfort
them who are in any Trouble, by the Comfort wherewith we ourfelves
are comforted of GOD.

BOSTON; N. E. Printed by JOHN DRAPER. 1752.

A FUNERAL SERMON

On the HONOURABLE

Mrs. *KATHERINE DUMMER*.

PSAL. LXXIII. 26.

My Flesh and my Heart faileth : But GOD is the Strength of my Heart, and my Portion forever.

THIS Psalm is the Representation of a good Man battling with Temptations, and coming off victorious. To see the Wicked prosper, and the Holy disappointed and afflicted, has often been a Perplexity to the best Men in the World. *Job's* peevish Friends knew not what to make of it ; and what they could not explain they absolutely denied : They affirmed *Job* must needs be a Hypocrite, or they could never account for the strange Providence towards Him. *David* more than once was harrassed with the same Difficulty : He fretted to see the Wicked at Ease, while the Pious were labouring in great Disquietude, and seemed not to be the Care of a good Providence. And here in my Context, *Asaph* is almost confounded with the same Problem, till a Divine Ray of
Light

Light from the Sanctuary, difpels the Gloom, and dif-
covers the Truth.   See the Ends of the Men : Wait to
obferve the Conclufion of the Matter : for the End
crowns the Work, and (in the trite Maxim) *No Man
can be pronounced happy till he be dead.*   On the one
Hand, what is the End of the Wicked ? See v. 19, 20.
*How are they brought into Defolation, as in a Moment !
They are utterly confumed with Terrors.   As a Dream
when one awaketh, fo, O LORD, when thou awakeft,
thou fhalt defpife their Image.*   Here is the Image of the
wicked Man's Death, and Deftruction after it.   But
open the Scene the other Way, and fee what we can
obferve there.   This is the Text and the Verfe preceeding.   *Whom have I in Heaven but thee ?   and there is
none upon Earth that I defire befides thee.   My Flefh and
my Heart faileth, but GOD is the Strength of my Heart
and my Portion forever.*   What a different Account is
here of the Holy and the Impious ?   How unlike their
Ends, and how various a Face do they wear ?   V. 27,28.
*For lo, they that are far from thee, fhall perifh : thou
haft deftroyed all them that go a whoring from thee.   But
it is good for me to draw near to GOD : I have put
my Truft in the LORD GOD, that I may declare all
thy Works.*

I know there are fome Expofitors who exceedingly
curtail and limit the Senfe of the infpired Pfalmift in the
Text before us.   When he talks of his Flefh and his
Heart failing, they would underftand it only as an Expreffion of Longing and vehement Defire.   As if he had
faid, I am at a Diftance from the Tabernacle of GOD,
and my Flefh and my Heart faileth with Longing to
enjoy GOD there ;   for He *is the Strength of my Heart
and my Portion forever.*   But fure this is a moft im-
poverifhed Sentence in this Interpretation.   I am fully
convinced that the Pfalmift here fpeaks of his Portion
and Strength in GOD, under all the Decays and Ruins
of

of Humane Nature. Suppoſe his Body deſerted by its
Props, and his Fleſh fails under him : Suppoſe his Spirits diſſipated and gone, his Courage flags, and his
Heart beats irregular and reluctant : Suppoſe this World
retreats from his View, and the eternal World opens
before him, then *GOD is the Strength of* his *Heart, and
his Portion forever.* This is, I think, the true genuine
Meaning of the Pſalmiſt in this Place, without any
Thing ſtrained, or forced, or miſapplied.

My Fleſh and my Heart faileth : *But GOD is the
Strength of my Heart, and my Portion forever.* The
Text is, you ſee, divided into two Parts. One expreſ-
ſing the Neceſſities of *Aſaph* : And the other his Relief
under thoſe Neceſſities. And, that I may treat the
Matter juſtly, I ſhall therefore divide my Diſcourſe into
two Parts, agreable to the two Diviſions mentioned.
1. *I ſhall repreſent to you a Man under theſe Circumſtances of my Text : His Fleſh and his Heart failing him.*
2. *I ſhall ſhew the Relief of the pious Man at ſuch Sea-
ſons : GOD the Strength of his Heart, and his Portion
forever.*

I. *I am to repreſent to you a Man under the Circumſtances of my Text : His Fleſh and his Heart failing Him.*

Sometimes this is true in Regard to *Danger* and *Diſtreſs* in which a Man may be involved. His Fleſh upon
him may have Pain, and his Soul within him may
mourn. He may be under the greateſt Difficulty and
Confuſion. Affliction may preſs from all Quarters :
Dangers may threaten ; and his Courage fail at the Proſpect. Outward Wants, and inward Deſertions ; Perſe-
cutions from the Hand of Men, or Temptations from
the Hand of *Satan*, may tire him out. His Fleſh may
be wearied, and his Heart faint, and he may cry out with
Trembling, *I ſhall one Day periſh by the Hand of* Saul.
He

He may be in Pain of Body, and in Terror of Mind, and in all Refpects of Grief and Anguifh anfwer the Exclamation of my Text, *My Flefh and my Heart faileth me.* My Strength wears, my Body pines, and my Refolution holds out no longer.

Again, Sometimes the *Flefh and the Heart* may fail thro' *Defire* and *Expectation. Hope deferred, maketh the Heart fick.* And it is a Phrafe often ufed, the Flefh and Heart failing, to exprefs the impatient Ardors of intenfe Defire. It is a bold, lively and poetical Figure ; and you frequently meet with it in the facred Text. See Deut. xxviii. 32. *Thine Eyes fhall look and fail with longing for them all the Day long.* See the glowing Fervour, *Cant.* v. 6. *My Soul failed when he fpake ; I fought him—I called him.* — And this is a beautiful and natural Defcription of warm Defire. The fond Wifh, the panting Hope, the ardent Expectation of fome great Good : And yet the Time delayed : *Now the Flefh and the Heart fails.* See Pfal. xxxviii. 9, 10. *LORD, all my Defire is before thee ; and my Groaning is not hid from thee. My Heart panteth, my Strength faileth me : as for the Light of mine Eyes, it alfo gone from me.* When the Soul fprings unbounded to a beloved Object ; and yet the Bleffing abfent, or deferred : When the holy Soul reaches after the fenfible Prefence of GOD, and yet he hides his Face, and defers his Vifits, then it cries out inconfolable, *My Flefh and my Heart faileth me.* See Pfal. lxiii. 1, 2. *O GOD, thou art my GOD, early will I feek thee : My Soul thirfteth for thee, my Flefh longeth for thee in a dry and thirfty Land, where no Water is : To fee thy Power and thy Glory, fo as I have feen thee in the Sanctuary.*

Further, Sometimes the *Flefh and the Heart fail* thro' too great *Tranfport* and *Extafy.* Joy may overpower the Heart, and the Flefh may fail under it. So our
Father

Father *Jacob*, at the News of his dear *Joseph*'s Advancement in the Land of *Egypt*, whom he had so long given over, and so often wept as dead ! He could no longer support the growing Rapture, but sunk under the Weight of Joy. Read the moving History, *Gen.* xlv. 25, 26, 27, 28. *And they went up out of Egypt, and came into the Land of Canaan unto Jacob their Father, and told him saying, Joseph is yet alive, and he is Governor over all the Land of Egypt. And Jacob's Heart fainted, for he believed them not. And they told him all the Words of Joseph, which he had said unto them : And when he saw the Wagons which Joseph had sent to carry him, the Spirit of Jacob their Father revived. And Israel said, It is enough; Joseph my Son is yet alive : I will go and see him before I die.* And in like Manner the Queen of the South, when she came to hear the Wisdom of *Solomon*, and saw his Magnificence and unheard-of Glory, she fainted, unable to sustain the Pleasure of the Sight. See 1 King. x. 4, — 9. *And when the Queen of Sheba had seen all Solomon's Wisdom, and the House that he had built, and the Meat of his Table, and the fitting of his Servants, and the Attendance of his Ministers, and their Apparel, and his Cup-bearers, and his Ascent by which he went up unto the House of the* LORD : *there was no more Spirit in her. And she said to the King, It was a true Report that I heard in mine own Land, of thy Acts, and of thy Wisdom. Howbeit, I believed not the Words, until I came, and mine Eyes had seen it : and behold, the half was not told me : thy Wisdom and Prosperity exceedeth the Fame which I heard. Happy are thy Men, happy are these thy Servants, which stand continually before thee, and that hear thy Wisdom. Blessed be the* LORD *thy* GOD *which delighted in thee, to set thee on the Throne of Israel ; because the* LORD *loved Israel for ever, therefore made he thee King, to do Judgment and Justice.* This is the Effect of Joy wound up too high. The feeble Body,

B and

and the trembling Heart are not made for thefe intenfe
Pleafures, in this mortal and finful State.   Even the Joys
of Religion may fometimes fwell too wide for the Breaft
of the good Man :   And he may cry out as did one of
the dying Martyrs, _It is enough_! _Lord, held thy Hand_ ;
the Clay can bear no more !   And fo the Text may be
alfo read, _My Flefh and my Heart faileth_ ; for _GOD is
the Strength of my Heart, and my Portion forever._   This
may be the Reafon why the Pfalmift's Heart failed him :
GOD was his Portion ; his eternal Portion ; and therefore he rejoiced with Joy unfpeakable and infupportable.

Laftly.   _My Flefh and my Heart faileth :_   What a
beautiful and natural Defcription is this of _Sicknefs_ and
Death !   Here is a moft natural Reprefentation of the
Change made by decaying Nature, the near Profpect of
Death, and the wafting Havock of the Grave.

See then a Perfon bloffoming in Rofey Health and
Youthful Vigour, with all the active Powers of Nature
found and lively in him.   His Bones are moift with
Marrow, his Cheeks are full, his Eyes fparkle, his
Heart beats ftrong, and his Pulfes leap high from all their
purple Springs.   Every Limb appears ftrong, and every
Joint moves eafy.   His Breath flows free, his Sinews
brace firm, and his Animal Spirits dart thro' his Nerves,
and beat the vital Road inceffant from the Brain to the
Heart.

This Flefh now looks, you think, very unlikely to
decay and fail.   Add to all this, that the Strength of the
Heart equals the Firmnefs of the Flefh.   The Mufcles
are all elaftick, and. the Courarge holds out unfhaken.
All the Man appears in full Beauty, Health and Vigour :
and every Veffel performs its Functions in perfect Order
and Œconomy.

And

And would you think now that this fair Frame muſt be the Victim of Diſeaſe and Death! That this ſhapely Fabrick muſt be ſhaken down, and drop its ſcattering Honours! A Heart ſo ſtrong, and a Fleſh ſo fair, would you imagine to be ſo eaſily overthrown, and that it ſhould ſink ſo ſuddenly! And yet ſo it is, this Fleſh and this Heart muſt fail us.

Perhaps on a ſudden, while we are in full Purſuit of our Buſineſs : while we walk careleſs thro' a Street, or ſmile joyful in Company ; in the midſt of Hurry, or in the Moment of Diverſion, we may ſuddenly fall down dead. Our Fleſh and Heart may fail at once, and give us no Warning. At once our Breath may gaſp away, our Pulſes ſtop, our Heart may forget to beat, and our Souls leap out, and down ſinks the feeble Fleſh, a ghaſt-ly Load of Clay. Young, and ſtrong, and fair as you now ſeem, this may be your Doom : the Flouriſh may wither, the Glory may fade, and the Fleſh and Heart fail at once.

But ſuppoſe we eſcape a ſudden Death, yet muſt our Fleſh and our Heart fail by ſlow Degrees, and in the Lea-ſure of a lingering Sickneſs. Shall I lead you to the Death-Bed of an expiring Mortal, and ſhow you the Proſpects there, the ſad Proofs and Iiluſtrations of my Doctrine. See then a poor Man under the Languiſhments of a waſt-ing Fever, and behold how his Fleſh fails him. How the Life leaves his Eyes, his Noſtrils are pinched in, and his Lips parched up, and his fur'd Tongue rolls amidſt gathering black Filth, clammy in his thirſty Mouth. His Temples appear wan and ſallow ; his pale Hands tremble ; his faint Voice heſitates ; his looſe Teeth chat-ter : and faultring Accents, and broken Murmurs expreſs the deep Neceſſities of Nature ; beg to be turned in the Bed ; and crave for the cool Draught. How different is this Shadow of a Man from the Friend we lately knew!

The

The Cheeks hollow that were foft and round ; The Eyes funk that were full and vivid ; The Voice hoarfe that was fweet and tuneful ; The Ribs prominent that were hid in Flefh ; and the Limbs pined that were fhaped in exact Proportion. See the melancholy Object ; and how unlike his former Self : Once fair and full, and now quite altered ; his Flefh having all failed him.

But does not his Heart fail him too, at this difmal Seafon ? Yes. His Pulfes undulate, intermit and fink deep. His Heart dilates, and contracts with Pain: It pants, and throbs, and flutters in his Breaft. Its ftrong Mufcles relax, and the Blood coagulates in its Hollows. His Lungs hang flabby, and catch the Air by Fits, which rattles in the Wind-pipe, and cools upon the Lips. Now the Friends whifper foft about the Curtains, and the Phyfician infinuates his Danger in ambiguous Hints, and doubtful Forms of Speech. Now the Minifter prays for the departing Spirit, and faithfully warns the dying Man to prepare for the Change juft before him. Here lies the Carcafe half dead, panting, fainting, cold, and haftening to the State of a Corpfe. The Profpects of Life are wholly over ; the Eternal World in a near View, and the Soul, no longer to be retained, fhakes it's Wings to be gone. And now afk the poor Man how he feels, and will he not tell you, *O Sir, my Heart fails me ! It is one Thing to think of Death at a Diftance, and another to fee it fo near. O what would I give for an affured Pardon ! When I reflect how carelefs I have lived, and fee I am now dying, my Courage is all gone : my Heart finks and dies within me.*

Here now is the Picture of a dying Man. This is the bold Youth that a few Days ago could defy Heaven and out-brave Omnipotence, with Lewdnefs and Intemperance, Oaths and Blafphemy. Where is his Fortitude now, that intrepid Air, and undaunted Front, with which

which he ufed to ridicule poor-fpirited Virtue, and gave a Sanction to his Vices ? Alas, he appears not what he was. He trembles at the Approach of Death, his Body wafts ; and his Courage finks ; his *Flefh and his Heart fail* him.

Thus I have given you the Cafe of Human Nature ; how brittle is it, and how foon diffolved ! The Holy and the Impious are alike in this, they muft all die ; and their Flefh and their Heart muft fail together. Of the Wicked this is a true Account, *Job.* xi. 20. *But the Eyes of the Wicked fhall fail, and they fhall not efcape, and their Hope fhall be as the giving up of the Ghoft.* And of the Pious it is alike evident and certain, *Pfal.* xii. 1. *Help, Lord, for the godly Man ceafeth ; for the Faithful fail from among the Children of Men.*

Thus far then I have only led you to the fick Bed, and the Coffin, will you now travel a little further, and take a folitary Walk among the Tombs ? Here are the Evidences of my Doctrine thick fcattered thro' all the hollow Ground. Here a Harveft of Grave-Stones rifes up over the green Turf, from a thoufand Corpfes beneath, to inform us whofe Body lies under, the Flefh all failed, and the Bones haftening after it. Here are Spectacles, how ghaftly and loathfome ? And what fad Proofs of my Propofition ? The Skin once fo fair, broken and dropt away : The Flefh fo foft, gathered into a Mafs of Corruption ; or mouldered to black Clay ; or dried to fine Duft : The Bones fo firm, loofened from one another, and lying in dark Diforder thro' the Coffin. The Flefh and the Skin gone, you fee the Place where the *Heart* once was, thro' the opening Ribs : And lo ! Nothing now but a Lump of noifom Clay, or black Mold, lies in the hollow Trunk. Only enter a Tomb, and lift up the Lid of a Coffin, and all this prefents to your View ; and a doleful Voice comes from thence,

My

MY FLESH AND MY HEART FAILETH! But I may not ftay too long in this damp and barren Region : Only I obferve to you, that thus far the Proof of the Doctrine has been growing : And Death and the Grave proclaim the Truth, the *Flefh and* the *Heart fail.*

I fhall juft add here, that this is true alfo in the Infirmities of *Old Age.* Suppofe we efcape early Death, and fudden Difeafe, yet fee old Age coming on, with all its gloomy Train of Attendants, and now the funk Heart labours, and the feeble Flefh totters to its Fall. Cold Palfies fhake the Limbs, the Ears grow deaf, and the Eyes dim ; the whole Animal Nature diffolves by Piecemeals, and down goes the hoary Head with Sorrow to the Grave. See the lively and poetical Defcription of it, in *Eccl.* xii. 1, — 7. *Remember now thy Creator in the Days of thy Youth, while the evil Days come not, nor the Years draw nigh, when thou fhalt fay, I have no Pleafure in them ; While the Sun, or the Light, or the Moon or the Stars be not darkened, nor the Clouds return after the Rain : In the Day when the Keepers of the Houfe fhall tremble, and the ftrong Men fhall bow themfelves, and the Grinders ceafe becaufe they are few, and thofe that look out of the Windows be darkened, and the Doors fhall be fhut in the Streets, when the Sound of the grinding is low, and he fhall rife up at the Voice of the Bird, and all the Daughters of Mufick fhall be brought low ; alfo when they fhall be afraid of that which is high, and Fears fhall be in the Way, and the Almond-tree fhall flourifh, and the Grafhopper fhall be a Burden, and Defire fhall fail : becaufe Man goeth to his long Home, and the Mourners go about the Streets : Or ever the filver Cord be loofed, or the golden Bowl be broken, or the Pitcher be broken at the Fountain, or the Wheel broken at the Ciftern. Then fhall the Duft return to the Earth as it was : and the Spirit fhall return unto GOD who gave it.*

I

I have now gone thro' the firſt Part of my Deſign, and repreſented to you the State of Man, his Fleſh and his Heart failing. It remains that I briefly ſpeak to the ſecond Point.

II. *When our Fleſh and our Heart faileth, the only Relief can be this of my Text,* G O D *the Strength of our Heart and our Portion forever.* Happy was it for *Aſaph* that he could make ſuch a Speech, and had ſuch a Ground of Comfort. Let us here run over the former Heads, and ſee how the Fact can be made out.

Suppoſe our Hearts fail us in *Danger* and *Diſtreſs,* yet if *G O D is* our *Strength and* our *Portion forever,* here is inſtant Succour and Support : We can have no *Diſtreſs* that he cannot enable us to bear : nor any *Danger* that he cannot ward off from us. If we are in Want, Here is a rich Portion for us. If we are bereaved, Here is a Subſtance that endures, a Portion forever. If we are in Hazard, we can have no Fear that this will leave us : And if we are deſtitute of every other Good, Here is infinitely enough to ſupply our Neceſſities, and ſatisfy our Deſires.

But ſuppoſe our Wiſhes graſp at a diſtant Good, and our Eyes look and fail with Longing : now, gracious Soul, renew your Choice of GOD, and let this Comfort you, Aſk your ſelf, ' What is it I pant after ? What is ' there truly Excellent in the Thing I deſire ? It was ' my GOD gave it all this Beauty, and from his Ful-' neſs they have all received. Is he not then infinitely ' better ? nay has he not in him the ſame Lovelineſs, ' but infinitely brighter ? Well then, If He is my Por-' tion, I have enough. I can at any Time ſlake my ' Thirſt here, and receive *above all* I can *aſk or think.*

Now indeed your Flesh and your Heart may fail another Way. You may cry out, *Who am I, O LORD GOD, and what is my House, that thou hast brought me hitherto!* You may be swallowed up, and even faint away with a Transport too big ; a pure Extafy too intenfe for mortal Flesh and Blood. GOD your Portion : the Infinite GOD : and Yours ! O Rapture too wide for the Breast of Man ! Well may his *Flesh and* his *Heart fail*, for GOD *is* his *Portion forever.* It is well he is *the Strength of* the *Heart* too, or the Joy would be too vast ; It would fwell the Breast, It would ftretch the Heart-Strings, and lick up the Soul.

But alas, After all this facred Delight, muft not the holy Man die, and faint in the Agonies of Expiring Nature ? After all his Communion with GOD, fee how the poor Man gafps away his Breath, and ftruggles in the laft Convulfions. See the Languors of his Eyes, and the Labour of his Heart, and lo ! no Difference between the Righteous and the Wicked : For we fee that *Wife Men die, likewife the Fool and the Bruitifh Perfon perifh, and how dieth the wife Man ? as the Fool : One Event happeneth to them all.* But Oh ! ftop the Rafh Judgment, and fee the Difference. Amidft all this Pain and Agony, the Shipwrack of diffolving Nature, O how calm within, how ravifhed is the holy Soul ! His *Flefh and* his *Heart fail* him, it is true : But at once his Courage returns, and his GOD *is the Strength of* his *Heart.* All the good Things of this World leave him ; and he has Nothing more to do with his Inheritance on Earth : But now his GOD fills his Soul, and becomes his Portion forever. Death, which puts a Period to all the Poffeffions of a wicked Man, cannot at all affect the Portion of the Holy. Nor Life, nor Death can feperate him from the Love of GOD, which is in CHRIST JESUS our Lord. It is no Matter what the outward Circumftances of his Death are, all is fecure within. *Mark the*

*the perfect Man, and behold the Upright ; for the End
of that Man is Peace.*

Shall we be a little particular here, and enquire into
the Force of the Text ?   Man, as Scripture † and Philofophy feem to agree, is compounded of three Parts, the
Spirit, the *Soul*, and the *Body*. There is a fpiritual Part,
a rational and immortal *Spirit*. There is the animal and
fenfitive Principle, a *Soul*, which we fee the Beafts have
in common with us. And there is the vifible and grofs
Body. That which is in fome Places called the *Soul*, is
in others called the *Life* ; and in my Text is termed
the *Heart*. This feems to be the Link between the immortal Spirit, and the earthly Body, and connects them
both together. This is the Medium by which the rational
Spirit perceives fenfible Objects, and acts upon them.
What becomes of this middle Principle when the Body
dies, has been a Problem among Philofophers. Some
have imagined it to die with the Body, as does the Soul
of the Brute ; and others have made ftill more whimfi-
cal Conjectures * about it. But my Text feems to have
provided better for it, and to infinuate, that it goes with
the intelligent, rational Spirit ; accompanies it into the
other World ; and attends it as it's Vehicle, to fupply

† 1 *Thef.* v. 23.
* For Inftance, *Homer* tells us, after the Body of *Hercules* had been
confumed on the *Funeral Pile*, that the *Soul* was with the *Shades* in
the *Regions of the Dead below* : and the *Spirit* was among the *Gods* in
Heaven. Vid. O.*dys.* L. xi. v. 600.   And fo in the *Iliad.*
　'*Tis certain when the Man diffolves in Death,*
　The Heavenly Mind *furvives th' expiring Breath :*
　The Soul *too glides, the groffer Body dead,*
　A femblant Form, and unfubftantial Shade.
And *Paracelfus*, and other more modern Philofophers of the *Enthufiaftic
Turn*, fuppofe that as the *immortal Spirit* afcends to *GOD* the Judge ;
and as the *Body* returns to its firft Principles of *Earth* and *Water* : So
this *middle Soul*, after the Death of the *Body*, wanders for a Time in
the Air, longer or fhorter, according to the Strength of its Conftitution, and then diffolves, as the Flame of a Candle goes out, and re-
verts to is original Elements of *Air* and *Fire*.

C

in

in fome Meafure, the want of the Body till the Refurrection.   So that when the Man's Flefh fails, and hisBody
pines on towards the Grave ; and when his Heart fails,
that is, perhaps, this middle Spirit which connects the
Soul and Body together, then GOD is the Strength of the
Heart, this *fenfitive Soul,* and keeps it from diffolving,
that like the Cloathing of the Spirit, it may attend it into
the other State.   *For we that are in this Tabernacle do
groan, being burthened ; not for that we would be un-
cloathed, but cloathed upon, that Mortality might be
fwallowed up of Life,* 2 Cor. v. 4.   So that while the *Spirit
of a Beaft goeth downward to the Earth, the Spirit of a
Man goeth upward, is given up, to GOD who gave it.*

But if this fhould be thought a precarious Interpretation, I am very willing to underftand the Text in the
common Acceptation.   Here then you fee a dying Man,
his Flefh failing, pining, falling down :   His Heart at
the fame Time failing too ; ceafing to beat with Life, or
rife with Comfort or Courage : and under all this, GOD
ftrengthens his Servant to bear the Burthen, and gives
Comfort and Revival to the Heart : Anon the Man dies
in Earneft ; and then this fame GOD becomes his *Portion
forever,* in another World.

But look into the Grave, and fee if this Portion in
GOD, and Support from him will hold good there too.
See the wide Havock of Death, and the ignominious
Ruins of humane Nature, fcattered in thefe filent Vaults.
But O how joyful and certain a Truth revives our
Hopes in my Text !   Lo, now *GOD is the Strength of
my Heart and my Portion forever.*   Therefore *my Heart
is glad, and my Glory rejoiceth, my Flefh alfo fhall reft in
Hope.*   This Duft remains ftill the Ruins of a Temple of
GOD.   This fleeping Carcafe, and mouldering Clay,
continues to be a Member of CHRIST ; in a gracious
Covenant with him ; a near Relation, and a clofe Union
                                                          to

to him. GOD regards the dead, decayed Body, and watches the fcattering Atoms, as they wander from it, with a complacent and exact Eye : He will recollect them ; He will replace them ; He will infpire them anew to Life ; and dart the Soul again into its old Manfion, refined, illuftrious, immortal. What tho' the Flefh be all failed, and the Bones be all wafted, and there be not fo much as the Sign of the Heart remaining ? Yet for all fhall the Text prove divinely true, and GOD be *the Strength of* our *Heart, and* our *Portion forever.* Job xiv. 14, 15. *If a Man die fhall he live again ? All the Days of my appointed Time will I wait till my Change come. Thou fhalt call, and I will anfwer thee ; thou wilt have a Defire to the Work of thy Hands.* Thus fhall we be called from the Grave, thus fhall we anfwer the Call, thus fhall our GOD regard us and defire us ; thus fhall he raife and fill us ; thus fhall we *behold his Face in Righteoufnefs, and be fatisfied when we awake with his Likenefs.* When he fhall appear, we fhall appear with him inGlory. He who will renew ourStrength, will be our Portion forever.

I have now offered the devout Hints I intended under the Doctrinal Confideration of the Words, and I conclude with a few Deductions from them.

INF. 1. From what we have heard we conclude the Advantages of fincere Religion. What an ample and enduring Inheritance makes up the Portion of the good Man ? GOD is his Portion forever. What a wife Choice has he made ? And how happy and fatisfied is he ? If GOD is his, and CHRIST is his, all is his. Here is a Poffeffion, how wide ! how vaft ! how indefinite and interminable ! See the Catalogue of his Goods, the Inventory of his Eftate, 1 Cor. iii. 21, 22, 23. *All Things are your's : whether Paul, or Apollos, or Cephas, or the World, or Life, or Death, or Things prefent, or Things*

to

to come ; *all are yours, and ye are CHRIST's, and CHRIST is GOD's.* Thus large are his Poſſeſſions ; and they are as laſting as they are large. The *Pleaſures of Sin* are but *for a Seaſon* ; but here are *Pleaſures forever-more.* The Riches of Earth *flee away* ; but theſe are *durable Riches.* No earthly Good can ſatisfy an immortal Mind : but in this GOD there is *Fulneſs of Joy.* If we had all the Pleaſures of Senſe, and all the Improvements of the Mind, deſtitute of the Love of GOD, and a Portion in him, miſerable Wretches were we : For theſe will all ceaſe, and decay, and fail under us. *Charity never faileth* ; *but whether there be Propheſies, they ſhall fail* ; *whether there be Tongues, they ſhall ceaſe* ; *whether there be Knowledge, it ſhall vaniſh away.* Nay, *our Fleſh and our Heart ſhall fail : But GOD is the Strength of our Heart, and our Portion forever.* O bleſſed Man then, who has choſen this good Part which can never be taken away ! Theſe ſhall be *ſatisfied with the Fatneſs of thy Houſe, and thou ſhalt make them to drink of the Stream of thy Delights.*

2. Hence the Folly and Miſery of Sinners. Will they yet *have Confidence in the Fleſh ?* How wrong do they judge ! How fooliſhly do they chooſe ! How miſerably are they diſappointed ! They reject GOD, and chooſe the Creature : They give away their Felicity in him, and chooſe theſe for their Portion. Ah ! miſ-judging, abandoned Men, what have you done ? They ſay to the Almighty, depart from us ; and at the ſame Time purſue the World, and gratify their Senſes, and heap up Treaſures in a vain Earth. Poor Men, when Death ſhall quickly call you away, *whoſe ſhall all theſe Things be ?* When your Fleſh and your Heart fail, what Portion have you in Reſerve ? *What will become of your Hope, when GOD ſhall take away your Soul ?* No Portion in GOD ; no Treaſure in another Life ; no Joys in Reverſion,—behold the gloomy Hour of Death, and how the

poor

poor Soul trembles upon the Edges of the eternal World ! and in it leaps, to hideous Darknefs and eternal Flames. Now all his gilded Hopes fail him : His Eyes grow dim to the Sweets of Light, and the Charms of Beauty : His Ears wax deaf to Strings of Mufick, and tuneful Airs : His Flefh trembles and his Heart faints, and no Dawn of Comfort to refrefh the Shades, or chafe the Horrors. Nothing laid up for this difmal Seafon : and now naked, abandoned, forlorn, the Soul appears before a GOD, whofe Anger is incenfed, whofe Arm is almighty, whofe Juftice is inexorable, and whofe Exiftence is eternal. Inftead of GOD the Strength of the Heart and the Portion forever, they fhall have their *Portion with Hypocrites* : *there fhall be Weeping and Gnafhing of Teeth. This is thy Lot, and the Portion of thy Meafure from me, faith the Lord, becaufe thou haft forgotten me, and trufted in Falfhood.*

And now what remains but the Exhortation.

3. Hence let us all choofe our Portion in GOD. This, my Brethren, is the only folid and enduring Subftance : for all Things elfe will fail you. But if this be your Choice, you will be full ; you will be fatisfied ; you have an Happinefs commenfurate to your Defire, and parallel with your Exiftence.

This has been the Wifdom of the Juft all along, as you find in the facred Records. *Abraham* and *Mofes,* and *David* and *Afaph,* and all the ancient Worthies, were famous for this Grace. It was this very Thing diftinguifhed them from the wicked World. And now their Flefh and their Heart have failed them, he *ftill* remains the Strength of their Heart and their Portion forever. The Time would fail me, fhould I mention the Names of the Fathers, who, being dead, yet fpeak the Truth of my Doctrine ; their GOD ftill remaining, *the GOD of Abraham, the GOD of Ifaac, and the GOD of Jacob* ;

Jacob; *not the GOD of the Dead but of the Living.*
They chofe GOD ; and now they are gone to him, and
receive him as their Portion. Their Faith we are to
follow, confidering the End of their Converfation.

But above all, Let us *look off* unto JESUS, who is the
brighteft Example of this : and whofe dying Agony proclaimed his Choice of GOD alone —*My GOD*! *my GOD!*

And now would we make GOD our Portion ? See
the Way. We muft go to him fheltered by the Wings
of JESUS. He muft make our Peace for us, and then
prefent us in his own Merits to GOD. Now GOD will
be well-pleafed with us, and after all ourRebellions, adopt
us as his Sons : and *if Children, then Heirs, Heirs of
GOD, and Joynt-Heirs with JESUS CHRIST, to an
Inheritance incorruptible, undefiled, and that fadeth not
away, referved in Heaven for us.* GOD himfelf will be
the *Portion of our Inheritance* : and what can we wifh for
more ? We muft bid adieu to our Poffeffions on Earth ;
—But *when all thefe Things fail, we fhall be received into
everlafting Habitations.*

It is with this Satisfaction that we part with our pious
Friends ; and this is the *Confolation of GOD* which I
bring to the mourning Family here before him, under
the great Bereavement of the laft Week, in the Death
of the Honourable Mrs. *Dummer.* The Honours of her
Blood and Alliance ; the Dignity and Gracefulnefs of her
Perfon ; the Superiority and Improvements of her
Genius ; and her Politenefs and Elegance of Converfation, are befide the Decorum of the Pulpit. My Bufinefs
is not to celebrate the Dead, but to inftruct the Living.
As therefore it becomes me to omit thefe, fo it were
criminal Silence not to fpeak of an Example of fuch diftinguifhed Charms, for Piety to GOD, and Benevolence
to Men. You, the Congregation in this Place, can witnefs
to

to the fteady, I had almoft faid *unrivaled*Conftancy of her
Attendance here. When faw you her Seat empty? Perhaps moft of you ftill found her *before* you daily *waiting*
in the Temple. No Difficulties of Heat,or Cold, or Rain,
or Tempeft would fhe plead as an Excufe to prevent her.
Follow her from hence to her Family, and her Clofet :
And what a Beautiful and Regular Œconomy in the
one ! and what an uniform Retirement to the other ! To
thofe around her, *She opened her Mouth with Wifdom* ;
and on her Tongue was the Law of Kindnefs : While all obferved her Defigns to cultivate her own Mind, and be a
Blefling in her Turn to others. She flung an additional
Lufter on her Hufband *when he was known in the Gates,*
and fat at the Head *of the Elders of the Land.* In all Matters of Honefty and Juftice,fhe had a peculiarDelicacy; ard
was exact to a great Degree of Nicenefs. Her Faith as a
Chriftian fhe kept inviolate : and while fhe paid a fteady
and univerfal Regard to the Divine Laws ; none profeffed
a greater Attachment to the Righteoufnefs and Merits of
JESUS alone, for her Acceptance with the Holy GOD.
One would have expected that fuch a Principle, and fuch
Practices fhould be magnified by a Peace in Death : and
fo it moft remarkably appeared. Tho' in her Life-Time
She was held much in Bondage thro' Fear of Death ; and
in former Illneffes, expreft great Anxieties, left She
fhould deceive herfelf in Affairs of Eternity ; yet, thro'
all the painful Hours of her Laft Sicknefs, She obtain-
ed the entire Victory. I never left her without her
earneftly preffing me in a low whifper, not to be obferved by the Company, efpecially her Hufband, whofe
Heart fhe knew could not bear it, *O Sir, Lift not up one*
Petition for my Return to fuch a World as this : And yet
to *her* a World of as eafy and pleafant Circumftances as
any of the Children of *Adam* have found it. It was She
that lead me to the Review of this Text, for your
Entertainment this Day : When, with all her Prefence
of Mind about her, She directed to the Place and ordered

ed it to be read for the Solace of her dying Hours, *Whom have I in Heaven but Thee?* *And there is none upon Earth that I desire besides thee* : *My Flesh and my Heart faileth: But GOD is the Strength of my Heart, and my Portion forever.* This was the Language of her Health, and the Experience of her last Moments. O, said she to me, *I long, I long to be in a World where I shall do Nothing but love, and admire, and adore my GOD thro' Eternity!* So she finished. And what can we, our Friends, left a little while behind, desire more than such an happy Death, after such an Exemplary Life. This glorious Support, must I in a particular Manner, offer to *Your* HONOUR, while you *mourn* with such abundant *Hope* : and can, looking ardently forward, as the great Ruler of the ancient People of GOD, say, *I shall go to her, but she shall not return to me.* In the Course of *Your* HONOUR's past Life, and particularly by this Bereavement, you have *seen an End of all Perfection.* And now, prest down as you must needs be, *The Eternal GOD be your Refuge, and underneath the Everlasting Arms.* *GOD remember you for Good, according to all the Good which you have done for this People; and spare you according to the Greatness of his Mercy, in CHRIST JESUS.*

But O the joyful Hour ! when we shall meet again, with our departed Friends, in the Palaces of Endless Glory ! There we shall remember, and recount the sacred Hours. spent together in the imperfect Worship of the World below : and, in quite another Manner, unite in the *Hallelujahs* of Heaven, without a jarring String, or an absent Voice, or a wandering Thought thro' the Round of a vast Eternity ! There is no more Separation, no more Death, no more Sin, what shall I say ? No more Temptation to Sin forever : *And GOD shall wipe away all Tears from our Eyes.*

𝔞 𝔐 𝔈 𝔑.

Mr. Byles's

S E R M O N

At the

O R D I N A T I O N

Of his Son.

THE Man of GOD throughly furnished to every Good Work.

A

SERMON

PREACHED AT THE

ORDINATION

Of the Reverend

Mr. *MATHER BYLES,*

To the PASTORAL OFFICE

In the First Church of CHRIST in *New-London,* Nov. 18. 1757.

To which is added the CHARGE given Him upon that Occasion.

● ～～～～～～～～～～～～～～～～～～～～ ●

BY His FATHER.

● ～～～～～～～～～～～～～～～～～～～ ●

Prov. xxiii. 15, 16. *My Son, as thine Heart shall be wise, my Heart shall rejoice, even mine. Yea, my Reins shall rejoice, when thy Lips speak right Things.*

✳✳

NEW-LONDON:

Printed and Sold by NATHANAEL GREEN, and TIMOTHY GREEN, *junr.* MDCCLVIII.

AN

Ordination SERMON.

II. TIM. III. 17.

----*That the Man of GOD may be perfect, throughly furnished unto all good works.*

THE Apoſtle *Paul* is here writing a Letter of Inſtructions to his Beloved Son *Timothy*, to furniſh him for the Work of the Miniſtry, and the Service of the Church. *Timothy* was a young Man of pious Deſcent, and peculiarly happy in that religious Education which he had received from his gracious Anceſtors. He was now called to the Miniſtry in the Church of CHRIST, and theſe are the Charges which *Paul* the aged gives to the youthful Paſtor. The Apoſtle concludes his awful Addreſſes, with an Encomium upon the Scriptures, and referring his Pupil to them. *From a Child thou haſt known* them, ſays he : And they were given, *That the Man of GOD might be perfect, throughly furniſhed to every good Work.*

The Words teach us, firſt, that *The Miniſter is the Man of GOD.* From him Miniſters derive their Commiſſion, and they come in his Name. To him they

they are given up and confecrated ; and his Doctrines they bring ; and his Image they bear in their holy Examples. *The Man of GOD*, is the ancient and venerable Style for the Prophets infpired, and the Angels appearing in Humane Shape. *Mofes* and *Elias*, the moft diftinguifh'd Prophets, were furnamed *the Men of GOD* : And the Meffenger promifing the Birth of *Samfon*, is fometimes the *Man of GOD*, and fometimes the *Angel of the LORD.* This reverend and auguft Style for infpired Prophets, and defcending Angels, under the Old Teftament, is in the New, applied to the humble Minifter in the Gofpel Church. The devoted Paftor is the Man of GOD. 'Tis a high Title ; a grand Appellation : But yet to us it belongs, and we claim it who are dedicated to GOD, and folemnly fet apart for his fpecial Service.

The Gofpel Minifter is the Man of GOD, for he is *called by GOD* into the Miniftry --*Called as was* Aaron ; not indeed in a miraculous and fupernatural Manner, as was ufual in the early Days of Infpiration : But yet called by the Providence and the Spirit of GOD, and by thefe led into his Office. GOD gives the Man a Turn of Soul, a Bent of Genius this Way ; he naturally inclines to this facred Work, and he burns to do Good to Souls, and edify the Church in more immediate Efforts and conftant Labours. Thus while the Propenfity of his Heart, and Impreffions from GOD, determine his Choice of this Divine Employment ; The concurring Circumftances of Providence, and the Election of fome Church make it clear that Heaven invites him into his Office : In the Voice of the People is the Call of GOD.

And now he is *folemnly fet apart for the Service of GOD.* He comes under a peculiar Confecration to the Work of Heaven. He is fanctified by Prayer,

and

and bleſſed in the Name of God ; he is led out before the great Congregation, dedicated by the Impoſition of Hands, and the Preſbytery pronounce over him, in the Name of Christ, *This is a Man of GOD.*

Now his whole *Life is to be devoted to GOD.* Now all his Powers, and all his Actions belong immediately to Christ and the Church. Now he is emphatically a Man of God ; and belongs to Him as his peculiar Property. He muſt now be for God, and for none other : *Whoſe I am, and whom I ſerve.*

Now boldly he *comes in the Name of GOD,* and acts by His Authority and Commiſſion. He brings the Doctrines of God, and declares His Will : The Repreſentative of God, and in ſome lower ſenſe, an Ambaſſador from him. God ſends him with his expreſs Mandates, and he comes literally a Man of God.

Now *ſee how he Lives* ; the Piety of his Soul, and the Luſter of his Example, go with him from the Cloſet to the Family ; from his Study to his Viſits ; from his Daily Converſations to his Labours in the Pulpit ; and ſee how he breathes and favours of God. Do not his ſerious Deportment, and his gracious Language, conſpire to proclaim him a Man of God ? How like God is he, in the Courſe of his Life, and the Temper of his Mind ?

But tho' I may not ſtay upon theſe Thoughts, yet as I would have my Diſcourſe as practical as I can, I know not how to leave them without ſome devout Reflections.

I. How *honourable* is the Work of the Miniſtry ? 'Tis an elevated Dignity, and a ſublime Character to be a Man of God. Strange ! that ſuch Duſt, and ſuch Sinners as we are, ſhould be rais'd to it ! 2. What

2. What an Inconfiftent Thing is a *wicked Minifter*? An unholy Divine ; a blind Watchman ; a wolfifh Shepherd ; an ignorant Angel ; a Star of Darknefs ; what Nonfenfe is this ! An ungodly Man of GOD ! what a Solecifm ? what a Monfter ? How it founds, to have a Minifter of CHRIST, an Idoliter of the World ? An Example to the Flock, a Slave to his Lufts ? A Preacher of the Gofpel, Profane, Lewd, Vicious ? Nothing can be more odious, more abfurd. Rom. ii. 21. *Thou that preacheft a Man fhould not Steal, doft thou Steal? Thou that fayeft a Man fhould not commit Adultery, doft thou commit Adultery? Thou that abhoreft Idols, aeft thou commit Sacriledge ?* With what Heart or Face can the impudent Wretch publickly condemn a Sin which his confcious Soul tells him, Thou art guilty of ? How can he fay the Unbeliever is condemned ; while his own Confcience replies, *Thou art the Man?* How can he perfwade Men to renounce a Portion here below, whofe own Mind choofes thefe idle Poffeffions ? (a) *But thou, O Man of GOD ; flee thefe Things : and follow after Righteoufnefs, Godlinefs, Faith, Love, Patience, Meeknefs.*

3. Let the pious Minifter bear this his Character much in Mind, *I am a Man of GOD.* Let him think upon all Occafions, what Wifdom, Gravity, Inftruction, Holinefs fhould always wait upon one in my Station ? Let his facred Office be much in his Eye : guard his Heart, feafon his Converfation, and regulate his Actions. When he is tempted let him think, Should a Man of GOD do fo ? *Shall fuch a Man as I flee ?* When he is afflicted, abufed, perfecuted, let him think, How fhould a Man of GOD bear, refign and be exemplary ? let this Thought run through his Study and his Life ; How prayerful, how watchful, how deligent fhould

I be, who lay Claim to the Title, *a Man of GOD.* (*a*) *O LORD GOD, keep this forever in the Imagination of the Thoughts of the Heart of thy Servant, and prepare His Heart unto thee?*

But I muſt not tarry here : The ſecond Doctrine that waits for our Conſideration, is this.

II. Miniſters of CHRIST muſt labour to be *Perfect* in their ſacred Work. *That the Man of GOD may be* Perfect, *throughly furniſhed unto all Good Works.*

Perfection, in the ſtrict Senſe of the Word, is not attainable by us in our preſent State. No Miniſter was ever Perfect in his Work. His Knowledge, his Labour, his Piety, were always ſomewhere defective. Even our Apoſtle himſelf, who came as near the Character as any Man, yet had his Foils and Deficiencies. *Not,* ſays he, (*b*) *as though I had already attained, or were already Perfect.* However, this ſhould be our Endeavour, to come as near Perfection as ever we can : and furniſh our ſelves for all our Work, as much as we are able.

Shall I here give you the Idea of a Perfect Miniſter ? I mean, of ſuch an one as may be in Reality, and not meerly Ideal. A Man furniſhed for his Work : but a mortal Man ſtill. A Man of like Paſſions, Frail and Sinful : But Sanctified and Prepared ?

Attend then, while, in the Name and Fear of GOD, I attempt to inſtruct you, my Son ; and to affect my ſelf with the Character I would wiſh to attain ; which I gaze at, and labour after, and go before you in.

The Man of GOD Perfect : Before the firſt Thing in his Character is, He muſt be a Regenerated, *Holy*

B

Holy Man. (a) Walk before me, and be thou Perfect.
He muſt have gone through a Converſion to GOD.
He muſt have an Experimental Acquaintance with
the Doctrines of Repentance, Faith, Love to GOD,
and Benevolence to Mankind. He muſt feel upon
his own Soul, a deep Impreſſion of thoſe Truths
which he preaches to others. Beſure he can never
be a Perfect Miniſter, who is not ſo much as a
good Chriſtian. But more than this : He muſt
be a Man of *eminent Sanctity.* It will not do for
him to reſt in the lower Forms of Chriſtianity.
He muſt *fear* GOD *above many.* A Fault might
be excuſed in another, that would be intolerable
in him. That which might paſs for Mirth and
Humour in a common Man, would in him be
Froth, and Levity, and Grimace : The Buffoon
grafted on the Divine. No ; He muſt be Grave,
Temperate, Sober, Meek. He muſt ſhine as an
Example in every Eye : and lead the Way to every
Duty in his Practice, which he recommends and
urges in his Sermons. His Life muſt be a Tran-
ſcript of his Sermons ; a living Comment upon them.
How abaſh'd muſt he needs look, to hear his
Actions cited, to confront his Doctrines ? This
then is the firſt Thing : This muſt be laid in the
Baſis of the ſacred Character. It is a dark Thing
for a Man to come into the Miniſtry, the Sins of
his Youth not repented of : and a Stranger to
vital Religion. But this is not all.

Natural *Good Senſe, Learning,* and *Improvement
of Mind,* enter into the Idea of a finiſhed Miniſter.
A Man may be an honeſt Chriſtian, and but a
miſerable Preacher. *Paul* was a Scholar, before he
commenced a Divine : And the other Apoſtles
were immediately inſpired from Heaven, to ſupply

(a) *Gen. xvii.* 1.   their

their Defects in humane Learning. He that gives
Light to others, had need have double Light himfelf.
A Minifter then, fhould be a Man of univerfal
Knowledge. Efpecially, he fhould have an intimate
Acquaintance with his Bible ; and be a thorough
Student in Divinity, in all its Branches and Connections.
He fhould be able to reafon upon the Points of
his Faith. He fhould underftand the Controverfies
of the Polemical Syftems ; and be a ready Cafuift
to the doubting Mind. He fhould have a Good
Tafte for Writing : And be truly Learned, without
Pedantry ; and truly Eloquent, without Stiffnefs and
Affectation. The Style of the Pulpit fhould be
Solemn and Manly : but yet it were well to be Rich
and Polite : Dull Thoughts, in grov'ling Language,
are far from the Majefty which becomes the Defk:
  I muft not digrefs from my facred Subject, to
treat here of Rhetorick and Oratory. This is not
a Seafon, or a Place for fuch Speculations. However, a Word or two falls within the Compafs of
my prefent Subject : That the Man of GOD may be
Perfect, throughly furnifhed. I may venture to fay
therefore, a publick Speaker fhould be a Perfon of
graceful Deportment, elegant Addrefs, and fluent
Utterance. He muft ftudy an eafy Style, expref-
five Diction, and tuneful Cadences, to win the
Affections and Attention of his Audience. The
Preacher muft *feek out acceptable Words.* So *Aaron*
the Prieft, under the Old Teftament, and *Apollos*
the Preacher, under the New, are remark'd for
Talents at Eloquence and Perfwafion. It is a *Shame*,
that any fhould fo pervert the Words of the Apoftle
Paul, 1 *Cor.* ii. 9. as to make them condemn Politenefs, and a good Style. The Apoftle there fays,
that his *Motives* and his Preaching, were not thofe

which the Wifdom of Man gave him, but he received them from God ; and they were different from the Politicks of a vain World. When he fays, he *fpeaks not with the enticing Words of Man's Wifdom*, he certainly could not mean, he was not Beautiful and Rich, in his Divine Compofures : for Nothing can be more finifh'd Oratory, than many of *Paul's* Sermons. As well might Method as Style be condemned : for both are the Effects of Art ; and of the Two, the former is moft fo. Idle Flourifh and noify Declamation, affected Witticifms and trifling Quotations, it is true, are difguftful in the Preacher ; and fo they are in the Author too : But regular Pronunciation and fmooth Periods, the adjufted Accent and the tuneful Cadence, lively Diction and decent Gefture, fhould all confpire to make the Man of God Perfect, throughly furnifhed for the good Work of the Pulpit. Not to mention the gallant Prophecies of the Old Teftament : Read the Sermon at *Athens* ; the Speech to *Feftus* ; the infpired Epiftles ; the fublime Revelations ; and I boldly pronounce, the Man who can condemn, magnificent Sentiments, in charming Language, muft have no Tafte, or no Confcience. The Truth is, I never met with any who condemn'd a polite Style, but either thofe who could not write in one ; or thofe who cenfured it with fuch a Pomp of Rhetorick, as at the fame Time fhow'd, they affected Nothing more, than to be thought Mafters in it. However, if by enticing Words of Man's Wifdom, be underftood, ratling Periods, uncouth Jargon, affected Phrafes and finical Jingles ; let them be condemned : let them be hifs'd from the Defk, and blotted from the Page. A proud young Novice, making the Pulpit a Stage, on which he fancies to difplay his
own

own Powers, would never make a fecond Attempt, did he know how the better Parts of his Congregation felt for him. Let this then be the Rule, in the Compofition of our Sermons: What Tendency has this Sentence? to glorify Christ, or to exalt Self? This one Thought, well purfued, would prune many a luxuriant Harrangue, and curtail many a florid Volume. 'Twould much better promote the Preachers Fame, and the Hearers Patience. But I defift here: I am but propofing Rules for Self, and the Improvement of my Son.

The next thing to furnifh the Man of God, and make him Perfect, is a Talent at *entertaining and ufeful Converfation.* He muft not live always in the Pulpit: He muft vifit, as well as preach. He fhould therefore have a modeft Affurance, a graceful Behaviour, and a furnifh'd Mind. He fhould know what to fay, and when to fay it ⋅ how to lead in Converfation, and how to follow. His Manner fhould be Grave, Chearful, Free, and Manly. The Clown, or the Churl, would fet but awkwardly on the Minifter. He fhould be able to divert : But he fhould never forget to improve his Company. He fhould fuffer no Vice to go forward where *he* is : Or if he cannot hinder, he fhould not fail to refent it. The Minifter who can tamely bear Wickednefs to proceed, without doing what he prudently may to ftop it ; is either a Hypocrite, or a Daftard. In a Word, fo fhould a Minifter behave and converfe, that all Companies fhould fee him enter with Pleafure ; and none leave him without Regret, nor without Inftruction.

From the Character thus far, you fee how many Graces muft unite, to adorn the Mind of a finifh'd Minifter. Add to thefe, he muft be a Man of

Prudence

Prudence and Courage ; of fteady Principles, and uniform Conduct ; of Patience, Zeal, Diligence and Perfeverance. In fhort, all the Excellencies of a fuperiour Mind, and a moft elevated Chriftian, much confpire to render him Perfect and Compleat.

But, O Man of God ! how great a Part of thy Work and thy Character lies unfeen ; *hid from the Eyes of the World ?* known only to God, and thy own Soul ? What mighty Labours attend him, invifible in his Clofet, retired from Men ? His Neighbours perhaps fancy him fitting eafy among his Books, when he is ftriving in Prayer, refifting Temptation, and encountering the Powers of Darknefs. The Study of the Minifter is the Field of Battle : Here he plays the Hero ; tries the Dangers of War, and repeats the Toils of Combate. How many maffy Volumes muft he go through, to enrich his Thought ? What Pains muft he take to compare, to digeft, to underftand, or to confute the various Pages of his Author ? How often muft he watch when others fleep ? and his folitary Candle burn, when the Midnight-Darknefs covers the Windows of the Neighbourhood ? And now, if after all, he fhould happen to excel, a Thoufand to One but he fees it, is proud of it, and the Refentment of Christ, blafts his Miniftry. 'Tis well, if after *having preach'd to others, he himfelf becomes not a Caft away* : Left, being *lifted up with Pride, he fall into the Condemnation of the Devil.* Senfible of his ftupendous Danger ; what Prayers and Watchings, what Faftings and Vigils, does his anxious Soul go through, proftrate in the Duft before God, to procure and keep a humble Temper ! Thefe are Things, it may be, out of the ordinary Road of Chriftianity : But, thou, O Man of God,

it

it becomes thee, to be no Stranger to the secret and arduous Duties.

This should be the generous *Emulation*, even among the Men of God, to excel one another in Labours and Humility. *Covet earnestly the best Gifts*, is a general Direction, to Ministers as well as People. Let who will run away with the Riches and the Applause : Be thine, O Man of God, the Diligence, and the Wisdom, and the Zeal. Let others divide the Name and the Revenues among them ; be it ours, to surpass in Labours, in Piety, and Improvements of the Mind. Let others look high, and talk big, and be renown'd : Let our Ambition turn another Way *(a) Are they Ministers of CHRIST? I am more : in Labours more abundant, in* Sufferings *above Measure : In Weariness and Painfulness ; in Watchings often : in Hunger and Thirst ; in Fastings often ; in Cold and Nakedness :* Temptations resisted within, and the *Care of the Churches from without.* A noble, a sublime Character ; and to this the Man of God should reach and aim. But I must not enlarge.

A Third Doctrine from the Words is this.

III. The Ministerial Office *abounds with Good Works. That the Man of GOD*, &c.

Every Christian has his *Works* to do ; Religion in general is a *Good* Work : But no Man has more Work lying upon his Hands, or better Work than the Minister. Not only his *General Calling* leads him, in common with his Christian Neighbours, to adore God, and do Good to Man : But it is Part of his *Particular Work*, to pray ; to visit the Sick ; to preach the Word ; to study his Bible ; to administer the Seals of the Covenant ; and manage the Affairs of the Church. His whole Life, must

(a) 2 Cor. xi. 23.   be

be fpent in good Works, and the immediate Service of CHRIST. (*a*) *He* then *that defires the Office of a Bifhop, defires a Good Work.* Still, I haften onward, and ftudy Brevity. —

The laft Doctrine, I fhall take Notice of here, is from the Reference of the Words, to the fore-going Context : And as it is taken from an Allufion, I fhall but juft mention it.

IV. *The Holy Scriptures are the Compleat Rule for a Minifter, in all the Parts of his Character and Office.* Thefe were given, *that the Man of GOD might be Perfect, throughly furnifhed to every Good Work.*

Here he fees all the Lineaments of his Character ; all the Branches of his Work. This is the Magazine, whence he draws his Treafures ; The Arfenal, whence he fetches his Weapons. If he is not Perfect, throughly furnifhed ; the Fault lies in himfelf, not in his Bible. That is compleat, though he is de-ficient. *The Law of the LORD is Perfect* : tho' he may *underftand* it *but in Part*.

It were eafy and pleafant here, did I not aim at the utmoft Brevity, Firft, to demonftrate the *Divine Authority of the Scriptures* ; and then their *Perfection, every Way, to accomplifh the Man of GOD.* I might felect the various Parts of his Character, as they ly fcattered in the facred Pages ; and the feveral Parts of his Work. I might read you in Order great Part of thefe Epiftles to *Timothy* ; and add the Epiftle to *Titus* : and in a Manner repeat what I have already faid, and anticipate the folemn Charge, I am going to pronounce. But, here too I forbear, and fhall conclude with a brief Appli-cation.

1. To

(*a*) 1 *Tim.* iii. 1.

1. To you, my Sons, who are *preparing for the Miniftry.* You fee what a holy, what an arduous, what an important Affair you are undertaking. How much Furniture is requifite for one in the facred Office? You will therefore conclude, that now is the Time for you, to accomplifh your felves for this mighty Work. How careful muft you be, to do Nothing now, that fhall hereafter be repeated, to blemifh your Character, and hinder your Opportunities to do Good? Now is the Time, to lay up Treafures in your Soul ; to fill your Mind with Ideas ; to polifh your Style ; and above all, to obtain the Sanctification of your Heart. Now you have *Time* ; now you are at Leifure ; and now, fhould you fo habituate your felves to Diligence, as to make it natural, againft the Time that conftant Labours roll upon you.

2. The Addrefs turns to You, my Fathers and Brethren, *already in the Miniftry.* To you the Text fpeaks : You now perceive the Truth, and feel the facred Force of it. You fee your Miniftry demanding a Thoufand good Works, to be every Day performed. You feel the Neceffity of being furnifhed for every Part of it. Your confcious Hearts bear Record to the Labours I defcribe ; the facred Labours of the Clofet, the Vifit, the Pulpit ; The Work of the Brain, and the Work of the Pen ; the Hand, the Eyes, the Tongue full of Employment. Memory, Invention, Fancy and Judgment, unite and exhauft themfelves in your daily Bufinefs. O what Prayer, what Agonies, what Temptations and Combates, do you hourly go through ? And how often fainting, are you ready to give out ; while your earneft Voice cries out to your Saviour for Help ? How often are you at a lofs to find

C out

out the Truth, difguifed with fo much Error, in fuch artful Colours ; more efpecially in your younger Studies ? To you then the Text fpeaks. It calls you to ftudy the Scriptures, impartially, diligently, ferioufly, and with much humble Prayer : So you will find the holy Ghoft, who at firft infpired them, daily enlighten you to underftand them ; and ftrengthen you to obey them. *Who is fufficient for thefe Things,* without Almighty Aids ? Here then be our conftant Truft, and our daily Prayer ; fo fhall *He* fay, *My Grace is fufficient for thee* ; fo fhall *we* fay, *I can do all Things through C H R I S T who ftrengthens me.*

3. Let me exhort you, *the dear Flocks of CHRIST,* to give all your Help to your poor Minifters. You hear how great their Work is, and how many Accomplifhments are neceffary for them : O *!* will you not help them all you can ? Will you not pray for them, and take every other Care from their Minds, that they may give themfelves wholly to the Preparations and Labours of their holy Office ? *Finally, Brethren, pray for us :* And you, particularly, the dear Flock, who have invited us upon this Occafion. Will you refolve, to make the Work of your Paftor as eafy to him as may be ? *This my Son is young and tender.* 'Tis a great Sacrifice that I make, in yielding to your irrefiftible Importunity, and confenting to his Settlement at fuch a Diftance from me : But your Unanimity and Ardor have overcome me ; and I refign to what appears the Allotment of God. May the fame Spirit of Peace and Love continue ; and I fhall not repent that I have confented. Upon you, and upon your Children, I leave my Bleffings.

But

But why do I, the moſt improper Perſon in the World, venture thus to addreſs others : When this Day, my Thoughts are ſo over-born, upon my own Account ; and for you, my Son. 'Tis not to you, my Brethren, my Fathers, that I venture to preach. No ; 'tis for Self, and for Thee, I ſtudy, I preach, I weep. And *what, my Son ? and what the Son of my* Youth *? and what, the Son of my Vows ? For thee I prayed, and GOD has granted me the Petition which I aſked of Him.* Begin your Miniſtry, in ſuch humble Language as this. " O " my Soul ! look inward, and feel the Weight of " the Important Charge before thee. What am I " going about ? So imperfeɛt, ſo unfurniſh'd, to " take the Charge of a Church, and enter the " Work of the Miniſtry ? How ſhall I, the chief " of Sinners, attempt the high Style of a Man " of GOD ? How ſhall I, my own Soul ſo polluted, " have the Souls of ſo many committed to my " Care ? To me, who am leſs than the leaſt of all " Saints, ſhall this Grace be given, that I ſhould " preach the unſearchable Riches of CHRIST ! " Will he count me faithful, putting me into " the Miniſtry ? O LORD GOD ! who am I, and " what is my Houſe, that thou haſt called me " hitherto ? I conſider the Difficulty and Solemnity " of the Work I am undertaking ; and my Heart " ſinks at the vaſt Proſpeɛt. I conſider, how a " Man of GOD ſhould be prepared and accom- " pliſhed ; and I bluſh and tremble at my own " Unpreparedneſs. I conſider the Glories of that " JESUS, whoſe Goſpel I bring ; and when I ſee " the Seraphims vail their Faces before Him ; and " hear them repeat, Holy, Holy, Holy, to Him ; " wo is me, for I am dumb, for I am of

C 2   " unclean

" unclean Lips, unworthy and unable to bear a
" Part in the Worſhip ; ſo dark, ſo guilty, I am
" not worthy to be called a Miniſter, or to appear
" thus in a holy Aſſembly. O Congregation ! pray
" for me. My Fathers in the Miniſtry, aſſiſt me
" with your Prayers : Bleſs me, even me, O my
" Fathers ! And particularly, you, the dear People,
" whoſe Souls I this Day receive at the Hands
" of CHRIST ; be not you wanting in this Duty.
" Strive together with me, in your Prayers to
" G o D for me. Aſk of the Father of Lights,
" that he would furniſh me, and accept me to
" miniſter to your Salvation. You have called me
" to be your Paſtor, and I have accepted your
" Call : And now, will you leave me alone, without
" your Help, without your Prayer ? My People,
" your Souls, and the Souls of your Children lye
" at Stake : My Fidelity, or my Idleneſs, may be
" your Salvation or Perdition. Pray for me then,
" be inſtant in Prayer, be earneſt and unwearied
" in it, that I may be approved by my Judge,
" and faithful to you. Pray, that the Spirit of CHRIST
" may fall upon me, and dwell richly in me ; ſo ſhall I
" go my Way rejoicing, upheld in all my Labour, and
" ſucceſsful in it ; ſo ſhall I be clear from the Blood
" of all Men ; ſo ſhall I both ſave my own Soul,
" and them that hear me ; when the great Shep-
" herd ſhall appear, I ſhall receive the Crown from
" Him ; the Paſtor and the People ſhall rejoice
" together ; and I riſe at your Head, having loſt
" none of your Souls ; and, preſenting you to the
" dear Saviour, ſay, *LORD, here am I, and the*
" *Children which thou haſt given me.* "
    You derive from Anceſtors who have been emi-
nent in the World, and in the Church of CHRIST .
                                            Labour

Labour to ferve your Lord, and fhine as they did. Methinks, I am now doing the Part of *Aaron*, when he put the facred Veftments on his Son, and prepared to lie down and die. Take the Satisfaction of your Father's Teftimony, to the Diligence, and exemplary Piety, of your Infancy and Childhood ; and hear Me join, in the dying Words of your excellent Mother, when fhe laid her Hands upon your Head, and gave your laft Blefling. " You have been a moft dutiful Child to me, and " have often made my Heart to rejoice. God will " blefs you, and reward you. And remember, " thefe are great Words for a dying Parent to " fpeak. " Engage chearfully in all your Work, looking at this Recompence of Reward. — *For they who inftruct, fhall fhine as the Brightnefs of the Firmament : and they who turn many unto Righteoufnefs, as the Stars for ever and ever.*

The

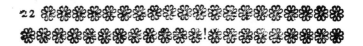

The Charge.

WHEREAS you, upon whom we now lay our Hands, have been immediately called to the Paſtoral Office in this Church of Our Lord Jesus Christ, and have thus publickly accepted it; We do, in the Name of that glorious Lord, thus ſolemnly Ordain and ſeparate you, to the Work of the Goſpel Miniſtry in general, and *now* as a Paſtor of this Church in particular.

We Charge you before God, and the Lord Jesus Christ, who ſhall judge the Quick and the Dead at His Appearance and His Kingdom; and before the e-leƈt Angels, *thoſe who ſtand by*, and are Witneſſes of this Tranſaƈtion; that you take heed to your Mi-niſtry, to fulfil it.

Preach the Word; be inſtant, in Seaſon, out of Seaſon; reprove, rebuke, exhort, with all Long-ſuf-fering and Doƈtrine.

Adminiſter the Seals of the New Teſtament, the Sacraments of Baptiſm and the Lord's Supper.

Bleſs the Congregation, in the Name of the Lord; putting his Name upon them, that they may be bleſſed.

Diſpenſe the Diſcipline of the Church of Christ; them that ſin, rebuke before all, that others alſo may fear; without preferring one before another, doing nothing by Partiality.

Give thy ſelf to Reading, to Meditation, to Prayer, and to all the Parts of your holy Work, as it is in the Oracles of God laid down before you: Give thy ſelf *wholly* to theſe Things, and may your Suc-ceſſes appear to all.

And

And the Doctrines which thou haſt heard of me, before many Witneſſes ; the ſame commit thou to faithful Men, who ſhall be able to inſtruct others. Lay Hands ſuddenly on Man ; neither be Partaker of other Men's Sins. keep thy ſelf pure.

And now, we bleſs you in the Name of God : and we point you to the Aids of his SPIRIT. If, my Son, thou keep this Charge of JESUS, unrebukable before Him, or in humble Sincerity ; when He, the chief Shepherd, ſhall appear, you ſhall receive from Him, the Crown of Glory that fadeth not away.

F I N I S.

ERRAT. Pag. 14. lin: 5. for *much* read *muſt*

The Vanity of every Man at his best Estate.

A Funeral

SERMON

On the Honorable

WILLIAM DUMMER, Esq.

Late Lieutenant GOVERNOR and COMMANDER IN CHIEF,
over the Province of the

Maſſachuſetts-Bay in *New-England*,

Who died OCTOBER 10, 1761.

Aged 84 Years.

By Mr. BYLES.

Eccl. xii. 7, 8. *Then ſhall the Duſt return to the Earth as it was, and the Spirit ſhall return to God who gave it. Vanity of Vanities, ſaith the Preacher, all is Vanity.*

Printed by GREEN & RUSSELL, in BOSTON, 1761.

Psal. XXXIX. 5.

*Verily every Man at his beſt ſtate is altoge-
ther Vanity.*

THESE words are very plain, and very full,
and very mortifying. Man, a noble and
reaſonable creature, of a curious body and
an immortal ſpirit, may he not be a little proud of his
talents, his capacities, his enjoyments, and his rever-
ſions?---No; he is an empty and a brittle thing :
Man is vanity.---Yes, *ſome men* : perhaps the gene-
rality. But are there not others exempted from the
character? The wiſe, the learned, the rich and noble, the beautiful and ſtrong ; perſons of wide fame
or high authority, princes and emperors at the head
of mankind, are theſe ſo too ? Yes ; *every man* is
vanity.----*Sometimes* perhaps, in ſome circumſtances
and

and at fome certain feafons : But not in his faireſt appearance, and brighteſt glory. The king ſick, or the ſcholar aſleep may be fo : but is the rich in the midſt of his poſſeſſions, the general at the head of his army.---Yes, every man at his *beſt eſtate* is vanity.--- Allow men ; *all* men, and all men in their *beſt eſtate*, are *vain* : a little vain it may be. Nay, *vanity* itſelf, in the abſtract. Well, granted, in a *few* things, per- haps in many : But ſure the idea may ſtop here. Nav he is *altogether vanity*. Theſe are aſſertions perhaps : a bear *hypotheſis* : a ſpeculation only, not well ground- ed. A topick of amuſement or diſpute, but not demonſtrated concluſion.---Nay, it is moſt certainly ſo. *Verily* every man at his beſt eſtate, is altogether vanity.

NEVER was a ſentence more ſtrong and forcible. Every word has an emphaſis upon it. Man, not barely *vain*, but in the abſtract, *vanity*. Not in a little but *altogether vanity*. Not in his worſt condition ; but in his *beſt ſtate*. Not ſome few ; but *every man*. And all this not a precarious aſſertion, but a moſt cer- tain truth. VERILY *every man at his beſt eſtate is alto- gether vanity*. This lies before us to illuſtrate and improve.

1ſt THEN

1ſt THEN; I am to illucidate and demonſtrate the propoſition, that every man at his beſt eſtate, is altogether vanity. And here I might premiſe, that man, at his firſt creation, was not vanity, in that compleat ſenſe, in which he is ſince. He was made a little lower than the angels and crowned with glory and honour. There was a real glory abiding on him: ſomething ſolid and ſubſtantial; till ſin broke, and ſoften'd, and deſtroyed his frame. By his fall from GOD he became *vain in his imaginations*: and hence he diffuſed vanity and the curſe through the lower creation.---So was the *creature made ſubjeсt to vanity*, by the tranſgreſſion of *Adam*, the lord of this ſubjeсted earth. He became vain firſt, in that bold attempt after godhead, when he eat the forbidden fruit. The vain man fancied that he had divinity within his reach: and the ſerpent fed the illuſion. Gen. iii. 5. *For* GOD *doth know, that in the day you eat thereof, that your eyes ſhall be opened; and ye ſhall be as gods, knowing good and evil.* Raviſhed with the gaudy phantom, the fooliſh, preſumptuous creature catch'd at it, tried to graſp it to his boſom, and hug and enjoy the bliſs: But how diſappointed was he! It glided from his arms, it mocked his careſs, it appeared nothing but a gilded cloud, a fleeting ſhadow; meer vanity. So that even then, at his beſt eſtate indeed; while he ſtood fair as a cedar in the garden of GOD, he was deceived by vanity;

nity ; and confeſt himſelf vanity. *Man being in honour abideth not.* But ſince the fall, O what compleat vanity is the race of *Adam ? Verily every man at his beſt eſtate is altogether vanity.* Let us, if you pleaſe, inſtance a little, and ſee if the aſſertion cannot be made out. Take the man in all the fine lights in which your fancy can place him, and let us try what we can make of it.

1ſt IN his beſt eſtate of *riches,* he is no better than vanity. No worldly man ever did arrive at all the riches which his vain mind wiſh'd for. But form the idea better than the fact.

SUPPOSE a man poſſeſt of all the wealth of the earth.---Suppoſe him ſeated in the midſt of plenty, his tables cover'd with all kinds of luxuries, and all round ſtand his unnumber'd ſlaves to execute his ſovereign orders. His coffers are mines of gold and ſilver. They teem with coin, and blaze with jewels.---He is *cloathed in purple and fine linen,* he ſets upon an ivory throne, in the midſt of a marble palace. Round about are his gardens, his orchards, his groves and his fields ſpreading in an endleſs proſpect. Iſſuing from theſe, he enters into magnificent cities, and walks through ſtreets of his own houſes ; every one, as he paſſes,
bringing

bringing in tribute and revenues. In a word, the treafures of the world pour into his magazines, and he fhall be the proprietor of all regions where the fun vifits.

WELL, here is an ideal rich man : fuch an one as never was really in the world : but we fet him in his beft eftate, that we may keep to the text, and attend to the conclufion. See the overgrown wretch then : and what do you behold ! Why firft of all, a huge lump of vanity, a proud, haughty, difdainful mortal, valuing himfelf upon the moft adventitious and exterior thing in the world. For all this his riches, he may be an ideot, a fot, a villain without honour or confcience. He may be fick and in pain ; he may be defpifed and hated ; no man may have a good thought of him ; and at laft he may die young, after he has loft all his wealth too, and not have a friend to clofe his eyes.

WHAT think you now ? Is this beft eftate vanity or not ? See the fucceeding verfe of my context : *Surely every man walketh in a vain fhew : furely they are difquieted in vain : he heapeth up riches and knoweth not who fhall gather them.*

THUS

Thus you see the sacred conclusion of the Holy Ghost upon riches, that they also are vanity : That man at his best estate in these is no better himself than vanity. Never let us call them *substance* any more.

2. Consider the man at his best estate of *honour*, and lo ! here he is also vanity. Suppose he is lifted to the pinnacle of earthly dignity, seated upon the supream throne, and gazed up at by a whole world of conquered nations. Suppose him rolling in his gilded chariot, thro' a *range* of triumphal arches, with a thousand fettered monarchs marching in procession, before the ravish'd victor. Round about are torn standards and broken armour, the trophies of his success, and the monuments of his glory. And now, applauded by millions he rides along, while the sky echoes with his name and his honours. But what is this hero now, but another demonstration of my doctrine : Man at his best estate, and vanity ? Amidst all this vain pomp and glitter, may not his mind be uneasy, and his body in pain. May he not think, " These people who acclaim me to day, may hiss me " to-morrow." Or may he not remember amidst all, that in a few hours more death will strip him of all, hurl him from all, and *this poor skirt be all the great conqueror carries away*, and six foot of earth be all he
takes

takes up. The dignity of this earth then is no security against this abasing character inscribed upon it,
vanity. The most honourable are no more secured
than the vilest and most abject : But of both alike it
is the scripture assertion, Psal. lxii. 9. *Surely men of*
low degree are vanity, and men of high degree are a lie :
to be laid in the ballance they are altogether lighter than
vanity. Near o'kin to this is the next head.

3. At his best estate of *fame* and *reputation*, man is
altogether vanity. Suppose the man not only to be
raised above all in outward marks of respect and dignity : but every one shall love him in their hearts ;
they shall respect and admire him : They shall talk
every where of his excellencies, and every one believe
what they say. They shall spread his fame far and
wide, and he shall be nniversally known, and as uni-
versally valued, from the most judicious critick to the
lowest plebean.

Well ; and what can be a fairer picture of vanity
in the whole world ? What is more uncertain, than
the esteem of men ; the breath of common fame ?
What more swelling and more empty ? 'Tis vanity in
the abstract : an idle bubble, blown up by the uncertain breath of others, that breaks in the attempt to
catch it.   B   A Man

A Man the moſt applauded by others, may be the moſt miſerable creature in the world, in the ſenſations of his own mind. All the pompous titles of an oriental monarch, are but great ſwelling words of vanity. A ſmall tranſition will bring us to ſay,

4. Man at his beſt eſtate of *power* and *authority*, is altogether vanity. This carries in it a diſtinct idea from honour and fame : For a man may receive the higheſt marks of dignity, and titles of honour, and may be really eſteemed, and univerſally applauded, and yet his authority and command may be very ſmall. He may have great influence to attract, and but ſmall power to oblige.

But ſuppoſe a man advanced to the throne of ſupream empire ; a ſovereign monarch, abſolute and arbitrary in all his edicts. --- On his breath hang the ſouls of millions. In his ſecret breaſt is depoſited the march of armies, and the fate of nations. Peace, or battles, retreat, or bloodſhed, or ſafety, or deſtruction, wait the mandates of his deſpotick voice.

Suppose he has not a rebel in his vaſt empire ; or if he had thouſands he has power to cruſh them in an inſtant, and only would appear the greater by
the

the bold, fuccefslefs oppofition. And now what's the confequence ? why juft the fame ftill, advanc'd to the beft eftate, he ftill remains vanity. Notwithftanding all his authority, may he not be a flave to his own lufts ? May not ambition, revenge, luxury, prefumption and defpair tyranize over him by turns, and claim a divided government in his foul ? And after all, may he not, *muft he not* refign it in death ! At once the blaft is given, and the bubble breaks.

5. MAN at his beft eftate of *pleafure* is altogether vanity.----Suppofe him furrounded with every object, fair to the eye, tuneful to the ear, delicate to the touch, fragrant to the fmell, and delightful to the tafte. Suppofe the generous wines flow round ; and the fprightly concert ftrikes up : wit and laughter fhall wake the genius and fhake the hall. The gay turn, the fly remark, the fmart reply ; ingenuity, mirth and good humour fhall be heard from all corners.

AND O what a fcene of abundant vanity have I here open'd ! Here's a room full of dying creatures, upon the edges of eternity, juft ftepping into it, and O how fenfelefs ! abandon'd ! frantick ! Noife and clamour, thoughtlefs impertinence, and empty jefting, fenfual gratifications and idle game, make up that ftrange mon-

fter

ster call'd *earthly pleasure*. O how unfit for the choice
of such creatures as we ! how unequal to the capacities of a reasonable soul ! how short-liv'd, and uncertain, and transient ! The *pleasures of sin are but for a
season* : and even while they last, are vain and unsub-
stantial too. Eccle. ii. 1, 2, 3. *I said in my heart, go
to now, I will prove thee with mirth, therefore enjoy plea-
pleasure : and behold this also is vanity. I said of laughter,
it is mad : and of mirth, what doth it ? I sought in mine
heart to give myself unto wine, and to lay hold on folly.*

6. MAN at his best estate of *body* is altogether vanity.
----In the former trials, I suppos'd the man to have
all exterior advantages : but now if you please you
shall approach to add interior to them. Suppose then
amidst all this plenty, this dignity, fame, power, and
mirth, the man enjoys a strong and regular gust of
appetite, to taste the various delights. Suppose him
strong, lively, active, of a firm constitution and warm
blood, glowing with the flush of youth, and hardy in
the vigour of health : yet in this sense is the conclusion sacred, Eccl. xi. 9. *Childhood and youth are vanity.*
Suppose him in the bloom of years, beauty adorns his
cheeks, and proportion shapes his limbs, and every one
gazes with eyes of approbation and love. Yet then is
the conclusion also true. Prov. xxxi. 30. *Favour is
deceitful, beauty is vain.* Poor vain creature, why are
these

thefe confcious airs, and that fluttering attire ? Muft
not all this beauty fade ? In a few moments more, will
not thofe fair colours vanifh from your face, and the
eyes fix, and the lips turn pale ? So a bubble fhines,
and dances upon the fmiling furface of the flood, and
in an inftant difappears, the beautiful round is loft,
and its place is no more found.

7. MAN, at his beft eftate of *foul* is altogether vanity.
The thought now rifes, and the conclufion grows
ftrong. We may eafily conceive a plentiful eftate,
outward honours, fcenes of mirth, and a healthy body,
and yet pronounce vanity upon all, while the *mind*
was not adapted to tafte the pleafure : But fuppofe it
is, yet fure now the point is made out, and the man is
altogether vanity. Suppofe the owner of ten thoufand
volumes has rode poft through his pages, yet may not
the fine library line the walls of a narrow foul ? Has
the man a fmattering of half a dozen languages ; tho'
he fpeaks in the tongues of men and angels, and have
not genius, he is but as *founding brafs, and a tinkling
cymbal.* Nothing fo empty and noify as a vain pedant.

BUT this reaches not the cafe neither ; fuppofe
then once more, a vaft *genius,* with all the ideas of
learning and fpeculation laid up in its faithful memory. Suppofe a bright imagination, a quick invention,

tion, a penetrating fagacity, a correct judgment ; a meer SOLOMON, excelling all mortals in wifdom and knowledge----The firft thing we obferve upon this is, *in his much wifdom is much grief, and as he increafeth knowledge he increafeth forrow.* How vain muft the wifeft man be, if he is puft up with his own learning ? After all his large acquifitions, how much more remains unknown to him, than he already knows ? There's hardly a fool upon earth, but would puzzle the conceited philofopher, with queftions upon the moft common fubject. And after all, one little turn of brain ; one fmall apartment difturb'd, one minute cell overthrown, and down falls all this ftupendous fabrick of intellect, and the poor creature becomes ftupid, or wanton, or raving. 1 Cor. iii. 20. *And again,* the LORD *knoweth the thoughts of the wife, that they are vain. Vain man would be wife !* I fhall attempt but one labour more, and with this trial I fhall form the conclufion of the whole matter.

8. Confider man in his beft eftate of virtue and *morality,* deftitute of the principle of renewed nature, and here too the point will be given, he *is altogether vanity.* You take notice, I here fay, *virtue* and *morality* as diftinguifhed from *holinefs* and *true piety.* 'Tis the pagan ethicks and not the chriftian fanctity that is

the

the prefent fubject. Well: but will not morality make us happy ? Is not virtue a real good ; the *fummum bonum* ? The calm philofopher; who could debate upon fenfual pleafure, and deliberately pronounce vanity upon it all: Yet even he, dazzled by falfe lights, and the appearance of truth in his argument, will never confent to have his beloved virtue pronounced vain too. Let us fee a little then how far this conclufion will hold. Suppofe a moralift, who indulges no inordinate appetite or hurtful paffion : Suppofe he endeavours after a generous love to mankind, and of all the fecond table of the law can fay, all thefe have I kept from my youth. Yet muft it be faid, there is fomething wanting, vanity within, fome chafm remaining unfill'd. The voice of eternal truth himfelf pronounces, *yet thou lackeft one thing.* Aye, but fuppofe he is even fuperftitious in his regards to the firft table too, fo far as man in a ftate of fallen nature proceeds unfanctified by the Spirit of God, the vanity fhall only be better finifhed, and make a finer fhow. Would you fee the very picture of vanity ; the very *image and fuperfcription* of it, I'll fhow it you. Look into Luk. xviii. 11. *The pharifee flood and prayed thus with himfelf ;* God, *I thank thee that I am not as other men are, extortioners, unjuft, adulterers, or even as this publican. I faft twice in the week, I give tithes of all that I poffefs.* If one was looking out for an emblem of vanity,

nity, I know not how it were poffible to find a better.

Virtue then, and morality, if it go no further, is but a vain appearance of good : this may puff a man up, but it can never be fatisfying, becaufe it can never be compleat. I know not how to help it, but till it is *full* it muft be *hollow*. Eccl. iv. 4. *Again I confidered every* right work, *this is alfo vanity and vexation of fpirit.* The moft accomplifhed philofopher among the heathen, and the exacteft moralifts they could boaft, were for the moft part, the vaineft things under heaven. They almoft lived wholly to themfelves. Even their pompous talk upon the publick and the love of one's country, has fuch evident marks of vain glory upon it, that it is difcovered in almoft every page by an attentive eye. Is even the dying fpeech of a *Socrates* unftained with it ? The luft of fame feems to be the grand fpring of their gaudy oratory, and hardy undertakings in what they call'd the cafe of virtue. The modeft *Virgil* himfelf is eafily detected. He ftumbles at the very threfhold of his heroic lines, and the vain *egolift* appears full.——*Ille ego qui quondam*——unlefs the vain criticks can prove the lines to be none of his : as fome of them have attempted.

And among thofe called chriftians, can the cafe be different ? The bare moral man may be lovely in his
accomplifh-

accomplifhments, but morality alone will not fave him. He may *here* lofe it totally, and all his hopes from it *hereafter* will prove as *the fpider's web.*

BUT I muft do the argument juftice. Man in his beft eftate of *faith* too, fhort of faving, is ftill only vanity. He *only feems* to be religious, but *that man's religion is vain. If he have all faith, fo as that he be able to remove mountains,* and it *work not by love,* it is but a thin appearance and empty noife. *Wilt thou know, O vain Man, that faith without works is dead!* The foul is wanting, and what you fee is a vain phantom without fubftance. A dead thing you know is vain. Hence the facred phrafe for the univerfal empire of death, is, *the creature alfo is fubject to vanity.* I have now confider'd man in his beft eftate indeed, and lo, he is ftill vanity.

THUS you have run through the feveral divifions of mankind, and what is the upfhot of the matter? What a mortifying conclufion is drawn from the confeft premifes? At his beft eftate of *riches* he is vanity, for he may be defpifed: add *honour* to his riches, and he is vanity ftill, for it may reach but a little way. Add extent of *fame* to thefe, and he is ftill vanity for want of *authority* to fupport it. If he has all thefe, he may ftill remain vanity, becaufe he is deftitute of fen-

C   fua

fual pleafures. Let him be furrounded with joyous objects, yet they will be in vain if he wants *vigour of appetite*, and health of body. If he enjoys thefe, yet he miffes the nobler *enjoyments of the mind*, and therefore is wretched vanity. Suppofe he has the higheft pleafures of *genius*, yet he may be a flave to vice: Or if he is a moral and a virtuous man, but not regenerated by the Spirit of God ; yet in vain does he look for happinefs, when *death* fhall proclaim him a *finner* againft God. Upon the whole, man at his beft eftate, is altogether vanity. So when our Father Adam had but two fons in the world, the name of one of them, and the beft of them too, was *Abel*, that is vanity. And *being dead he yet fpeaketh* this great truth, that the beft of the fons of Adam are vanity, that man at his beft eftate is altogether vanity. Vanity ! that is a bubble, a bladder of wind and water fluttering in the air, fair indeed, of moft correct and perfect fhape, exactly round, high and fhining : but hollow, frail, eafily and fuddenly broken, gone in a moment, and remembred no more. And *what is your life* but fuch a gilded vapour, *appearing for a little time and then vanifhing away.*

Vanity ! what's that ? In the language of fcripture it is a ftrange fort of a *thing* : I would rather fay, of a *word*. A non-entity, more thin than a chimera, more unfubftantial than a fhadow : *lefs than nothing and*

and vanity. And yet this is the condition of man ; all nations of men ! *every man at his best estate* ! Are we now ready to improve the doctrine ? And from what we have heard, we infer,

1. IF in his *best estate* man is altogether vanity, no wonder he is so in his *common* and his *worst estate.* In his sicknesses he may well *possess months of vanity.* Job vii. 3. In pain, ignominy, and reproach ; in the vicissitudes of providence, and the little portions of comfort, with the deep mixtures of afflictions, he may well be called vain, and see and acknowledge it himself.

2. Is every man at his best estate vanity---O the mercy of GOD *to regard man* ! What are we before him ? Worms ! that's too much, dust and ashes ! that's too much ; nothing ! that's too much ; *less than nothing and vanity. What is man that thou art mindful of him, or the son of man that thou visitest him ?* Even the angels are little before him, and he *charges them with foolishness* : But man is lower than they, nay altogether vanity : And yet, O the amazing notice he takes of us ! Herein is goodness and condescention mysterious and inconceivable !

3. Is man at his best estate vanity----O the grace of CHRIST

CHRIST to *become man !* What a wonder was it that he should take this nature into one person with the Son of GOD ! He took the nature, under all its vain circumstances, excepting that one article, sin. He became the same frail, and brittle, and mortal man that we now are. Here now was man at his best estate, and yet hear what he says, Psal. xxii. 6. *But I am a worm and no man.* How strange grace was this, that he who was all the fulness of the godhead bodily, should thus empty himself, and wear such an appearance of vanity, in the nature of man ? And yet so it was, and he cries out under it, Psal. cii. 2. *My days are like a shadow that declineth.* Thus our LORD *made himself of no reputation, and took upon him the form of a servant,* and all this for our salvation.

4. From what we have heard, we infer, *pride was not made for man.* So empty, so frail, so deceitful a thing, to boast and glory, and admire itself : This is vanity with a witness ! A creature dropping to dust, and falling into a filthy grave, to set up for strength and beauty, honour and applause ! Was ever any thing more absurd and ridiculous ? So might an emmit crawl in state, and value itself upon its imaginary possessions, and conceited accomplishments : So might a shadow, lengthened by the setting sun, admire to find
                                                            itself

itſelf grown ſo tall, while in the ſame moment it was going to vaniſh, blended in the gathering twilight, and loſt in night and darkneſs. Far be from ſuch thin appearances pride, ambition, or vain glory.

5. *WHAT a vain world is this*, when man, the very head of it, is altogether vanity ? So ſome read the text : *Surely all is vanity, every man at his beſt eſtate.*

AND methinks it is no unfair concluſion, if man, the nobleſt creature on the earth,is altogether vanity,the earth itſelf muſt needs be a vain empty place. There's the appearance of good here : but 'tis not at all the leſs vain for that ; but rather the more ſo.---So Satan ſhew'd our LORD *all the kingdoms of the world, and all the glory of them, in a moment of time* ; and it was well he did ſo ; for had he not ſeen them in a moment, the ſhow would all have been over. For the *faſhion of this world paſſeth away.*

6. AND to conclude : Let us *not truſt to any thing in this world. Truſt not in man : for wherein is he to be accounted of. Curſed be the man that truſteth in man, and maketh fleſh his arm.* Not the wiſeſt, the greateſt, the beſt of men, are fit for our ſteady confidence : *Truſt not in princes, whoſe breath is in their noſtrils. His*
breath

breath goeth forth, he returneth to his earth, and in that very day his thoughts perish. Truft not in uncertain riches, or in a frail life. Jam. iv. 13, 14. *Go to now ye that fay, to-day or to-morrow we will go into fuch a city, and continue there a year, and buy, and fell, and get gain : Whereas ye know not what shall be on the morrow : for what is your life ? It is even a vapour that appeareth for a little time, and then vanisheth away.* O awakened foul, look back, and reflect inward, and fay, I have now *feen an end of all perfection.* From this time will I feek a *better country, that is an heavenly.* O bleffed JESUS, *from thy fulnefs let me receive, and grace upon grace.* Thefe things are *but for a feafon :* But *JESUS CHRIST, the fame yefterday, to-day, and forever.*

THUS I have finifhed what I intend on my fubject in general : But what an illuftration and example has the providence of heaven now given of it in the funeral of the Honourable Mr. DUMMER. In him we have, in many refpects, feen *man at his beft eftate :* while the great GOD, has, by the dart of death, fixt on it the infcription, VANITY. How nobly, for a fhining courfe of years, did he fill the firft chair of government in the province, with fuperior wifdom, and, I think, unrivalled acceptance and applaufe ! How did he retire from it, followed with the gratitude and bleffings of a whole people ! In the calm leifure of

his

his recefs, in what amiable and venerable lights did
he fhine in his domeftic and amicable connections!
His fteady family devotions, his ftated retirements to
his clofet, his applications to the entertaining and pious pages of various kinds, his friendly entertainments, and his works of piety and charity, filled up
his ufeful hours. This church can witnefs to the
conftancy and folemnity of his exemplary attendance
on the divine worfhip : while his honors to CHRIST
will be ftill feen here, on the communion table, and in
the coftly volume from which the word of GOD is read
every Lord's-day. His death was of a piece with his
life, in the large donations to publick and pious
ufes in his laft will. So he fhone living and dying : And what a ftriking inftance of *man at
his beft eftate !* ----- But lift up the lid of the coffin,
and fee what is come of all that was mortal. Is
this he whom we remember in the politenefs and
dignity of former years ! How broken with long difeafe ! with excruciating pains ! with age ! with death!
Is this the unblemifhed magiftrate, the PATRIOT
GOVERNOR ; loyal to his prince, and the father to his
country ! How changed from him in the bufy fcenes
and enterprize of active life ! now *lying ftill and quiet,
fleeping and at reft ; with kings and counfellors of the
earth, which built defolate places for themfelves.* Deaf
and unconfcious is he to all the honours of his applauding

plauding country. The immortal mind indeed remains, and remains to pronounce *vanity* upon all that is not immortal. Duty and affection have obliged me thus much to the deceased : But the bufinefs of the pulpit is with the living.

SEE, *you in the elevated ftations* of life, the period of all your glory. So you *die like men, and fall as one of the princes.* You in *advanced years,* if you reach fourfcore, fee 'tis *labour and forrow* : *foon cut off and you fly away.* You, the *mourning relatives* of the departed, will you prepare to mingle your duft with his ? Will you be ambitious to meet him in a fairer inheritance ? While *we* who were happy in his friendfhip and affection, complain with you, *lover and friend haft thou put far from me, and my acquaintance into darknefs.* Will you *all* attend, my brethren, the high and the low, the rich and the poor together ; *fee the end of man, and the living lay it to heart*: while the *preacher himfelf,* upon the furvey of the whole, now pronounces, and clofes all the argument, Eccl. the firft and the laft verfes, *Vanity of vanities, faith the preacher, vanity of vanities, all is vanity. Let us hear the conclufion of the whole matter ; fear GOD, and keep his commandments, for this is the whole of man.*

F I N I S.

A POEM

On the 𝕯𝕰𝕬𝕿𝕳

Of His late M A J E S T Y

King *G E O R G E,*

Of glorious Memory :

A N D   T H E

A C C E S S I O N

Of our prefent S O V E R E I G N

King GEORGE *II.*

To the *Britifh* T H R O N E.

By Mr. *B Y L E S.*

Ergo agite, et cuncti lætum celebremus honorem :
Pofcamus ventos, atque hæc mea facra quotannis
Urbe velit pofita templis fibi ferre dicatis.
Virg. Æn. vj

A Poem

On the Death of King GEORGE I.

And

Accession of King GEORGE, II.

SAY, mournful Mufe, declare thy rifing woe;
What heaves thy heart; and whence thy forrows flow;
Why in thy face fuch anxious grief appears;
And o're thy eye-balls fwim the fpeaking tears.
O George, thy death my flowing numbers mourn,
Thy facred afhes, and diftinguifh'd urn:
Thee every mufe, and every grace deplores,
From *Thame's* banks, to thefe *Atlantick* fhores;
Each bard, his grief in gliding accents fhews,
And faireft eyes diftill their cryftial dews.

O! were my breaft flufh'd with an equal fire,
Vaft as my theme, and ftrong as my defire!
Then, mighty George, then fhould my notes arife,
And fpreading mufick echo round the skies;
Thy name, in tuneful meafures lead along,
Should dance, harmonious, thro' my flowing fong;
The raptur'd mufe thy awful form reveal,
Defcribe thy counfels, and thy actions tell;

Bid

Bid dying founds thy ravifh'd life bemoan,
Or fhouting nations hail thee to thy throne;
Each varying fcene, with various numbers crown'd,
Should earth, and fea, and air, & heaven refound!

Long e're his *Albion* triumph'd in his reign
His fword glar'd dreadful o'er the *Hungarian* plain
Witnefs, ye troops, thro' whofe wide ranks he ran,
Rouz'd the fierce war, and call'd the tumult on:
Say, how divinely then his afpect fhow'd,
What conduct fhone, what dauntlefs courage glow'd
When man to man, and fmoke oppos'd to fmoke,
Flames flafh'd at flames, at thunder thunder broke,
When death, indignant, drove his iron car,
Thro' the dire havock of the raging war:
Ev'n now, behold! the intrepid Heroe flies
To meet the monfter with undaunted eyes:
Till fmiling vict'ry, and immortal peace,
Hung o're his head, and bid the battle ceafe.

Record, O heavenly Mufe, the illuftrious day
When joyful *Britain* own'd the fovereign fway;
Conceal'd for ever, lye the acts that ftain
The laft black months of Anna's gloomy reign;
When fecret treafon work'd, when juftice fled,
And loud deftruction threaten'd o'er our head:
'Twas then, by heaven ordain'd, his happy hand,
From ruin refcu'd the devoted land;

The

The ftorm was hufht, the clam'rous factions laid,
And peaceful-olive fpread its wealthy fhade.
So when dark clouds hang heavy o'er the main
And, bellying down, diftend with floods of rain ;
To heave them on, the winds their forces try,
While they, flow-failing, labour up the sky ;
The thickning volumes fpread the heavenly dome,
And as they pafs, project a folemn gloom:
Difolving now, a drizling dew diftills,
Dampens the vales, and fprinkles round the hills;
Still, gathering ftrength, the airy fluces low'r,
And on the fields, defcends a copious fhow'r,
Laft, furious grown, down rufh the rapid rains,
And pour impetuous, fpattering on the plains.
If then the fun breaks out, the fhadows fly,
And the gay rainbow arches o're the sky

Hail, happy Albion! heavens peculiar care,
See thy Deliverer to thy fhoars repair !
Flourifh ye fields, ye groves exalt your heads,
Where Thames's currant murmurs o're the meads ;
And thou, Augusta, fparkling in my eyes,
Let thy tall towers, and fhinning turrets rife;
Where riches glitter ; mirth for ever fings ;
And fmiling plenty fpreads her golden wings ;
For thee, Peru her beamy face difplays ;
For thee the orient fhores of Ganges blaze ;
A thoufand pleafures crown thy flowry plains,
While George divinely o're thy kingdom reigns.
But

But oh! at once the heavenly fcenes decay,
And all the gaudy vifions fade away.
He dies!—— my Mufe, the difmal found forbear:
In every eye debates the falling tear:
A thoufand paffions o'er my bofom roll,
Swell in my heart, and fhock my inmoft foul.
He dies!——let nature own the direful blow,
Sigh, all ye winds, with tears, ye rivers, flow,
Let the wide ocean, loud in anguifh, roar,
And tydes of grief pour plenteous on the fhore;
No more the fpring fhall bloom, or morning rife,
But night eternal wrap the fable fkies.

Enough, my Mufe, give all thy tears away;
Break, ye dull fhades; and rife the rofey day:
Quicken, O Sun, thy chariot dazling-bright,
And o'er thy flaming empire pour the light:
O Spring, along thy laughing lawns be feen
Fields always frefh, and groves for ever green:
Let *Britain*'s forrow ceafe, her joys enlarge,
The *Firft* revives within the *Second* GEORGE.
Hail! mighty Prince, O fhining Sovereign hail!
Fain would the Mufe lifp her prophetick tale;
In myftic lays, thy future years relate,
And fing the records of unripen'd fate;
Bid Thee, in fame's triumphant chariot ride,
And CAROLINA glitter by thy fide.
Fair Princefs, Thou! in whofe majeftick eyes
Dawn heavenly beauties, and immortal joys;

By

By thee, shall *Albion* future triumphs own,
And a long race of Hero's grace her throne :
Here, FREDERICK in the bloom of years shall stand;
Here youthful WILLIAM blossom o'er the land;
Thou ANNA, here, with charms celestial crown'd
And all thy heavenly Sisters flame around.

Ev'N our far shores confess the big delight,
Where the faint sun rolls down his golden light;
The dancing billows leap along the main,
Proud of th' extent of GEORGE's happy reign;
Applauding thunders shake the air around,
Waves shout to waves, and rocks to rocks resound;
Each human breast glows with resistless fire,
And ev'ry Angel strikes his sounding lyre.

O live, auspicious PRINCE! live, radiant QUEEN!
Long let your influence guild the glorious scene:
And you, fair Off-spring, form'd for high command,
Flourish, ye blooming Honours of the land !
But when from the dim courts below you fly,
To the bright regions of the upper sky,
Where trees of life, by living riv'lets team,
Wave their talls heads, and paint the running stream,
May round your heads, crowns flash celestial-bright,
And regal purple change for robes of light ;
Taste charms still new, and joys without decay,
While endless years in raptures roll away.

§‡‡‡§‡‡‡§‡‡‡§‡‡‡§‡‡‡§‡‡‡§‡‡‡§‡‡‡§‡‡‡§

A POEM

Presented

To His Excellency

William Burnet, Esq;

On his Arrival at *BOSTON*,
July 19. 1728.

By Mr. *BYLES.*

Hic sua præferri quamquam vetat alta paternis;
Libera fama tamen, nullisque obnoxia jussis,
Invitum præfert unaque; in parte repugnat.
　　　　　　　　　　Ovid. Met. L. XV. v. 852.

Published by Order of his *Excellency* the Governour.

To His Excellency

Governour *BURNET*,

On his Arrival at *BOSTON*.

WHILE rifing Shouts a gen'ral Joy proclaim,
And ev'ry Tongue, O BURNET, lifps thy
Name;
To view thy Face, while crowding Armies run,
Whofe waving Banners blaze againft the Sun,
And deep-mouth'd Cannon, with a thund'ring Roar,
Sound thy Commiffion ftretch'd from Shore to Shore
Accept the tuneful Labours of my Mufe,
To bend frefh Laurels round your fhaded Brows
With your Deferts, to raife the facred Fire,
And in your Praifes ftring her joyful Lyre.

A 2

Long have we wish'd the golden Hours to rise,
And with diftinguifh'd Purple paint the Skies,
When, thro' our wondring Towns, in Raptures gay,
The pompous March fhould fhape it's fhining Way;
While breathing Trumpets try their filver Strains,
And whirling Chariots fcour along the Plains;
When the glad City fhould unfold it's Gates,
And the long Triumph grace the glowing Streets.
O Burnet! how we bad the Minutes run,
Urg'd the flow Hours, and chid the lingring Sun!
Impatient, met each Poft, and call'd aloud,
' When will his Wheels fmoke rat'ling o'er the Road?
' When fhall we fay, *He's come!* with big Delight,
' And with his Afpe*t* feaft our longing Sight?

Welcome, Great Man, to our defiring Eyes;
Thou Earth! proclaim it; and refound, ye Skies!
Voice anfw'ring Voice, in joyful Confort meet,
The Hills all echo, and the Rocks repeat:
And Thou, O *Bofton*, Miftrefs of the Towns,
Whom the pleas'd Bay, with am'rous Arms, furrounds,
Let thy warm Tranfports blaze in num'rous Fires,
And beamy Glories glitter on thy Spires;
Let Rockets, ftreaming, up the Ether glare,
And flaming Serpents hifs along the Air;

Sublime

Sublime, thy Joys thro' the high Heav'ns be fhown,
In foreign Lights, and Stars before unknown :
While rival Splendors deck the Earth below,
And o'er the Streets the daz'ling Windows glow.

But You, O *Cambridge*, how can you forbear
In gliding Lays to charm each liftning Ear !
You, where the Youth purfue th' illuftrious Toil,
Where the Arts flourifh, and the Graces fmile,
Make Burnet's Name in lafting Numbers fhine,
Ye foft Recefles of the tuneful Nine !
Speak the glad Day, with ev'ry warbling String,
When firft You blefs'd the Indulgence of his Wing ;
Say, how prophetick Rapture fiez'd Your Tongue,
When You, on Fire, Your future Glories fung.
By Him protected, by his Pattern led,
Each fmiling Art fhall lift her beauteous Head.
Divinity, in op'ning Volumes, lies,
O *Wigglefworth*, to thy enlightned Eyes;
And *Greenwood*'s Hand with wond'rous Skill, difplays
Nature unveil'd, and fhews her lovely Face :
Long fhall the noble Sciences declare
Thy Bounties, Hollis ; and a BURNET's Care.

In Burnet's Face our future Fame appears,
And Arts and Graces lead his flowing Years.

For

[4]

For him, Ye Mufes, tune immortal Verfe,
And mighty Themes, in lofty Lays, rehearfe,
Proud in his Praifes, wind your golden Strings,
And in high Raptures clap your waving Wings.
Thou Sun, for him, fhalt each fair Year adorn,
Bid the Spring bloffom, and the Summer burn,
Teach rip'ning Fruits to paint Autumnal Scenes,
And fmile and blufh amidft the living Greens.
Ev'n the rough Winter feigns a youthful Tread;
And, in low Homage, bows his rev'rend Head :
The Northern Tempefts fhall forget to roar,
And gentle Waves, foft-murm'ring, kifs the Shore.

Now Aftronomic Tubes, aloft fhall rife,
Shake off their Duft, and level at the Skies,
Defcry new Glories in the fhining Spheres,
And BURNET's Name be read on future Stars.
The Pencil now, in wondrous Lines, fhall flow,
And, warm with Life, bid the touch'd Canvas, glow,
Mufick, fweet Daughter of the Choirs above,
Shall, foft-defcending, down the Ether move ;
With heavenly Airs the breathing Flute infpire,
The Viol ftring, and bend the warbling Wyre.

But chief, Ye Pages, open to the Light,
Where wond'ring Angels roll their ravifh'd Sight ;

Ye

Ye facred Pages, eafy to his Soul,
Spread the dark Mazes of your myftic Roll.
No more You fleep, hid in an awful Gloom,
Your Shades all fcatter, and your Beauties bloom;
Years yet unborn, your op'ning Scenes unfold,
And all your dawning Clouds are edg'd with Gold.
So when the *Shekinah*, myfterious, ftood
High o'er *Arabia's* divided Flood,
(When down the Sands below the Prophet led,
And the Waves foam'd fublime above his Head,)
Whilft Clouds and Darknefs *Egypt's* Hoft amaz'd,
O'er *Ifrael's* Ranks immortal Glory blaz'd.

And Thou, my Mufe, affume a joyful Air,
Remind his Candor, and forbid thy Fear.
Tell him You come before the Fount of Day,
And from the Source of Light, demand a Ray.
Gracious, He'll grant the Favour thou haft pray'd,
And fling the Blaze of Glories from his Head.
As on the fragrant Windings of the Shore
Where *Perfia* glitters with her golden Ore,
Up the high Hills the early People rife,
And to the Eaft turn their defiring Eyes,
Till beamy *Phœbus* guilds the rofey Skies,
Then, all at once, their founding Shouts unite,
Hail the bright Car, and blefs the lovely Light

Pleas'd

Pleas'd with their Prayer, he Paſſes o'er the Land,
And ſcatters Bleſſings with a laviſh Hand;
The Fields all brighten, as he onward moves,
And his fair Glories fluſh the gladen'd Groves;
O'er all the Earth the flaming Splendor flows,
Like one great Ruby, all the Ocean glows:
To BURNET thus I ſue, He thus complies,
And thus his ſoft Indulgence ſooths my Eyes.

On the DEATH

OF THE

QUEEN.

A P O E M.

Infcribed to His EXCELLENCY

Governour BELCHER.

By the Reverend Mr. *BYLES*,

Non Ego illam mihi dotem duco effe,quæ dos dicitur :
Sed pudicitiam, et pudorem, et fedatum cupidinem,
Deum metum, parentum amorem, et cognatum concordiam :
Tibi morigera, atque ut munifica fim bonis, profim probis.
                                    Alcm. in Plaut. Amphit.

BOSTON in *NEW ENGLAND* :
Printed by J. DRAPER, for D. HENCHMAN in Cornhill. 1733

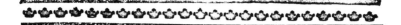

On the 𝔇𝔢𝔞𝔱𝔥
OF THE
QUEEN.

To His EXCELLENCY
Governour B E L C H E R

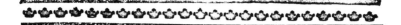

Hile from each foul the forrows
copious flow,
And weepingNations heave with
mighty woe;
Whilſt ev'ry lyre to mournful notes is ſtrung,
And CAROLINA flutters on each tongue:
The mourning Muſe, to conſolation deaf,
Swells the ſad conſort with melodious grief.

Ten

Ten flow'ry springs on golden plumes have flown,
Since she, triumphant, hail'd thee on thy throne.
Oh CAROLINE *!* Oh Princess now no more!
Each heart bleeds inward, and all eyes deplore.
Stretch'd pale in death thy lovely limbs are laid,
Thy beauty, *Albion,* and thy joys are fled *!*
To thee, our tears their filial torrents bring,
And ev'ry passion opens ev'ry spring :
Lost to despair, in wild laments we moan,
And distant regions echo groan for groan.

'Twas she, adorn'd by Virtue's heav'nly charms,
In rosey beauty blest her Prince's arms;
Her lover with a pious eye she view'd,
And CESAR at her feet successless su'd :

Imperial

Imperial purple her calm eyes difdain,
And *Roman* Eagles wav'd their wings in vain ;
Infpir'd, Religion's dictates to difcharge,
She gave her felf to *Britain* and to GEORGE.

Say, rais'd *Britannia,* how her gentle air,
Adorn'd the palace, and improv'd the fair.
Difcord, and party-rage grew tame, to gaze,
And noify factions clamour'd in her praife.
Domeftick life th' illuftrious Pattern grac'd ;
On Royal milk the Royal infants feaft :
Form'd by her hands the Monarch race were feen,
The rip'ning Hero, and the future Queen.
Far fom vain courts her filent footfteps roam,
Where chofen volumes deck'd the facred dome:

B   Still

Still loud applauſes of the joyful age,
Purſu'd her thro' the lonely Hermitage·
Here, in high raptures, her immortal mind,
O'er *Newton*'s Orbs expatiates, unconfin'd ;
Familiar gueſt! ſhe viſits all the Skies,
From world to world, from ſun to ſun ſhe flies ;
Thence ſmiles at Mimick crowns whichSultans
      wear
In the mock empires of this little ſtar.

Such was the Queen! ſhe was — but is no
      more ! ——
Wide wounds the woe, and ſpreads from ſhore
      to ſhore :
                                        Groans

Groans the hoarfe Ocean as the tydings fly,
Wave roars to wave, and rocks to rocks reply,
She was, but is no more — loft all relief !
Now all her graces greaten all our grief.
Ev'n our far land its anguifh loud proclaims,
We felt her influence, and we bleft her beams.

But, *BELCHER*, firft in Grief as in Com-
    mand ;
With early zeal you kift her beauteous hand ;
Your honours to the deftin'd Queen you paid,
Ere the crown flafh'd, far-beaming, on her head
The Mufe reluctant, by your Order fings,
Elfe had fhe filent wept, and broke her ftrings.
                         What

What fame to *us* reports, by *you* were feen,
The glance attractive, the majeftick mien,
The Angel form each milder feature wears,
That look obliging, thofe defcending airs.
Collected in her innocence fhe ftood,
Devout to Heav'n, to men divinely good,
You faw— now fee the fated end of all :
How the F A I R fades, and how the MIGHTY fall*!*

See the pale cheek its faded blufh refign,
The dying eyes with tranfient luftre fhine ;
Hoarfe the funk voice, the breaft no longer warm,
And death gains faft o'er ev'ry mortal charm.
O Virtue, now thy joys are all fincere !
Th' exulting Queen demands the final pray'r,

(Eternal

(Eternal glories op'ning to her view,)
Waves her joy hand, and bids theGlobe adieu.

See, in the Regal vaults, the ſhatter'd lead,
Whoſe gaping ſeams diſcloſe the Royal dead.
Were theſe, O Muſe, triumphantSov'reigns once!
This skin all ſhrivel'd! and theſe naked bones!
No more reſentful, great E L I Z A, reſt,
Support in peace the *Scottiſh Mary's* cheſt!
Whilſt cloſe, by Glorify'd M A R I A's ſhrine,
We place the duſt of Heav'nly C A R O L I N E.
Ye Living,hear what mouldringMonarchs ſay!
" *For endleſs joys give mortal dreams away.*

THE
COMET:
A
POEM.

BOSTON: Printed and Sold by B. GREEN and Comp.
in *Newbury-Street*, and D. GOOKIN, at the Corner of
Water-street, Cornhil. 1 7 4 4.

THE
C O M E T.

ESCEND, *Urania*, and infpire my verfe,
I raife my fong to fing your kindred ftars;
I aim to rove where glitt'ring comets ftray,
Trace the bright wand'rers thro' th' Æ-
therial way,
And all around th' Almighty's pow'r proclaim,
Where worlds can roll, or funs inceffant flame.

See! heav'nly mufe, view with attentive eyes,
The ruddy wonder of the ev'ning fkies!
From ftar to ftar, the burning ruin rolls,
Beams thro' the Ether, and alarms the poles:
Around the earth the wond'ring nations gaze,
On the dire terrors of the lengthen'd blaze,
While, trailing on, they dream its fparkling hair,
Shakes famine, earthquake, peftilence and war:
Illufions vain! remote from human things,
Where other planets roll in other rings
It travels vaft; and all around proclaims
A world in chaos, or an earth in flames.

So,

So, thro' the Ether, fwept the ancient earth,
Ere time, and form, and beauty firft had birth,
Unfhap'd and void, thro' fpace immenfe it roam'd,
Till fpoke the GoD——— and *Eden* inftant bloom'd.

What ruin ! what confufion might be hurl'd,
By fuch a ball, upon our guilty world ?
Witnefs, ye waves, which in the deluge fpread,
Whelm'd o'er the earth, and ftretch'd the nations dead.
Down heav'n's high fteep, wide-fpread the fteaming train
Rufh'd on the fields, and pour'd the floods of rain ,
The dark abyfs, attracted into day,
Gufh'd o'er the mountain-tops, and ror'd away ;
The toft ark, tott'ring, thro' its fabrick fhook,
Involv'd in clouds and darknefs, foam and fmoke,
By tempefts plung'd along from fteep to fteep,
Bounds to the clouds, or dafhes down the deep.
Ye angels ! guard her thro' the ftormy fcene,
Till the gay rainbow arch the heav'ns ferene.

But, O my mufe, fwift muft the time come on,
When frefh infpir'd, and fervid from the fun,
The flagrant Stranger fhapes a diff'rent path,
And from its annual orbit drags the earth.
Ye fancy, mortals ! diftant as ye are,
All calm and placid round the failing ftar,

     In

In gentle rays ferenely gleams the head,
And eafy lufter thro' the train is fpread:
Ah, ye perceive not what loud tumult reigns
Thro' the hot regions of its wild domains ;
What hideous thunder the wide Ether fhocks,
Of tumbling mountains, and of crafhing rocks:
Fierce feas of flame beat round the burning fhores,
And ev'ry tempeft raves, and every furnace rofes.
To this devoted earth it marches on,
And midnight blazes with the glare of noon ,
Big, and more big, it arches all the air,
A vault of fluid Brafs the fkies appear:
From their foundations, where they ancient ftood,
Down rufh the mountains in a flaming flood ;
The min'rals pour their melted bowels out,
The rocks run down, the flying rivers fpout ;
The earth difolves thro' its disjointed frame,
Its clouds all lighten, and its Etna's flame ;
The fea exhales, and in long volumes hurl'd,
Follows the wand'ring globe from world to world :
Now at the fun it glows, now fheers its flight
Thro' the cold defarts of eternal night,
Warns every creature thro' its tracklefs road,
The fate of finners, and the wrath of GOD.

POEMS.

THE

Conflagration,

Applied to that grand Period or Cataſtrophe of
our World, when the Face of Nature is to
be changed by a Deluge of Fire, as formerly
it was by that of Water.

THE

God of Tempeſt

AND

Earthquake.

BOSTON, Printed;
And Sold by D. Fowle *in* Ann-ſtreet, *and by* Z. Fowle
in Middleſtreet.

❖❖❖HE ſentiments of authors are various in regard to the cauſe
❖ ❖ whence the Conflagration is to ariſe, and the effects it is to
❖❖❖ produce. Divines will have it take its riſe from a miracle,
as a fire from heaven ; but philoſophers contend for it being produced
from natural cauſes : ſome think an eruption of the central fire ſufficient for the purpoſe ; others look for the cauſe in the atmoſphere.
The aſtrologers account for it from a conjunction of all the planets in
the ſign Cancer, as they ſay the deluge was occaſioned by the conjunction in Capricorn : but others aſſure themſelves that the world is to
undergo its conflagration from the near approach of a comet in its re-
return from the ſun ; as theſe huge bodies, by the intenſity of their
heat, and their wandering tranſverſe motion acroſs the earth's orbit,
threaten to produce the moſt ſignal changes and revolutions in the
ſyſtem of things.
                              New Dictionary of Arts and Sciences.

The Conflagration.

IN some calm Midnight, when no whisp'ring Breeze
Waves the tall Woods, or curls th' undimpled Seas,
Lull'd on their oazy Beds, the Rivers seem
Softly to murmur in a pleasing Dream ;
The shaded Fields confess a still Repose,
And on each Hand the dewy Mountains drowse :
Mean time the Moon, fair Empress of the Night !
In solemn Silence sheds her Silver Light,
While twinkling Stars their glimm'ring Beauties shew,
And wink perpetual o'er the heav'nly blue ;
Sleep, nodding, consecrates the deep Serene,
And spreads her brooding Wings o'er all the dusky Scene :
Through the fine Ether moves no single Breath ;
But all is hush as in the Arms of Death.
  At once, Great GOD ! thy dire Command is giv'n,
That the last Tempest shake the Frame of Heav'n.
Strait thick'ning Clouds in gloomy Volumes rise,
Gather on Heaps, and blacken in the Skies ;
Sublime through Heav'n redoubling Thunders roll,
And gleamy Lightnings flash from Pole to Pole.
Old Ocean with presaging Horror rores,
And rousing Earthquakes rumble round the Shores ;
Ten thousand Terrors o'er the Globe are hurl'd,
And gen'ral Dread alarms a guilty World.
  But Oh ! what Glory breakes the scatt'ring Glooms ?
Lo ! down the op'ning Skies, he comes ! he comes !
The Judge descending flames along the Air ;
And shouting Myriads pour around his Carr :

Each

Each ravifh'd Seraph labours in his Praife,
And Saints, alternate, catch th' immortal Lays ;
Here in melodious Strains bleft Voices fing,
Here warbling Tubes, and here the vocal String,
Here from fweet Trumpets Silver Accents rife,
And the fhril Clangour echo's round the Skies.
   And now, O Earth ! thy final Doom attend,
In awful Silence meet thy fiery End.
Lo ! rifing radiant from his burning Throne,
The Godhead, thund'ring, calls the Ruins on.
" Curft Earth ! polluted with the Prophets Blood,
" Thou, the vile Murd'rer of the Son of GOD,
" Full ripe for Vengeance, Vengeance be thy Due,
" Perifh in Flames, refine, and rife anew !
Thus as he fpeaks, all Nature owns the GOD,
Quiver the Plains, the lofty Mountains nod.
The hollow winding Caverns echo round,
And Earth, and Sea, and Air, and Heav'n refound.
   Now ratt'ling on tremendous Thunder rolls,
And loudly crafhing, fhakes the diftant Poles ;
O'er the thick Clouds amazing Lightnings glare,
Flames flafh at Flames, and vibrate through the Air ;
Roaring Vulcanoes murmur for their Prey,
And from their Mouth curls the black Smoke away ;
Deep groans the Earth, at its approaching Doom,
While in flow Pomp the mighty Burnings come.
As when dark Clouds rife flowly from the Main,
Then, in fwift Sluices, deluge all the Plain,
Defcending headlong down the Mountains Sides,
A thoufand Torrents roll their foamy Tides,
The rufhing Rivers rapid roar around,
And all the Shores return the dafhing Sound :

Thus

Thus awful, flow, the fiery Deluge low'rs,
Thus rufhes down, and thus refounding rores.
But O ! what Sounds are able to convey
The wild Confufions of the dreadful Day !
Eternal Mountains totter on their Bafe,
And ftrong Convulfions work the Valley's Face ;
Fierce Hurricanes on founding Pinions foar,
Rufh o'er the Land, on the tofs'd Billows rore,
And dreadful in refiftlefs Eddies driv'n,
Shake all the chryftal Battlements of Heav'n.
See the wild Winds, big-bluftring in the Air,
Drive through the Forefts, down the Mountains tare,
Sweep o'er the Vallies in their rapid Courfe,
And Nature bends beneath th' impetuous Force.
Storms rufh at Storms, at Tempefts Tempefts rore,
Dafh Waves on Waves, and thunder to the Shore.
Columns of Smoke on heavy Wings afcend,
And dancing Sparkles fly before the Wind.
Devouring Flames, wide-waving, roar'd aloud,
And melted Mountains flow a fiery Flood :
Then, all at once, immenfe the Fires arife,
A bright Deftruction wraps the crackling Skies :
While all the Elements to melt confpire,
And the World blazes in the final Fire.
  Yet fhall ye, Flames, the wafting Globe refine,
And bid the Skies with purer Splendour fhine,
The Earth, which the prolifick Fires confume,
To Beauty burns, and withers into Bloom ;
Improving in the fertile Flame it lies,
Fades into Form, and into Vigour dies :
Frefh-dawning Glories blufh amidft the Blaze,
And Nature all renews her flow'ry Face.

With

With endlefs Charms the everlafting Year
Rolls round the Seafons in a full Career ;
Spring, ever-blooming, bids the Fields rejoice,
And warbling Birds try their melodious Voice ;
Where e'er fhe treads, Lillies unbidden blow,
Quick Tulips rife, and fudden Rofes glow :
Her Pencil paints a thoufand beauteous Scenes,
Where Bloffoms bud amid immortal Greens ;
Each Stream, in Mazes, murmurs as it flows,
And floating Forefts gently bend their Boughs.
Thou, *Autumn*, too, fitt'ft in the fragrant Shade,
While the ripe Fruits blufh all around thy Head :
And lavifh Nature, with luxuriant Hands,
All the foft Months, in gay Confufions blends.

The holy Nation here tranfported roves
Beneath the fpreading Honours of the Groves,
And pleas'd, attend, defcending down the Hills,
The murm'ring Mufick of the running Rills.
Anthems divine by ev'ry Harp are play'd,
And the foft Mufick warbles thro' the Shade.

Hither, my Lyre, thy foft Affiftance bring,
And let fweet Accents leap from String to String :
Join the bright Chorus of the future Skies,
While all around loud Hallelujah's rife,
And to the tuneful Lays the echoing Vault replies.

This blcffed Hope, my ravifh'd Mind infpires,
And through my Bofom flafh the facred Fires :
No more my Heart its growing Joy contains,
But driving Tranfports rufh along my Veins ;
I feel a Paradife within my Breaft,
And feem already of a Heav'n poffefs'd.

✳✳✳✳✳

The God of Tempest and Earthquake.

1.

THY dreadful Pow'r, Almighty GOD,
  Thy Works to speak conspire ;
This Earth declares thy Fame abroad,
  With Water, Air, and Fire.

2.

At thy Command, in glaring Streaks,
  The ruddy Light'ning flies ;
Loud Thunder the Creation shakes,
  And rapid Tempests rise.

3.

Now gathering Glooms obscure the Day,
  And shed a solemn Night ;
And now the heav'nly Engines play,
  And shoot devouring Light.

4.

Th' attending Sea thy Will performs,
  Waves tumble to the Shore,
And toss, and foam amidst the Storms,
  And dash, and rage, and rore.

5.

The Earth, and all her trembling Hills,
  Thy marching Foot-Steps own ;
A shudd'ring Fear her Entrails fills,
  Her hideous Caverns groan.

6.

My GOD, when Terrors thickest throng,
  Thro' all the mighty Space,
And rat'ling Thunders rore along,
  And bloody Lightning, blaze :

7.

When wild Confusion wrecks the Air,
  And Tempests rend the Skies,
Whilst blended Ruin, Clouds and Fire
  In harsh Disorder rise :

8.

Amid the Hurricane I'll stand
And strike a tuneful Song ;
My Harp all trembling in my Hand,
And all infpir'd my Tongue.

9.

I'll shout aloud, " Ye Thunders. I roll,
" And shake the sullen Sky ;
" Your founding Voice from Pole to Pole
" In angry Murmmurs try.

10.

" Thou Sun ! retire, refufe thy Light,
" And let thy Beams decay ;
" Ye Lightnings, flash along the Night,
" And dart a dreadful Day.

11

" Let the Earth totter on her Bafe,
" Clouds Heav'ns wide Arch deform ;
" Blow, all ye Winds, from ev'ry Place,
" And breathe the final Storm.

12.

" O JESUS, hafte the glorious Day,
" When thou shalt come in Flame,
" And burn the Earth, and wafte the Sea,
" And brake all Nature's Frame.

13.

" Come quickly, *Bleffed Hope*, appear,
" Bid thy fwift Chariot fly ;
" Let Angels warn thy coming near,
" And fnatch me to the Sky.

14.

" Around thy Wheels, in the glad Throng,
" I'd bear a joyful Part ;
" All *Hallelujah* on my Tongue,
" All Rapture in my Heart.

F I N I S.

POEMS

ON

Several Occasions

By Mr. BYLES.

Nunc itaque et verfus et cætera ludicra pono.
Hor. Lib. 1. Epift. 1. v. 10.

BOSTON: Printed and Sold by S. Kneeland and T. Green, in Queenftreet, 1744.

PREFACE.

THE Poems collected in thefe Pages, were for the moſt Part written as the Amuſements of looſer Hours, while the Author belonged to the College, and was unbending his Mind from ſeverer Studies, in the Entertainments of the Claſſicks. Moſt of them have been ſeveral
Times

PREFACE.

Times printed here, at *London*,
and elsewhere, either seperate-
ly, or in Miscellanies : And the
Author has now drawn them
into a Volume. Thus he gives
up at once these lighter Productions, and bids adieu to the
airy Muse.

POEMS

ON

Several Occasions.

The Almighty CONQUEROR.

I.

AWake my Heart, awake my Tongue,
 Sound each melodious String ;
In num'rous Verse and lofty Song,
 To thee, my GOD, I sing.

II.

Omnipotent Redeemer-LORD,
 What Wonders haft thou done !
My flowing Numbers shall record,
 The Vict'ries thou haft won.

B   III. I

III.

I glow in Raptures all divine,
  As with the Theme I rife,
Your tuneful Aids, fictitious Nine,
  No more fhall tempt my Eyes.

IV.

Lo! rob'd with Light, J e s u s defcends
  The Graves tremendous Gloom ;
Day blufhes round him where he tends,
  And dawns amid the Tomb.

V.

Sudden from off that difmal Bed,
  The fcatt'ring Shadows fly ;
The dark Dominions of the Dead
  Confefs the Stranger, *Joy.*

VI.

Hark! how in hideous Howls complains
  The conquer'd Tyrant *Death* ;
He roars aloud, and fhakes his Chains,
  And grinds his Iron Teeth.

VII. Immortal

VII.

Immortal Vigour fill'd the **Man,**
Almighty Pow'r the GOD,
When, arm'd with Thunders, down he ran
To *Satan*'s dire Abode.

VIII.

Then Hell's grim Monarch faw, and **fear'd,**
And felt his tott'ring Throne ;
He rag'd, and foam'd, and wildly ftar'd,
And feiz'd his nodding Crown.

IX.

In vain he rav'd, and roll'd his Eyes,
And held his Crown in vain :
Swift on his Head the Lightning flies,
With everlafting Pain.

X.

At once th' old Serpent's Craft was crufh'd,
Beneath thy fiery Frown,
When Thou, great GOD, refiftlefs rufh'd,
And hurl'd the Monfter down.

XI. Thy

XI.

Thy Fetters, in the deep Abyſs,
　His tort'red Members wring :
There let him writhe, and coyl, and hiſs,
　And dart his pointleſs Sting.

XII.

Theſe were the Victims of thy Hate,
　When Fury fiuſh'd thy Face ;
But who, dear Saviour, can relate
　The Conqueſts of thy Grace !

XIII.

Ceaſe, ceaſe my Tongue, be ſtill, my Lyre,
　Be ſilent every String :
This is a Theme, O heav'nly Choir,
　Too great for you to ſing.

The GOD of Tempeſt.

I.

THY dreadful Pow'r, Almighty GOD,
　Thy Works to ſpeak conſpire ;
This Earth declares thy Fame abroad,
　With Water, Air, and Fire.

II. At

II.

At thy Command, in glaring Streaks,
  The ruddy Light'ning flies ;
Loud Thunder the Creation ſhakes,
  And rapid Tempeſts riſe.

III.

Now gathering Glooms obſcure the Day,
  And ſhed a ſolemn Night ;
And now the heav'nly Engines play,
  And ſhoot devouring Light.

IV.

Th' attending Sea thy Will performs,
  Waves tumble to the Shore,
And toſs, and foam amidſt the Storms,
  And daſh, and rage, and roar.

V.

The Earth, and all her trembling Hills,
  Thy marching Footſteps own ;
A ſhudd'ring Fear her Entrails fills,
  Her hideous Caverns groan.

VI. My

VI.

My GOD, when Terrors thickeſt Throng
 Thro' all the mighty Space,
And ratt'ling Thunders roar along,
 And bloody Lightnings blaze :

VII.

When wild Confuſion wrecks the Air,
 And Tempeſts rend the Skies,
Whilſt blended Ruin, Clouds and Fire
 In harſh Diſorder riſe :

VII.

Amid the Hurricane I'll ſtand,
 And ſtrike a tuneful Song ;
My Harp all-trembling in my Hand,
 And all inſpir'd my Tongue.

VIII.

I'll ſhout aloud, " Ye Thunders ! roll,
 " And ſhake the ſullen Sky ;
" Your ſounding Voice from Pole to Pole
 " In angry Murmurs try.

IX. Thou

IX.

" Thou Sun ! retire, refuse thy Light,
   " And let thy Beams decay ;
" Ye Lightnings, flash along the Night,
   " And dart a dreadful Day.

X.

" Let the Earth totter on her Base,
   " Clouds Heav'ns wide Arch deform :
" Blow, all ye Winds, from ev'ry Place,
   " And breath the final Storm.

XI.

" O Jesus, haste the glorious Day,
   " When thou shalt come in Flame,
" And burn the Earth, and waste the Sea,
   " And break all Nature's Frame.

XII.

" Come quickly, *Blessed Hope !* appear,
   " Bid thy swift Chariot fly :
" Let Angels tell thy coming near,
   " And snatch me to the Sky.

XIII.

XIII.

" Around thy Wheels, in the glad Throng
 " I'd bear a joyful Part ;
" All *Hallelujah* on my Tongue,
 " All Rapture in my Heart.

The Complaint and the Confolation.

I.

WHERE fhall I find my LORD, my LOVE,
 The Sov'REIGN of my Soul ?
Penfive from Eaft to Weft I rove,
 And range from Pole to Pole.

II.

I fearch the fhady Bow'rs, and trace
 The Mazes of the Grove,
Dear LORD, to fee thy beauteous Face,
 And tell thee how I love.

III.

For Him, about the flow'ry Fields
 My wand'ring Footfteps ftray,
When dewy Morn each Mountain guilds,
 And purples o'er the Sea ;

IV. Till

IV.

Till Ev'ning bids the Weftern Clouds
   With glittering Edges flame,
To the foft Winds, and murm'ring Floods,
   I ftill repeat his Name.

V.

Ev'n in the filent Shades of Night
   My Song the Foreft fills ;
When the fair Moon with folemn Light
   Has filver'd o'er the Hills.

VI.

Jesus my Fair ! aloud I cry,
   For thee, for thee I burn ;
Jesus, the echoing Vales reply,
   Jesus, the Rocks return.

VII.

Ah thou my Life, when fhall I tafte
   That Heav'n of endlefs Charms ?
When fhall I pant upon thy Breaft ;
   And languifh in thy Arms ?

C   VIII.

VIII.

Oh! how I long to clasp thee close,
　　Close in a strong Caress!
Joyful my latest Breath I'd loose
　　For so divine a Bliss.

IX.

Ye ling'ring Minutes, swiftly roll,
　　And rise, the happy Day,
When on his Bosom, thou my Soul,
　　Shalt all dissolve away.

X.

Then shall my flutt'ring Heart be fixt,
　　The Muse no more complain,
But with the Choirs immortal mixt,
　　Resound a heav'nly Strain.

The Altogether Lovely.

I.

OFT has thy Name employ'd my Muse,
　　Thou LORD of all above:
Oft has my Song to thee arose,
　　My Song, inspir'd by Love.

II. My

II.

My Heart has oft confefs'd in Flame,
  And melted all away :
Thou art by Night my hourly Dream,
  My hourly Thought by Day.

III.

Each Feature o'er thee is a Charm,
  And ev'ry Limb a Grace ;
Divinely beauteous all thy Form,
  Divinely fair thy Face.

IV.

Thy Love to me how large ! how full !
  How kind are thy Commands !
Take, O my Love, take all my Soul
  For ever in thy Hands.

V.

Thofe bleeding Hands, which on the Crofs
  Were ftretch'd for my Carefs :
In the dear Thought my Life I loofe ——
  Was ever Love like this !

VI. Weep

VI.

Weep, weep my Eyes, let gushing Tears
  Stream in an endless flow :
Love on his dying Lips he wears,
  His Wounds Compassion show.

VII.

Now he remembers me, and speaks,
  I hear his Voice ; *Forgive :*
In the dead Pale that spreads his Cheeks ;
  Ten thousand Beauties live.

VIII.

Lord, my Affections all are thine,
  Warm'd with a grateful Fire ;
And thou, O best Belov'd, art mine,
  My Hope, and my Desire.

IX.

Conspiring Love, conspiring Charms,
  Confess thee all my Joy :
Come, heav'nly Fair, come to my Arms
  And all my Pow'rs employ.

The

The Comparison, the Choice, and the Enjoyment.

I.

WHO on the Earth, or in the Skies,
 Thy Beauties can declare ?
Jesus, dear Object of my Eyes,
 My Everlasting Fair.

II.

Mortals, for you this is too great,
 Too bright, and too sublime :
This, Angels labour to repeat ;
 And sink beneath the Theme.

III.

Behold, ye Beauties here below,
 And clasp him in your Arms ;
Can ye such heav'nly Graces show,
 Or rival him in Charms ?

IV.

Though now, delighted, we can trace
 Your Colours as they lye,
When he appears, from off your Face
 The fading Colours fly.

V. When

V.

When all your Charms in vain we feek,
  And all your Joys are fled,
Beauty blooms rofey on his Cheek,
  And dances round his Head.

VI.

In vain your fofteft Smiles appear,
  Or lovely Blufhes rife :
Eternal Tranfports center here,
  Heav'n brightens in thefe Eyes.

VII.

Unveil, almighty Love, thy Face,
  Thy Features let me fee ;
At once I'll rufh to thy Embrace,
  I'll fpring at once to thee.

VIII.

With infinite Delight, I'll lay
  My Head foft on thy Breaft :
My Eyes fhall o'er thy Beauties ftray ;
  My Arms furround thy Waift.

IX. Thus

IX.

Thus fix'd for ever --- O the Joys !
  Th' unutterable Blifs !
Now where's your Pleafure, earthly **Toys** ?
  Can ye compare with This !

X.

No more from thy Embrace I'll roam,
  My L o r d, my Life, my Love,
I fee the Scenes of Joys to come
  In long Proceffion move.

XI.

Now, vaft Eternity, roll on,
  O fathomlefs Profound !
Ye endlefs Ages, fwiftly run,
  Your nevei-ceafing Round.

On a very profane Compliment in a noble and devout Poem.

A H ! Ceafe, *vain Mufe*, forbear thy hardy
  Lays,
Nor urge the Thunder on thy guilty Bays,
                                        How

How durſt thou thus debaſe the SAVIOUR's
    Blood,
And raiſe a Mortal o'er the Throne of GOD :
Melodiouſly-Profane, prefer his Name,
And, gay in Eloquence, thy Judge blaſpheme?
O'er the black Lines remain perpetual Gloom,
And Flames, and deep Oblivion be the Doom.
Round the dire Rant ſhall ſudden Lightnings
    rage,
And kindling Vengeance blaſt the impious Page.
So when th' Arch-Angel left his heav'nly Song,
And mock'd his Maker with a Seraph's Tongue,
MESSIAH, terrible in Wrath! aroſe,
And hurl'd him down to Hell's tremendous
    Woes,
Where Seas of Fire with roaring Storms reſound,
And endleſs Darkneſs ſpreads its brooding Hor-
    rors round.

HYMN

H Y M N to C H R I S T *for our* Regeneration *and* Refurrection.

I.

TO Thee, my Lo r d, I lift the Song,
    Awake, my tuneful Pow'rs :
In conftant Praife my grateful Tongue
    Shall fill my foll'wing Hours.

II.

Guilty, condemn'd, undone I ftood ;
    I bid my GOD depart :
He took my Sins, and paid his Blood,
    And turn'd this wand'ring Heart.

III.

Death, the grim Tyrant, feiz'd my Frame,
    Vile, loathfome and accurft :
His Breath renews the vital Flame,
    And Glories change the Duft.

IV.

Now, Saviour, fhall thy Praife commence ;
    My Soul by Thee brought Home,
And ev'ry Member, ev'ry Senfe,
    Recover'd from the Tomb.

D   V. To

V.

To Thee my Reafon I fubmit,
   My Love, my Mem'ry, Lord,
My Eyes to read, my Hands to write,
   My Lips to preach thy Word.

GOLIAH's *Defeat.*

In the Manner of Lucan.

WHEN the proud Philiftines for War de-
      clar'd,
And *Ifrael's* Sons for Battle had prepar'd,
Before the Heathen Camp a Monfter ftalk'd,
And awful frowning, in the Valley walk'd.
With hideousStrides he travers'd all theGround,
And o'er the Hills the Country view'd around
His brawny Flefh, and his prodigious Bones,
Befpoke him one of *Anak's* mighty Sons.
Death and Defiance fat upon his Brow,
Revenge and Hell his glaring Eye-balls fhow.
                                             Then

Then his dire Hand uplifted to the Skies,
Thunder his Voice, and Lightning in his Eyes,
He cry'd aloud with such a dreadful Sound,
As shook the Heav'ns, and rent the trembling
    Ground
" Attend, ye Armies ; *Israel,* hear ; 'tis I
" Despise yourPow'r, and all your Hosts defy
" What! not a Man among you dares attempt
" The gloriousFight,or urge the knownEvent?
" His despicable Flesh shall make a Feast,
" For rav'nous Fowl, and each voracious
    Beast.

Behold, Concern and dire Amaze appear ⎫
Thro' all theHost, when they hisAccents hear, ⎬
Shudd'ring Anxiety, and black Despair. ⎭
Pale are their Faces, in their Hearts is dread,
And panick Terror o'er the Field is spread.
Ghastly Confusion reigns, and not a Knight
Dares undertake to *think* upon the Fight.

Now

Now a young Shepherd, *David* was his Name,
To fee his Brethren in the Army, came :
But when *Goliah*'s threatning Words he heard,
A gen'rous Anger in his Looks appear'd.
To *Saul* the King, his hafty Footfteps go,
And loud he claims for Combat with the Foe.
Th' aftonifh'd Chiefs, the daring Challenge hear,
And give Confent with Wonder and with Fear.
Inftant the blooming Youth defcends a Brook,
And in his Shepherd's Bag five Pebbles took ;
He waits impatient, till his longing Eyes,
The gloomy Giant iffuing forth defcries,
With his tall Plume high-nodding in the Skies.
He roar'd loud Curfes as he onward went,
Tortur'd the Air, and fhook the Firmament.
David undaunted heard the Voice with Smiles,
And ran triumphant to the mighty Spoils.
Downward *Goliah* caft a carelefs Glance,
And faw the Stripling on the Ground advance.
As from fome lofty Tow'r, tall Men below
Acrofs the Streets like little Puppets go :

So

So look'd young *David* to *Goliah's* fize,
And, deep beneath, fcarce reach'd his loftyEyes.
Sublime, the Monfter faw him with difdain,
Like a fmall Infect run along the Plain.
At firft, collected in himfelf he ftood,
‘ Himfelf, an Army ! and his Spear, a Wood ! ’
His Helmet like a fiery Meteor fhone,
Blaz'd high amidft the Heav'ns ; another Sun.
His flaming Buckler with his Arm did rife,
Streak'd Rainbows on the Clouds, and flafh'd
    about the Skies.
Then, with uplifted Roar, aloud he howls,
And fhakes all Nature to the diftant Poles.
" What daring Mortal this who treads theField,
" And thinks himfelf fo fmall to be conceal'd ?
" Hence, fly my Rage, young Stripling quickly
    fly,
" Or, by theGods! byDagon! Thou fhalt die.
" This Hand, rafhYouth, thy mangled Carcafe
    tares,
" And hurls thy fcatter'dLimbs above theStars.

‘ For

" For Birds and Beafts, thyEntrails ſpread the
    Plains,

" And on the Pavement ſmoke thy batter'd
    Brains !

" Not all thePow'rs above my Wrath ſhall brave ;

" Thy God may pity, but he cannot ſave.

Fearleſs, the Hero heard the thundring Peals
Drive thro'theRocks,and rattling roundtheHills.
Diſdain flaſh'd dreadful from his martial Eyes,
And thus aloud his dauntleſs Tongue replies.

" Ceaſe,emptyVaunter,ceaſethy impiousBreath,

" This Stone ſhall fly commiſſicn'd with thy
    Death :

" Your's is the Sword and Spear you vainly
    boaſt,

" The Vict'ry's mine,for mine's the LORD OF
    HOST !

He ſaid ; then whirl'd his Sling, the Pebble
    flung,
It flew impetuous, and triumphant ſung ;

On

On his broad Front it ſtrook the Wariour full,
And Death drove furious thro' his craſhing
    Scull.
Down fell the mighty Bulk ; Hills, Fields
    and all,
Shook when he fell, and echo'd to the Fall.
In Duſt and Blood awhile his Members roll,
Then Night eternal ruſh'd upon his Soul.
A Length enormous in the Plains he ſhow'd.
' Like a vaſt Iſland in a Sea of Blood.

O D E, *for* Palatine *Tune.*

I.

HEav'nly Love, our Boſoms ſeize !
    Ye ſoft ſeraphick Pow'rs,
      Come, join your Songs with ours ;
Gently as the dying Breeze
Whiſpers o'er the Midnight-Seas,
    Or breathes along the Shores.

II. Let

II.

Let the tender Echoes round
        The facred Song improve,
        And fweetly onward move :
Loft in Extafy of Sound,
Let the feather'd Choirs refound
        Thro' all the tuneful Grove.

III.

Jesus, 'tis to Thee we fing,
        Thou, the celeftial Fair,
        Soft to our Breafts repair ;
Elfe we break each joyful String,
With fad Notes the Vales fhall ring
        Abandon'd to Defpair.

IV.

Oh ! thy Love our Paffion warms!
        Come blefs our longing Sight.
        Come, over-pow'r us quite :
Put on all thy wondrous Charms,
Come and fill our ravifh'd Arms,
        And Heav'n is lefs Delight.

Written

Written in M I L T O N's *PARADISE LOST.*

HAD I, O had I all the tuneful Arts
Of lofty Verſe ; did ev'ry Muſe inſpire
My flowing Numbers, and adorn my Song !
Did MILTON's Fire flaſh furious in my Soul ;
Could I command the Harmony, the Force,
The glitt'ring Language, and the true Sublime
Whoſe mingledBeauties grace his glowing Lays,
Then ſhould my Lines glide languiſhingly flow,
Or thundring roar, and rattle as they fleet,
Or, lovely-ſmiling, bud immortal Bloom,
As various as the Subjeᷓ they deſcribe,
And imitate the Beauties which they mark.
Thus with ambitious Hand, I'd boldly ſnatch
A ſpreading Branch from his immortal Laurels.

But, O my Muſe, where ſhall thy Song begin ?
Or where conclude ? ten thouſand Glories charm
My raviſh'd Heart, and dance before my Sight.
O MILTON ! I'm tranſported at thy Name !
My Soul takes Wing at once ; or ſhoots away,
Born eager by a Tyde of Thought along.

E   Some-

Sometimes big Fury fwells thy awful Verfe,
And rolling Thunder burfts along thy Lines.
Now Hell is open'd, and I fee the Flames
Wide-waving, blazing high, and flutt'ring dance:
Now clanking Chains amaze my lift'ning Ears,
And hideous Spectres fkim before my Sight,
Or in my wild Imagination ftare.

Here *Satan* rears his mighty Bulk on high,
And tow'rs amid th' infernal Legions ; fill'd
With Pride, and dire Revenge ; daring his Looks ;
Rage heaves his lab'ring Breaft, and all around
His fiery Eye-balls formidably roll,
And dart deftructive Flames ; with dreadful
      Blaze
The ruddy Ligh'ning rapid runs along,
And guilds the gloomy Regions of Defpair,
With Streaks tremendous.   Here affaults my
      Sight
The grefsly Monfter *Death*, He onward ftalks
With horrid Strides, Hell trembles as he treads ;
                                    On

On his fierce Front a bold defiance low'rs ;
Bent is his Brow, in his right Hand he fhakes
His quiv'ring Lance. How fell the Fiend
    appears
In ev'ry Profpect, wrathful or ferene ?
Pleas'd, *horrible he grins a gaftly Smile* ;
And *Erebus* grows blacker as he Frowns.

  But tell, immortal Mufe, O Goddefs ! tell
The joyful Dread, the terrible Delight,
Which fill my Mind, when I behold theRanks,
Th' embatt'led Ranks of mighty Cherubim,
In dreadfulQuadrate croud thePlains of Heav'n.
I hear, I hear the Trumpets loud Alarms ;
The keen Vibration cuts the yielding Air,
And the fhril Clangors ring around the Sky.
I fee the bold intrepid Cohorts move ;
From ev'ry Scabbard flies a flaming Sword,
Wav'd by the mighty Combatants on high,
So flafhing radiant from a gloomy Cloud,
Long Lightnings flourifh with a livid Glare.
Now on at once th' immortal Hero's rufh,

         And

And with a sudden Onset shake the Field.

Hark ! how confus'd Sounds thicken in theAir,

Mingling, tumultous,and perplex'd, and rough,

Of Shouts, and Groans, and grating Clang of
    Arms,

The twanging Bow, the Jav'lins deadly Hifs,

Loud-clafhing Swords, and Spears encountring
    Spears.

Helms found on Helms, on Bucklers Bucklers
    ring,

Vaft waving Wings high in the Air are heard,

Whilft loud-refounding Feet beat thick the
    Ground,

And all the jarring Sounds of War unite,

In direful Difcord, and outragious Roar.

Behold, my Mufe, where *Michael* bends his
    Courfe,

Starts his fwift Car, and bounds impetuous on,

With rapid Rage it rattles thro' the Ranks,

Smokes o'er theField,and drives theWar along.

But

But who can tell the Raptures which I feel,
When fix'd in deep Aftonifhment, my Eyes
Behold Messiah, dread Messiah ! arm'd
With all the dire Artillery of God ?
Unnumber'd Seraphim around him throng,
Clap their expanded Wings, and fhout aloud ;
Heav'ns mighty Concave echo's to their Voice,
The everlafting Hills return the Sound.
Oh ! how I feel the noble Ardor warm
My beating Breaft, and thrill along my Veins !
My charging Spirits pour around my Heart ;
My Eyes bright-fparkling with immortal Fires.
His flying Chariot fhakes the tott'ring Sky,
Swift all the vaft Expanfe behind him rolls,
Refiftlefs Thunders rattle from his Hand,
Devouring Lightnings fhoot beneath his Feet,
Ten thoufand Terrors thicken where he bends.
What Havock! What Confufion fpreads the
   Plain !
What Myriads fall by his defcending Bolts,
Dafh'd to the Ground, and crufh'd beneath his
   Wheels ?

                                    Tumult

Tumult and Ruin, Horror, Rage and Death,
Play round his Sword, and fhake their fhaggy
    Wings :
Hell flames before him, wild Defpair ftalks on,
And purple Vict'ry hovers o'er his Head.
GreatGOD! whatVengeancekindled in thyEyes!
WhatThunders bellow'd! and what Lightnings
    blaz'd !
When *Satan*, daring Chief of all thy Foes !
Was feiz'd, as trembling and agaft he ftood,
Seiz'd by thy mighty Hand, and rais'd aloft,
Then headlong hurl'd down the high Steep of
    Heav'n ?
At the dire Sight his bold compeers amaz'd,
Confounded, fhiver ev'n amidft the Flames,
Forget to Fight, drop all their idle Arms,
Swift from thy Fury fly away, and down
Down from the tow'ring Battlements they rufh
Precipitant, into the Dark profound,
Whilft *Chaos* loud rebellows to the Fall.

   No more--- my fainting Mufe folds up her
    Wings,
Unable to fuftain fo ftrong a Flight---
                The

'The Battle only *Raphael* fhould relate,
Or Milton in fuch Strains as *Raphael* fings.

Let fofter Subjects now command my Mufe,
Let fofter Numbers fmoothly flow along,
And bloom, and bloſſom as the Ever-greens,
That deck the flow'ry Face of Paradife.
O Milton, *Eden* opens by thy Art,
And with redoubl'd Beauty wanton fmiles.
I'm charm'd, I'm ravifh'd,all my Souldiſſolves,
I loofe my Life amid the heav'nly Scenes ;
That in gay Order from thy Pencil flow.
O beauteous Garden ! O delightful Walks !
In you forever, ever will I ftray,
Glide o'er thy flow'ryVales,climb thy fair Hills,
And thro' thy fragrantLawns tranfported tread.
I'd trace the mazy Windings of thy Bow'rs,
And in the Gloom of thy furrounding Groves
Ask the cool Shadow, and the fanning Breeze.
Here rifing Perfume fhould regale my Smell,
And heav'nly Harmony tranfport my Ears ;

While

While all the Trees around, to court a look,
Flourifh luxuriant with unfading Charms.
Rofes, and Violets, and Daffodils,
And gaudy Tulips of a thoufand Dyes,
Shall fpring profufely round ; the Lilly too,
Ambitious, offer its unfullied White,
To grace a Garland for fair Innocence.
Ye feather'd Songfters of the Spring, arife,
Difplay your fpangledPlumes, where twinkling
     Gems,
With blended Beauties, caft a doubtful Blaze,
And, keenly-flafhing, ftrike the Gazer's Sight.
Let your fweet Voices warble thro' the Grove,
While in concording Harmony I hear
The purling Murmurs of the bubbling Brooks.
Mean time the embroider'd Banks on either
     Hand
Shall open all their everlafting Sweets,
Their verdant Honours, and their flow'ryPride,
As the pure floating Volumes wind along.
Here the firft Pair, divinely reign'd fupream,
And funk reclining on the flow'ry Turff.
                 Hail,

Hail, happy *Adam*, Heav'n adorns thy Soul,
Full blefs'd. And thou, immortal Mother, Hail!
O heav'nly-fair, divinely-beauteous *Eve* !
Thee to adorn what endlefs Charms confpire ?
Cæleftial Coral blufhes on thy Lips,
No op'ning Rofe glows with fo bright a Bloom.
Thy Breath abroad diffufive Odor fpreads,
A gay Carnation purples o'er thy Cheeks,
While thy fair Eyes roll round their radiant Orbs,
With winning Majefty, and nat'ral Art.
Thy waving Treffes on thy Shoulders play,
Flow loofely down, and wanton in the Wind.
You, am'rous *Zephires*, kifs her fnowy Breaft,
Flit foftly by, and gently lift her Locks.
Forgive, fair Mother, O forgive thy Son,
Forgive his vain Redundance of Expreffion,
Fir'd by thy Beauty, and by MILTON's Song.
Here could the ravifh'd Fancy rove perpetual,
Amid the Raptures, the tranfporting Blifs,
That in foft Meafures move for ever round.---

F

But,

But, O my Mufe, fhake off thefe idle Dreams,
Imaginary Trances ! vain Illufions !
Count the gay Stars, and number all the Sands,
And ev'ry Drop that in the Ocean floats :
But never hope to fum th' unnumber'd Charms,
That fwim before thy ever-ravifh'd Eyes,
When they on thee, O MILTON, give a glance.
In vain thou ftriv'ft to lifp his lofty Praife ;
Imperfect Accents flutter round thy Tongue,
And on thy Lips unfinifh'd, MILTON dies.
His mighty Numbers tow'r above thy Sight,
Mock thy low Mufick, and elude thy Strains.

❉❀❉❀❉❀❉❀❉❀❉❀❉❀❉❀❉❀❉❀❉❀❉❀❉

To the Memory of a young Commander flain in a
Battle with the Indians, 1724.

DEfcend, immortal Mufe, infpire my Song,
Let mournful Numbers gently flow along:
And thou, my Lyre, in folemn Notes complain,
And in fad Accents foftly fpeak thy Pain ;
Let melting Mufick tremble on thy Strings,
While in concording Sounds the Goddefs fings ;

Sings

Sings haplefs *Alpeus* in the gloomy Grave,
Alpeus the Gay, the Beauteous and the Brave ;
Alpeus, who with the Thirft of Glory fir'd,
Couragious in his Country's Caufe expir'd.

At the dear Name a forrowful Delight,
Recalls the Youth back to my longing Sight.
Ah, lovely Youth ! once flufh'd with ev'ry Grace,
A thoufand Charms adorn'd thy fmiling Face ;
A lilly White was on thy Forehead fpread,
And in thy Cheeks cæleftial rofey Red ;
O'er all thy Features no Defect was found,
But blooming Beauty ever hover'd round ;
And, whilft without, unnumber'd Charms com-
　　bin'd,
Unnumber'd Graces deck'd thy manly Mind.

Thus *Alpeus*, wert thou once by all beheld,
Like fome fair Flow'r, the Glory of the Field :
But now, alas ! ftop'd is thy fcatter'd Breath,
Thy Beauties rifled in the Arms of Death ;
From thy pale Cheeks the fading Colour flies,
And leaden Slumbers feal thy heavy Eyes.

So fome bright Bird repeats his Lays of Love,
And fings melodious in a golden Grove ;
When ftrait a Bullet, with a thund'ring Sound,
Burfts thro' the Air, and gives the deadly Wound;
Then, inftant from the blooming Bough im-
    pell'd.
He falls, and feebly flutters on the Field.

But, O my Mufe, forbear thefe Strains, and tell
How great he fought, and how divine he fell.
Say, how intrepid he maintain'd his Ground,
And with what Vigour fcatter'd Deaths around.
Now on the Waves in the fmall Bark he ftood,
And ting'd the Billows with th' Oppofers Blood ;
Now, daring, on the thickeft War he bore,
Broke thro' the Ranks, and gain'd the diftant
    Shore.
His Sword, like Light'ning, glitter'd from above,
When dreadful on, th' undaunted Hero drove,
And with fuch Sounds deftructive Thunder roars,
As his fwift Lead impetuous onward pours.
Now on the Left he bent, now to the Right
The youthful Warriour led along the Fight.

                          You

You Pagan Troops, could fcarce his Rage fuftain,
Tho' your dire Numbers blacken'd all the Plain.
Till feeling in his Breaft the fiery Wound,
The finking Youth drop'd fainting to the
    Ground ;
In quick fhort pants ebb'd out his quiv'ring
    Breath,
While o'er his Eye-lids hung the Shades of
    Death.

  Thrice happy Youth, fleep in thy filent Bed,
While blifsful Vifions dance around thy Head ;
Let living Verdure flourifh o'er thy Tomb,
And let unfading Flow'rs for ever bloom.
Mean time the Mufe thy Story fhall relate,
And fnatch thy Actions from the Jaws of Fate,
Declare th' unrival'd Wonders of thy Youth,
Nor cloud with Fable the refulgent Truth ;
So coming Ages fhall thy Deeds admire,
And late Pofterity thy Praife confpire.
Long as the Morning paints the blufhing Skies,
Or Nature in the Spring renew'd fhall rife ;
                  Whilft

Whilst the gay Sun pours down in radiant
    Streams,
The golden Glory of his blazing Beams ;
So long, O *Alpeus*, shall thy envy'd Name
Glow in the Records of immortal Fame :
There stand confess'd among the meaner Fires,
As *Syrius* shines amid the lesser Stars.

Written in Dr. WATT's *Poems* ; *given to a*
young Lady.

I.

WHILE rosey Cheeks their Bloom confess,
    And Youth thy Bosom warms,
Let Vertue, and let Knowledge dress,
    Thy Mind in brighter Charms.

II.

Daily on some fine Page to look
    Lay meaner Sports aside ;
And let the Needle, and the Book,
    Thy useful Hours divide.

III. Let

III.

Let Heav'nly Love from WATTS's Lays,
  Infpire thy youthful Blood ;
Nor let a mortal Rival feize
  That Heart ordain'd for God.

An ELEGY *addrefs'd to His Excellency Governour*
  BELCHER : *On the* Death *of his Brother-
  in-Law, the Honourable* DANIEL OLIVER, *Efq;*

PEnfive, o'ercome, the Mufe hung down her
    Head,
And heard the fatal News,-- "*The Friend is dead.*
Dumb, fixt in Sorrow, fhe forgot her Song,
The Tune forfook her Lyre, the Voice her
    Tongue,
'Till, BELCHER, You command her Strains to
    rife,
You ask, fhe fings ; You dictate, fhe replies ;
That well-known Voice awakes her dying Fires,
And inftant, at your Call, the Pow'r infpires.

Then

Then let our Griefs in mingling Streams
      deſcend,
You mourn the Brother, and I weep the Friend
He's dead------ O vaſt unutterable Woe !
Gone, gone for ever from theſe Seats below :
No more his gracious Lips our Souls ſhall move,
And lift us to the holy Joys above ;
No more the Church his ſacred Tranſports feel,
His ſtrong Devotion, and his fervent Zeal ;
No more his Face ſhines with the conſcious
      Calms,
Of Faith, and Pray'rs, and gen'rous Deeds, and
      Alms :
Ah ! fainting, pale, ebbs out his quiv'ring Breath,
And OLIVER the good deſcends to Death.

      Thus while the Friends their private Loſs
         deplore,
Lament unpity'd, unreliev'd, ye Poor.
Who, round his Gates, your daily Bleſſings paid,
Warm by his Cloaths, or from his Table fed.
Profuſe, his lib'ral Hand their Pray'r prevents,
(So ſhower'd the ancient *Manna* round the Tents)
                                          Witneſs

Witnefs, ye confcious Nights, whofe Shades he
 chofe,
Unknown, to fee, and fuccour Humane Woes :
Invifible, he trod the homely Cott,
The Hungry eat, th' Opprefs'd to groan forgot,
The Sick perceiv'd the fudden Cordial fave,
All blefs'd the Gift, nor faw the Hand that gave.
From Men, with Art and facred Caution hid,
The Mufe, from Heav'n infpir'd, reveals the Deed.

 You painted Roofs, and pompous Rooms of
 State,
Where, in the Senate, the grave Patriot fate,
Say, how his fteady Conduct grac'd your Board ;
Juft were his Thoughts, and prudent ev'ry Word ;
Serene, delib'rate, undifguis'd by Art,
His Tongue was faithful, and fincere his Heart.
Statefmen, th' unblemifh'd Counfellor bemoan,
And from his fair Example form your own.
So muft your Greatnefs fink, your Glories fade,
And, blended, in the common Duft be laid.
Nor Wealth, nor Titles, nor Fame's gentle Charms,
Can bribe your Life from Fate's relentlefs Arms :

   G   *VIRTUE*

VIRTUE, fair Goddefs ! only can allow
Conquefts o'er Death, and crown the Victor's
    Brow.

Mindlefs of Grandieur, from the Crowd he fled,
Sought green Retirements, and the filent Shade.
Ye bow'ry Trees, which round his Manfion
    bloom,
Oft ye conceal'd him in your hallow'd Gloom:
Oft he enjoy'd, in your fublime Abode,
His Books, his Innocence, his Friend, his GOD.
Now, fad, I wander o'er the lofty Scat,
And trace the Mazes of the foft Retreat.
View the fair Profpects, round the Gardens rove,
Bend up the Hill, and fearch the lonely Grove ;
But ah ! no more his Voice falutes my Ear,
Nor in his Hands the blufhing Fruits appear :
Yet is his Image in each Scene convey'd,
And bufy Fancy forms his gliding Shade,
I feem to meet him in the flow'ry Walks,
And, thro' the Boughs, his whifpering Spirit talks.
Eager I call, the dear Delufion flies,
Grief feals my Lips, and Tears fuffufe my Eyes.

                              O

O far, far off, above the Ken of thefe,
The rifing Mountain, and th' afpiring Trees,
In the gay Bow'rs that crown th' Eternal Hills,
His fpotlefs Soul, in deathlefs Pleafure, dwells ;
Tuneful replies, while Choral Seraphs play,
And in bright Vifions fmiles the Hours away.
He vifits now no more this dull Abode,
But talks with Angels, and beholds his GOD.

 Now ceafe, the flowing Tears, the Fun'ral
  Strains.
Let joyful Sounds revive the vocal Plains.
What tho' the Body in the Tomb be laid,
Ghaftly and breathlefs, in the awful Shade ?
Tho' by our Eyes, his Form no more confefs'd,
Pleas'd by the Friend, and by the Chriftian blefs'd?
We view the bright Reverfion in the Skies,
When the dead Saint, wak'd to new Life, fhall
 rife.
Mean time, the heav'nly Mufe embalms his Name,
And gives him up confign'd to endlefs Fame :
Thefe faithful Lines thy Abfence ftill bemoan,
And this Infcription grace thy mould'ring Stone.

     Here,

" Here, Paffenger, confin'd, reduc'd toDuft,
" Lies what was once, religious, wife, and juft.
" Steady and warm in Liberty's Defence,
" True to his Country, loyal to his Prince :
" In Friendſhip faithful, gen'rous to Defert,
" A Head enlightn'd, and a glowing Heart.

❀❀❀❀❀❀❀❀❀❀❀❀❀❀❀❀❀❀❀❀❀❀

To a Friend, on the Death of a Relative.

WHILE Death his awfulTriumphs fpreads
　　　　around,
And crowded Nations fill the vaulted Ground ;
While ev'ry Rank, and State, and Sex, and Age,
Feel his keen Shafts, and fink beneath hisRage.
Mortals, prepare to try the doubtful State,
To yield the Battle, and refign to Fate.

　Late has the Monarch, with defpotick fway,
Refiftlefs fnatch'd thy favourite Fair away.
Gone, gone for ever from thy fond Carefs,
No more her much-lov'd Form thy Eyes ſhall
　　　　blefs,

　　　　　　　　　　　　　Her

Her Abfence ftill thy rifing Sighs deplore,
And in her Converfe you delight no more ;
Touch'd by your Woe, the Mufe her Tribute
    brings
And with graveAirs,in foothing Numbers,fings.

But facred is the Mufe ; by Heav'n fhe's led
T' inftruct the Living, not to blanch the Dead.
Ye Living, hear her tuneful Lips rehearfe
No trifling Themes, nor in ignoble Verfe.

And chief,bewife,ye bloomingYoung andFair,
See your fad Picture, and your Period here.
How foon the Beauties vanifh from yourForms,
Fall into Duft, and mingle with the Worms !
Beneath the Honours of a lonely Tomb,
In penfive Silence and a folemn Gloom,
Sleeps that fair Form in Death's relentlefsArms,
Whofe living Face once blufh'd with endlefs
    Charms.

But, Ah! No more her Cheeks the Rofes wear,
Nor on her lovely Lips the Smiles appear ;
Fix'd are thofe Eyes which once divinely roll'd,
The Limbs all ftiffen'd, and the Veins all cold ;
              That

That Voice is fled which charm'd Mankind
    before,
And that soft snowy Breast must pant no more,
So from your Lips the transient Breath shall fly,
Pale the fresh Cheek, and fix'd the rolling Eye;
The charming Face and beauteous Shape be laid,
All Pale and Breathless in the awful Shade.
To deck your Grave the Turff shall bloom
    around,
And the green Grass enamel all the Ground:
And still the flow'ry Emblem shall display,
The youthful Flourish and the swift Decay.
Ah, trust no more, ye Fair, your fading Face,
Let bright Religion court your warm Embrace,
To her soft Beauties be your Love inclin'd,
The deathless Beauties of th' immortal Mind.
So to new Charms your waking Dust shall rise,
And gay in Glory glitter up the Skies,
In heav'nly Tunes, with fresh Delights, shall sing,
And bloom and blossom in eternal Spring.

    But thou, fond Mourner, give thy Tears away,
See the Gloom end in everlasting Day;

See

See the fair Soul on Wings of Angels rife,
Above the ftarry Concave of the Skies :
Now here, now there fhe rolls her dazz'led Sight;
Struck at the Profpect with immenfe Delight.
Her down-caft Eyes the fulged Streets behold.
And view a Pavement rich with gleemy Gold :
Aloft, the Roof, fram'd by th' almighty Hands,
Glorious, on *Adamantine* Pillars ftands.
Here fplendid Thrones confound the aching
     Sight,
And pour abroad unfufferable Light ;
There in high Crowns a beamy Luftre plays,
And twinkling Jewels fhoot a tremblingBlaze,
The flowing Robes wave on like lambent
     Flames,
And flafh and fparkle with celeftial Gems.
Abroad, the Fields difplay their flow'ry Pride,
In whofe fair Bofoms living Waters glide.
Here the glad Saint in mazy Rapture roves
Through Bow'rs of Blifs, and gay immortal
     Groves.

                                      Here

Here JESUS ſhines unutterably bright,
And Storms of Glory beat upon the Sight ;
To theſe highScenes thy raviſh'dViews be giv'n
And bow conſenting to the Will of Heav'n.

Hymn at Sea.

I.

GReat GOD, thy Works our Wonder raiſe,
    To thee our ſwelling Notes belong ;
While Skies, and Winds, and Rocks, and Seas,
Around ſhall echo to our Song.

II.

Thy Pow'r produc'd this mighty Frame,
Aloud to thee the Tempeſts rore,
Or ſofter Breezes tune thy Name
Gently along the ſhelly Shore.

III.

Round thee the ſcaly Nation roves,
Thy op'ning Hands their Joys beſtow,
Thro' all the bluſhing coral Groves,
Theſe ſilent, gay Retreats below.

IV. See

IV.

See the broad Sun forfake the Skies,
Glow on the Waves, and downward flide!
Anon, Heav'n opens all its Eyes,
And Star-Beams tremble o'er the Tyde :

V.

Each various Scene, or Day or Night,
LORD, points to thee our ravifh'd Soul ;
Thy Glories fix our whole Delight :
So the touch'd Needle courts the Pole.

To an ingenious young Gentleman, on his dedica-
ting a Poem to the Author.

TO you, dear Youth, whom all the Mufes own,
    And great *Apollo* fpeaks his darling Son,
To you the Mufe directs her grateful Lays,
And brings the Tribute which you merit, Praife.

What various Vertues in your Perfon join,
Tho' great yet humble, modeft tho' divine ;
Tho' num'rous Graces glitter thro' your Song,
And heav'nly Accents dance around your
        Tongue ;

        H   Strong

Strong in your Mind while big Ideas roll,
And your vaſt Subject fills your lab'ring Soul.
Yet, from your Heights, how kind you conde-
      ſcend,
Forget your Greatneſs, and aſſume the Friend?
Your Friend, you fond approve, commend,
      admire,
Bleſs with the Criticks Light, and Poets Fire,
To crown your Friend, your gen'rous Hand allows
A Branch of Bays from your o'erſhaded Brows;
Unfading Wreaths, around my Temples ſpread,
By you unmiſs'd, adorn my joyful Head.
So your bright Father *Phœbus*, o'er the Skies
Profuſely ſcatters Light's eternal Dyes,
Unnumber'd Worlds from him receive their
      Days,
Yet ſtill he ſhines with undiminiſh'd Rays.

    Each Time I view this Product of your Art
Two diff'rent Paſſions ſtruggle in my Heart,
Which, like the ebbing, or the flowing Tyde,
Contracts with Envy, or dilates with Pride;
                Now

Now shrunk with Spight, now with Ambition
    swell'd,
Proud at your Praise, env'ous to be excell'd :
And as I meditate the doubtful Theme,
My clashing Passions strike a sudden Flame ;
The Muse takes Fire ---- Thoughts thick upon
    her throng,
Start the quick Words, and rapid run along.
So when in wat'ry Clouds hot Sulphur pent,
Runs here and there, and labours for a Vent.
Till kindling to a Blaze at the rough Jars,
Water with Fire, and Fire with Water wars ;
Then bursting forth, thick-flashing Lightning
    flies,
And ready Thunder rolls along the Skies.

Ah ! how can I the happy Title claim,
And of your Tutor boast th' immortal Name,
When in your Breast ten Thousand Raptures live,
And glow superiour to the Sparks I give ?
In vain you say I form'd your Infant Strains,
Taught you on stubborn Thoughts to fling your
    Chains,

Smooth'd

Smooth'd your harſh Voice,& bid yourNumbers
   glide
Like gentle Rills a-down a Mountains Side ;
Prun'd your young Wings,inſtructed you to ſkim
The level Lawn, or daring Soar ſublime ;
In vain all theſe, when ev'ry Judge will find
You fly aloft, unfetter'd, unconfin'd,
And ſee my diſtant Muſe, ſhort-panting, lag
   behind.
So the low Hen the Eagles Egg may hatch,
And feed the callow Care, and o'er him watch,
But when thick Feathers on his Back unite,
He ſpreads hisPlumes,& takes a tow'ringFlight,
Neglects his Nurſe, & claims his heav'nly Birth,
While ſhe,with flutt'ring Wings,hovers,—— and
   drops to Earth.

   But Oh ! forbear, thy laviſh Tongue be
   tame,
Nor fluſh my Features with a conſcious Flame,
Juſtice demands that I th' Applauſe refuſe :
Not I, but mighty POPE inſpir'd thy Muſe.

                   He

He, wondrous Bard ! whoſe Numbers reach our
    Shore,
Tho' Oceans roll between, and Tempeſts roar:
Huſh'd are theStorms,& ſmooth theWaters lie,
As his ſweet Muſick glides harmonious by ;
Raviſh'd, my Ear receives the heav'nly Gueſt,
MyHeart high-leaping,beats my pantingBreaſt:
Thro' all my Mind inceſſant Rapture reigns,
And Joys immortal revel in my Veins.
So the ſoft *SYRENS warbled o'er the Main,*
And ſo *ULISSES' Soul took Wing to meet the*
    Strain.

O Pope ! thy Fame is ſpread around the Sky,
Far as the Waves can flow, far as the Winds can
    fly !
Hail! Bard triumphant,fill'd with hallow'dRage,
Sent from highHeav'n to grace the happyAge
For thee a thouſand Garlands ſhall be wove,
And ev'ry Clime project a laurel Grove ;
Thy Name be heard in ev'ry artful Song,
And thy loudPraiſe employ each tunefulTongue.
                  Ev'n

Ev'n my young Mufe the noble Theme would
　　take,

And lifp imperfect what fhe cannot fpeak.

'Tis POPE, my Friend, that guilds our gloomy
　　Night,

And if I fhine 'tis his reflected Light :

So the pale Moon, bright with her borrow'd
　　Beams,

Thro' the darkHorrors fhoots her filverGleams.

POPE's are the Rules which you, my Friend,
　　receive,

From him I gather what to you I give.

When I attend to his immortal Lyre,

I kindle inftant with a facred Fire ;

Now here, now there, my Soul purfues his Song,

Hurried impetuous by his Pow'r along :

MyPulfe beats thick,urg'd by my drivingBlood,

And on my Breaft I feel the rufhing GOD.

But when to you I would the Flames convey,

In my cold Hands the holy Fires decay.

As when your Hand the Convex-Glafs difplays,

It clofe collects fome fcatter'd folar Rays ;

　　　　　　　　　　　　　　Tho'

Tho' cold the Glafs, where'er its Focus aims,
The Object fmokes, it reddens, and it flames:
So Pope, thro' me, fhines full upon your Mufe;
So cold *my* Breaft; and fo *your* Bofom glows.

Go on, fweet Poet, charm our lift'ning Ears,
Infufe new Joy, and fcatter all our Cares.
O let no Trifle tempt your noble Rage,
No mortal Theme your mighty Mufe engage;
But when harmonious to her Lyre fhe fings,
And with fwift Fingers ftrikes the trembling
   Strings.
Let facred Subjects fill the Air around,
And Angels waft to Heav'n the Extacy of Sound.
Write for *ETERNITY*! --- what Pleafures thrill
Thro' all my Veins and urge my flying Quill
As that I name? what Tranfports fire my Mind,
When I behold its wond'rous Scenes combin'd?
Here, the laft Trumpet fhakes the founding Air,
There, gloomy glow the Regions of Defpair:
Now, on this Earth devouring Flames increafe,
And bellowing Burnings boyl the hiffing Seas:
       Then

Then, melting Joys my fwiming Eyes confefs,
And Saints diffolve away in endlefs Blifs :
While hymningCherubs try their tuneful Strains,
And charm, with Notes like yours, the heav'nly
      Plains ;
Exalted high, the Saviour-God is known,
And dazling Glory blazes round his Throne;
Around his Head a beamy Luftre plays,
Where glittering Jewels blend their trembling
      Rays ;
Eternal Day breaks from his radient Eyes,
And flames divinely o'er the fhining Skies:
Thus fits the GOD, with awful Honours crown'd
While everlafting Ages wheel their mighty
      Round ! -------

But, paufe my Mufe; ceafe my unartfulSong :
The Beauties which I ftrive to praife I wrong.
The Scenes fo faft upon my Fancy flow,
Convinc'd, I own Eternity a *NOW.*

Thus let your pious Mufe employ herFlame,
Then, lafting as yourTheme, fhall be yourFame:
                                                    Thus

Thus let your Poesy refine, improve,
And match the Musick of the Choirs above ;
Still from your Lips let such soft Notes arise,
And Songs of Seraphs sound beneath the Skies ;
Till, as your Muse, your Soul expands her
    Wings,
And to their bright Abodes, exulting, springs :
There, there your Voice shall deathless Strains
    resound,
And be amid th' immortal Chorus drown'd.
So some full Spring a trickling Rill bestows,
That makes melodious Murmur as it flows ;
It widens as it wanders on its Course,
And as it glides it gathers greater Force ;
Still on it runs, and nought its Stream controuls,
It now a Riv'let, now a River rolls.
Now its strong Tyde, with unresisted Sway
Rushes impetuous down and foams away ;
It pours along, and all its Banks out-braves
Till the vast Sea absorbs its undistinguish'd
    Waves.

The BLOOM *of* LIFE, fading *in a happy* DEATH.

I.

GReat GOD, how frail a Thing is Man !
   How fwift his Minutes pafs !
His Age contracts within a Span ;
   He blooms and dies like Grafs.

II.

Now in his Breaft frefh Spirits dart,
   And vital Vigour reigns :
His Blood pours rapid from his Heart,
   And leaps along his Veins.

III.

His Eyes their fparkling Pleafure fpeak,
   Joy flutters round his Head ;
While Health ftill bloffoms on his Cheek,
   And adds the rofey Red.

IV.

Thus the fond Youth fecurely ftands,
   Nor dreams of a Decay ------
At once he feels Death's Iron Hands,
   His Soul is fnatch'd away.

V. Down

V.

Down to the Earth the Body drops,
    Whence it was fram'd at firft,
Forgets its former flatt'ring Hopes
    And haftens to its Duft.

VI.

No more we view the wonted Grace ;
    The Eye-Balls roll no more :
A livid Horror fpreads the Face
    Where Beauty blaz'd before.

VII.

So the young *Spring*, with annual Green,
    Renews the waving Grove ;
And Riv'lets thro' the flow'ry Scene
    In Silver Mazes rove.

VIII.

By tuneful Birds of ev'ry Wing,
    Melodious Strains are play'd ;
From Tree to Tree their Accents ring,
    Soft-warbling thro' the Shade.

 IX. The

IX.

The painted Meads, and fragrant **Fields,**
  A ſudden Smile beſtow :
A golden Gleam each Valley guilds**,**
  Where numerous Beauties blow.

X.

A Thouſand gaudy Colours fluſh
  Each od'rous Mountain's Side :
Lillies turn fair, and Roſes bluſh,
  And Tulips ſpread their Pride.

XI.

Thus flouriſhes the wanton Year,
  In rich Confuſion gay,
Till *Autumn* bids the Bloom retire,
  The Verdure fade away.

XII.

Succeeding Cold withers the Woods,
  While hoary *Winter* reigns,
In Fetters binds the frozen Floods,
  And ſhivers o'er the Plains.

XIII, And

XIII.

And muſt *my* Moments thus decline ?
  And muſt *I* ſink to Death ?
To Thee my Spirit I reſign,
  Thou Sov'REIGN of my Breath.

XIV.

JESUS my Life has dy'd, has roſe :
  I burn to meet his Charms !
Welcome the Pangs, the dying Throes,
  That give me to his Arms.

❀❀❀❀❀❀❀❀❀❀❀❀❀❀❀❀❀❀❀❀

A Poem on the Death of King GEORGE I.
And Acceſſion of King GEORGE II.

SAY, mournfulMuſe,declare thy riſingWoe,
  What heaves thy Heart ; and whence thy
    Sorrows flow ?
Why in thy Face ſuch anxious Grief appears ;
And o'er thyEye-balls ſwim the ſpeakingTears :
O GEORGE, thy Death my flowing Numbers
    mourn,
Thy ſacred Aſhes, and diſtinguiſh'd Urn :
                Thee,

Thee, ev'ry Mufe, and every Grace deplores,
From *Thames's* Banks, to thefe *Atlantick*Shores,
Each Bard his Grief in gliding Accents fhews,
And faireft Eyes diftill their cryftal Dews.

O ! were myBreaft flufh'd with an equalFire,
Vaft as my Theme, and ftrong as my Defire !
Then, mighty GEORGE, then fhould my
  Notes arife,
And fpreading Mufick echo round the Skies ;
Thy Name, in tuneful Meafures led along,
Should dance, harmonious, through my flow-
  ing Song ;
The raptur'd Mufe thy awful Form reveal,
Defcribe thy Counfels, and thy Actions tell ;
Bid dying Sounds thy ravifh'd Life bemoan,
Or fhouting Nations hail thee to thy Throne ;
Each various Scene, with varying Numbers
  crown'd,
Should Earth, and Sea, and Air, and Heav'n
  refound.

Long

Long ere his *Albion* triumph'd in his Reign
His Sword glar'd dreadful o'er th' *Hungarian*
    Plain,
Witnefs, ye Troops, thro' whofe wide Ranks
    he ran,
Rowz'd the fierce War, and call the Tumult on :
Say, how divinely then his Afpect fhow'd,
What Conduct fhone ! what dauntlefs Courage
    glow'd !
When Man to Man, and Smoke oppos'd to
    Smoke,
Flames flafh'd at Flames, at Thunder Thunder
    broke,
When Death indignant, drove his Iron Car,
Thro' the dire Havock of the raging War ;
Say, Goddefs, how th' intrepid Hero flies,
To meet the Monfter with undaunted Eyes ;
'Till fmiling Vict'ry, and immortal Peace,
Hung o'er his Head, and bid the Battel ceafe !

Record, O heavenly Mufe, the illuftrious Day,
When joyful *Britain* own'd his fov'reign Sway.
                      Conceal'd

Conceal'd for ever, lie the Acts which stain
The laft blackMonths, the Shades of ANNA's
      Reign ;
When fecret Treafon work'd, when Juftice fled,
And loud Deftruction threatned o'er our Head,
'Twas then, by Heav'n ordain'd, his happy Hand
From Ruin refcu'd the devoted Land,
The Storm was hufh, the clam'rous Factions laid,
And peaceful Olive fpread its wealthy Shade.
So when darkClouds hang heavy o'er theMain,
And bellying down, diftend with Floods of Rain,
To pufh them on, the Winds their Forces try,
While they, flow-failing, labour up the Sky ;
The thickning Volumes fpread the heavenly
      Doom,
And as they pafs, project a folemn Gloom :
Diffolving now, a drifling Dew diftills,
Dampens the Vales, and fprinkles round theHills;
Still gathering Strength, the airy Sluces low'r,
And on the Fields defcends a copious Show'r,
Laft, furious grown, down rufh the rapidRains,
And pour impetuous, fpatt'ring on the Plains.
                    If

If then the Sun breaks out, the Shadows fly,
And the gay Rainbow arches o'er the Sky.

Hail! happy *Albion*, Heav'ns peculiar Care,
See thy Deliv'rer to thy Shores repair!
Flourifh, ye Fields; ye Groves, exalt yourHeads,
Where*Thame*'s Currant murmurs o'er theMeads!
And thou, *Augufta*, fparkling in my Eyes,
Let thy tall Tow'rs, and fhining Turrets rife,
Where Riches glitter, Mirth for ever fings,
And fmiling Plenty fpreads her golden Wings:
For thee, *Peru* her beamy Face difplays,
For thee the orient Stores of *Ganges* blaze;
A thoufand Pleafures crown thy flow'ry Plains,
While GEORGE divinely o'er thy Kingdom
    reigns.

But, Oh! at once the heav'nly Scenes decay,
And all the gaudy Vifion fades away.
He dies ---- my Mufe, the difmal Sound forbear:
In ev'ry Eye debates the falling Tear;
A thoufand Paffions o'er my Bofom roll,
Swell in my Heart, and fhock my inmoft Soul.

K   H*e*

He dies ---- Let Nature own the direful Blow,
Sigh, all ye Winds; with Tears, ye Rivers, flow;
Let the hoarfe Ocean, loud in Anguifh rore;
And Tides of Grief pour plenteous on the Shore:
No more the Spring fhall bloom, or Morning rife,
But Night eternal wrap the fable Skies.

Enough, my Mufe, give all thy Tears away,
Break, ye dull Shades; and rife, the rofey Day.
Quicken, O Sun, thy Chariot dazling-bright,
And o'er thy flaming Empire pour the Light.
O Spring, along thy laughing Lawns be feen
Fields always frefh, and Groves for ever green:
Let *Britain*'s Sorrows ceafe, her Joys enlarge,
The *firft* revives in thee the *fecond* GEORGE.
Hail! mighty Prince, O fhining Sov'reign, hail!
Fain would the Mufe lifp her prophetick Tale,
In myftic Lays thy future Years relate,
And fing the Records of unripen'd Fate;
Bid thee in Fame's triumphant Chariot ride,
And CAROLINA glitter by thy Side:

Fair

Fair Princefs, thou, in whofe majeftick Eyes,
Dawn heav'nly Beauties, and immortal Joys:
By thee, fhall *Albion* future Triumphs own,
And a long Race of *Hero's* grace her Throne;
Here FREDERICK in Bloom of Years fhall
       ftand,
Here youthful WILLIAM bloffom o'er the
       Land;
Thou ANNA, here, with Charms celeftial
       crown'd,
And all thy heav'nly Sifters flame around.

Ev'n our far Shores confefs the big Delight,
Where the faintSun rolls down his golden Light;
The dancing Billows leap along the Main,
Proud of th'Extent of GEORGE's happy Reign;
Applauding Thunders fhake the Air around,
Waves fhout to Waves, and Rocks to Rocks
       refound;
Each humane Breaft glows with refiftlefs Fire,
And ev'ry Angel ftrikes his founding Lyre.

      K 2   O

O live, auſpicious Prince; live, radiant Queen,
Long let your Influence guild the glorious Scene:
And you, fair Offspring, form'd for high Com-
　　mand,
Flouriſh, ye blooming Honours of the Land:
So when from the dim Courts below you fly
To the bright Regions of the upper Sky;
Where Trees of Life by living Riv'lets team,
Wave their tall Heads, and paint the running
　　Stream,
May round your Heads Crowns flaſh, celeſtial-
　　bright,
And regal Purple change for Robes of Light;
Taſte Charms ſtill new, and Joys without Decay,
While endleſs Years in Raptures roll away.

To His Excellency Governour BURNET, *on his
Arrival at* Boſton.

WHile riſing Shouts a gen'ral Joy proclaim,
　　And ev'ry Tongue, O BURNET, liſps
thy Name;

　　　　　　　　　　　　　　To

To view thy Face, while crowding Armies run,
Whofe waving Banners blaze againft the Sun,
And deep-mouth'd Cannon, with a thund'ring
      Roar,
Sound thy Commiffion ftretch'd from Shore to
      Shore ;
Accept the tuneful Labours of the Mufe,
To bend frefh Laurels round your fhaded Brows,
With your Deferts, to raife the facred Fire,
And in your Praifes ftring her joyful Lyre.

Long have we wifh'd the goldenHours to rife,
And with diftinguifh'd Purple paint the Skies,
When, thro' our wondring Towns, in Raptures
      gay,
The pompous March fhould fhape it's fhining
      Way ;
While breathingTrumpets try their filverStrains,
And whirling Chariots fcour along the Plains ;
When the glad City fhould unfold it's Gates,
And the longTriumph grace the glowingStreets,
O Burnet ! how we bad the Minutes run,
Urg'd the flowHours, and chid the ling'ringSun !
                Impatient,

Impatient, met each Post, and call'd aloud,
" When will his Wheels smoke rattling o'er the
      " Road ?
" When shall we say, *HE'S COME !* with big
      Delight,
" And with his Aspect feast our longing Sight ?

Welcome, great Man, to our desiring Eyes,
Thou Earth ! proclaim it ; and resound, ye Skies !
Voice answ'ring Voice, in joyful Consort meet,
The Hills all echo, and the Rocks repeat :
And thou, *Bostonia*, Mistress of the Towns,
Whom the pleas'd Bay, with am'rous Arms,
      surrounds,
Let thy warm Transports blaze in num'rous Fires,
And beamy Glories glitter on thy Spires ;
Let Rockets, streaming, up the Ether glare,
And flaming Serpents hiss along the Air ;
Sublime, thy Joys thro' the high Heav'ns be
      shown,
In foreign Lights, and Stars before unknown :
While rival Splendors deck the Earth below,
And o'er the Streets the daz'ling Windows glow.
                       But

But You, O *Cambridge*, how can you forbear
In gliding Lays to charm each liftning Ear ?
You, where the Youth purfue th' illuftrious Toil,
Where the Arts flourifh, and the Graces fmile,
MakeBuRNET'sName in laftingNumbers fhine,
Ye foft Receffes of the tuneful Nine!
Speak the glad Day, with ev'ry warbling String,
When firft you blefs'd th' Indulgence of his
   Wing;
Say,how prophetickRapture feiz'd yourTongue,
When you, on Fire, your future Glories fung.
" By him protedted, by his Pattern led,
" Each fmiling Art fhall lift her beautiousHead.
" Divinity, in op'ning Volumes, lies,
" O *Wigglefworth*, to thy enlightned Eyes;
" And *Newton*'s Hand with wond'rous Skill
   " difplays
" Nature unveil'd, and fhews her lovely Face:
" Long fhall the noble Sciences declare
" Thy Bounties, HOLLIS: and a BURNET's
   Care.

        In

In BURNET's Face our future Fame appears,
And Arts and Graces lead his flowing Years.
For him, ye Mufes, tune immortal Verfe,
And mighty Themes, in lofty Lays, rehearfe,
Proud in his Praifes, wind your golden Strings,
And in high Raptures clap your waving Wings.
Thou Sun, for him, fhalt each fair Year adorn,
Bid the Spring bloffom, and the Summer burn,
Teach rip'ning Fruits to paint autumnal Scenes,
And fmile and blufh amidft the living Greens.
Ev'n the rough Winter feigns a youthful Tread;
And, in low Homage, bows his rev'rend Head;
The Northern Tempefts fhall forget to roar,
And gentle Waves, foft-murmuring, kifs the
    Shore.

Now Aftronomic Tubes aloft fhall rife,
Shake off their Duft, and level at the Skies,
Defcry new Glories in the fhining Spheres,
And BURNET's Name be read on future Stars.
The Pencil now, in wondrous Lines fhall flow,
And, warm with Life, bid the touch'd Canvas,
    glow,
                                    Mufick,

Mufick, fweet Daughter of the Choirs above,
Shall, foft-defcending, down the Ether move;
With heavenly Airs the breathing Flute infpire,
The Viol ftring, and bend the warbling Wyre.

But chief, Ye Pages, open to the Light,
Where wond'ring Angels roll their ravifh'd
  Sight;
Ye facred Pages, eafy to his Soul,
Spread the dark Mazes of your * myftic Roll.
No more You fleep, hid in an awful Gloom,
Your Shades all fcatter, and your Beauties bloom;
Years yet unborn, your op'ning Scenes unfold,
And all your dawning Clouds are edg'd with
  Gold.
So when the *Shekinah*, myfterious ftood
High o'er *Arabia*'s divided Flood,
(When down the Sands below the Prophet led,
And the Waves foam'd fublime above his Head)
Whilft Clouds and Darknefs *Egypt*'s Hoft
  amaz'd,
Thro' *Ifrael*'s Ranks immortal Glory blaz'd.
    L   **And**

* *His Effay on the Prophefies.*

And Thou, my Muse, assume a joyful Air,
Recall his Candor, and forbid thy Fear;
Tell him You come before the Fount of Day,
And from the Pow'r of Light, demand a Ray:
Gracious, He'll grant the Favour thou hast
       pray'd,
And *fling the Blaze of Gloeies from his Head.*
As on the fragrant Windings of the Shore
Where *Perfia* glitters with her golden Ore,
Up the high Hills the early People rife,
And to the Eaft turn their defiring Eyes,
Till beamy *Phœbus* guilds the rofey Skies,
Then, all at once, their founding Shouts unite,
Hail the bright Car, and blefs the lovelyLight:
Pleas'd with theirPrayer,he paffes o'er theLand,
And fcatters Bleffings with a lavifh Hand;
The Fields all brighten, as he onward moves,
And his fairGlories flufh the gladden'd Groves;
O'er all the Earth the flaming Splendor flows,
And, like a Ruby, all the Ocean glows:
To BURNET thus I fue, He thus complies,
And thus his foft Indulgence fooths my Eyes.

To His EXCELLENCY the GOVERNOUR.

SIR,

A S Your EXCELLENCY *has long honou-red me with a particular Friendfhip, Gratitude demands that I attempt your Service: And as you are now in Mourn-ing from the Stroke of Heaven, the greatest Refpect I can pay you, is, to affift your Improvement under the Hand of* GOD.

In order to this, the Mufe has once more refu-med her Lyre : And her Averfion to Flattery you will receive as her beft Complement. Inftead of copious Panegyrick upon the Dead, I have chofen rather, in folemn Language, to admonifh the Li-ving ; And when others, perhaps, would have embraced fo fair an Opportunity for an Encomium on your EXCELLENCY, *I have only taken the Freedom of an Exhortation. I know you will be pleafed to obferve, that while I employ the Numbers of the* Poet, *I never forget the Character of the* Divine.   *I am,*

May it pleafe your EXCELLENCY,

Your *Excellency's*

affectionate Nephew,

and moft humble Servant,

Bofton, October
13. 1736.

M. BYLES.

To His EXCELLENCY *Governour* BELCHER,
on the Death *of His* L A D Y.

BELCHER, once more permit the Muſe
   you lov'd,
By honour, and by ſacred Friendſhip mov'd,
Wak'd by your woe, her numbers to prolong,
And pay her tribute in a Funeral ſong.

From you, great Heav'n with undiſputed
   voice,
Has ſnatch'd the Partner of your youthful joys.
Her beauties, ere ſlow Hectick fires conſum'd,
Her eyes ſhone chearful, and her roſes bloom'd:
Long ling'ring ſickneſs, broke the lovely form,
Shock after ſhock, and ſtorm ſucceeding ſtorm,
Till Death, relentleſs, ſiez'd the waſting clay,
Stopt the faint voice, and catch'd the Soul away.

No more in Converſe ſprightly, ſhe appears,
With nice decorum, and obliging airs:
Ye Poor, no more expecting round her ſtand,
Where ſoft compaſſion ſtretch'd her bounteous
   hand:
         Her

Her Houſe her happy ſkill no more ſhall boaſt,
" Be all things plentiful, but nothing loſt.
Cold to the tomb ſee the pale corpſe convey'd,
Wrapt up in ſilence, and the diſmal ſhade.

Ah! what avail the ſable velvet ſpread,
And golden ornaments amidſt the dead?
No beam ſmiles there, no eye can there diſcern
The vulgar coffin from the marble urn :
The coſtly honours, preaching, ſeem to ſay,
" Magnificence muſt mingle with the clay.

Learn here, ye Fair, the frailty of your face,
Raviſh'd by death, or nature's ſlow decays :
Ye Great, muſt ſo reſign your tranſient pow'r,
Heroes of duſt, and monarchs of an hour!
So muſt each pleaſing air, each gentle fire,
And all that's ſoft, and all that's ſweet expire.

But you O BELCHER, mourn the abſent Fair,
Feel the keen pang, and drop the tender tear:
The GOD approves that nature do her part,
A panting boſom, and a bleeding heart.
Ye

Ye baser arts of flattery, away !
The Virtuous Muse shall moralize her lay.
To you, o Fav'rite Man, the Pow'r supream
Gives wealth, and titles, and extent of fame ;
Joys from beneath, and blessings from above ;
Thy Monarch's plaudit ; and thy people's
     love :
The same high Pow'r, unbounded, and alone,
Resumes his gifts, and puts your mourning
     on.
His Edict issues, and his Vassal, *Death*,
Requires your Consort's, ------ or YOUR flying
     breath.
Still be your glory at his feet to bend,
Kiss thou the SON, and own his Sov'reign
     hand ;
For his high honours all thy pow'rs exert,
The gifts of Nature, and the charms of Art :
So over Death the conquest shall be giv'n,
Your Name shall live on earth, your Soul in
     heav'n.

                         Mean

Mean time *my* Name to *thine* ally'd fhall
ftand,

Still our warm Friendfhip, mutual flames
extend ;

The Mufe fhall fo furvive from age to age,
And Belcher's name protect his *Byles's* page.

❈❈❈❈❈❈❈❈❈❈❈❈❈❈❈❈❈❈❈❈❈

To Pollio, *on his preparing for the Prefs a
Treatife againft the* Romifh *Church.*

LOng had the *Romifh* Darknefs mock'd the
Eyes,

And Smoke and Locufts hover'd round the Skies ;
Like fome dire Plague th' infectious Errors run,
They ftalk'd thro' Midnight, and devour'd at
Noon.

Confederate Schools fecur'd the dark Retreats,
With facred Lies, and confecrated Cheats ;
Amazing Change ! Obedient to the Prieft,
Bread leaps to Flefh and omniprefent Pafte !
To fill their Coffers all their Fancies team ;
Ev'n Purgatory proves a golden Dream ;

All

All Merchandife thro' their wide Market rolls,
From rotten Carcaffes, to humane Souls.

'Tis thine, O *Pollio*, in juft Rage to rife,
And from the Monfter fnatch the thin Difguife,
With skilful Hand the fraudful Schemes difplay,
And all the bold Impofture.open lay.
How ftrong thy Pages are in maffy Senfe,
VaftHoards of Thought, and manlyEloquence!
Extenfive Learning, and in Reaf'ning cool,
And, like thy Converfation, rich and full !

Thy Converfation ! --- here the Mufe could
    ftay,
And in big Pleafures fmile the Hours away.
The Mufe familiar, fhall the State forget.
The Schools, the Court, and fecret Cabinet,
But milder Numbers fhall in Thee commend
The gentle, and the condefcending Friend.
If, in grave Words, you facredThoughts beftow,
A deep Attention fets on ev'ry Brow ;
If thro' the Sciences your Fancy ftrays,
With Joy we follow thro' the flow'ry Maze ;
                                    Or

Or if you Mirth, and hum'rous Airs affume,
An univerfal Laughter fhakes the Room.
Each comes with Pleafure ;   while he ftays
    admires ;
Goes with Regret, nor unimprov'd retires.

Forgive me, *Pollio*, if the forward Mufe,
Forgets her Rank, and too familiar grows :
Forgive, if fhe ambitious fhould relate,
How free you talk, how intimate I fet ;
O, let my Name with thine together ftand,
And let me boaft the Honours of thy Friend,
My Name, by Thee fhall laft to future Days,
And *Pollio*'s Page protect his *Byles*'s Lays.

On the Death of the Q U E E N.

To His Excellency Governour B E L C H E R.

WHile from each Soul the Sorrows copious
    flow,
    And weeping Nations heave with mighty
    Woe ;

M   Whilft

Whilſt ev'ry Lyre to mournful Notes is ſtrung,
And CAROLINA flutters on each Tongue :
The mourning Muſe, to Conſolation deaf,
Swells the ſad Conſort with melodious Grief.
Ten flow'ry Springs on golden Plumes have
    flown,
Since ſhe, triumphant, hail'd thee on thy Throne.
Oh CAROLINE ! Oh Princeſs now no more !
Each Heart bleeds inward, and all Eyes deplore.
Stretch'd pale in Death thy lovely Limbs are
    laid,
Thy Beauty, *Albion*, and thy Joys are fled !
To Thee, our Tears their filial Torrents bring,
And ev'ry Paſſion opens ev'ry Spring :
Loſt to Deſpair, in wild Laments we moan,
And diſtant Regions echo Groan for Groan.

  'Twas ſhe, adorn'd by Virtue's heav'nly
    Charms,
In roſey Beauty bleſs'd her Prince's Arms ;
Her Lover with a pious Eye ſhe view'd,
And CÆSAR at her Feet ſucceſsleſs ſu'd :

                  Imperial

Imperial Purple her calm Eyes difdain,
And *Roman* Eagles wav'd their Wings in vain;
Infpir'd, Religion's Dictates to difcharge,
She gave her felf to *Britain*, and to GEORGE.

Say, rais'd *Britannia*, how her gentle Air
Adorn'd the Palace, and improv'd the Fair.
Difcord, and Party-Rage grew tame, to gaze,
And noify Factions clamour'd in her Praife.
Domeftick Life th' illuftrious Pattern grac'd;
On royal Milk the royal Infants feaft:
Form'd by her Hands the Monarch-Race were
      feen,
The rip'ning Hero, and the future Queen.
Far from vain Courts her filent Footfteps roam,
Where chofen Volumes deck'd the facred Dome:
Still loud Applaufes of the joyful Age,
Purfu'd her thro' the lonely Hermitage.
Here, in high Raptures, her immortal Mind,
O'er *Newton's* Orbs expatiates, unconfin'd;
Familiar Gueft! fhe vifits all the Skies,
From World to World, from Sun to Sun fhe flies!

Thence

Thence ſmiles at mimickCrowns which Sultans
 wear
In the mock Empires of this little Star.

 Such was the Queen! ſhe was ---- but is no
 more !-----
Wide wounds theWoe, and ſpreads fromShore
 to Shore ;
Groans the hoarſe Ocean as the Tydings fly,
Wave roars toWave, and Rocks toRocks reply,
She was, but is no more ---- loſt all Relief !
Now all her Graces greaten all our Grief.
Ev'n our far Land it's Anguiſh loud proclaims,
We felt her Influence,and we bleſs'd herBeams.

 But, *BELCHER*,firſt inGrief as inCommand ;
With early Zeal you kiſs'd her beauteousIland ;
Your Honours to the deſtin'd Queen you paid,
Ere theCrown flaſh'd, far-beaming,on herHead.
The Muſe reluctant, by your Order ſings,
Elſe had ſhe ſilent wept, and broke her Strings.
What Fame to *us* reports, by *you* were ſeen,
The Glance attractive, the majeſtick Mein,
       The

The Angel-Form each milder Feature wears,
That Look obliging, thofe defcending Airs.
Collected in her Innocence fhe ftood,
Devout to Heav'n, to Men divinely Good,
You faw----now fee the fated End of all :
How the Fair fades, and how the Mighty fall.

See the Pale Cheek its faded Blufh refign,
The dying Eyes with tranfient Luftre fhine ;
Hoarfe the funk Voice, the Breaft no longer
   warm,
And Death gains faft o'er ev'ry mortal Charm.
O VIRTUE ! now *thy* Joys are all fincere !
Th' exulting Queen demands the final Pray'r,
(Eternal Glories op'ning to her View,)
Waves her gay Hand, and bids the Globe adieu.

See, in the regal Vaults, the fhatter'd Lead,
Whofe gaping Seams difclofe the royal Dead.
Were thefe, O Mufe, triumphant Sov'reigns
   once !
This Skin all fhrivel'd ! and thefe naked Bones !
No more refentful, great ELIZA, reft,
Support in Peace the *Scottifh Mary*'s Cheft !
       Whilft

Whilſt faſt by WILLIAM's and MARIA's Shrine,
We place the Duſt of heav'nly CAROLINE.

Ye living, hear what mould'ring Monarchs ſay !
" *For endleſs Joys give mortal Dreams away.*

✿✿✿✿✿✿✿✿✿✿✿✿✿✿✿✿✿✿✿✿✿✿✿✿

To the Reverend Dr. WATTS, *on his Divine*
POEMS.

I.

SAY, ſmiling Muſe, what heav'nly Strain
  Forbids the Waves to roar ;
Comes gently gliding o'er the Main,
  And charms our liſt'ning Shore !

II.

What Angel ſtrikes the trembling Strings ;
  And whence the golden Sound !
Or is it WATTS-----or GABRIEL ſings
  From yon celeſtial Ground ?

III.

'Tis Thou, Seraphick WATTS, thy Lyre
  Plays ſoft along the Floods ;
Thy Notes, the anſ'wring Hills inſpire,
  And bend the waving Woods.

        IV. The

IV.

The Meads, with dying Mufick fill'd,
  Their fmiling Honours fhow,
While, whifp'ring o'er each fragrant Field,
  The tuneful Breezes blow.

V.

The Rapture founds in ev'ry Trace,
  Ev'n the rough Rocks regale,
Frefh flow'ry Joys flame o'er the Face
  Of ev'ry laughing Vale.

VI.

And Thou, my Soul, the Tranfport own,
  Fir'd with immortal Heat;
While dancing Pulfes driving on,
  About thy Body beat.

VII.

Long as the Sun fhall rear his Head,
  And chafe the flying Glooms,
As blufhing from his nuptial Bed
  The gallant Bridegroom comes:

VIII. Long

VIII.

Long as the dufky Ev'ning flies
  And fheds a doubtful Light,
While fudden rufh along the Skies
  The fable Shades of Night :

IX.

O WATTS, thy facred Lays fo long
  Shall ev'ry Bofom fire ;
And ev'ry Mufe, and ev'ry Tongue
  To fpeak thy Praife confpire.

X.

When thy fair Soul fhall on the Wings
  Of fhouting Seraphs rife,
And with fuperior Sweetnefs fings
  Amid thy native Skies ;

XI.

Still fhall thy lofty Numbers flow,
  Melodious and divine ;
And Choirs above, and Saints below,
  A deathlefs Chorus ! join.

XII. To

To our far Shores the Sound fhall roll,
  (So *Philomela* fung)
And Eaft to Weft, and Pole to Pole
  Th' eternal Tune prolong.

To P I C T O R I O, *on the Sight of his Pictures.*

AGES our Land a barbarous Defart ftood,
  And favage Nations howl'd in ev'ry Wood;
No laurel'd Art o'er the rude Region fmil'd,
Nor blefs'd Religion dawn'd amidft the Wild;
Dulnefs and Tyranny confederate reign'd,
And Ignorance her gloomy State maintain'd.

An hundred Journies now the Earth has run,
In annual Circles, round the central Sun,
Since the firft Ship the unpolifh'd Letters bore
Thro' the wide Ocean to the barb'rous Shore.
Then Infant-Science made it's early Proof,
Honeft, fincere, tho' unadorn'd, and rough;
Still thro' a Cloud the rugged Stranger fhone,
Politenefs, and the fofter Arts unknown:

No heavenly Pencil the free Stroke could give,
Nor the warm Canvaſs felt its Colours live.
No moving Rhet'rick rais'd the raviſh'd Soul,
Flouriſh'd in Flames, or heard it's Thunder roll;
Rough horrid Verſe, harſh, grated thro' the Ear,
And jarring Diſcords tore the tortur'd Air ;
Solid, and grave, and plain the Country ſtood,
Inelegant, and rigorouſly good.

Each Year, ſucceeding, the rude Ruſt devours,
And ſofter Arts lead on the following Hours ;
The tuneful Nine begin to touch the Lyre,
And flowing Pencils light the living Fire ;
In the fair Page new Beauties learn to ſhine,
The Thoughts to brighten, and the Style refine,
Till the great Year the finiſh'd Period brought ;
PICTORIO painted, and MÆCENAS wrote.

Thy Fame, PICTORIO, ſhall the Muſe rehearſe,
And ſing her Siſter-Art in ſofter Verſe :
'Tis your's, great Maſter, in juſt Lines to trace
The riſing Proſpect, or the lovely Face.

In

In the fair Round to fwell the glowing Cheek,
Give Thought to Shades,and teach thePaints to
   fpeak.
Touch'd by thy Hand, how *Sylvia*'s Charms
   engage !
And *Flavia*'s Features fmile thro' ev'ry Age.
In *Clio*'s Face, th' attentive Gazer fpies
Minerva's reafoning Brow, and azure Eyes,
Thy Blufh, *Belinda*, future Hearts fhall warm,
And *Celia* fhine in *Citherea*'s Form.
In hoary Majefty, fee CATO here ;
Fix'd ftrong in Thought,thereNEWTON's Lines
   appear ;
Here in full Beauty blooms the charmingMaid ;
Here *Roman* Ruins nod their awful Head ;
Here glotingMonks their am'rousRights debate,
The *Italian* Mafter fits in eafy State,
VANDIKE and RUBENS fhow their rivalForms,
And CÆSAR flafhes in the Blaze of Arms.

   But ceafe,fondMufe,nor the rudeLays prolong,
A thoufand Wonders muft remain unfung ;

Crowds of new Beings lift their wond'ring Heads,
In conscious Forms, and animated Shades.
What Sounds can speak, to ev'ry Figure just,
The breathing Statue, and the living Bust ?
Landskips how gay ! arise in ev'ry Light,
And fresh Creations rush upon the Sight ;
Thro' fairy Scenes the roving Fancy strays,
Lost in the endless, visionary Maze.

Still, wondrous Artist, let thy Pencil flow,
Still, warm with Life, thy blended Colours glow,
Raise the ripe Blush, bid the quick Eye-balls roll
And call forth every Passion of the Soul.
Let thy soft Shades in mimick Figures play,
Steal on the Heart, and catch the Mind away.
Yet *Painter*, on the kindred Muse attend,
The Poet ever proves the Painter's Friend.
In the same Studies Nature we pursue,
I the Description touch, the Picture you ;
The same gay Scenes our beauteous Works adorn,
The purple Ev'ning, or the flamy Morn :

Now,

Now, with bold Hand, we strike the strong
    Design;
Mature in Thought, now soften every Line;
Now, unrestrain'd, in freer Airs surprize,
And sudden, at our Word, new World's arise.
In gen'rous Passion let our Breasts conspire,
As is the Fancy's, be the Friendship's Fire;
Alike our Labour, and alike our Flame:
'Tis thine to raise the Shape; 'tis mine to fix
    the Name.

E P I T A P H.

BEneath, the PROPHET lays his rev'rend
    Head,
Amid, these awful Mansions of the Dead.
No more the PATRIOT shall assert the Laws,
Nor in the Senate plead his Country's Cause:
Around the CHURCH, no more the list'ning
    Throng,
Gaze on his Eyes, and hang upon his Tongue:
No more his *healing Hand* shall Health restore,
Elude the Grave, and baffle Death no more.

                                  In

In *Eden*'s flow'ry Vales the Spirit roves,
Where Streams of Life roll thro' immortal
    Groves :
Fix'd in deep Slumbers, here the Dust is giv'n,
'Till the laſt Trumpet ſhake the Frame of Heav'n :
Then freſh to Life the waking Saint ſhall riſe,
And in new Triumphs glitter up the Skies ;
With ſmiling Joys, and heav'nly Honours
    crown'd,
Bid endleſs Ages wheel their mighty Round.

✿✿✿✿✿✿✿✿✿✿✿✿✿✿✿✿✿✿✿✿✿✿

E P I T A P H.

SO fades the Fair, the tranſient Roſes fled,
    (No Charms but *Virtue* bloom around the
    Dead)
The *Patriot* ſo forgets his Land's Defence,
His fine Address, and flowing Eloquence :
    " Ye Living, learn ; Your *Graces* ſo conſume,
    " Beauty and Genius mingle in the *Tomb.*

           E P I T A P H.

E P I T A P H.

READER, fuch as Thou *art*, fuch once She
    ftood,
As foft, ingenious, beautiful and good ;
Such as She *is* Thou quickly muft become,
Stiff, fenfelefs, loathfome, mould'ring in a Tomb.
Yet fhall Thefe Limbs with Charms renew'd
    afcend,
Bright from the Duft, and by the Grave refin'd ;
  " Like Her be *Virtuous*, You like Her fhall
  " fhine
  " Young, fair, gay, active, deathlefs and
  " divine.

❀❀❀❀❀❀❀❀❀❀❀❀❀❀❀❀❀❀❀❀❀❀

E P I T A P H.

PROBUS beneath in peaceful Slumber lies ;
    PROBUS, the juft, the active, and the wife.
His manly Frame contain'd an equal Mind,
Faithful to GOD, and gen'rous to Mankind.
High in his Country's Honours long he ftood,
Succour'd Diftrefs, and gave the Hungry Food.
                   In

In Friendſhip ſteady, in Devotion warm,
A loyal Subjeƈt, and a Patriot firm.
Thro' ev'ry Age his dauntleſs Soul was try'd,
Great while he liv'd, but greater when he dy'd.

✿✿✿✿✿✿✿✿✿✿✿✿✿✿✿✿✿✿✿✿✿

To a young Lady.
Written with a Silver Pen, preſented by her
to the Author. 1725.

L ET grov'ling Rhymers court an awkward
  Muſe,
Their Genius urge, and give their Fires a looſe,
Invoke *Apollo Delia*'s Name to ſing,
And aſk a Quill from *Cupid*'s am'rous Wing ;
But I, more happy, ſpeak a brighter Flame,
A nobler Pen, and a diviner Dame.

You, fair BELINDA, ev'ry Boſom fire,
Tune ev'ry Voice, and ſound on ev'ry Lyre :
Where e'er you point the Lightning of your
    Eyes,
Viƈtim's fall thick, and Fate reſiſtleſs flies ;

                                    From

From all your Form a thoufand Glories dart,
And feather'd Mifchiefs ftrike on ev'ry Heart :
This flenderQuill, from your fairHand,can prove
An Arrow wing'd withConqueft and withLove ;
Can, ev'n in my unartful Fingers fhine,
And with warm Beauties Grace each flowing
    Line,
While ev'ry Reader feels th' immortal Strains,
Thrill thro' his Heart,and glow along hisVeins.

  But you, O charming Maid, throw by thefe
    Arms,
Forget your Features, and neglect yourCharms .
Tho' rifing Lillies on your Temples fpread,
And Rofes ftrew your Checks with fainter red,
Yet look difdainful on a fading Face,
Boaft brighter Glories, and a nobler Grace ;
Ye Virtues ! drefs her with a conftant Care,
And to an Angel raife the fmiling Fair.

       O   *Written*

Written in the Blank Leaf of a POEM intitled
Ætna.

THat firſt of Beauties in your Numbers ſhines,
    You ſuit your Theme with correſpondent
    Lines.

As ſounding Etna thunders from below,
And Smoke, majeſtick, hovers round its Brow,
While its tall Head ſhines with eternal Snow :
    Each various Scene your anſw'ring Lines
    unfold,
So *rough* you write, ſo *cloudy*, and ſo *cold*.

The following EPIGRAM *was written upon a Pile
of Building, erected in* Paris *by* Louis XIVth *after
the Peace with Queen* ANNE.

PAR domus hæc Urbi eſt, Urbs orbi : neutra
        triumphis
Et belli et pacis, par, Ludovice, tuis.

Anſwer'd.

VATES eſt Mendax, Verſus mentitur uterque,
    Nam minor urbs orbe eſt et minor urbe domus.
                                            Velbera

Verbera tot Verax habeat, quot præmia Mendax,
   Sic quæ non meruit præmia uterque feret.
Utraque fi injufta eft Merces, erit utraque juri
   Et belli et. pacis, par, Ludovice, tuo.

Tranflated.

THIS Palace like a City lifts its Heads,
And like a World the ample City fpreads.
O *Louis* how thy Monuments increafe ?
Alike thy Trophies both of War and Peace !

The Anfwer.

How far from Truth the fhamelefs Bard
   declines !
And like Him lie his ignominious Lines.
In the wide World the leffer City ftands,
And lefs than That the boafted Pile afcends.
   Now, for thefe Truths, had I as many Stripes,
As for his Lies the flatt'ring Poet bribes,
O *Louis*, 'twould to future Times declare
Alike thy Juftice both of Peace and War.

The CONFLAGRATION.

IN some calm Midnight, when no whisp'ring
    Breeze
Waves the tall Woods, or curls th'undimpled Seas,
Lull'd on their oazy Beds, the Rivers seem
Softly to murmur in a pleasing Dream ;
The shaded Fields confess a still Repose,
And on each Hand the dewy Mountains drowse :
Mean time the Moon, fair Empress of the Night !
In solemn Silence sheds her silver Light,
While twinkling Stars their glimm'ring Beauties
    shew,
And wink perpetual o'er the heav'nly blue :
Sleep nodding, consecrates the Deep serene,
And spreads her brooding Wings o'er all the
    dusky Scene :
Thro' the fine Æther moves no single Breath ;
But all is hush as in the Arms of Death.

At once, Great GOD ! thy dire Command is
    giv'n,
That the last Tempest shake the Frame of
    Heav'n.   Strait

Strait thick'ning Clouds in gloomy Volumes rife,
Gather on Heaps, and blacken in the Skies ;
Sublime through Heav'n, redoublingThunders
    roll,
And gleamy Lightnings flafh fromPole toPole.
Old Ocean with prefaging Horror rores,
And roufing Earthquakes rumble round the
    Shores ;
Ten thoufandTerrors o'er the Globe are hurl'd,
And gen'ral Dread alarms a guilty World.

   But Oh ! what Glory breaks the fcatt'ring
    Glooms ?
Lo ! down the op'ningSkies, he comes ! he comes !
The Judge defcending Flames along the Air ;
And fhouting Myriads pour around his Car :
Each ravifh'd Seraph labours in his Praife,
And Saints, alternate, catch th' immortal Lays ;
Here in melodious Strains bleft Voices fing,
Here warblingTubes, and here the vocal String,
Here from fweet Trumpets filver Accents rife
And the fhril Clangour echo's round the Skies.

       And

And now, O Earth ! thy final Doom attend,
In awful Silence meet thy fiery End.
Lo ! rifing radiant from his burning Throne,
The God-Head, thund'ring, calls the Ruins on.
" *Curſt Earth polluted with the Prophets Blood,*
" *Thou, the vile Murd'rer of the Son of GOD,*
" *Full ripe for Vengeance, Vengeance be thy due,*
" *Periſh in Flames, refine, and riſe anew.*
Thus as he ſpeaks, all Nature owns the GOD,
Quiver the Plains, the lofty Mountains nod,
The hollow winding Caverns echo round,
And Earth, and Sea, and Air, and Heav'n refound.

Now ratt'ling on, tremendous Thunder rolls,
And loudly craſhing, ſhakes the diſtant Poles.
O'er the thick Clouds, amazing Lightnings
    glare,
Flames flaſh at Flames, and vibrate through the
    Air.
Roaring Vulcanoes murmur for their Prey,
And from their Mouth curls the black Smoke
    away.

                  Deep

Deep groans the Earth, at its approaching Doom,
While in flow Pomp the mighty Burnings come.
As when dark Clouds rife flowly from the Main,
Then, in fwift Sluices, deluge all the Plain,
Defcending headlong down the Mountains fides,
A thoufand Torrents roll their foamy Tides,
The rufhing Rivers rapid roar around,
And all the Shores return the dafhing found :
Thus awful, flow, the fiery Deluge low'rs,
Thus rufhes down, and thus refounding rores.

But O ! what Sounds are able to convey
The wild Confufions of the dreadful Day !
Eternal Mountains totter on their Bafe,
And ftrong Convulfions work the Valley's Face.
Fierce Hurricanes on founding Pinions foar,
Rufh o'er the Land, on the tofs'd Billows rore,
And dreadful in refiftlefs Eddies driv'n,
Shake all the chryftal Battlements of Heav'n.
See the wild Winds, big bluft'ring in the Air,
Drive thro' the Forefts, down the Mountains tare,
Sweep o'er the Vallies in their rapid Courfe,
And Nature bends beneath th' impetuous Force.
                                             Storms

Storms rush at Storms, at Tempests Tempests rore,
Dash Waves on Waves, and thunder to the Shore.
Columns of Smoke on heavy Wings afcend,
And dancing Sparkles fly before the Wind.
Devouring Flames, wide-waving, rore aloud,
And melted Mountains form a fiery Flood :
Then, all at once, immenfe, the Fires arife,
A bright Deftruction wraps the crackling Skies :
While all the Elements to melt confpire,
And the World blazes in the final Fire.

Yet shall ye, Flames, the wafting Globe refine,
And bid the Skies with purer Splendour shine ;
The Earth, which the prolifick Fires confume,
To Beauty burns, and withers into Bloom ;
Improving in the fertile Flame it lies,
Fades into Form, and into Vigour dies :
Frefh-dawning Glories blush amidft the Blaze,
And Nature all renews her flow'ry Face.
With endlefs Charms the everlafting Year
Rolls round the Seafons in a full Career ;
Spring, ever blooming, bids the Fields rejoyce,
And warbling Birds try their melodious Voice :
Where-

Where-e'er fhe treads, Lillies unbidden blow,
Quick Tulips rife, and fudden Rofes glow;
Her Pencil paints a thoufand beauteous Scenes,
Where Bloffoms bud amid immortal Greens,
Each Stream, in Mazes, murmurs as it flows,
And floating Forefts gently bend their Boughs,
Thou, *Autumn*, too, fitt'ft in the fragrant Shade,
While the ripe Fruits blufh all around thyHead;
And lavifh Nature, with luxuriant Hands,
All the foft Months, in gay Confufion, blend's,

The holy Nation here tranfported roves
Beneath the fpreading Honours of the Groves,
And pleas'd, attend, defcending down the Hills,
The murm'ring Mufick of the running Rills.
Anthems divine by ev'ry Harp are play'd,
And the foft Mufick warbles thro' the Shade.

Hither, my Lyre, thy foft Affiftance bring,
And let fweet Accents leap fromString toString;
Join the bright Chorus of the future Skies,
While all around loud *Hallelujah's* rife,
And to the tuneful Lays the echoing Vault
    replies.   P   This

This bleſſed Hope, my raviſh'd Mind inſpires,
And through my Boſom flaſh the ſacred Fires :
No more my Heart it's growing Joy contains,
But driving Tranſports ruſh along my Veins ;
I feel a Paradiſe within my Breaſt,
And ſeem already of a Heav'n poſſeſs'd.

❀❀ ❀❀❀❀❀❀❀❀❀❀❀❀❀❀❀❀❀❀❀❀❀❀❀

E T E R N I T Y.

NO more of murm'ring Streams, or ſhady
Groves,
Of fleecy Flocks, or of their Shepherds Loves ;
No more fair *Myra*, on thy Name I'll dwell,
Nor in ſoft Notes to you my Paſſion tell :
Theſe trifling Themes, no more ſhall tempt my
Tongue,
A nobler Subject aſks th' advent'rous Song ;
Scenes of eternal Wonders court my Eyes,
And bid the Muſe on ſoaring Pinions riſe.

As in the Stars their lanquid Light's decay,
When the fullSun burſts forth and pours theDay,
So from my Mind the meaner Topicks run,
When vaſt ETERNITY comes rolling on.

ETERNITY,

ETERNITY, O thou unfathom'd Deep,
In thy dark Womb, what hidden Wonders sleep ?
How am I lost in thee ! who can explain
The past Revolvings of thy mazy Reign ?
Or who his Mind is able to dilate
To the long Periods of thy future Date ?
Strange Labyrinths my puz'led Soul confound,
And winde mysterious in an endless Round.

Before this System own'd the central Sun ;
Or Earth its Race about its Orbit run,
When Light ne'er dawn'd, nor Form display'd
     its Face,
But shapeless Matter fill'd th' unmeasur'd Space ;
E'er *Chaos* self with jarring Discords rung
Or the rude Elements were together flung ;
Then, then, ETERNITY, thy Pow'r was known,
Then did'st thou sit on thy unshaken Throne,
Thy Scepter flourish'd, never to decay ;
IMMENSITY the Kingdom of thy Sway.

Anon, Creation rose in infant Bloom,
And smiling Light dispel'd the horrid Gloom.

Hea'vns

Heav'ns mighty Vault was like a Curtain thrown,
Where the Stars twinkled, and the Ether shone.
Time leap'd to Life, and sped his March from
          far,
Seated on Motion, his triumphal Car ;
Through all the Worlds of Light his Axil rung,
And rolling Wheels resistless smok'd along ---
Yet, O ETERNITY, all Time to Thee,
Is a small Bark that floats in an unbounded Sea.

But, O my Muse, with wondring Eyes, behold
Scenes that remain, and Ages yet untold.
Look ! where Duration yet unborn appears,
In the long Train of still succeeding Years !
The vast Extension stretches unconfin'd,
My Thoughts perplexes, and o'erpow'rs my
          Mind.

The Day shall come when this stupendous Ball
Shall haste to Ruins, and to nothing fall.
When Thou, Great GOD, shalt in the Clouds
          descend,
Lift up thy Hand, and swear that Time shall end.
                              Hark !

Hark ! the dread Trumpet breathes the mighty
    Sound,
The fwelling Accents through the Air rebound ;
See ! the Graves teem ; the wakingSaints arife ;
And the new Bodies glitter up the Skies ;
Then the laftFlames, commiffion'd,downward
    pour,
Melt the rough Rocks, confume the burning
    Shore,
While the Sea bubbles in its final Roar.
All Nature finks, and every World deftroy'd,
Leaves a wafte Darknefs, and a traftlefs Void.
NowfaintingTime,in onevaftWrecko'erthrown,
Sinks dying down, and gives its lateft Groan ;
ETERNITY who firft its Being gave,
Its fruitful Mother once, becomes its Grave :
So Streams which from theSea their Birth obtain,
Flow fwift along, there to be loft again.

    But, Oh ! what Profpefts open to my View !
What diftantScenes,my wond'ringEyes purfue ;
I fee the gloomy, ever burning Caves,
Where, in eternal Storms, the melted Brimftone
    raves ;   Loud

Loud roar the Flames, while rifing Cries refound,
And endlefs Shreeks, and Blafphemies go round :
There Sinners waken from their idle Dreams,
And raging Devils curfe the glowing Flames.
There coyls th' Old Serpent, ftrugling with his
        Chain,
Still hiffes dire, and bites the Brafs in vain.
ETERNITY, thy Breath the Flame infpires,
And adds new Torment to th' inceffant Fires.

Far other Scenes my joyful Lays invite,
And heav'nly Vifions fwim before my Sight,
I hear foft Mufick glide along the Air,
And Songs of Seraphs echo in my Ear.
I fee the pious Souls with Pleafure crown'd,
And o'er the holy Hills Delights abound.
But Oh ! the Raptures which my Pow'rs confefs
When JESUS fhines in his refulgent Drefs !
From his wide Wounds perpetual Streams of
        Light,
For ever rufh, and ftrike the dazled Sight :
ETERNITY, here thy high Joys are known,
The top moft Gem in the REDEEMER's Crown,
               Ten

Ten thousand Raptures by thy Hands are giv'n;
Eternity, Thou art the Heav'n of Heav'n !

✿✿✿✿✿✿✿✿✿✿✿✿✿✿✿✿✿✿✿✿✿✿✿

Added by a Friend, upon reading the foregoing.

THere thou, O *Friend,* shall join th' Angelick
   Throng,
(The only Rivals of thy heav'nly Song)
Our Friendship there shall in Perfection shine,
And there, as here, thy Flames shall kindle mine.
There Jesus still shall animate thy Lays,
And thy sweet Tongue still celebrate his Praise.
His Praise, which here so oft thy Muse has sung,
While on thy Lips thy Friends transported hung;
Still ask'd the lofty Musick of thy Lyre,
And from thy Bosom catch'd the deathless Fire ;
For, from thy Hand, they own the borrow'd Bays,
And, like my Muse, confess thy gen'rous Rays.
In those bless'd Realms thy heav'n-born Soul shall
   stand ;
And sing superiour in the radiant Band ;

        And

And while thy Hands the Palm cæleſtial claim,
ETERNITY ſhall conſecrate thy Fame.

   While this great Thought employs my infant
      Muſe,
And ſhe with flutt'ring Wings the Taſk purſues,
On you, dear SIR, ſhe caſts her anxious Sight,
Indulge, propitious, and aſſiſt her Flight ;
To you the grateful Offering ſhe would bring,
You claim her Song who form'd her Voice to ſing.
Taught by your Rules, by your Example fir'd ;
She heard, ſhe learnt, and Inſtant was inſpir'd :
Still by your Influence ſhe exerts her Pow'rs,
And ev'ry varying Note ſhe ſtrikes is yours.
O cou'd I think in ſuch a lofty Vein,
And in juſt Numbers emulate your Strain,
Had I your Muſe which ev'ry Hearer warms,
For ever raiſes and for ever charms,
Tranſports your Friends, who urge its heav'nly
      Airs,
And drink the Harmony with raviſh'd Ears,
Then, all melodious ſhould my Accents flow,
Worthy ETERNITY --- and worthy You.

     T H E E N D.

THE

CONTENTS

Written

The CONTENTS.

The CONTENTS.

ERRATA.

Omitting a very few leſſer *Typographical* Errors,
thoſe which tend more to diſturb the Senſe,
are thus corrected.

PAge 23. Verſe 7. read *plain.*
　p 26. v. 5. from Bottom, r. *Lightning.*
　p. 64. v. 8. from Bottom, r. *Dome.*
　p. 74. v. 6. r. *Glories.*
　p. 103. v. 5. from Bottom, r. *Cryſtal.*
　p. 106. v. 4. from Bottom, r. *Lights.*

Eben. Miller jun 1752 (handwritten)

A
COLLECTION

OF

POEMS.

By several Hands.

B O S T O N: Printed and Sold by B. Green and
Company, at their Printing-House in *Newbury-street*;
and D. Gookin, in *Cornhil.* 1744.

E. Miller (handwritten)

A
COLLECTION
OF
POEMS.

To a GENTLEMAN *on the fight of fome of his* POEMS.

 AIL! charming Poet, whofe diftin-
    guifh'd lays,
Excite our wonder and furmount
    our praife :
Whom all the Mufes with frefh ar-
    dour fire,
And *Aganippe*'s chryftal ftreams infpire.
O ! were my genius equal to my will !
What melting words fhould from my lips diftill,
Smooth as the gentle flow from your foft quill.
On me the pow'r but throws his glancing beams,
You feel the vital vigour of his flames :
But tho' the fubject tow'rs above my fight,
I'll ftretch my wings, and dare the wondrous height.

But where, ye Nine, ſhall I begin my ſong,
Hurried impetuous by his fire along.
Loſt in a pleaſing maze I wandring rove,
Here crop a roſe, and there a tulip prove,
Nor ever fix'd my wanton footſteps ſtray,
But o'er the beauteous field take an unbounded play
If you attempt the Lyre in tender ſtrains,
And moving numbers warble o'er the plains,
The liſtning ſwains a deep attention ſhow
The winds are huſh'd, the rivers ceaſe to flow ;
With wonder ſilent are the bending trees,
Nor hear their boughs the murmurs of a breeze.

Like HORACE ſweet the tuneful harp you ſtring,
While in our ears th' enchanting accents ring.
Or like your WATTS's ſoft melodious lyre,
Who from the *Roman* ſnatch'd the immortal fire.
WALLER who beſt excell'd in handſome praiſe,
Joyful beholds your temples bear his bays.
Your Similes like ſparkling diamonds glow,
Which on their ambient gold a light beſtow,
And as the ſtars in meaſur'd numbers dance,
With ſprightly glory thro' the vaſt expanſe,
A lively luſtre gilds the heavenly blue,
Such your pure lines, ſuch your alluſions ſhew.

Happy the Poet whom the applauding town,
Admir'd in your fine lines, before his own.

And

And happy you, who while you ſtrive to raiſe
Your modeſt Friend, are compaſs'd round with praiſe.
H:, baſhful, with a veil conceals his face,
Nor on the world his living lightnings flaſh.
So Maids in whom the varied red and white,
The bluſhing roſe, and lilly fair unite,
Their lovely looks from gazing mortals hide,
Nor laviſh on the world their cheeks gay pride :
But conſcious of an ever-ſpringing bloom,
O'erſpread their features with a decent gloom.

You, like *Apollo*, ſhine with godlike rays,
And court the Virgin with melodious lays ;
Whoſe perſon to the wondring world unknown,
By you adorn'd with laurel wreaths, is ſhone.
Your Poem with unnumber'd graces gleams
Upon my ſoul, and darts promiſcuous beams :
Its numbers, like a ſtream, majeſtick glide,
When by its banks it rolls it ſilver tide,
While mourning Winds in murmurs ſoftly breathe,
And ſilent ſcenes an image paint of death.
Your thoughts for multitude like billows roul ;
And with the force of Lightning peirce the Soul.

May former Bards their juſt eſteem enjoy,
Nor I to raiſe your merit their's deſtroy.
You ſcorn a fame with borrow'd glory bright,
But ſhine like *Phœbus* in your native light

But

But sure the Nine more graceful garments show,
And softer accents from their fingers flow,
Since you with pity saw their rude attire,
And taught their hands to bend the sounding wyre.

No more shall foreign wits our clime despise,
And bless the indulgence of their milder skies.
Britannia's Bards, forever may ye feel
The inspiring Pow'r; and with his raptures swell.
May MILTON's force, and DRYDEN's smoothness join
With mingled lustre on your Isle to shine:
But still regard, with fond propitious eyes,
Your distant sons by your examples rise,
On us *Apollo* sheds his kindly light,
We too ascend *Parnassus* steepy height:
My friend can riding reign the furious horse,
And thro' the aerial kingdoms drive his course:
Can reach the glittering Regions of the sky,
Where the still tracts of purest ether ly;
Or thro' the flow'ry fields of nature rove,
And gather garlands to adorn his love.

And now, my Muse, attempt one labour more,
Let MILTON's fame resound from shore to shore:
MILTON who in his works immortal lives,
And in the deathless praise your Poem gives.
You imitate his airy rapid flights,
And mount with ardour to his godlike heights.

How

How fwift the vigour of your numbers fly,
When the dread chariot bounds along the fky ;
While o'er the azure plains MESSIAH's driven,
And hurls his foes precipitant from heaven !
His eyes majeftick flafh with flames of fire,
And kindle hell in thofe who dare his ire.
You lead me through the gay delightful fcenes,
Where paradife adorns the happy plains.
Here nature's wing'd inhabitants repair,
And chant their mufick thro' the ravifh'd air.
Here rilling ftreams in winding mazes move,
There tow'r the fhady honours of the grove.
There opening flow'rs breathe their refrefhing fweets,
And here the ripening fruit the finger greets :
While courtly Zephyres wave the trembling trees,
And fan their faces with a gentle breeze.
Bleft garden of primæval innocence !
(But now furrounded with a flaming fence)
How longs my panting Soul to ftretch my limbs,
Near the foft running of thy cooling ftreams,
Upon the verdure of a grafsy mead,
And rifing turf a pillow for my head,
Eafy my thought, my proftrate length to lay,
And wafte in chearful joys the fmiling day ?
Here dwelt the happy Pair diffolv'd in blifs,
And heard unmov'd the Serpent's harmlefs hifs,

While

While subject nature bow'd its humble neck,
And every charm confpir'd the place to deck.

Forgive, dear Friend, the ftraying of my verfe,
Which fhould your merit, not your thoughts rehearfe ;
But your defcription fo my fenfe invites,
I leave the Author for the things he writes ;
Viewing the copy of your wondrous mind,
I lofe the great Original behind.
Thus trav'llers walking thro' the *Italian* plains,
To fome great city, ftudious of their gains,
Loft in a thoufand charms which court their eyes,
Drink in the profpect with a vaft furprize,
Till thoughtlefs of their journey's deftin'd end,
They thro' the vales with high exultings tend.

But tho' the painter and the picture pleafe,
In praife of both my ftrains reluctant ceafe.
Nor can the labours of my vulgar Mufe,
Tho' You the theme a tedious length excufe.
You beft can ftretch along and lofty wing,
And with unfailing force for ever fing.
So *Phœbus* fhining with immortal gleams,
Shoots down the golden glory of his beams.
Nor when behind the hills his light retires,
Are in the ocean quenc'd his radiant fires,
But rifing to their fight, the inferiour world
Behold his flames with fiery vigour hurl'd.

An E L E G Y *on the long expected Death of Old*
J A N U S. [The New-England Weekly Courant.]

Mourn, alas ! for in the grave is laid
Old rev'rend JANUS with his double head.
Affist, ye nine, my mournful fong infpire,
　　And thou, O *Bacchus,* add thy gen'rous fire ;
Let high *Parnaffus* weep in ev'ry place,
And let each fummit celebrate a face :
Tears from all *Argus'* eyes this death demands,
While griev'd *Briareus* wrings his hundred hands.

Mourn, all ye fcribblers who attempted fame,
Screen'd by the umbrage of his pow'rful name :
Whofe works now ceafe each rolling week to rife,
A grateful cov'ring over fmoaking pies ;
Or when a fquib a holliday declares,
To mount in air, and blaze among the ftars.
You, woeful *Wights !* his loft protection mourn,
And let your griefs flow plenteous o'er his urn ;
Alas ! no more fhall your bright fouls be fhown,
In foreign fhapes, and features not your own :
No more you'll write beneath his fhade conceal'd,
But in full dulnefs be abroad reveal'd.

B　　　　　　　So

So when th' ambitious Aſſe around him ty'd,
The ſhaggy horrors of the Lion's hyde,
Wheree'er he ſtalk'd the beaſts forſook their prey,
And from the tawney terror fled away ;
When now forgetting what he was before,
He tries to ſcowl, and thinks it time to roar ;
He takes full breath, --- -- but, ah, it came to paſs,
That a loud bray confeſs'd the cover'd Aſſe :
In ruſh the ſhouting ſwains from ev'ry ſide,
Strip the vile beaſt, and bang his batter'd hyde.

But, O my muſe, ſome conſolation bring,
And in this doleful ditty ceaſe to ſing.
Few thought his rev'rend vitals were ſo ſtrong,
Or that th' old fellow could have liv'd ſo long.
For, many a month did to the world diſplay,
How all his parts were haſt'ning to decay ;
And (as 'tis uſual, e'er one's parting breath)
He lighten'd once or twice before his death ; *
For fire befure's in thoſe who verſes write ;
And where, *my friends*, is fire, unleſs there's light ?
Theſe melancholy ſignals firſt appear'd,
And his approaching end to all declar'd.

---

* Alluding to the two late poetical Courants.

So fome old oak upon a plain appears,
Bending beneath a mighty weight of years;
If then, from heav'n, commiffion'd ftorms arife,
Fly o'er the fields, and thunder through the fkies,
The tree aftonifh'd at the loud alarm,
Waves with the wind, and totters to the ftorm;
Its leafy honours all around are fpread,
And acorns rattle from its lofty head;
'Till it's huge trunk breaks with a crafhing found,
And the tall top lies level with the ground.

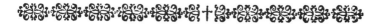

On the Foregoing.

Xcefs of vice won't fail to haften death!
How foon old JANUS yeilds his poif'nous
breath!
He's born, comes to his height, grows old and dies,
And his curf'd carcafe on a dunghil lies;
Juft fate of JANUS! all before the fun
Could fix times round his annual orbit run!
Of tory malice fpawn'd, by faction nurs'd;
Men can't be blefs'd by heav'n, but he is curs'd.

When heav'n incenfed will no more forbear
To fcourge the fins that waiting vengeance dare;

And ſatan comes commiſſion'd from above
To ſpread inteſtine jars, and baniſh love :
His willing aid old JANUS gives the fiend,
Joins hand in hand, and makes ſucceſs attend.
While he continu'd, as he firſt deſign'd,
To wrong the guiltleſs, and abuſe mankind,
Dull malice void of wit in proſe or rhyme
Could pleaſe enough to make him rich by crime.
To mock the pious, and the vile to praiſe,
The venerable ſinner's fame could raiſe.
By hatred, envy, party-rage, he lives,
And on the ſpoils of peace triumphant thrives.

But when our paſſions calm, and love deſcends,
When men are bleſs'd with peace, and faction ends,
When ſatan could not, by divine command
In party-ſpirit reign to plague the land ;
Old JANUS found at once his work was done,
And trembled for paſt crimes, tho' left alone ;
His reputation ſunk, he ſtarv'd, and griev'd,   ⎫
Ætna was in his ſoul while conſcience heav'd,   ⎬
And wild deſpair the haſt'ning change perceiv'd.   ⎭
In vain, he gaſps a while, repents, and dreams
Of new recruits of life from virtuous themes,
To poiſon ſo inur'd, when not ſupply'd,
He tries to live on wholeſome food, and dy'd.

He's

He's gone ! thanks for his death ! who dy'd to give
The world a poet who deferves to live.
*****, *Harvard*'s honour, and *New-England*'s hope
Bids fair to rife, and fing, and rival POPE.
No more let *Britain*'s fons in haughty fcorn
Say that our country wants ONE poet born.
The death of venerable JANUS fays,
He could no longer live upon *their* bays.
Could JANUS live again, he'd wifh to die ;
If in oblivion ***** would let him ly.

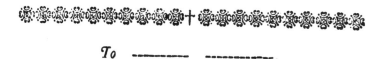

To ———— ————.

LONG has *New-England* groan'd beneath the
load,
    Of too too juft reproaches from abroad,
Unlearn'd in arts, and barren in their fkill,
How to employ the tender mufes quill :
At length our ***** aloft transfers his name,
And binds it on the radiant wings of fame ;
All we could wifh the youth, he now appears,
A finifh'd poet in his blooming years.

With anxious care, we fee the ftripling climb
Thofe heights we deem'd for mortals too fublime,
And dread a dang'rous fall ————   Yet

Yet fondly gaze, 'till he, above our fears,
Has loft th' attracting world, and fhines among the ftars.

Thence, may the Influence of thy heavenly rays, ⎫
(Our prefent joy, and hope of future days !)   ⎬
Infpire our imitation, as it does our praife.   ⎭
Rife yet, great genius, further onward go,   ⎫
But let our tender youth, whofe bofoms glow   ⎬
With bright ideas, be thy charge below ;   ⎭
Thy kindly afpect, fan their growing fire,
Till they, like thee, on wings of fame afpire,
And loudly, in harmonious lines proclaim   ⎫
New-England's fons, e'erwhile of barb'rous name, ⎬
A match for *Albion*, or the *Grœcian* fame.   ⎭

The C O M E T.

Efcend, *Urania*, and infpire my verfe,
I raife my fong to fing your kindred ftars ;
I aim to rove where glitt'ring comets ftray,
Trace the bright wand'rers thro' th' Æthereal way,
And all around th' Almighty's pow'r proclaim,
Where worlds can roll, or funs inceffant flame.

See !

See ! heav'nly mufe, view with attentive eyes;
The ruddy wonder of the ev'ning fkies !
From ftar to ftar, the burning ruin rolls,
Beams thro' the Æther, and alarms the poles :
Around the earth the wond'ring nations gaze,
On the dire terrors of the lengthen'd blaze,
While, trailing on, they dream its fparkling hair,
Shakes famine, earthquake, peftilence and war :
Illufions vain ! remote from humane things,
Where other planets roll in other rings
It travels vaft ; and all around proclaims
A world in chaos, or an earth in flames.

So, thro' the Æther, fwept the ancient earth,
Ere time, and form, and beauty firft had birth,
Unfhap'd and void, thro' fpace immenfe it roam'd,
Till fpoke the God------and *Eden* inftant bloom'd.

What ruin ! what confufion might be hurl'd,
By fuch a ball upon our guilty world ?
Witnefs, ye waves, which in the deluge fpread,
Whelm'd o'er the earth, and ftretch'd the nations dead.
Down heav'n's high fteep, wide-fpread, the fteaming train
Rufh'd on the fields, and pour'd the floods of rain ;
The dark abyfs, attracted into day,
Gufh'd o'er the mountain-tops, and roar'd away ;

The

The toſt ark, tott'ring, thro' it's fabrick ſhook,
Involv'd in clouds and darkneſs, foam and ſmoke,
By tempeſts plung'd along from ſteep to ſteep,
Bounds to the clouds, or daſhes down the deep,
Ye angels! guard her thro' the ſtormy ſcene,
Till the gay rainbow arch the heav'ns ſerene.

But, O my muſe, ſwift muſt the time come on,
When freſh inſpir'd, and fervid from the ſun,
The flagrant ſtranger ſhapes a diff'rent path,
And from its annual orbit drags the earth.
Ye fancy, mortals! diſtant as ye are,
All calm and placid round the ſailing ſtar,
In gentle rays ſerenely gleams the head,
And eaſy luſtre thro' the train is ſpread:
Ah, ye perceive not what loud tumult reigns
Thro' the hot regions of its wild domains;
What hideous thunder the wide Æther ſhocks,
Of tumbling mountains, and of craſhing rocks:
Fierce ſeas of flame beat round the burning ſhores,
And ev'ry tempeſt raves, and ev'ry furnace roars.
To this devoted earth it marches on,
And midnight blazes with the glare of noon;
Big, and more big, it arches all the air,
A vault of fluid braſs the ſkies appear:
From their foundations, where they ancient ſtood,
Down ruſh the mountains in a flaming flood;   The

The min'rals pour their melted bowels out,
The rocks run down, the flying rivers fpout;
The earth diffolves thro' its disjointed frame,
Its clouds all lighten, and its *Ætna's* flame;
The fea exhales, and in long volumes hurl'd,
Follows the wand'ring globe from world to world :
Now at the fun it glows, now fteers its flight
Thro' the cold defarts of eternal night,
Warns ev'ry creature thro' its tractlefs road,
The fate of finners, and the wrath of GOD.

Ad ———————— ————————.

Ucida, qui novit numeris conftringere jufis
L *Aftra poli folemq; perenni ducere curfu;*
Ille tibi Altifono *cantandi* carmine *Vires*
Permifit : dotefq; *Oro* tibi *adaugeat* Amplas.
Optimus Ille PARENS : At tu refonare memento,
Illius, *grato* dum Vivis *pectore Laudes ;*
Cumq; Augufta dabit tibi *adire palatia cæli,*
Ætherea claros cithara cantabis Honores
CHRISTI, *perpetuo qui folus* Carmine dignus.

C

The Translation.

H E whose high wisdom gilds the blue expanse,
Where the gay pole-star tries its measur'd
Dance,
Who to the sun appoints its annual bounds,
And leads him on his everlasting rounds ;
To you this GOD has granted to rehearse
In founding numbers, and exalted verse.
May he, *best parent !* ampler blessings shed,
With rich profusion o'er thy happy head.
But thou ! do thou remember to prolong
His grateful praises in thy flowing song.
Resound his name with all thy noblest strains,
While vital spirits pulsate thro' thy veins ;
So when thy soul, exulting, soars away
To the fair regions of eternal day,
Where heav'ns high tow'rs magnificently rise,
And shoot long glories down th' inferior skies
All rapture, thou shalt take th' æthereal lyre,
Thy hands divinely bend the warbling wire,
J E S U S still dwell harmonious on thy tongue,
Th' exhaustless subject of immortal song.

A

A poetical LAMENTATION, *occasioned by the* Death *of His late Majesty King* G E O R G E *the First.*

NOW, O ye nine! if all your pow'rs can paint
The scenes of woe which wake this loud
   complaint,
Breath from my muse such soft and solemn verse,
As suits to strew my matchless Sov'reign's hearse ;
And let my grief in mournful musick glide
To *Albion*'s shores, and join the gen'ral tide.

 While in this task I'd try the tenderest skill,
Beneath the subject sinks my quiv'ring quill,
Restless, my muse her awful theme surveys,
While wounded passions plead for present ease,
My grief grows wild, and strugling sorrows throng
To break in trembling accents from my tongue.

 O that in shade, which woful cypress rears,
My growing grief cou'd pour in dutious tears !
To waving woods the desp'rate cause reveal,
And learn my lays to each remurm'ring rill.
How oft in lonesom wilds, the widdow'd dove,
In melting moans laments its absent love,
While list'ning forrests seem to feel the wound,
And eccho dies beneath the doleful sound.

And

And ſhall my woe, more peircing than the ſighs
Of dying doves, or mourning matron's cries,
Now aſk in vain ſome ſympathetic groan,
From darkſome groves, reflecting moan for moan ?
Shall unrelenting rocks forbear to bleed,
While I proclaim the great *AUGUSTUS* dead !
AUGUSTUS-----ah ! ----my muſe, I feel the ſound
Ruſh thro' my ſoul, and all its pow'rs confound ;
Swift tow'rds my heart unuſual horror climbs,
And ſtrange convulſions ſeize my ſhudd'ring limbs :
In my cold veins the crimſon ſcarcely flows,
My ſlack'ning nerves their nat'ral aids refuſe,
From aking eyes the briny ſorrow breaks,
And liquid pearl, rolls down my faded checks,
The ling'ring remnant of my life's oppreſt,
And death-like damps bedew my lab'ring breaſt.

Had I the royal prophet's tuneful ſtrain
When *Iſrael's* breathleſs chiefs had ting'd the plain ;
Would but *Apollo's* genial touch inſpire
Such ſounds as breathe from ***** warbling lyre ;
Then, might my notes in melting meaſures flow,
And make all nature wear the ſigns of woe.
Content, my muſe muſt mourn with humbler ſtrings,
While *GEORGE's* death, and *Albion's* loſs ſhe ſings.

Now

Long had the fields resign'd their smiling dress,
And herds rov'd round for food in dumb distress,
When famish'd hills, in russet robes array'd,   *
Seem'd to presage some dire event decreed :
While fainting nature felt such ardent fire,
As if 'twas with this fever to expire ;
Then from the King of kings, a message flies,
To call his great vicegerent to the skies :
An hasty summons snatch'd our Sov'reign's breath,
His life is set, his glory dim'd with death. ---------
Let ev'ry gem which studs the *British* crown,
Look pale and wan, since *Albion*'s light is down :
No more you'll share its rays, nor mingling shed
Your trembling splendors round his sacred head.
No more the throne shall show that awful face,
Where majesty was mix'd with mildest grace :
Nor hostile realms revere their conqu'rour king,
Nor nations shroud beneath his shelt'ring wing.
That wond'rous form, which once could kingdoms sway,
Is now the grizly tyrant's helpless prey.

Rise gentlest winds, to give your sorrows vent
That distant climes may learn our desp'rate plaint ;
Whisper your woe, and languish as you flie,
And, when you've told the doleful tidings, die.

---

* An uncommon Drought at that Time.

With

With swelling grief, let restless billows roar
And loose their lives on each resounding shore.
While gathering damps surround each groaning hill,
And gushing riv'lets drench th' enamel'd vale.

Ye gaudy flow'rs and blossoms drop your dies,
No more let roses blush, nor lillies rise,
Nor teeming buds their knownless sweets disclose,
But, with untimely blasts, their bashful beauties loose.
No more let trees in verdant liv'ries tow'r,
Nor ripen'd fruit from bending branches pour,
But leafless twigs shall team with trembling drops,
And gently waving, shed their crystal crops :
While cluster'd vines, their withering arms unwind,
'Till all the ground's with scatter'd purple stain'd.

Ye wing'd musicians, leave your airy domes,
Sadden your notes, and pluck your painted plumes :
While woods and plains with dying flocks are strow'd,
Let scaly swarms in anguish lash the flood,
And floating squadrons, fold their canvas wings,
Since now no more they'l serve the best of kings.

Lock'd in the chambers of the distant skies
Let *Phœbus* mourn, 'till *Albion* dries its eyes,
While darkness silver *Cynthia*'s face invades,
And sickly planets close their twinkling lids.

While

While the high heav'n its mifty mantle wears,
And low'ring clouds weep down in fhowry tears,
Let the flow thunder roll in fun'ral peals,
As livid light the burfting fkies reveals;
Winding in ftreaky torches thro' the gloom,
To light the fleeping monarch's mould'ring tomb.

　While confort bells the thick'ning vapours break,
And deep complaints, in dying language fpeak,
Let the tall fteeples bow their gilded fpires,
As each fad found in circling waves expires.
Now let *Britannia*'s peers deplore their prince,
In pompous woe, and faint magnificence;
With arms revers'd, let martial mourners fhow,
Gloom in their cheeks, and fadnefs on their brow;
While the foft fex their tendereft forrows blend,
Wail with difhevel'd hair, and wringing hand,
Their blufhing charms eclips'd with fable veils,
As thro' the duft their decent mourning trails.

Come, hoary regifters of ancient times,
Whofe vital tide declines your wither'd Limbs;
Babes in the dawn of life, and you whofe veins,
The dancing fire of ripen'd youth contains;
With all *Parnaffus*, bring your laft perfume,
With bofoms bare, and mingled mournings come,
And fpread　in one wide ruin round your Sov'reign's
　　　tomb.

But ceaſe, my muſe, or weep in gentler ſtreams,
Behind this ſhady ſcene ſome comfort gleams;
Lift from the diſmal gloom thy aking eyes:
Refreſhment ſprings from whence thy ſorrows riſe.

When at the hour of *Brunſwick*'s ſwift diſcharge,
To heav'n ſeraphick guardians guide their charge;
Rapid, the news thro' trembling kingdoms runs,
And all the ſkies are peirc'd with piteous groans;
Then, as this light the dark'ned empire leaves,
Then, wondrous *W A L E S* the ſinking ſcepter ſaves:
Then, with her ſparkling iſſue, comes his QUEEN,
Like night's fair empreſs midſt her ſtarry train;
With cypreſs crown'd, they guild th' imperial ſeat,
And prop, tho' weak with woe, the tott'ring ſtate;
While intermingling joys, and grief impreſs
Their different dies, in ev'ry ſubjects face.
Albion reviv'd, yet longs with eager eye
To ſee their *Sovereigns* ſhine in cloudleſs majeſty.
So when in deep eclipſe, the riſing ſun,
Streaks with a duſky light his orient throne:
With ſully'd robes he mounts th' ætherial field,
And rules the day, with *Cynthia*'s ſable veil'd.
Languid, and faint, his muffled front appears,
While earth and air a ſemblant horror wears.
'Till rapid time unfolds his fulgid face,
And ſpreads his golden glories quick'ning rays.

Like Phœbus, *thus, acquiring unsought praise*
He catch'd at love ; and fill'd his arms with bays.

Waller.

BELINDA.   *A Pastoral.*

" YE tuneful nine, who all my soul inspire,
      " Whose numbers charm me, and whose
                  transports fire,
" Snatch me, O snatch me to some gentle seat,
" Where shady forests form a soft retreat.
" And thou, O spring, deck the surrounding bow'rs,
" Ye blossoms bloom, and flourish all ye flow'rs.
" BELINDA comes, I hear her heav'nly voice,
" Let the flow'rs flourish, and the blooms rejoice.

  " BELINDA fair my wanton fancy leads
" Where fainting breezes whisper o'er the meads,
" High leaps my heart, and ev'ry pulse beats love,
" While the dear name soft dies along the grove ;
" Her name, in echoes dances on the hills,
" Adds softer musick to the bubb'ling Rills,
" Bids each gay tree a livelier verdure show,
" The lillies whiten, and the roses glow,
" Scatters the gloomy horrors of the night,
" And gives a glory to the noon-day light.

D

" But

" But, ah ! fond youth, forbear thy am'rous ſtrain,

" Vain is thy paſſion, and thy numbers vain !

" Could'ſt thou e'er hope, preſumptuous, that the fair,

" With ſmiling eyes ſhould dawn upon thy pray'r,

" That panting, ſinking, with ſurrend'ring charms,

" The beauteous nymph ſhould bleſs thy circling arms?

" Ah ! no, ſome happier youth the fates have bleſt

" To reign, unrival'd, in her lovely breaſt ;

" Some happier youth, ah ! ſo ye pow'rs decree,

" Who never ſung, who never lov'd like me ;

" He, coldly aſking, ſhall obtain the prize,

" And bear the beauty from my trembling eyes,

" Shall, without rapture, on the goddeſs gaze,

" And uninſpir'd, behold her ſmiling face ;

" When her ſweet voice chimes in his taſteleſs ear,

" He'll hear indeed, but will regardleſs hear :

" While I, unhappy, ſhall the nymph deplore,

" Nor court the day, nor aſk a pleaſure more :

" Penſive, I'll wander through the lonely woods,

" And tell my ſorrows to the liſt'ning floods,

" Give to the hills and vales my paſſions vent,

" While the rough rocks repeat my loud complaint,

" The trees, attentive, ſhall forget to bloom,

" Nor a ray glimmer in their ſolemn gloom.

Thus STREPHON ſung to all th' admiring ſwains,
And moving numbers warbled o'er the plains ;

Sometimes,

Sometimes, elate, he fung the yielding fair,
Then mourn'd, and figh'd, abandon'd to defpair,
The fhepherds, fixt in deep attention hung,
And griev'd, or triumph'd, to the varying fong ;
They bleft th' harmonious accents of his lyre,
And the nice hand that touch'd the trembling wire,
Their hearts o'ercome with gen'rous paffions flam'd,
They curs'd his rival, and BELINDA blam'd.

When STREPHON thus---" Forbear rafh fwains forbear,
" Nor wifh the rival ill, nor fault the fair.
" O blefs BELINDA, all ye pow'rs above,
" And blefs the man, BELINDA deigns to love !
" But me, ah ! me ten thoufand pangs arreft,
" And mix tumultuous in my beating breaft,
" Muft that fair form (forbid it, O ye Skies !)
" Muft that fair form be ravifh'd from my eyes ?
" Shall fome more favour'd youth with haughty air,
" Far from my fight the lovely charmer bear ?
" Throw round her flender waift his ftupid arms,
" Nor own, ungrateful, the fuperiour charms ?
" From her gay bofom fnatch th' unfullied fnows,
" And from her blufhing cheeks, the op'ning rofe,
" Yet his cold lips tafte no exalted joys,
" Nor one glad fparkle languifh in his eyes ?
" Shall he ---- No more, my heart forgets to move,
" And life's warm ftream its circling maze to rove ;

" The

" The killing thought defaces all the ſcene,
" Fades evry flow'r, and withers ev'ry green,
" Augments the murmur of the running rills,
" And ſpreads a gloomier ſhadow o'er the hills.

Thus while he ſung the ſoft BELINDA's praiſe,
Hills, fields, and vales re-echo'd to his lays ;
The ſhepherds hearken'd 'till the god of light
Roll'd down his car ; and ruſh'd along the night.

A full and true Account of how the lamentable wicked
French *and* Indian *Pirates were taken by the valient*
Engliſh Men.

Good people all, pray underſtand
    my doleful ſong of woe :
It tells a thing done lately, and
    not very long ago.

How French-men, Indians eke, a troop,
    (who all had drunk their cogues)
They went to take an *Engliſh* ſloop :
    O the ſad pack of rogues !

The *Engliſh* made their party good,
    each was a jolly lad :
The Indians run away for blood,
    and ſtrove to hide like mad.

Three

Three of the fellows in a fright,
  (that is to fay in fears)
Leaping *into* the fea *out-right*,
  fows'd over head and ears.

They on the waves in woful wife,
  to fwim did make a ftrife,
[So in a pond a kitten cries,
  and dabbles for his life ;

While boys about the border fcud,
  with brick-bats and with ftones ;
Still dowfe him deeper in the mud ;
  and break his little bones.]

What came of them we cannot tell,
  though many things are faid :
But this, befure, we know full well,
  if they were drown'd, they're dead.

Our men did neither cry nor fqueek ;
  but fought like any fprites :
And this I to the honour fpeak
  of them, the valiant wights !

O did I not the talent lack,
  of *'thaniel Whittemore* ;
Up to the ftars ——i' th' almanack,
  I'd caufe their fame to foar.

Or

Or could I fing like father *French*,
    fo clever and fo high;
Their names fhould laft like oaken bench,
    to perpetuity.

How many prif'ners in they drew,
    fay, fpirit of *Tom Law* !
Two French-men, and papoofes two,
    three fannops, and a fquaw.

The fquaw, and the papoofes, they
    are to be left alive :
Two French, three Indian men muft die:
    which makes exactly five.

[Thus cypher, Sirs, you fee I can,
    and eke make poetry :
In common-wealth, fure fuch a man,
    how ufeful muft he be !]

The men were all condemn'd, and try'd,
    and one might almoft fay,
They'l or be hang'd, or be repriev'd,
    or elfe they'l run away.

Fair Maidens, now fee-faw, and wail,
    and fing in doleful dumps ;
And eke, ye lufty lubys all,
    arife, and ftir your ftumps.

This

This precious po'm fhall fure be read,
  in ev'ry town, I tro :
In ev'ry chimney corner faid,
  to *Portfmouth*, *Bofton* fro.

And little children when they cry,
  this ditty fhall beguile;
And tho' they pout, and fob, and figh,
  fhall hear, and hufh, and fmile.

The pretty picture too likewife,
  a-top looks well enough ;
Tho' nothing to the purpofe 'tis,
  'twill ferve to fet it off.

The poet will be glad, no doubt,
  when all his verfe fhall fay,
Each boy, and girl, and lafs, and lout,
  for ever, and for aye.

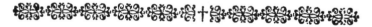

Some excellent Verfes *on* Admiral VERNON'S *taking the*
Forts and Caftles of Carthagena, *in the Month of*
March. 1742,3.

     ATtend all nations round about,
         who dwell on ev'ry fhore;
Where're old *Neptune's* waves can float,
    Or *Britain's* cannons roar.

                                    I found

I found great VERNON's spreading fame,
    round heav'ns expanded arch ;
Who thund'ring on the *Spaniards* came
    on the last ninth of *March.*

Four ships against two forts sail'd on,
    And took them as they stood ;
Tho' both the forts were built with stone
    and th' ships were made of wood.

St. *Philip* gone, and *Terra-Bomba,*
    (was ever seen the like----O !)
Resolv'd to cut the *Spaniard's* comb--a,
    they fir'd at *Boco-Chico.*

The *Spaniards* star'd at the loud ring,
    as at a rod stares dunce ;
Like frighted pidgeons they took wing,
    and vanish'd all at once.

Castle *Legrand* to guard the boom,
    stood threat'ning far and wide ;
Two men of war did boldly come
    and pour'd a whole broad-side.

But, gen'rous, give the foes their due,
    there was no sign of fear;
VERNON *fire on, a fig for you !*
    for not a man was there.

This

This caſtle was their greateſt ſtrain,
    Don *Blaſs* concluded right;
He ran away with all his men,
    and left the fort to fight.

Into his ſhip the hero got,
    then ſail'd away to town,
Then bid them fire, then bid them not,
    then run, then ſtop'd, then run.

So a young lady in new ſtays
    tail-neſtling keeps a rout;
And ſo a maggot in a cheeſe
    rolls wriggling round about.

You ſaid, Don *Blaſs*, you'd drink a glaſs
    with VERNON, could you catch him:
He's coming on, why do you run?
    pray can't you ſtay and pledge him?

Faſtned in *Carthagena* cloſe,
    no further can you fly;
Armies by land, or fleets let looſe
    will catch you by and by.

How dolefully with eighty guns,
    Don *Blaſs*'s ſhip was ſeen!
Taken from ſeventy *Spaniſh* Dons,
    by five and twenty men.

E

In

Don *Blaſs* beheld, he ſob'd and whin'd,
    his huge black whiſkers tore;
And had he not fear'd to be fin'd,
    he would have curs'd and ſwore.

In haſte they ſunk three men of war,
    to ſtop the channel up;
Each veſſel elſe they ſet on fire,
    viz. ſhip, brig, ſnow, and ſloop.

While theſe brave things were done at ſea,
    our ſoldiers work'd for blood,
Built on the land a battery,
    behind a hideous wood.

Wentworth commands, down go the trees,
    with horrible report;
Agaſt, the trembling *Spaniard* ſees
    the negroes and the fort.

As ghoſt ſtalks on by moon-light gleam
    ſtill terrible to nurſe,
So frightful did each ſoldier ſeem
    that went away from us.

Our picture ſhows all this with art,
    (was ever work ſo pretty!)
And ſoon you'l ſee the ſecond part,
    when we have took the city.

Carthagena's

Carthagena's *Downfall.*

Olly we fung the other day,
How poor *Don Blafs* fcuttled away;
Clofe up in *Carthagena* keeps,
And leaves his caftles and his fhips :
We promis'd foon, in jocund meafure,
To take the city and the treafure ;
So further to refrefh your heart,
Here, failors, fing the fecond part.

Jack Spaniard fees, fhiv'ring and fhaking,
All his fhips funk, and caftles taken ;
Nearer our men, and nearer creep,
Each takes his profpect glafs to peep.
And O ! what riches here were feen,
In ev'ry alley, ftreet, and lane !
In ev'ry corner mingling rays
Of filver, gold, and diamonds blaze.
All the tin pots were filver fine,
And filver wire was us'd for twine.
The land-bank bills were yellow mould,
And all the gridirons made of gold.
The fpits and fkewers of ev'ry fkullion,
And wooden cans were folid bullion.

E 2   Each

Each bed was velvet few'd together,
Stuff'd with leaf-gold without a feather.
Each cup-board groan'd beneath its weight,
For all the earthen ware was plate.
What endlefs wealth fpread o'er the ground!
What ftorms of guineas rain'd around!
Each foldier at a diftance views,
Hope fills his pockets, fleeves and fhoes;
Each heart beats faft, affur'd to come
Loaded with bags of money home.

Hark then! and fee! trumpets and drums,
Cannons and mufkets, fhouts and bombs;
Mafts cracking, tumbling city walls,
Steeples o'erturn'd by iron balls;
Ten thoufand dangers, deaths and harms,
And fhower of heads,trunks,legs and arms.
Whole magazines blown up on high,
And foldiers flying thro' the fky,
Till, left they fhould be all o'erthrown,
The *Spaniards* fent to buy the town.
Juft as we feiz'd all to our ufe,
Out comes a paltry flag of truce,
And after a fhort modeft parl'ing
Only paid down nine millions fterling.

PARTHA-

PARTHANISSA.

Dedicated to the Admirers of Italian Opera.

Arthaniſſa's beauty blooming,
 All my raviſh'd mind inſpires
Smiling feature, eyes conſuming
 Melt my heart with amorous fires.

Oft beneath the moon-ſhine walking,
 Parthaniſſa's name I've ſung ;
Babling echo's round me talking,
 Anſw'ring ſoftly to my tongue.

Flow'ry meadows, foreſts floating,
 You have heard my gliding ſtrains ;
Midnight owls forgot their hooting,
 When I warbled o'er the plains.

Bubling fountains gently rilling,
 Branches bending, purling ſtreams,
Whiſp'ring breezes ſweetly ſmelling,
 Huſh my ſoul in lulling dreams.

Come then, *Parthaniſſa* charming,
 With your ſmoothly-ſwimming air :
Parthaniſſa my breaſt warming,
 Come, my *Parthaniſſa* fair.

Tripping

Tripping artful, eafy moving,
    Sweep the furface of the green.
Take a heart fo tender, loving,
    Ever-beauteous little queen.

* * *

To a little Mafter.

D Ear little mafter, fet the tea ;
    Expect me at the hour of three :
And let me alfo, when I come,
Papa and *Mamma* find at home.

The ANSWER.

From Dr. Wenftanley's *Poems, printed at* Dublin. 1742.

C An you, much honour'd man, excufe
    The firft lifps of an infant mufe ?
Young as I am, my lips would patter
An inftant anfwer to your letter.

In gilded edge your lines appear,
So morning cloud fpeaks *Phœbus* near.
Ambition fets my mind on fire
And like *Apollo* you infpire :
Infpir'd, I only can indite :
——*Milton* and *Homer* could not write.

                       Here,

Here, Sir, your little nephew ſtands,
And pants, and burns to kiſs your hands :
Thoſe hands, from which ſo oft have come
The citron-peel, and ſugar-plumb.

See the tea-table ready dreſt,
Proud to receive ſo great a gueſt.
Peru, with ſilver tea-pots, ſmiles
And ſugar floats from weſtern iſles ;
Japan the glitt'ring tables lends ;
China her beauteous diſhes ſends ;
The tea on *Ganges*' borders grew :
All nations joyn to pleaſure you.
Compleat, if you adorn the room ;
-----*Papa and Mamma are at home.*

China, and *Ganges*, and *Japan*
Are words my *Papa* taught my pen.
He ſays, they're countrys to be found
In a ſtrange world below the ground ;
Where folks with feet erected tread,
And diſtant downward hangs the head :
Fearleſs, they topſy-turvey run,
With nought beneath----but ſkies and ſun.

This, all my nurſe's tales exceeds,
Of giants with an hundred heads !

                                    I know

I know of knights in ev'ry region,
Who fingly flew, at leaft, a legion ;
And fiery dragons too, trapan'd,
As big as twenty miles of land ;
Their fkin was brafs, their teeth were fteel ;
A nation was their common meal :
Of goblins pale, with faucer eyes,
To catch the naughty boy that cries :
I credit all of ghofts, they fay,
Who on a pins-point dance the haye ;
Unheard, unfeen, along they glide,
And ftately thro' a key-hole ride :
(So heroes made their pompous marches,
In chariots, thro' triumphal arches :)
Of hideous hags, who nightly fly,
On groves of broom-fticks thro' the fky :
Of faries, who the moon-fhine prize ;
And pigmies, half an inch in fize :
Thefe, as they're things I've feen the prints of,
I very fully am convinc'd of.

But that a veffel ever fails
Where nought grows upwards but cows tails ;
That fervants fent to fetch the claret,
Should find the cellar in the garret ;
That work-men the whole roof fhould fpread,
Before the leaft foundation's laid ;

That

That evening fees the rifing fun,
And when 'tis midnight, then 'tis noon,
That birds defcend the more they foar,
And hills rife downwards low'r and low'r;
And, that folks always walk fo ev'n,
They ne'er drop upwards down to heav'n,
Are things I can't believe not I :
----Tho' fure my *Papa* cannot lye.

But manners bids me haften home :
My country's common father, come,
Come, let me ftill your fondnefs prove,
And boaft in your's, a parent's love.
Your golden cane, I'll ftill beftride,
And rapid round the ftudy ride.
You fav'd me from the gafp of death,
When wheezing quinfies held my breath,
John lafh'd the dapples two-fold pair,
And whirl'd me thro' the winter air ;
Clos'd up in glafs, fecure I ride,
And mock the fnows on ev'ry fide;
Your coach convey'd me fafe from harms,
From nurfes, to my *Mamma*'s arms :
Here oft your goodnefs I commend,
And often blefs your bounteous hand ;
Here ftill my grateful paffions work,
And ftill I live to make my mark.

F

*

To ———————— ————————

With a Present of Peacock's Feathers.

S I R,

❀❀❀ O your hands the little muse,
❀❀❀ Again in grateful numbers flows ;
As oft as she can bend the string,
She still has some new gift to sing.
Now that a small return be made,
She calls the peacock to her aid.
Her voice, *his* train, accept together :
————You sent a hat, I send a feather.

Poor PAVO, stript of all his pride,
Affects a melancholly stride ;
He gives, to paint a bed for you,
His glitt'ring plumes of golden hue ;
No more you see him, haughty, spread
All *Argus'* eyes around his head ;
The heav'nly blue deserts his breast,
No jewels twinkle on his crest :
Alas ! how alter'd ev'ry feature,
Could you but see the naked creature !

On *Ovid's* verse I often look,
(Who wrote an *English* picture-book)
Such changes there I frequent see,
Narcissus-flow'r, and *Daphne*-tree.

Daphne,

Daphne, thy ſtory ſuits our caſe,
Half-maid ſhe runs, and ſprouts half bays;
Phœbus purſu'd, fir'd with her charms,
And catch'd the laural in his arms:
So *Pavo* fled, while *Servo* chas'd,
'Till ſeiz'd, and in his arms embrac'd;
The ſympathetic genius ſpread
His gloſs decay'd, his colours fled;
Sober he wanders round the houſe,
No more a peacock----- but a gooſe.

But tho' he ſtalks in diſmal plight,
Rueful and horrid to the ſight;
Thy groſer ſhade, *Alcides*, ſo *
Wanders a grimly ghoſt below;
The lighter ſoul with gods partakes
Immortal youth from *Hebe*'s checks.

See, what collected beauties ſhine
On yonder blazing counterpain!
Improv'd each ſingle feather ſhows,
And with redoubled luſtre glows:
So *Phœnix*, wonder of the eaſt!
Expires upon the genial neſt;
In fertile flame conſum'd ſhe lies,
Withers to bloom, to vigour dies.

---

* Vid. POPE's *Hom.* Odyſſ. B. XI. l. 743. Notes.

Accept this off'ring as 'tis meant;
Meaſure the payment by th' intent,
'Twill make a figure in your ledger,
Your Nephew,

S I R,

The little Major.

To ******** *Deſiring to borrow* Pope's Homer.

From a Lady.

THE muſe now waits from ***'s hands to preſs
Homer's high page, in *Pope's* illuſtrious dreſs:
How the pleas'd gooddeſs triumphs to pronounce,
The names of ***, *Pope*, *Homer*, all at once!

The ANSWER.

SOON as your beauteous letter I peruſe,
Swift as an echo flies the anſw'ring muſe;
Joyful and eager at your ſoft commands,
To bring my *Pope* ſubmiſſive to your hands.

Go, my dear *Pope*, tranſport th' attentive fair,
And ſooth, with winning harmony her ear.
'Twill add new Graces to thy heav'nly ſong,
To be repeated by her gentle tongue;
Thy brightning page in unknown charms ſhall grow,
Freſh beauties bloom, and fire redoubled glow;

With

With founds improv'd, thy artful numbers roll,
Soft as her love, and tuneful as her foul :
Old *Homer*'s fhade fhall finile if fhe commend,
And *Pope* be proud to write, as **** to lend.

Written in the blank Leaf of Mr. Addifon's CATO :
Given to a Lady.

O, gentle volume, teach the fair to love,
With *Marcia*'s elegance, and ftricteft virtue ;
Soften'd by fonder *Lucia*'s open temper :
Her heav'nly mind as faultlefs as her form.

Let ev'ry charm adorn the fav'rite youth,
Like *Juba* vig'rous, modeft, beautiful,
Divinely flufh'd with *Marcus*' glowing ardor,
Graceful as *Portius*, gen'rous and ferene,
And all great *Cato*'s foul dilate his breaft.

O happy pair, 'tis you alone fhall prove
The finifh'd tranfports of immortal love.

EPIGRAM *on a Pedantic Compofure.*
O ftrong conclufion, no connected fenfe,
Quotations here, not arguments, convince ;
Clearnefs and eloquence you vainly feek,
You afk for *reafon*, and he gives you *greek*.

When

When *Babel* aim'd above the skies to shine,
Their tongues confounded crush'd the proud design:
These pages show like their ambitious throngs,
And talk confusion in a thousand tongues.

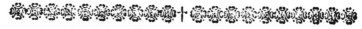

To his most honoured Mother, On New-Year's Day, 1737.

A piece for a Lad at writing School.

WHILE all around to your attentive eyes,
Conquests and triumphs in bright order rise, *
Be your's in softer victories to engage,
In vertue over death, in bloom o'er age;
Fresh trophies rising, as each year subsides,
Your sons all heroes, and your daughters brides.

COMMENCEMENT.

I Sing the day, bright with peculiar charms,
Whose rising radiance ev'ry bosom warms;
The day when *Cambridge* empties all the towns,
And youths commencing, take their laural crowns:
When smiling joys, and gay delights appear,
And shine distinguish'd, in the rolling year.

---

* *The Margin decorated with the Duke of* Marlborough's *Victories.*

While

While the glad theme I labour to rehearfe,
In flowing numbers, and melodious verfe,
Defcend immortal nine, my foul infpire,
Amid my bofom lavifh all your fire,
While fmiling *Phœbus*, owns the heavenly layes
And fhades the poet with furrounding bayes.
But chief, ye blooming nymphs of heavenly frame,
Who make the day with double glory flame,
In whofe fair perfons, art and nature vie,
On the young mufe caft an aufpicious eye :
Secure of fame, then fhall the goddefs fing,
And rife triumphant with a tow'ring wing,
Her tuneful notes wide-fpreading all around,
The hills fhall echo, and the vales refound.

Soon as the morn in crimfon robes array'd
With chearful beams difpels the flying fhade,
While fragrant odours waft the air along,
And birds melodious chant their heavenly fong,
And all the wafte of heav'n with glory fpread,
Wakes up the world, in fleep's embraces dead.
Then thofe whofe dreams were on th' approaching day,
Prepare in fplendid garbs to make their way
To that admir'd folemnity, whofe date,
Tho' late begun, will laft as long as fate.
And now the fprightly Fair approach the glafs
To heighten every feature of the face.

They

They view the rofes flufh their glowing cheeks,
The fnowy lillies twining round their necks.
Their ruftling manteaus huddled on in hafte,
They clafp with fhining girdles round their waift.
Nor lefs the fpeed and care of every beau,
To fhine in drefs, and fwell the folemn fhow.
Thus clad, in carelefs order mixt by chance,
In hafte they both along the ftreets advance ;
'Till near the brink of *Charles*'s beauteous ftream,
They ftop, and think the lingring boat to blame.
Soon as the empty fkiff falutes the fhore,
In with impetuous hafte they cluftering pour,
The men the head, the ftern the ladies grace,
And neighing horfes fill the middle fpace.
Sunk deep, the boat floats flow the waves along,
And fcarce contains the thickly crowded throng ;
A gen'ral horror feizes on the fair,
While white-look'd cowards only not defpair.
 Till row'd with care, they reach th' oppofing fide,
Leap on the fhore, and leave the threat'ning tide.
While to receive the pay the boat-man ftands,
And chinking pennys jingle in his hands.
Eager the fparks affault the waiting cars,
Fops meet with fops, and clafh in civil wars.
Off fly the wigs, as mount their kicking heels,
The rudely bouncing head with anguifh fwells,
A crimfon torrent gufhes from the nofe,
Adown the cheeks, and wanders o'er the cloaths.

Vaunting,

Vaunting, the victor's ftrait the chariots leap,
While the poor batter'd beau's for madnefs weep.

Now in calafhes fhine the blooming maids,
Bright'ning the day which blazes o'er their heads ;
The feats with nimble fteps they fwift afcend,
And moving on the crowd, their wafte of beauties fpend,
So bearing thro' the boundlefs breadth of heav'n,
The twinkling lamps of light are graceful driv'n ;
While on the world they fhed their glorious rays,
And fet the face of nature in a blaze.

Now fmoak the burning wheels along the ground,
While rapid hoofs of flying fteeds refound,
The drivers by no vulgar flame infpir'd,
But with the fparks of love and glory fir'd,
With furious fwiftnefs fweep along the way,
And from the foremoft chariot fnatch the day.
So at olympick games when heros ftrove,
In rapid cars to gain the goal of love.
If on her fav'rite youth the goddefs fhone
He left his rival and the winds out-run.

And now thy town, O *Cambridge !* ftrikes the fight
Of the beholders with confus'd delight;
Thy green campaigns wide open to the view,
And buildings where bright youth their fame purfue.

G

Bleft

Bleſt village ! on whoſe plains united glows,
A vaſt, confus'd magnificence of ſhows.
Where num'rous crowds of different colours blend,
Thick as the trees which from the hills aſcend :
Or as the graſs which ſhoots in verdant ſpires,
Or ſtars which dart thro' natures realms their fires.

How am I fir'd with a profuſe delight,
When round the yard I roll my raviſh'd ſight !
From the high caſements how the ladies ſhow !
And ſcatter glory on the crowds below.
From faſh to faſh the lovely lightening plays
And blends their beauties in a radiant blaze.
So when the noon of night the earth invades
And o'er the landſkip ſpreads her ſilent ſhades.
In heavens high vault the twinkling ſtars appear,
And with gay glory's guild the gleemy ſphere.
From their bright orbs a flame of ſplendors flows,
And all around th' enlighten'd ether glows.

Soon as huge heaps, have delug'd all the plains
Of tawny damſels, mixt with ſimple ſwains,
Gay city beau's, grave matrons and coquats,
Bully's, and cully's, clergymen and wits.
The thing which firſt the num'rous crowd employs,
Is by a breakfaſt to begin their joys.
While wine, which bluſhes in a chryſtal glaſs
Streams down in floods, and paints their glowing face.

And

And now the time approaches when the bell,
With dull continuance tolls a folemn knell.
Numbers of blooming youth in black array
Adorn the yard, and gladden all the day.
In two ftrait lines they inftantly divide,
While each beholds his partner on th' oppofing fide,
Then flow, majeftick, walks the learned *head*,
The *fenate* follow with a folemn tread,
Next *levi*'s tribe in reverend order move,
Whilft the uniting youth the fhow improve.
They glow in long proceffion till they come,
Near to the portals of the facred dome ;
Then on a fudden open fly the doors,
The leader enters, then the croud thick pours,
The temple in a moment feels its freight,
And cracks beneath its vaft unweildy weight,
So when the threatning Ocean roars around
A place encompafs'd with a lofty mound,
If fome weak part admits the raging waves,
It flows refiftlefs, and the city leaves ;
Till underneath the waters ly the tow'rs,
Which menac'd with their height the heav'nly pow'rs.

The work begun with pray'r, with modeft pace,
A youth advancing mounts the defk with grace,
To all the audience fweeps a circling bow,
Then from his lips ten thoufand graces flow.

The

The next that comes, a learned thefis reads,
The queftion ftates, and then a war fucceeds.
Loud major, minor, and the confequence,
Amufe the crowd, wide-gaping at their fence.
Who fpeaks the loudeft is with them the beft,
And impudence for learning is confeft.

The battle o'er, the fable youth defcend,
And to the awful chief, their footfteps bend.
With a fmall book, the laurel wreath he gives
Join'd with a pow'r to ufe it all their lives.
Obfequious, they return what they receive,
With decent rev'rence, they his prefence leave.
Difmifs'd, they ftrait repeat their backward way,
And with white napkins grace the fumptuous day.

Now plates unnumber'd on the tables fhine,
And difhes fill'd invite the guefts to dine.
The grace perform'd, each as it fuits him beft,
Divides the fav'ry honours of the feaft,
The glaffes with bright fparkling wines abound,
And flowing bowls repeat the jolly round.
Thanks faid, the multitude unite their voice,
In fweetly mingled and melodious noife.
The warbling mufick floats along the air,
And foftly winds the mazes of the ear;
Ravifh'd the crowd promifcuoufly retires,
And each purfues the pleafure he admires.

Behold

Behold my mufe far diftant on the plains,
Amidft a wreftling ring two jolly fwains ;
Eager for fame, they tug and haul for blood,
One nam'd *Jack Luby*, t'other *Robin Clod*,
Panting they ftrain, and labouring hard they fweat,
Mix legs, kick fhins, tear cloaths, and ply their feet.
Now nimbly trip, now ftiffly ftand their ground,
And now they twirle around, around, around ;
Till overcome by greater art, or ftrength,
Jack Luby lays along his lubber length.
A fall ! a fall ! the loud fpe&ators cry,
A fall ! a fall ! the echoing hills reply.

O'er yonder field in wild confufion runs,
A clam'rous troop of *Affric's* fable fons,
Behind the vi&ors fhout, with barbarous roar,
The vanquifh'd fly with hideous yells before,
The gloomy fquadron thro' the valley fpeeds
Whilft clatt'ring cudgels battle o'er their heads.

Again to church the learned tribe repair,
Where fyllogifms battle in the air,
And then the elder youth their fecond laurels wear.
Hail ! happy laurets ! who our hopes infpire,
And fet our ardent wifhes all on fire.
By you the pulpit and the bar will fhine,
In future annals ; while the ravifh'd nine

Will

Will in your bofom breathe cæleftial flames,
And ftamp *Eternity* upon your names.
Accept my infant mufe, whofe feeble wings
Can fcarce fuftain her flight, while you fhe fings.
With candour view my rude unfinifh'd praife
And fee my *Ivy* twift around your *bayes*.
So *Phideas* by immortal *Jove* infpir'd,
His ftatue carv'd, by all mankind admir'd.
Nor thus content, by his approving nod,
He cut himfelf upon the fhining god,
That fhaded by the umbrage of his name,
Eternal honours might attend his fame.

An Account of the Proceffion of the General Court into
　　Salifbury, *in the Year* 1737. *when the Affair of the*
　　Boundary Line was debated between the two Provinces
　　of the Maffachufetts *and* New-Hampfhire.

　　　Written by an Irifh *Poet to his Friend.*

Y dear joy, ye did never behold this fine fight,
　　As yefterday *morning* was feen *before night :*
　　Oh! I fear it means no good to your *neck,* nor
　　　　mine,
For they fay 'tis to *fix a right place* for the *line.*
You in all your *born days* faw, *nor I did not neither,*
So many fine *borfes* and men *ride* together.

　　　　　　　　　　　　　　　　　　　At

At the *head* the *low'r* houſe trotted *two* in a *row*,
Then all th' higher houſe pranc'd *up* after the *low*.
Then the governor's coach *gallop'd* on like the *wind*.
And the *laſt* that came *foremoſt* was troopers *behind*.

To ―――――― ――――――

T H E poet, when he ſaw his Pages full,
Pronounc'd the fancy cold, the numbers dull,
" Say, muſe, what wond'rous magick can I uſe,
" To raiſe to poetry this low ſunk proſe ?

The muſe reply'd, " See ! thro' the audience round,
" The force of action and the pow'r of ſound ;
" Quick beat the pulſes, ev'ry heart leaps high,
" Fixt the charm'd Ear, and raiſ'd th' attentive Eye :
" Let but the graceful orator pronounce,
" He'll read it into poetry at once.

Obedient thus to what the goddeſs ſpoke,
The volume humbly waits on *******.